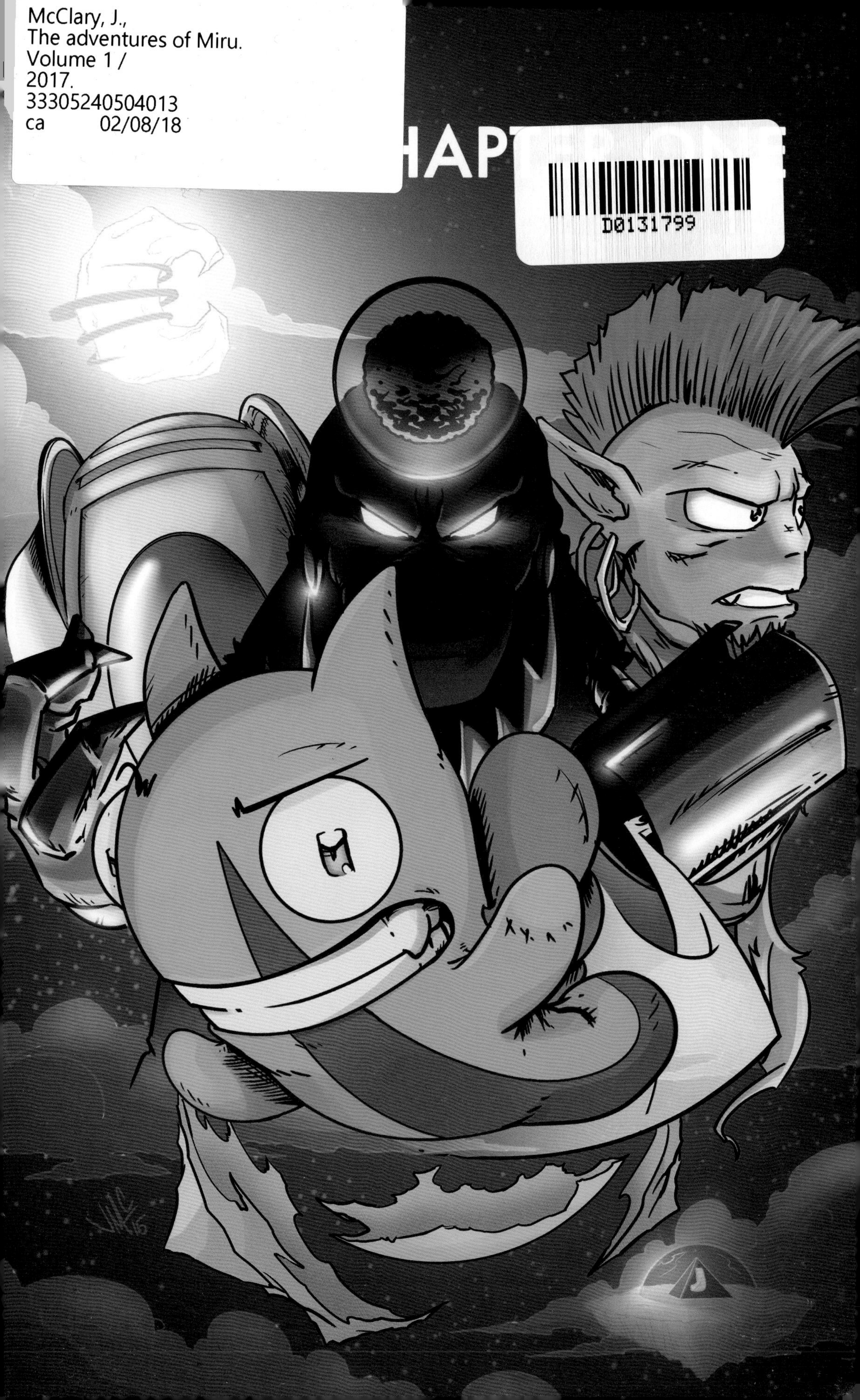

Bryan Seaton - Publisher/ CEO • Shawn Gabborin: Editor In Chief • Jason Martin: Publisher-Danger Zone • Nicole D'Andria: Marketing Director/Editor
Jim Dietz: Social Media Manager • Danielle Davison: Executive Administrator • Chad Cicconi: Elderly Dragon • Shawn Pryor: President of Creator Relations

THE ADVENTURES OF MIRU Vol. 1 TPB, SEPTEMBER 2017. Copyright Jemal McClary, 2016. Published by Action Lab Entertainment. All rights reserved. All characters are fictional. Any likeness
to anyone living or dead is purely coincidental. No part of this publication may be reproduced or transmitted without permission, except for review purposes. Printed in China. First Printing.

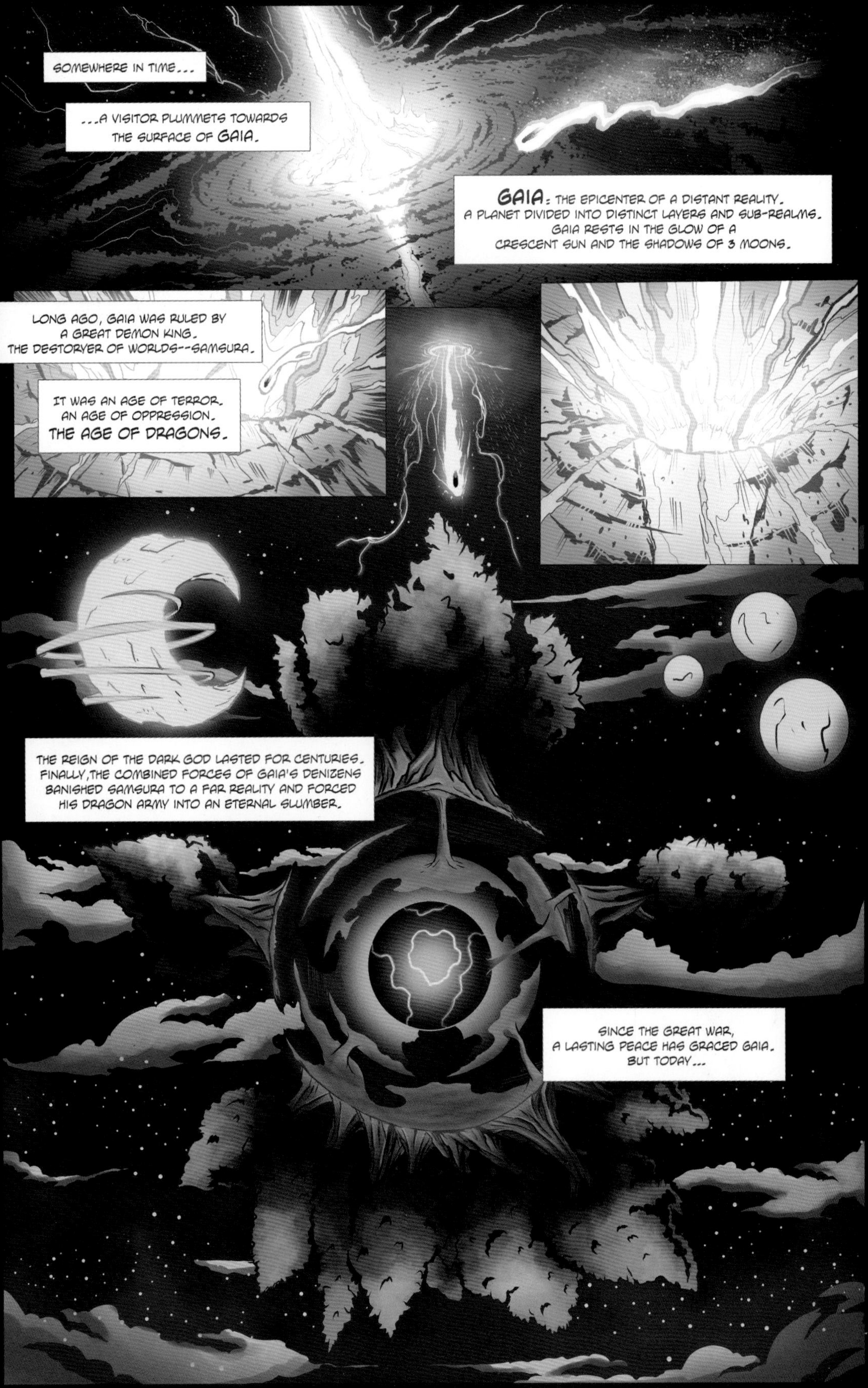
SOMEWHERE IN TIME...
...A VISITOR PLUMMETS TOWARDS THE SURFACE OF GAIA.
GAIA: THE EPICENTER OF A DISTANT REALITY. A PLANET DIVIDED INTO DISTINCT LAYERS AND SUB-REALMS. GAIA RESTS IN THE GLOW OF A CRESCENT SUN AND THE SHADOWS OF 3 MOONS.
LONG AGO, GAIA WAS RULED BY A GREAT DEMON KING. THE DESTORYER OF WORLDS--SAMSURA.
IT WAS AN AGE OF TERROR. AN AGE OF OPPRESSION. THE AGE OF DRAGONS.
THE REIGN OF THE DARK GOD LASTED FOR CENTURIES. FINALLY, THE COMBINED FORCES OF GAIA'S DENIZENS BANISHED SAMSURA TO A FAR REALITY AND FORCED HIS DRAGON ARMY INTO AN ETERNAL SLUMBER.
SINCE THE GREAT WAR, A LASTING PEACE HAS GRACED GAIA. BUT TODAY...

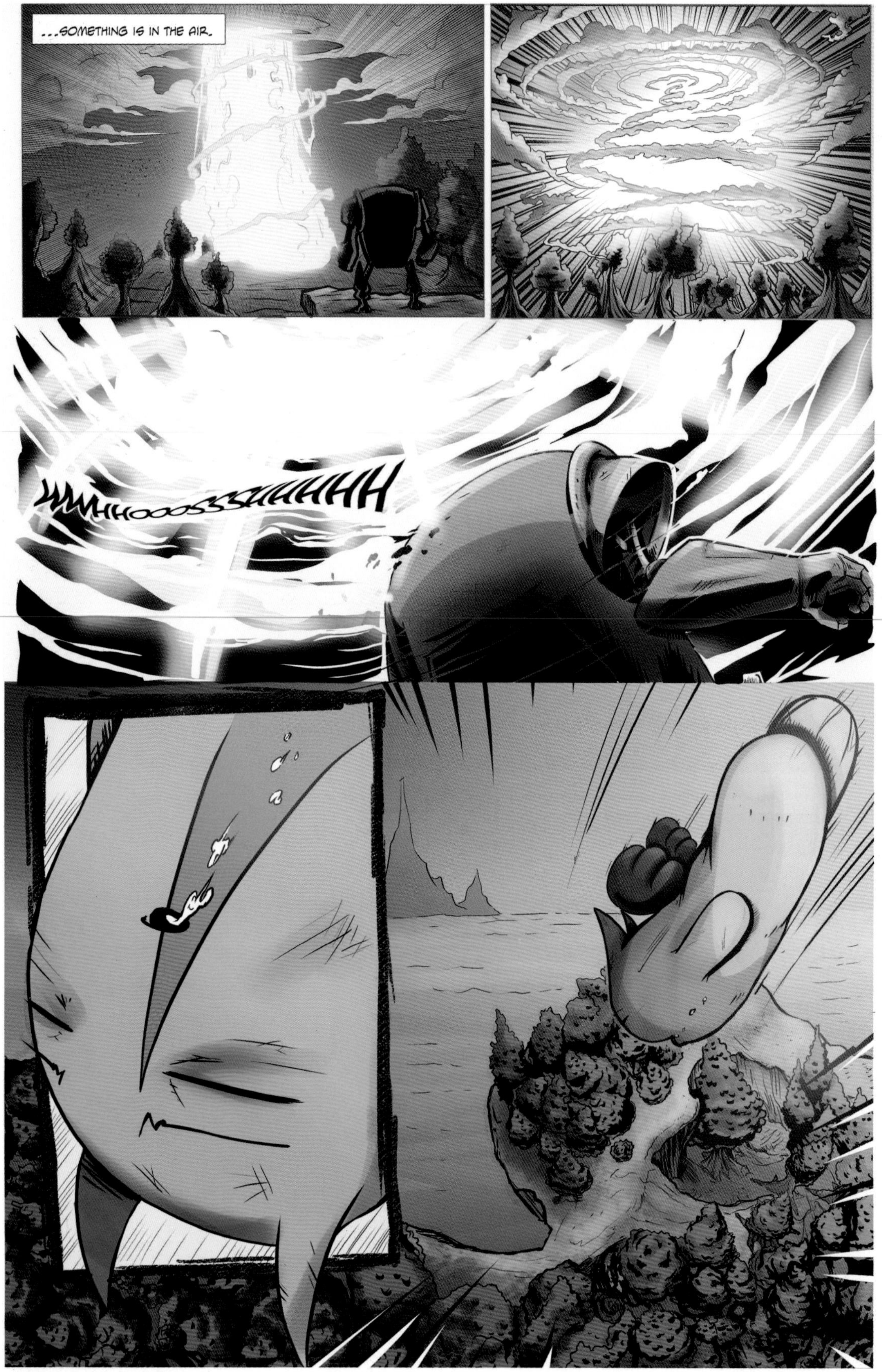
...SOMETHING IS IN THE AIR.
WHHOOOOSSSHHHHHH

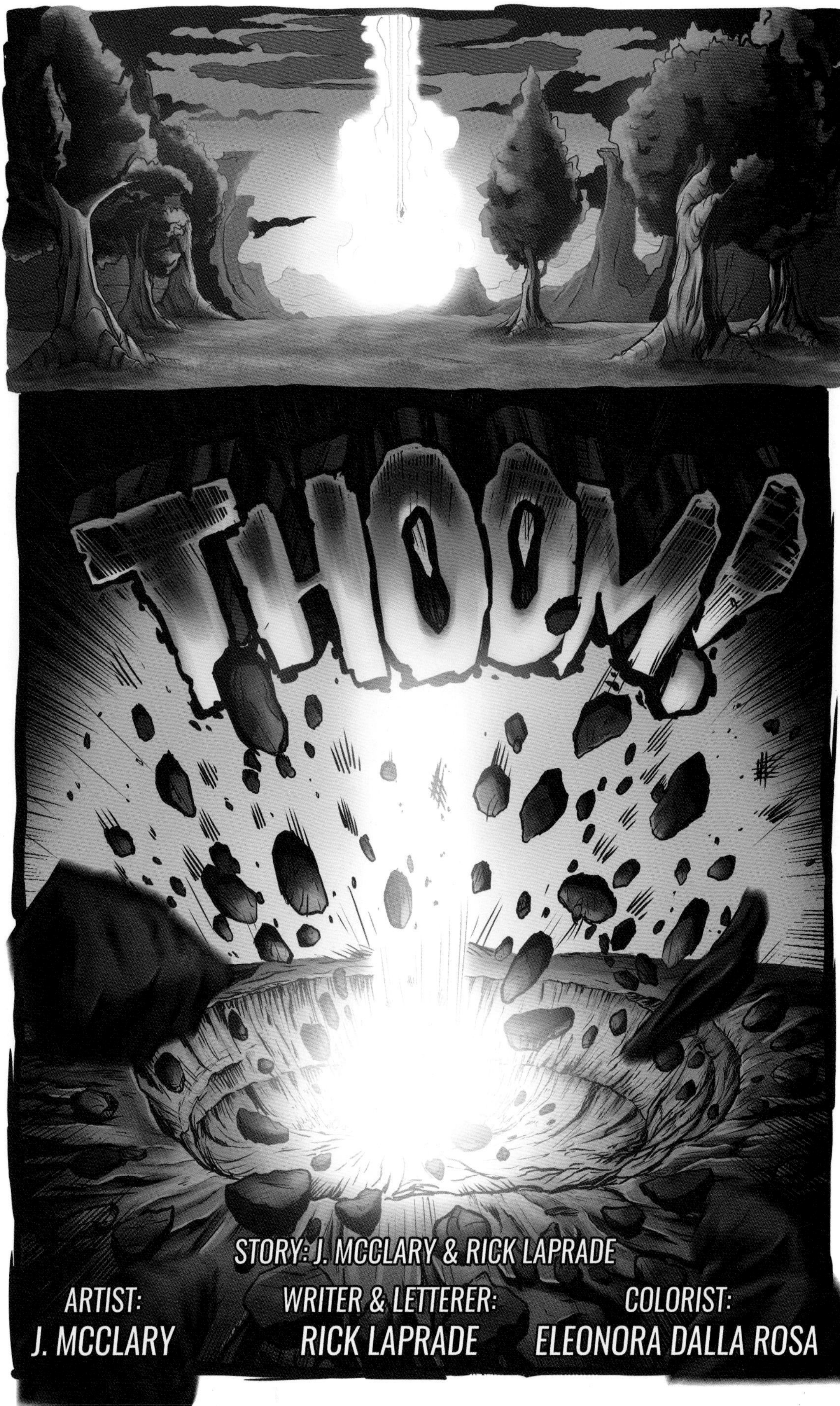
THOOM!
STORY: J. MCCLARY & RICK LAPRADE
ARTIST:
J. MCCLARY
WRITER & LETTERER:
RICK LAPRADE
COLORIST:
ELEONORA DALLA ROSA

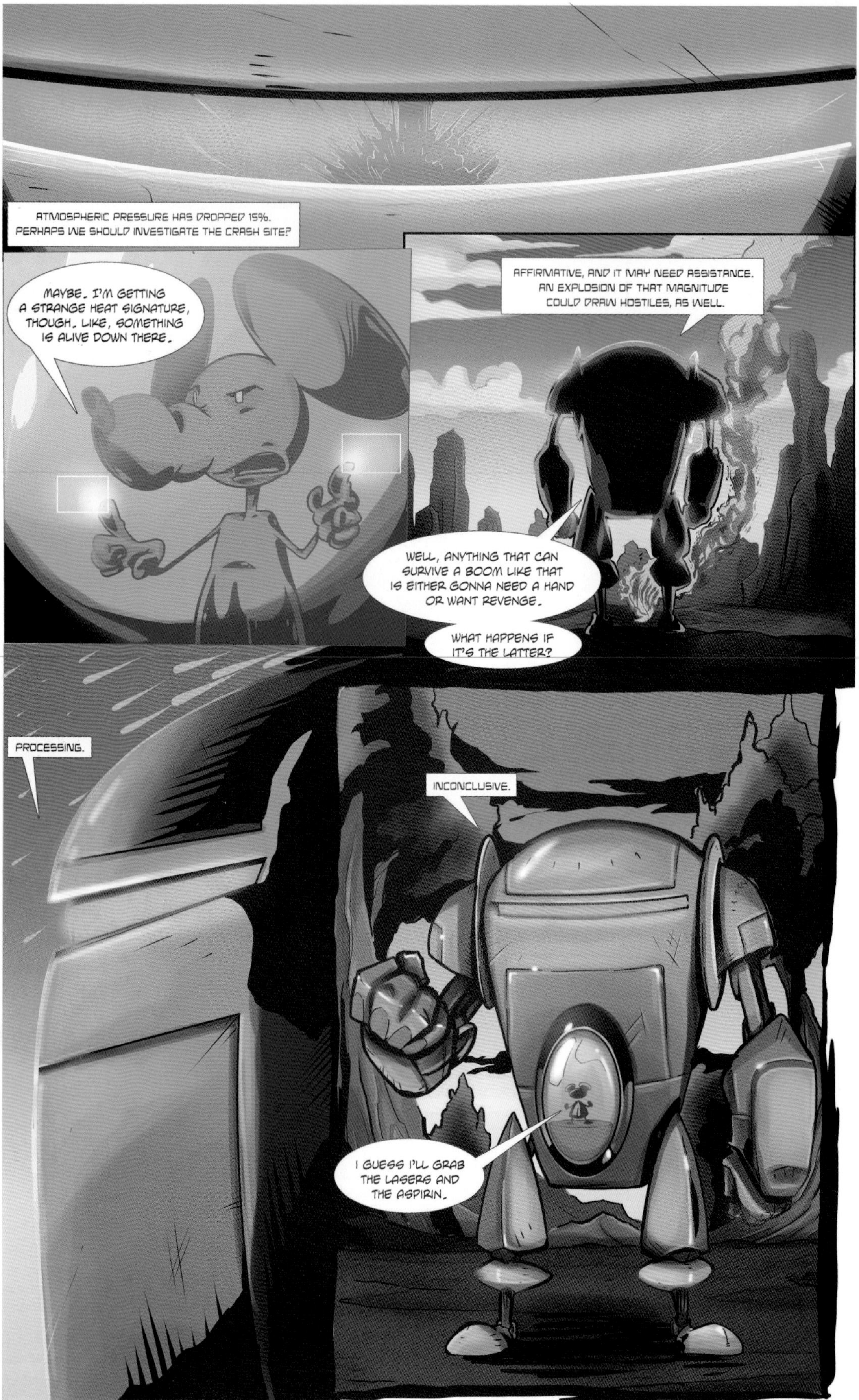
ATMOSPHERIC PRESSURE HAS DROPPED 15%. PERHAPS WE SHOULD INVESTIGATE THE CRASH SITE?
MAYBE. I'M GETTING A STRANGE HEAT SIGNATURE, THOUGH. LIKE, SOMETHING IS ALIVE DOWN THERE.
AFFIRMATIVE, AND IT MAY NEED ASSISTANCE. AN EXPLOSION OF THAT MAGNITUDE COULD DRAW HOSTILES, AS WELL.
WELL, ANYTHING THAT CAN SURVIVE A BOOM LIKE THAT IS EITHER GONNA NEED A HAND OR WANT REVENGE.
WHAT HAPPENS IF IT'S THE LATTER?
PROCESSING.
INCONCLUSIVE.
I GUESS I'LL GRAB THE LASERS AND THE ASPIRIN.

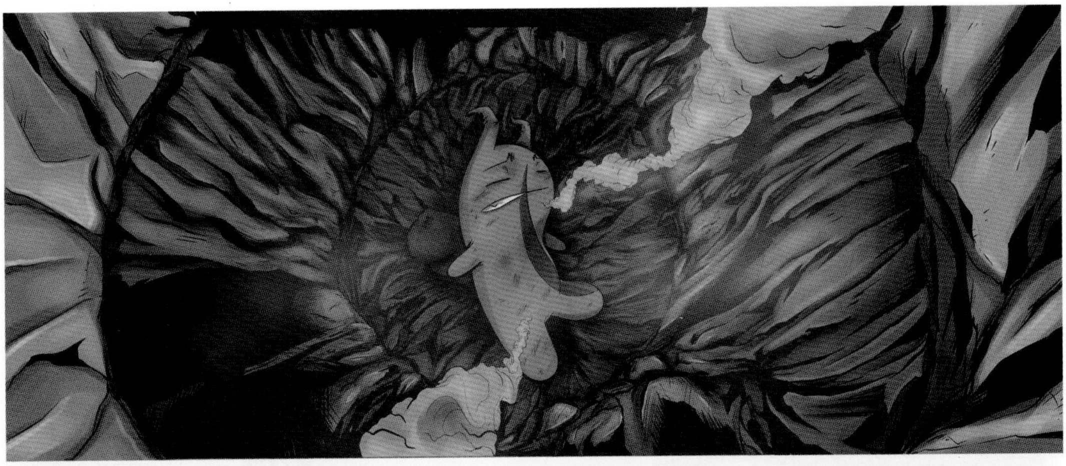

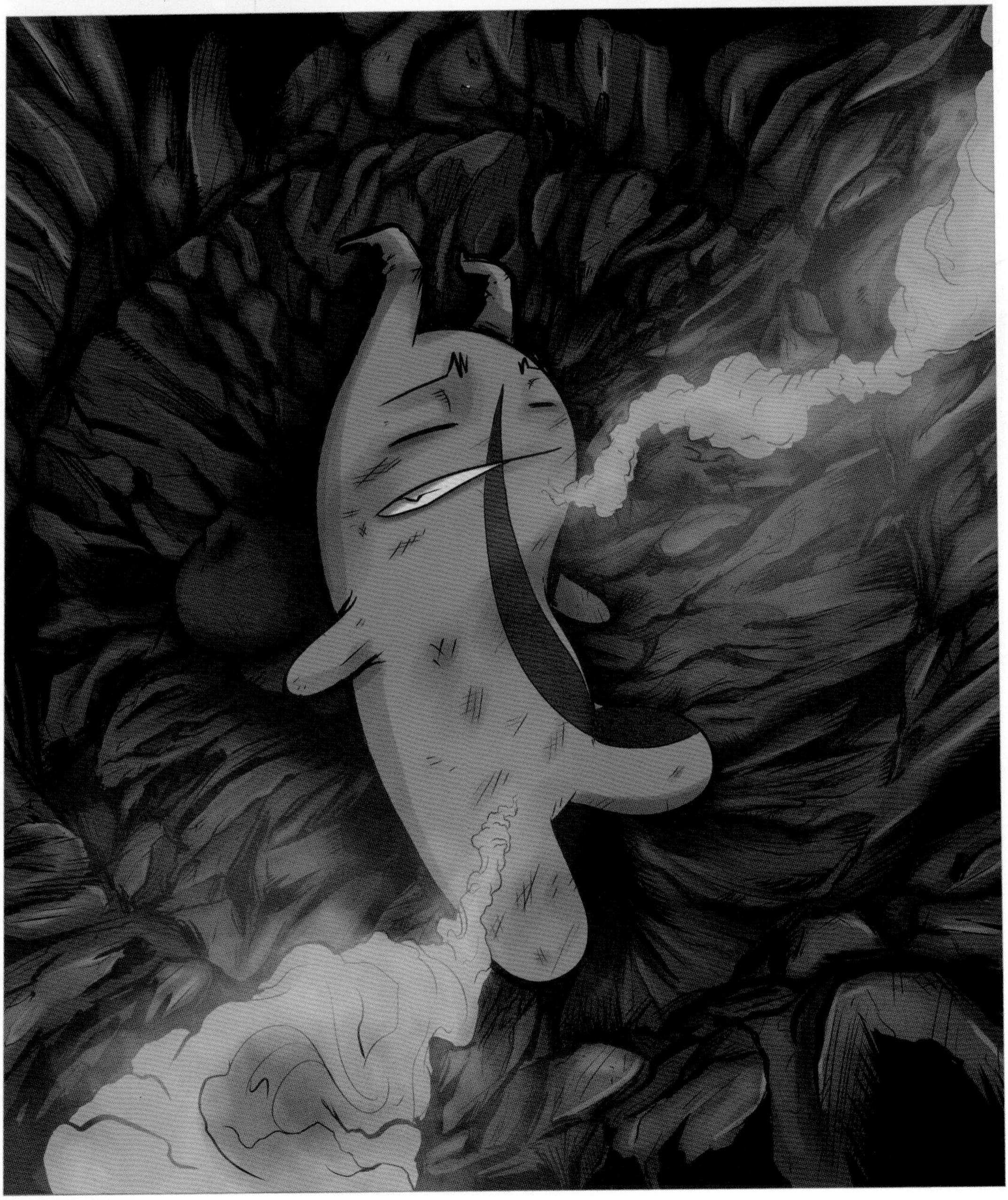

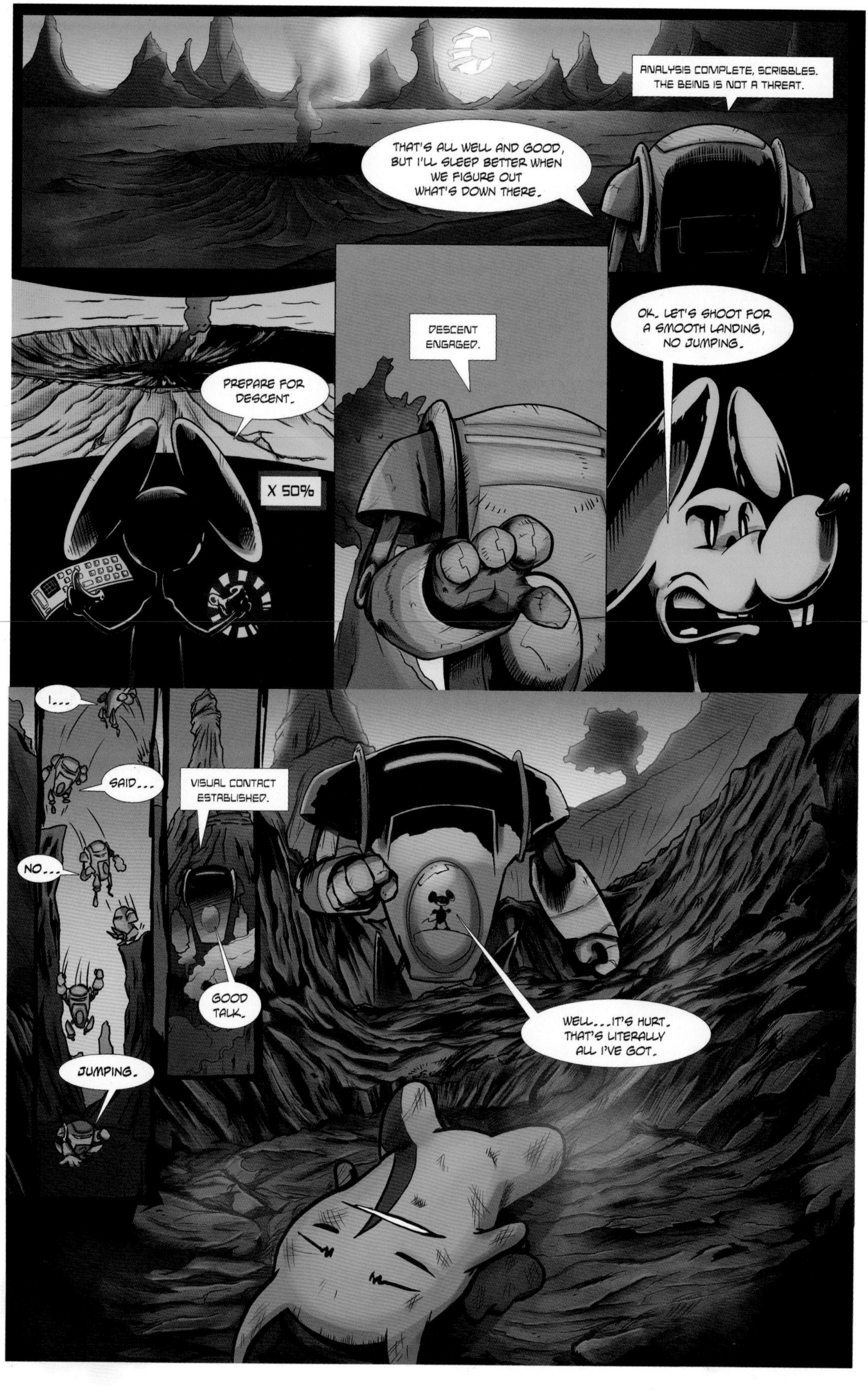
ANALYSIS COMPLETE, SCRIBBLES.
THE BEING IS NOT A THREAT.
THAT'S ALL WELL AND GOOD, BUT I'LL SLEEP BETTER WHEN WE FIGURE OUT WHAT'S DOWN THERE.
PREPARE FOR DESCENT.
X 50%
DESCENT ENGAGED.
OK. LET'S SHOOT FOR A SMOOTH LANDING, NO JUMPING.
I...
SAID...
NO...
JUMPING.
VISUAL CONTACT ESTABLISHED.
GOOD TALK.
WELL...IT'S HURT. THAT'S LITERALLY ALL I'VE GOT.

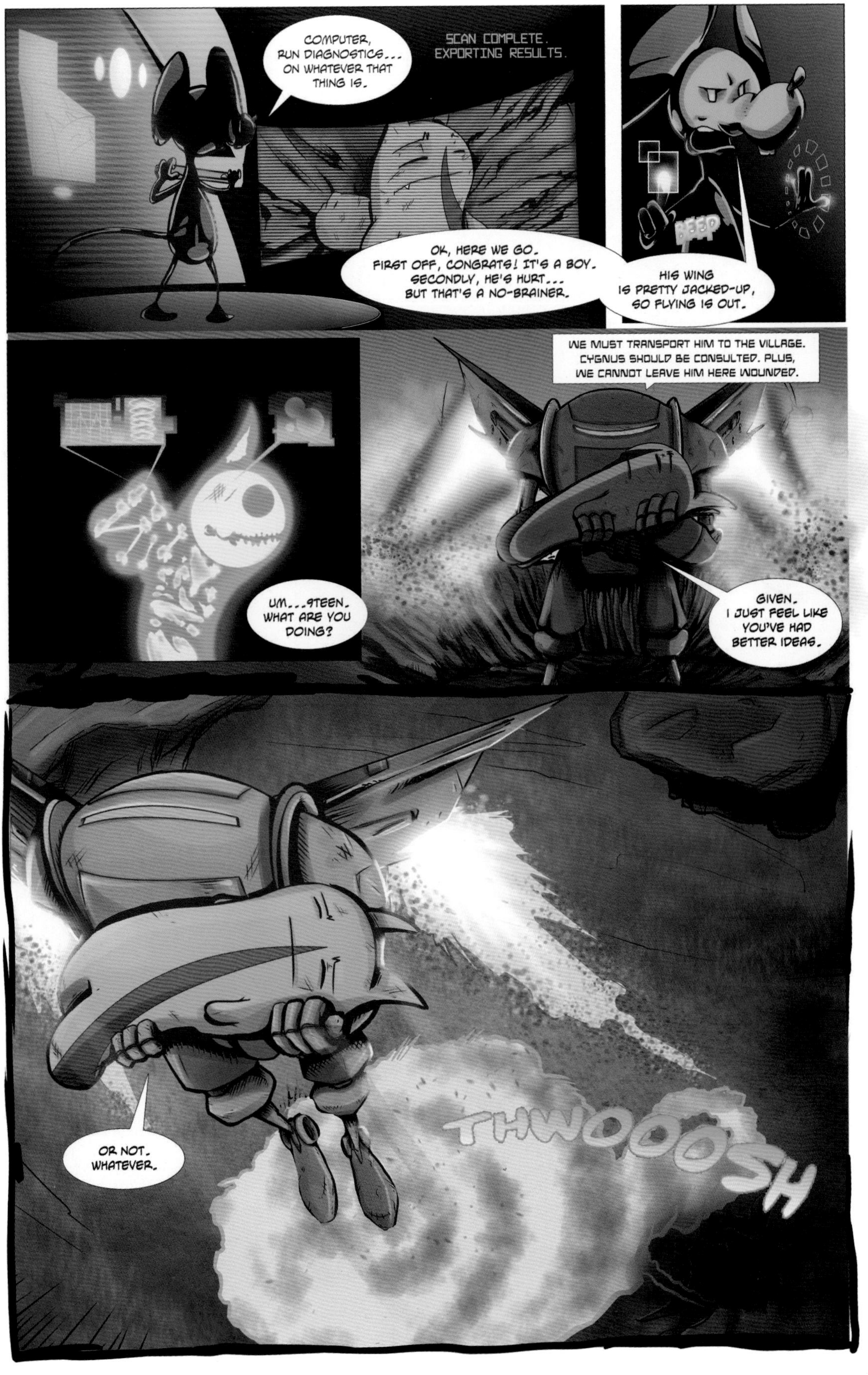
COMPUTER, RUN DIAGNOSTICS... ON WHATEVER THAT THING IS.
SCAN COMPLETE. EXPORTING RESULTS.
BEEP
OK, HERE WE GO. FIRST OFF, CONGRATS! IT'S A BOY. SECONDLY, HE'S HURT... BUT THAT'S A NO-BRAINER.
HIS WING IS PRETTY JACKED-UP, SO FLYING IS OUT.
UM...STEEN. WHAT ARE YOU DOING?
WE MUST TRANSPORT HIM TO THE VILLAGE. CYGNUS SHOULD BE CONSULTED. PLUS, WE CANNOT LEAVE HIM HERE WOUNDED.
GIVEN. I JUST FEEL LIKE YOU'VE HAD BETTER IDEAS.
THWOOOSH
OR NOT. WHATEVER.

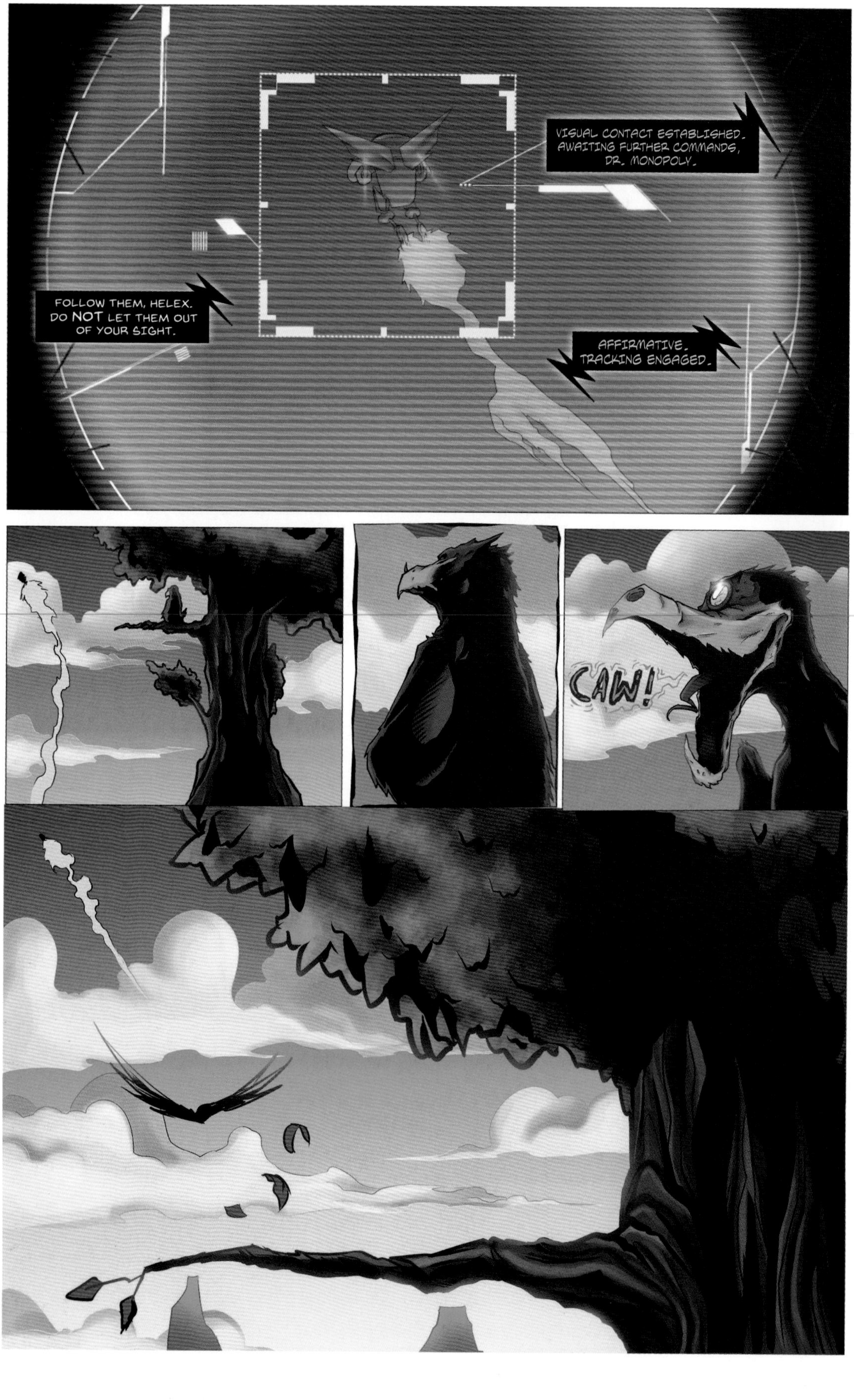
VISUAL CONTACT ESTABLISHED. AWAITING FURTHER COMMANDS, DR. MONOPOLY.
FOLLOW THEM, HELEX. DO **NOT** LET THEM OUT OF YOUR SIGHT.
AFFIRMATIVE. TRACKING ENGAGED.
CAW!

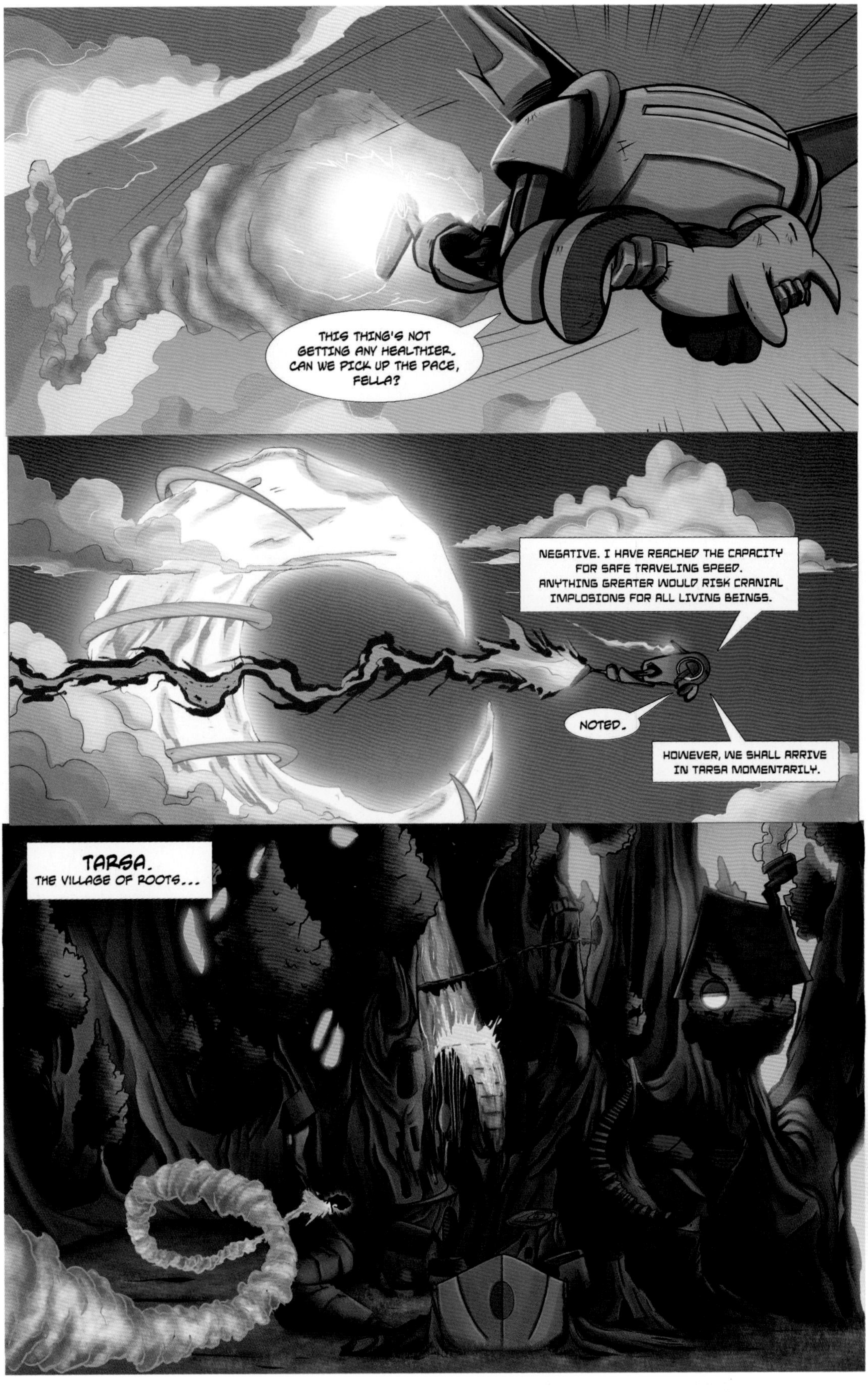
THIS THING'S NOT GETTING ANY HEALTHIER. CAN WE PICK UP THE PACE, FELLA?
NEGATIVE. I HAVE REACHED THE CAPACITY FOR SAFE TRAVELING SPEED. ANYTHING GREATER WOULD RISK CRANIAL IMPLOSIONS FOR ALL LIVING BEINGS.
NOTED.
HOWEVER, WE SHALL ARRIVE IN TARSA MOMENTARILY.
TARSA. THE VILLAGE OF ROOTS...

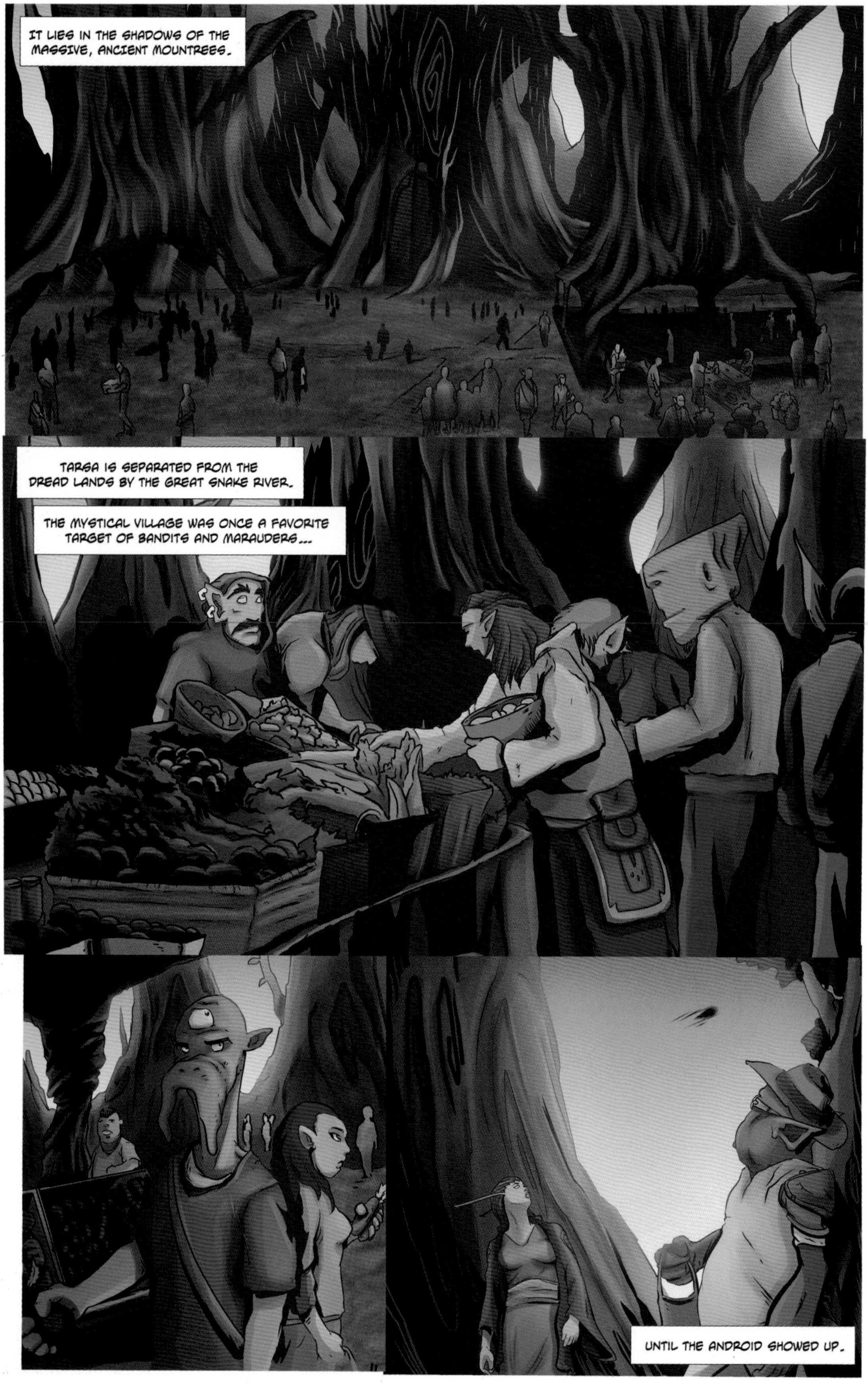
IT LIES IN THE SHADOWS OF THE MASSIVE, ANCIENT MOUNTREES.
TARSA IS SEPARATED FROM THE DREAD LANDS BY THE GREAT SNAKE RIVER.
THE MYSTICAL VILLAGE WAS ONCE A FAVORITE TARGET OF BANDITS AND MARAUDERS...
UNTIL THE ANDROID SHOWED UP.

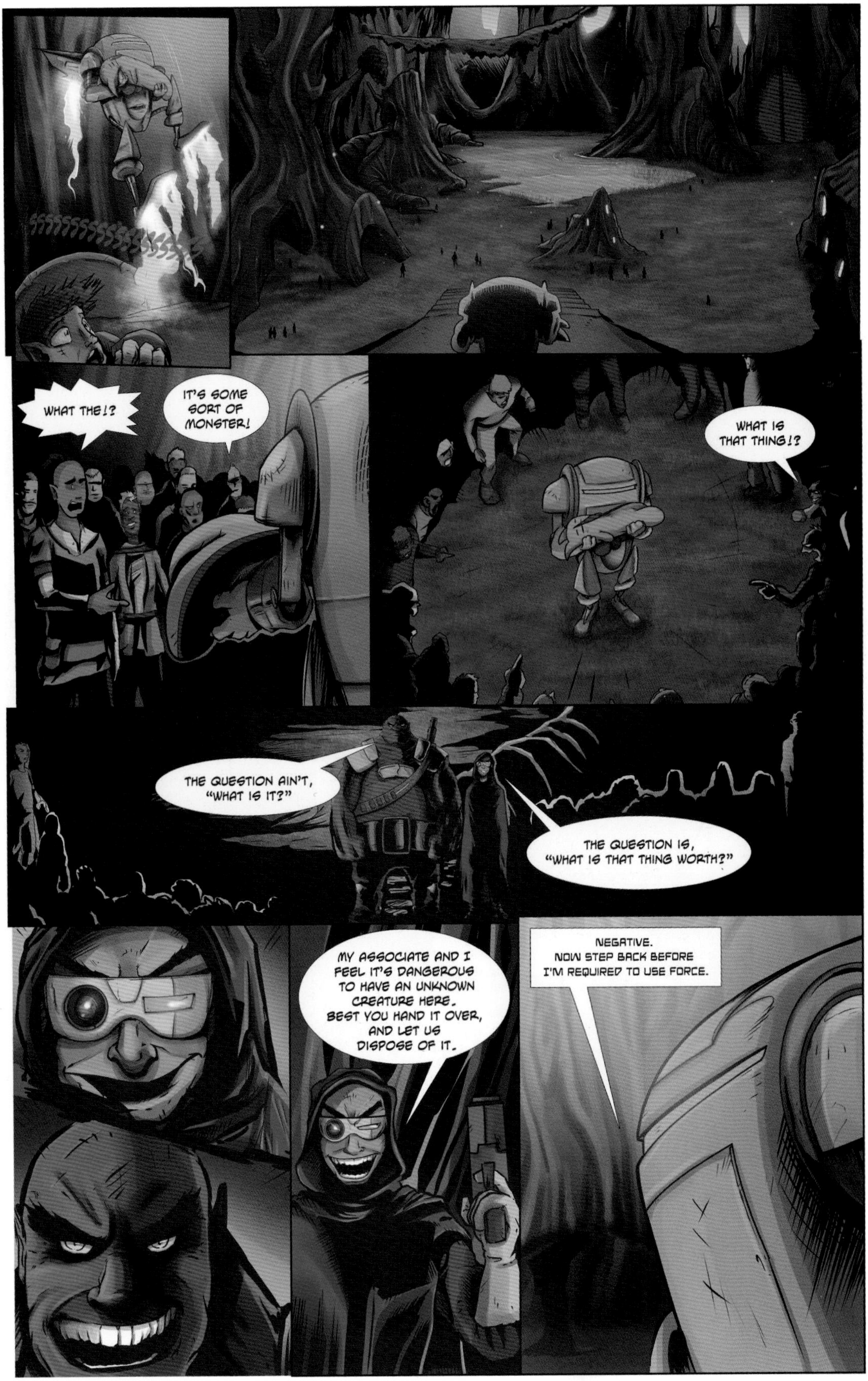
WHAT THE!?
IT'S SOME SORT OF MONSTER!
WHAT IS THAT THING!?
THE QUESTION AIN'T, "WHAT IS IT?"
THE QUESTION IS, "WHAT IS THAT THING WORTH?"
MY ASSOCIATE AND I FEEL IT'S DANGEROUS TO HAVE AN UNKNOWN CREATURE HERE. BEST YOU HAND IT OVER, AND LET US DISPOSE OF IT.
NEGATIVE. NOW STEP BACK BEFORE I'M REQUIRED TO USE FORCE.

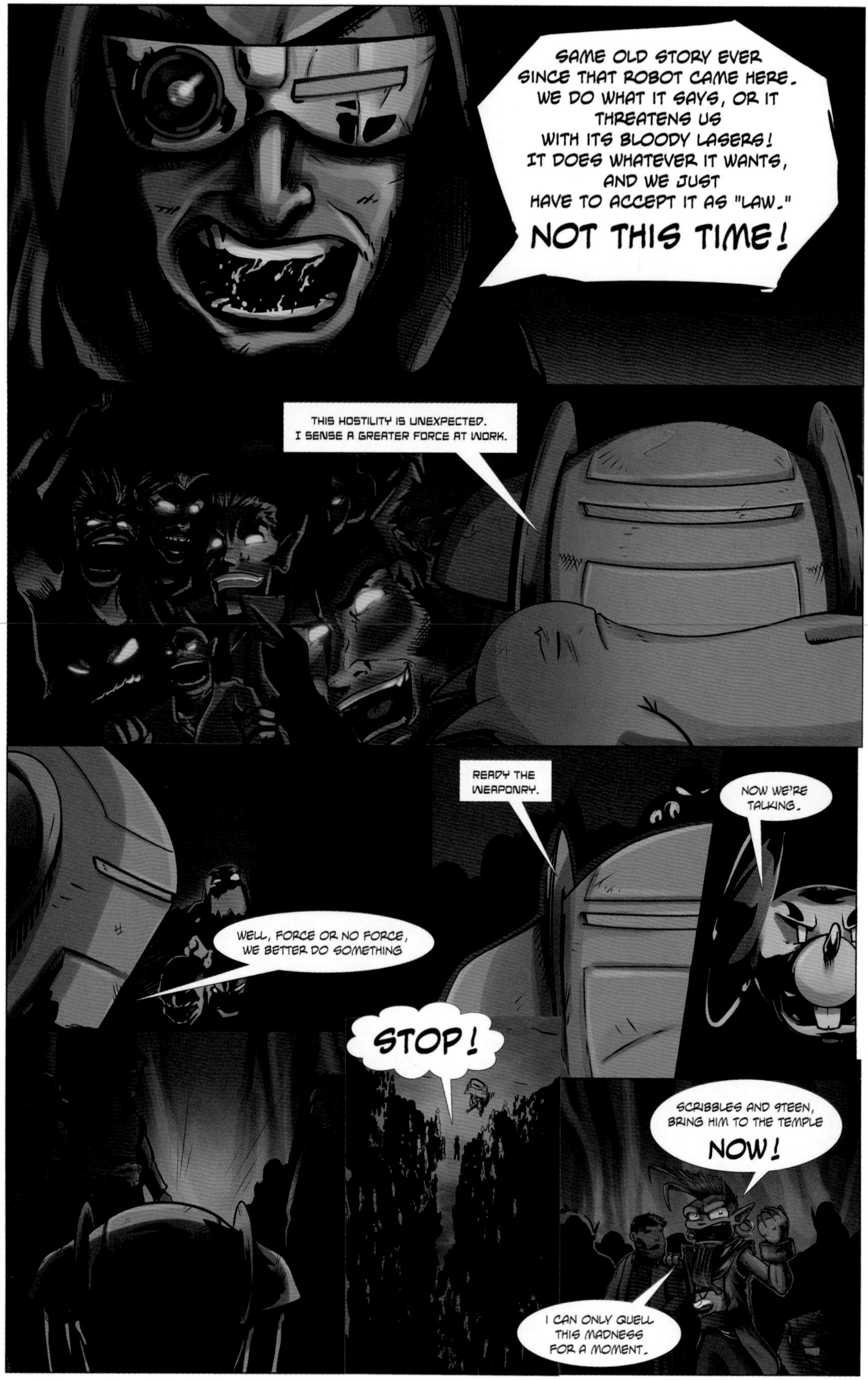
SAME OLD STORY EVER SINCE THAT ROBOT CAME HERE. WE DO WHAT IT SAYS, OR IT THREATENS US WITH ITS BLOODY LASERS! IT DOES WHATEVER IT WANTS, AND WE JUST HAVE TO ACCEPT IT AS "LAW." NOT THIS TIME!
THIS HOSTILITY IS UNEXPECTED. I SENSE A GREATER FORCE AT WORK.
WELL, FORCE OR NO FORCE, WE BETTER DO SOMETHING
READY THE WEAPONRY.
NOW WE'RE TALKING.
STOP!
SCRIBBLES AND STEEN, BRING HIM TO THE TEMPLE NOW!
I CAN ONLY QUELL THIS MADNESS FOR A MOMENT.

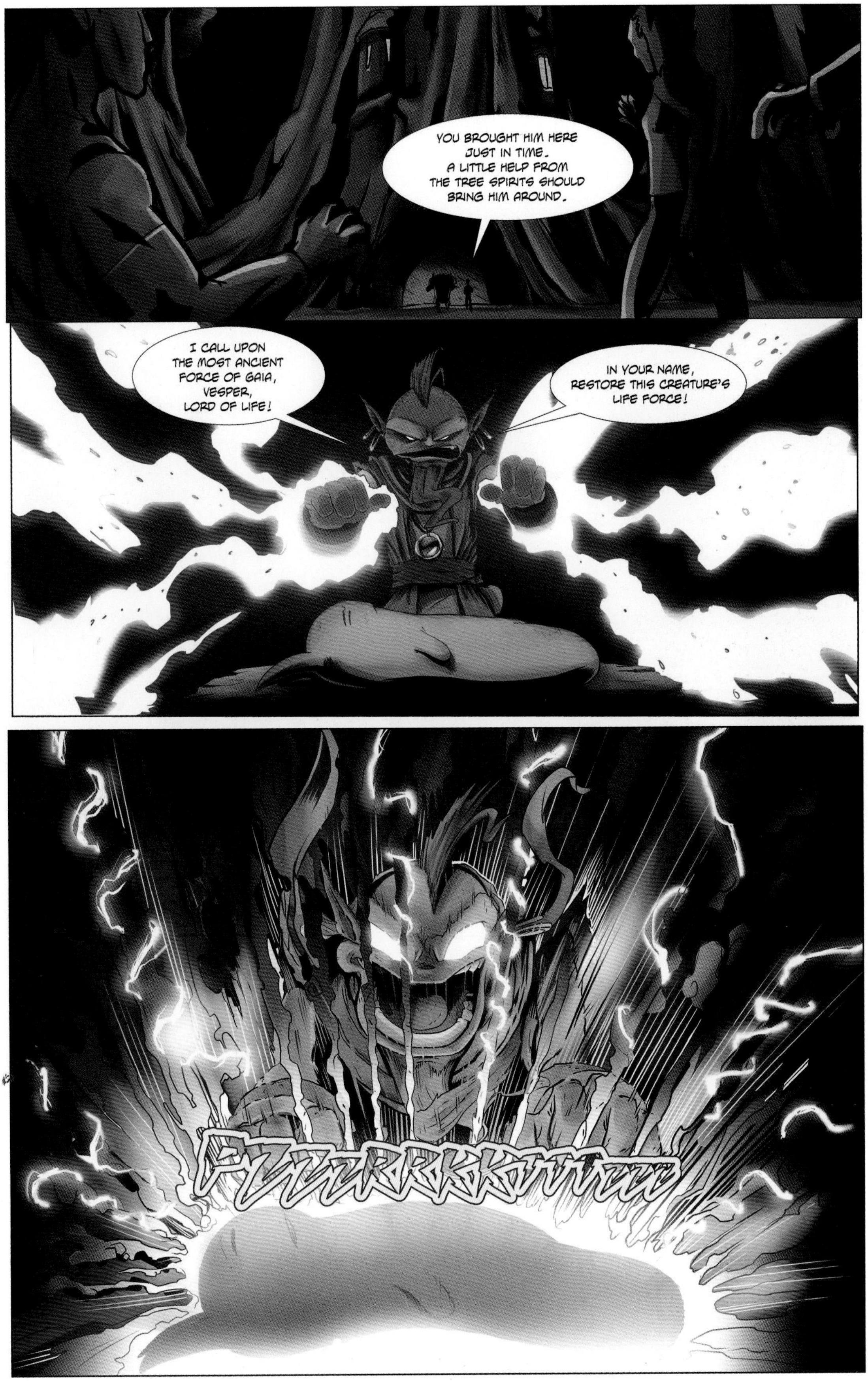
YOU BROUGHT HIM HERE JUST IN TIME. A LITTLE HELP FROM THE TREE SPIRITS SHOULD BRING HIM AROUND.
I CALL UPON THE MOST ANCIENT FORCE OF GAIA, VESPER, LORD OF LIFE!
IN YOUR NAME, RESTORE THIS CREATURE'S LIFE FORCE!

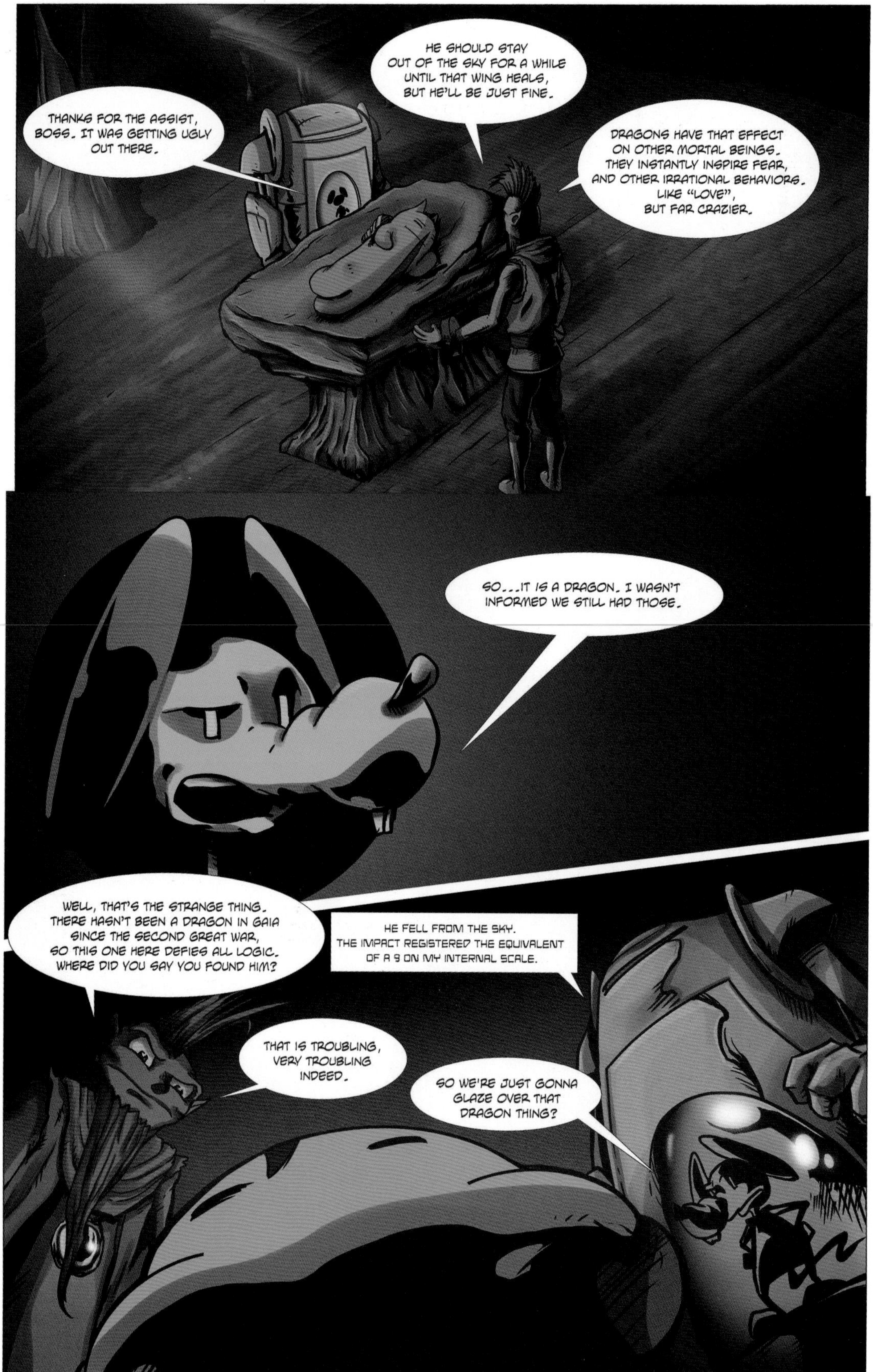
THANKS FOR THE ASSIST, BOSS. IT WAS GETTING UGLY OUT THERE.
HE SHOULD STAY OUT OF THE SKY FOR A WHILE UNTIL THAT WING HEALS, BUT HE'LL BE JUST FINE.
DRAGONS HAVE THAT EFFECT ON OTHER MORTAL BEINGS. THEY INSTANTLY INSPIRE FEAR, AND OTHER IRRATIONAL BEHAVIORS. LIKE "LOVE", BUT FAR CRAZIER.
SO...IT IS A DRAGON. I WASN'T INFORMED WE STILL HAD THOSE.
WELL, THAT'S THE STRANGE THING. THERE HASN'T BEEN A DRAGON IN GAIA SINCE THE SECOND GREAT WAR, SO THIS ONE HERE DEFIES ALL LOGIC. WHERE DID YOU SAY YOU FOUND HIM?
HE FELL FROM THE SKY. THE IMPACT REGISTERED THE EQUIVALENT OF A 9 ON MY INTERNAL SCALE.
THAT IS TROUBLING, VERY TROUBLING INDEED.
SO WE'RE JUST GONNA GLAZE OVER THAT DRAGON THING?

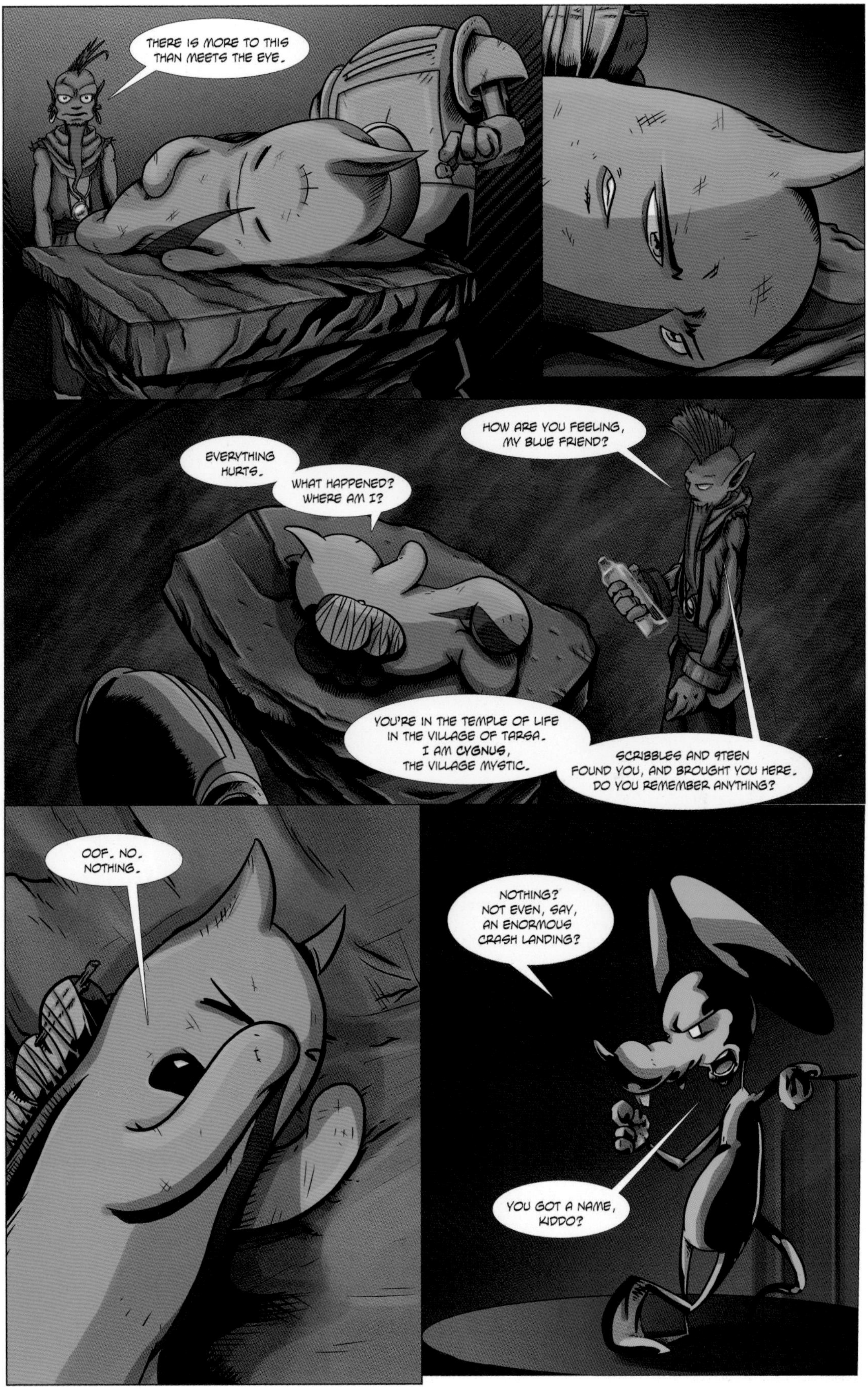
THERE IS MORE TO THIS THAN MEETS THE EYE.
HOW ARE YOU FEELING, MY BLUE FRIEND?
EVERYTHING HURTS.
WHAT HAPPENED? WHERE AM I?
YOU'RE IN THE TEMPLE OF LIFE IN THE VILLAGE OF TARSA. I AM CYGNUS, THE VILLAGE MYSTIC.
SCRIBBLES AND STEEN FOUND YOU, AND BROUGHT YOU HERE. DO YOU REMEMBER ANYTHING?
OOF. NO. NOTHING.
NOTHING? NOT EVEN, SAY, AN ENORMOUS CRASH LANDING?
YOU GOT A NAME, KIDDO?

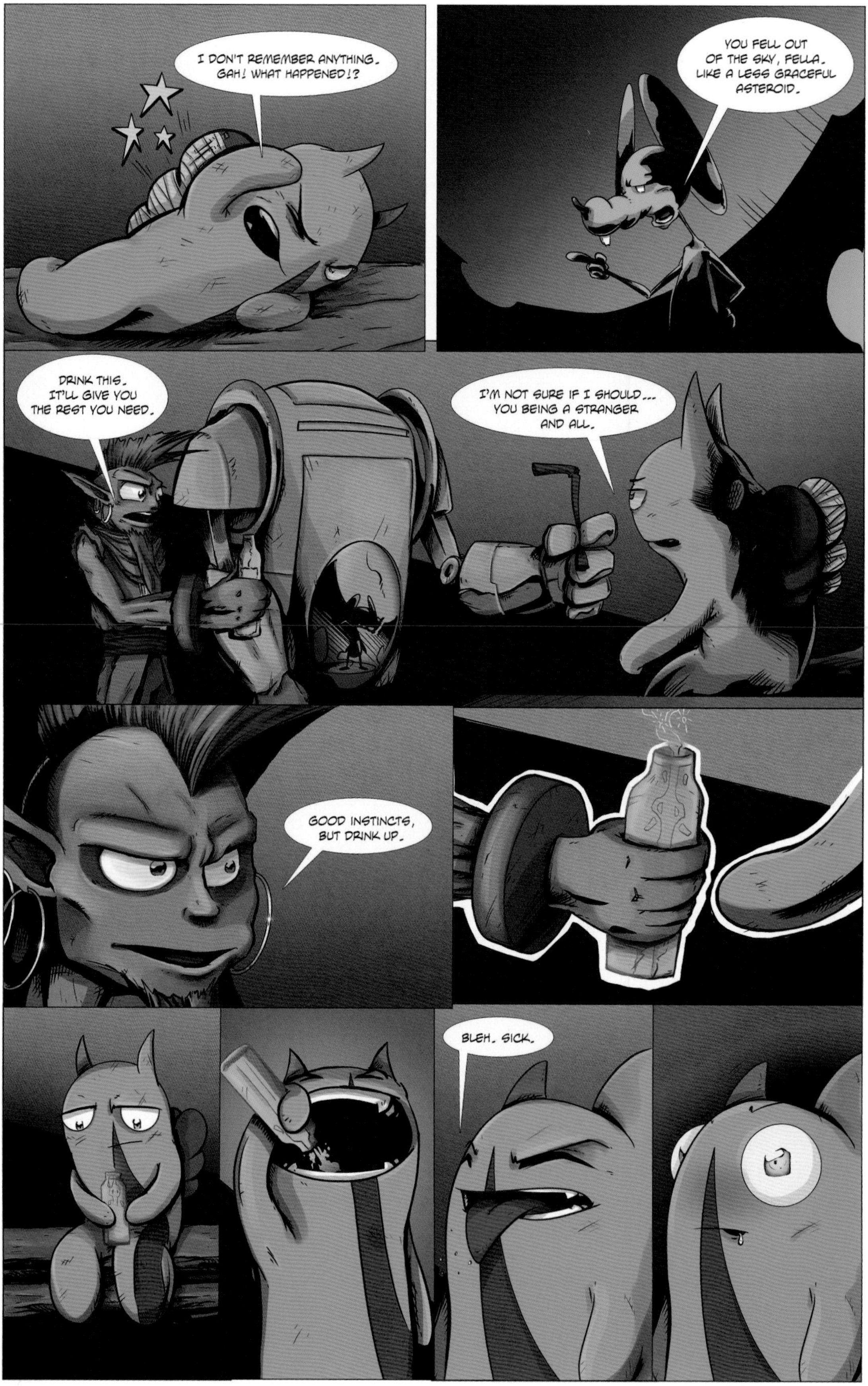
I DON'T REMEMBER ANYTHING. GAH! WHAT HAPPENED!?
YOU FELL OUT OF THE SKY, FELLA. LIKE A LESS GRACEFUL ASTEROID.
DRINK THIS. IT'LL GIVE YOU THE REST YOU NEED.
I'M NOT SURE IF I SHOULD... YOU BEING A STRANGER AND ALL.
GOOD INSTINCTS, BUT DRINK UP.
BLEH. SICK.

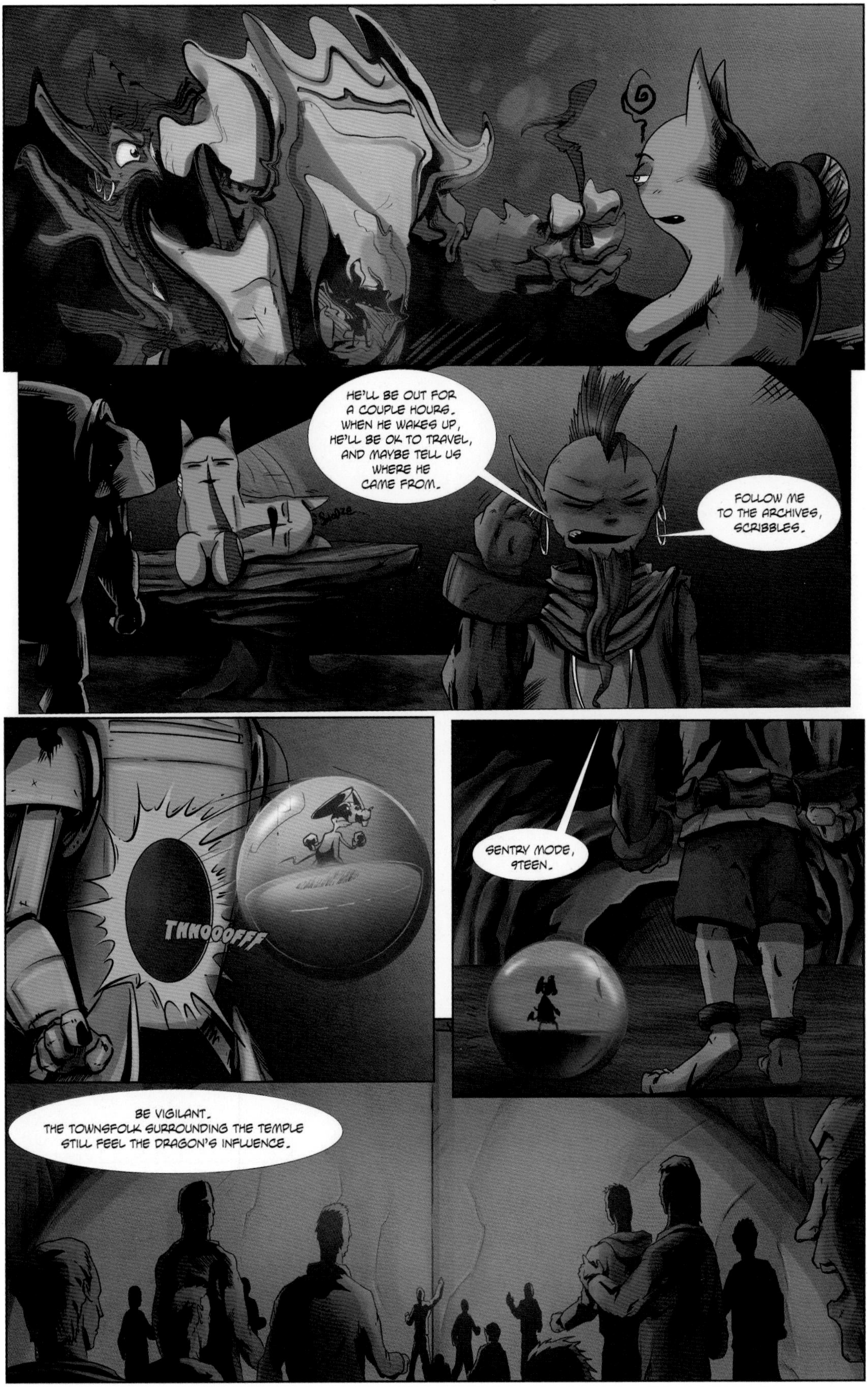
HE'LL BE OUT FOR A COUPLE HOURS. WHEN HE WAKES UP, HE'LL BE OK TO TRAVEL, AND MAYBE TELL US WHERE HE CAME FROM.
FOLLOW ME TO THE ARCHIVES, SCRIBBLES.
THNOOOOFFF
SENTRY MODE, 9TEEN.
BE VIGILANT. THE TOWNSFOLK SURROUNDING THE TEMPLE STILL FEEL THE DRAGON'S INFLUENCE.

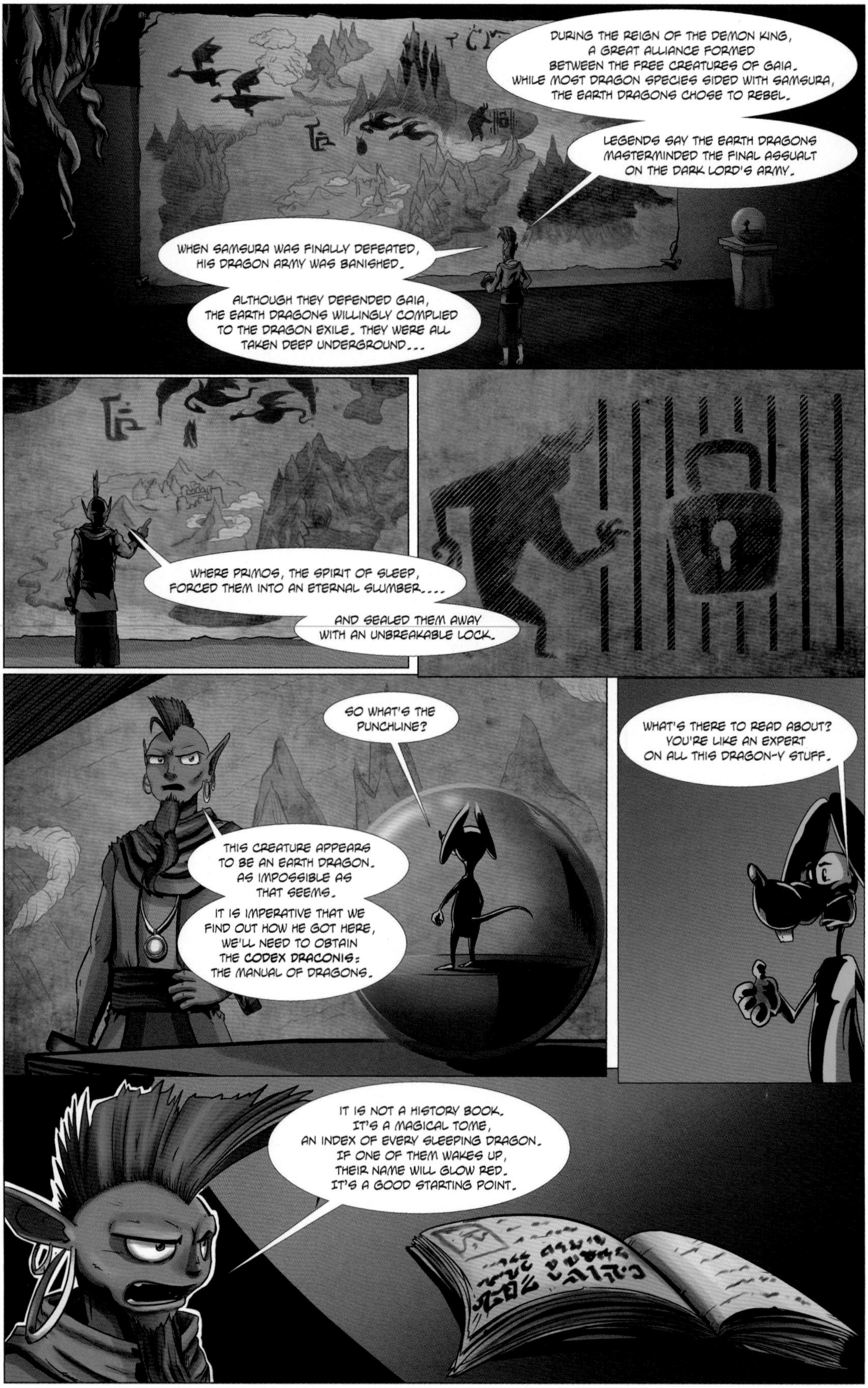
DURING THE REIGN OF THE DEMON KING, A GREAT ALLIANCE FORMED BETWEEN THE FREE CREATURES OF GAIA. WHILE MOST DRAGON SPECIES SIDED WITH SAMSURA, THE EARTH DRAGONS CHOSE TO REBEL.
LEGENDS SAY THE EARTH DRAGONS MASTERMINDED THE FINAL ASSUALT ON THE DARK LORD'S ARMY.
WHEN SAMSURA WAS FINALLY DEFEATED, HIS DRAGON ARMY WAS BANISHED.
ALTHOUGH THEY DEFENDED GAIA, THE EARTH DRAGONS WILLINGLY COMPLIED TO THE DRAGON EXILE. THEY WERE ALL TAKEN DEEP UNDERGROUND...
WHERE PRIMOS, THE SPIRIT OF SLEEP, FORCED THEM INTO AN ETERNAL SLUMBER....
AND SEALED THEM AWAY WITH AN UNBREAKABLE LOCK.
SO WHAT'S THE PUNCHLINE?
THIS CREATURE APPEARS TO BE AN EARTH DRAGON. AS IMPOSSIBLE AS THAT SEEMS.
IT IS IMPERATIVE THAT WE FIND OUT HOW HE GOT HERE, WE'LL NEED TO OBTAIN THE **CODEX DRACONIS**: THE MANUAL OF DRAGONS.
WHAT'S THERE TO READ ABOUT? YOU'RE LIKE AN EXPERT ON ALL THIS DRAGON-Y STUFF.
IT IS NOT A HISTORY BOOK. IT'S A MAGICAL TOME, AN INDEX OF EVERY SLEEPING DRAGON. IF ONE OF THEM WAKES UP, THEIR NAME WILL GLOW RED. IT'S A GOOD STARTING POINT.

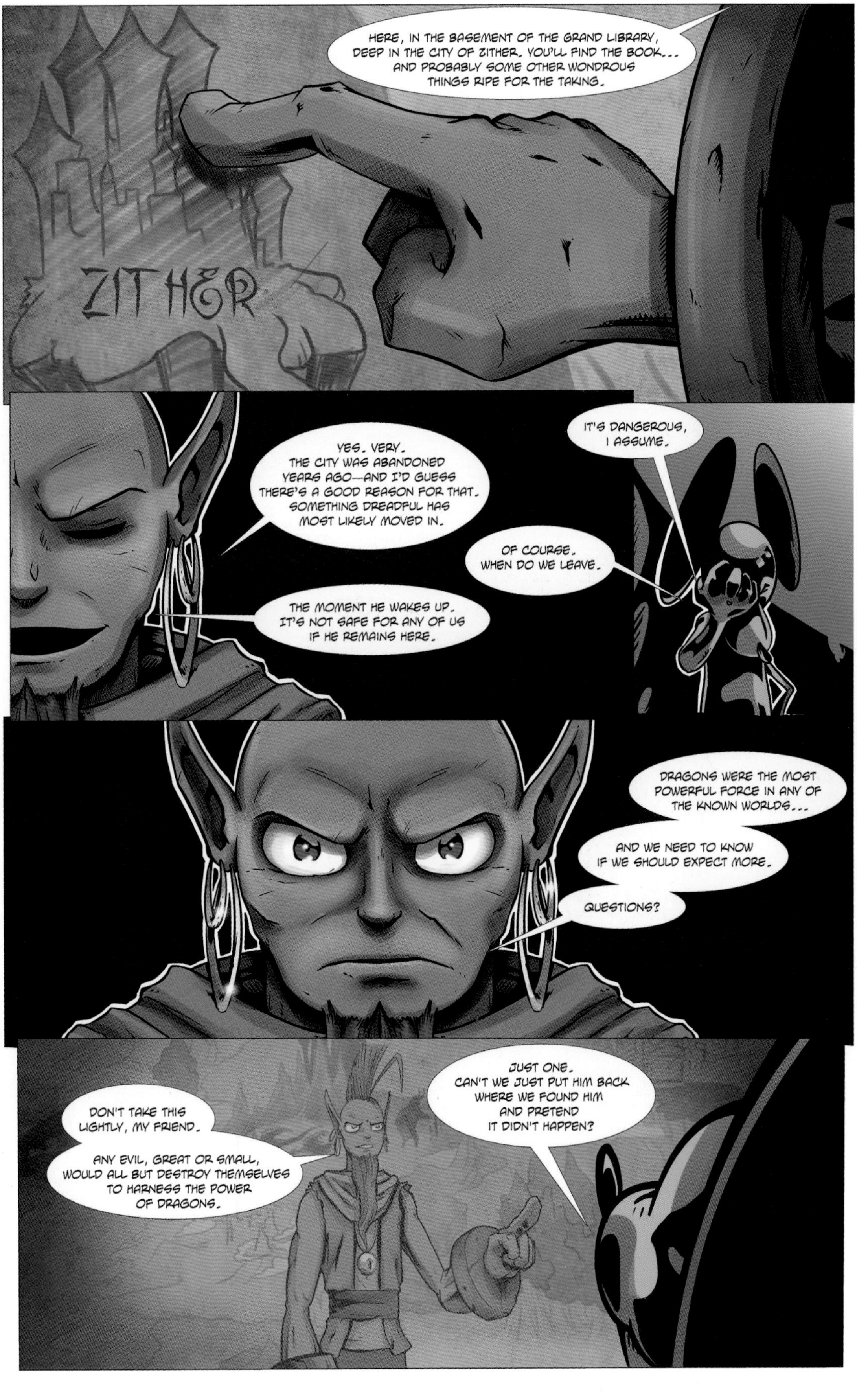
HERE, IN THE BASEMENT OF THE GRAND LIBRARY, DEEP IN THE CITY OF ZITHER. YOU'LL FIND THE BOOK... AND PROBABLY SOME OTHER WONDROUS THINGS RIPE FOR THE TAKING.
ZITHER
IT'S DANGEROUS, I ASSUME.
YES. VERY. THE CITY WAS ABANDONED YEARS AGO—AND I'D GUESS THERE'S A GOOD REASON FOR THAT. SOMETHING DREADFUL HAS MOST LIKELY MOVED IN.
OF COURSE. WHEN DO WE LEAVE.
THE MOMENT HE WAKES UP. IT'S NOT SAFE FOR ANY OF US IF HE REMAINS HERE.
DRAGONS WERE THE MOST POWERFUL FORCE IN ANY OF THE KNOWN WORLDS...
AND WE NEED TO KNOW IF WE SHOULD EXPECT MORE.
QUESTIONS?
JUST ONE. CAN'T WE JUST PUT HIM BACK WHERE WE FOUND HIM AND PRETEND IT DIDN'T HAPPEN?
DON'T TAKE THIS LIGHTLY, MY FRIEND.
ANY EVIL, GREAT OR SMALL, WOULD ALL BUT DESTROY THEMSELVES TO HARNESS THE POWER OF DRAGONS.

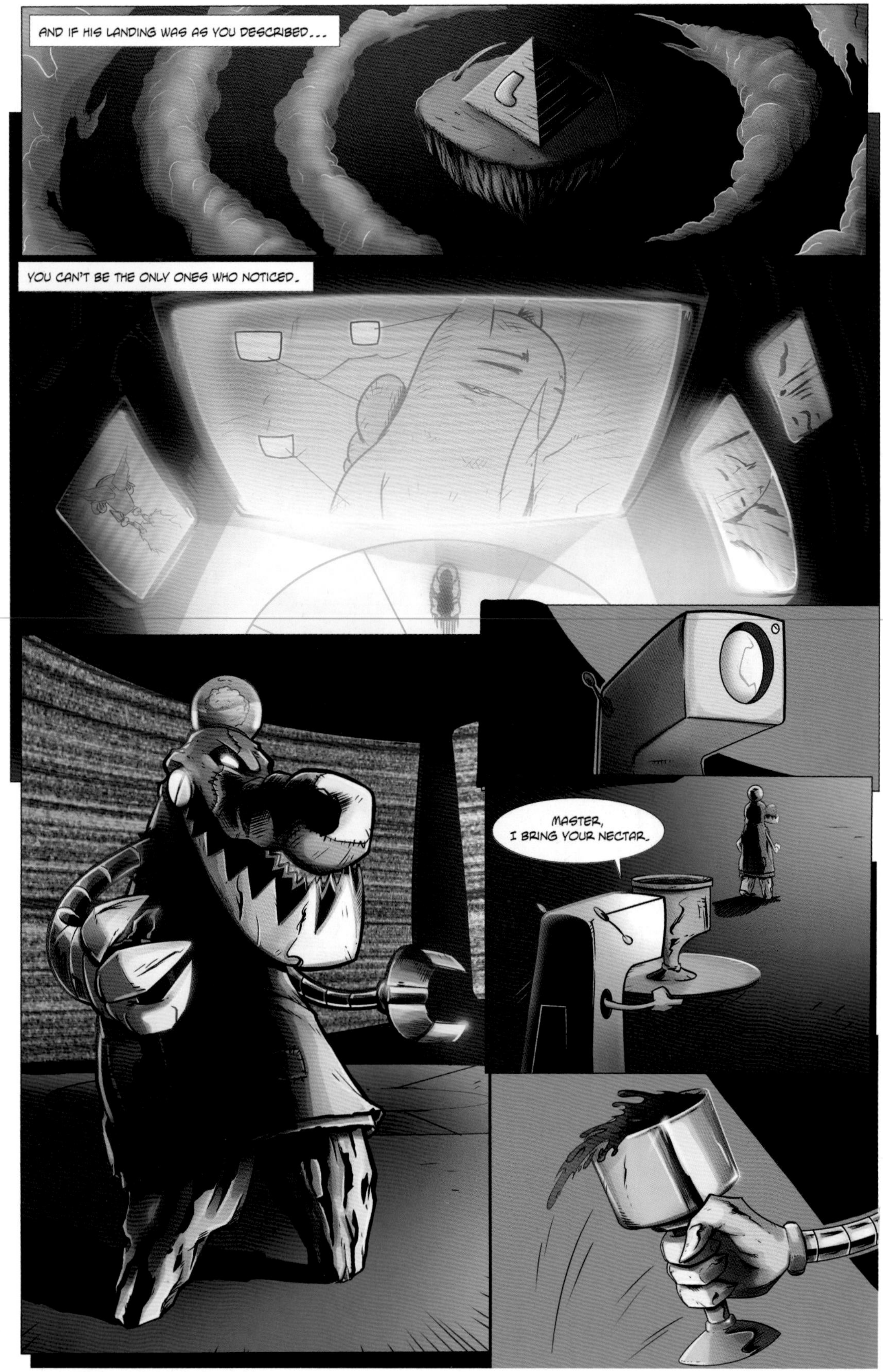
AND IF HIS LANDING WAS AS YOU DESCRIBED...
YOU CAN'T BE THE ONLY ONES WHO NOTICED.
MASTER, I BRING YOUR NECTAR.

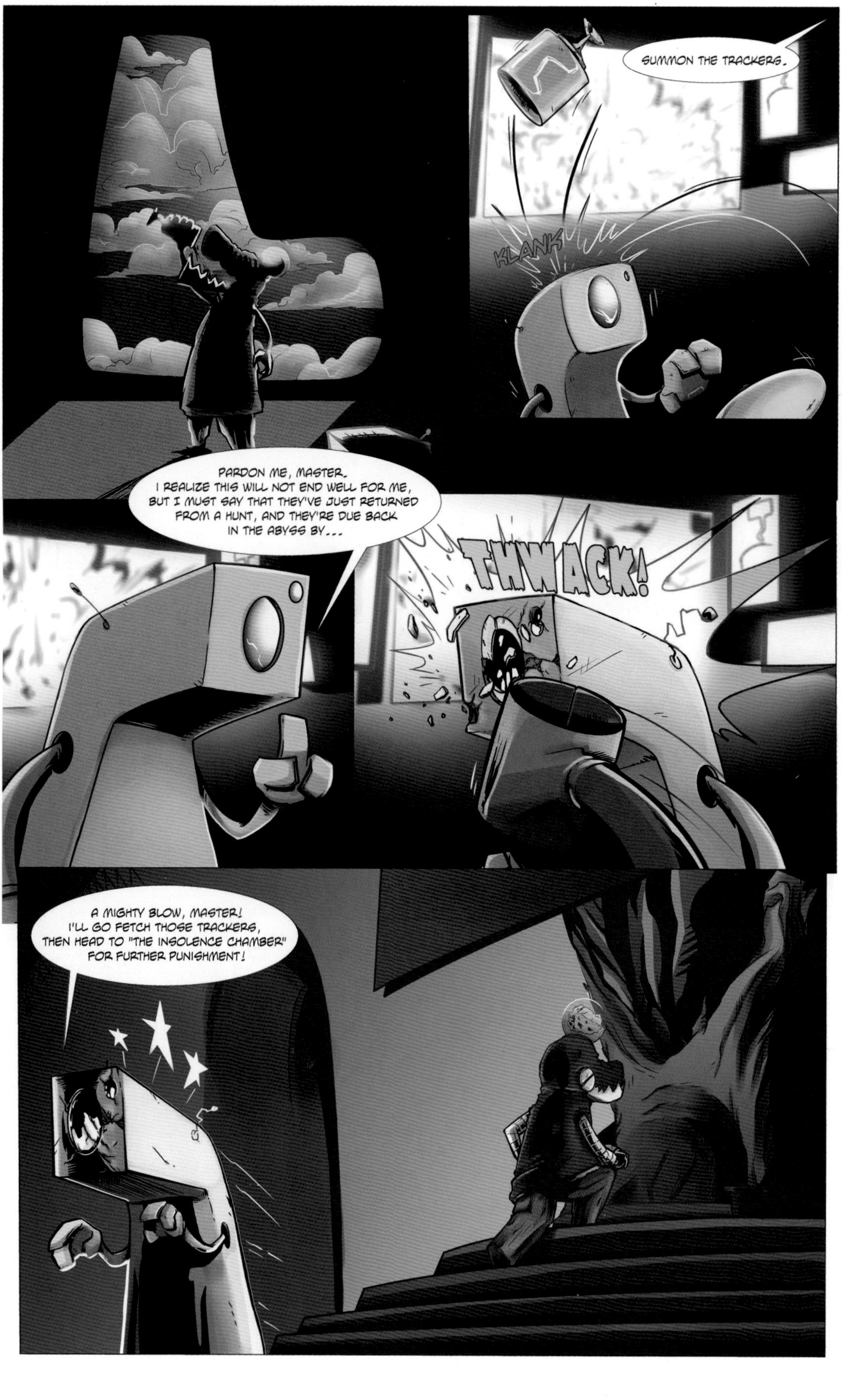
SUMMON THE TRACKERS.
KLANK
PARDON ME, MASTER. I REALIZE THIS WILL NOT END WELL FOR ME, BUT I MUST SAY THAT THEY'VE JUST RETURNED FROM A HUNT, AND THEY'RE DUE BACK IN THE ABYSS BY...
THWACK!
A MIGHTY BLOW, MASTER! I'LL GO FETCH THOSE TRACKERS, THEN HEAD TO "THE INSOLENCE CHAMBER" FOR FURTHER PUNISHMENT!

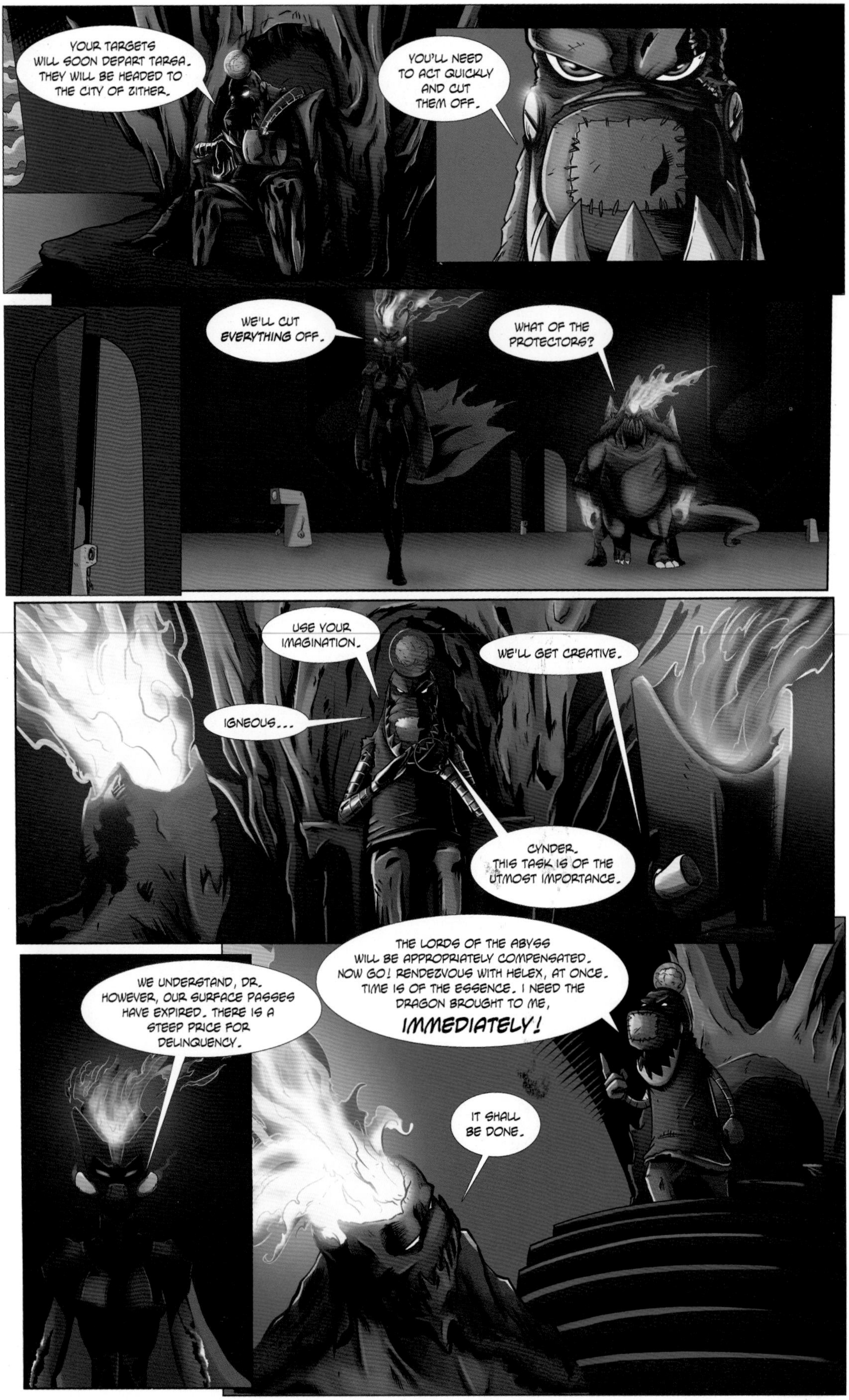
YOUR TARGETS WILL SOON DEPART TARSA. THEY WILL BE HEADED TO THE CITY OF ZITHER.
YOU'LL NEED TO ACT QUICKLY AND CUT THEM OFF.
WE'LL CUT EVERYTHING OFF.
WHAT OF THE PROTECTORS?
USE YOUR IMAGINATION.
WE'LL GET CREATIVE.
IGNEOUS...
CYNDER. THIS TASK IS OF THE UTMOST IMPORTANCE.
WE UNDERSTAND, DR. HOWEVER, OUR SURFACE PASSES HAVE EXPIRED. THERE IS A STEEP PRICE FOR DELINQUENCY.
THE LORDS OF THE ABYSS WILL BE APPROPRIATELY COMPENSATED. NOW GO! RENDEZVOUS WITH HELEX, AT ONCE. TIME IS OF THE ESSENCE. I NEED THE DRAGON BROUGHT TO ME, IMMEDIATELY!
IT SHALL BE DONE.

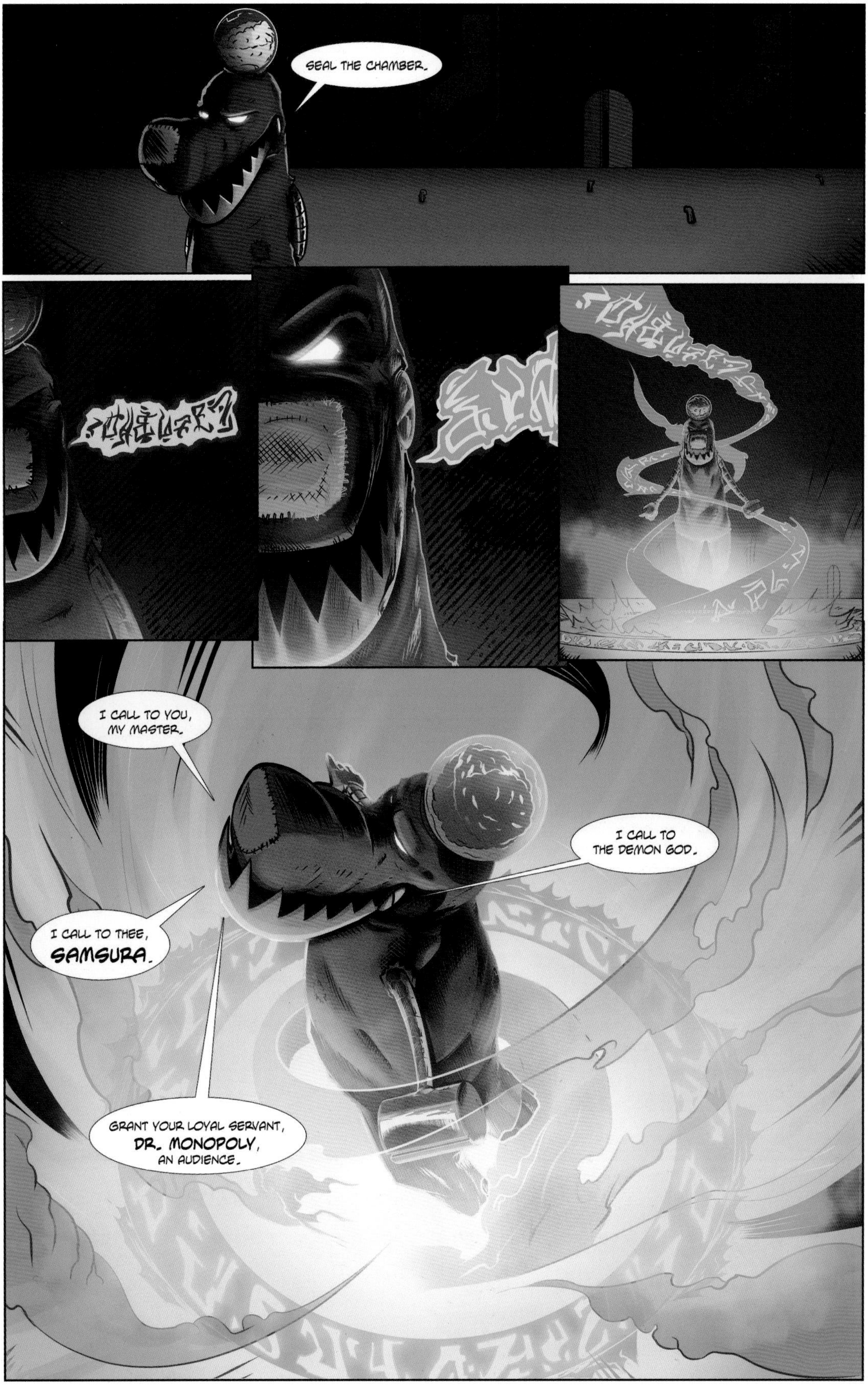
SEAL THE CHAMBER.
I CALL TO YOU, MY MASTER.
I CALL TO THE DEMON GOD.
I CALL TO THEE, SAMSURA.
GRANT YOUR LOYAL SERVANT, DR. MONOPOLY, AN AUDIENCE.

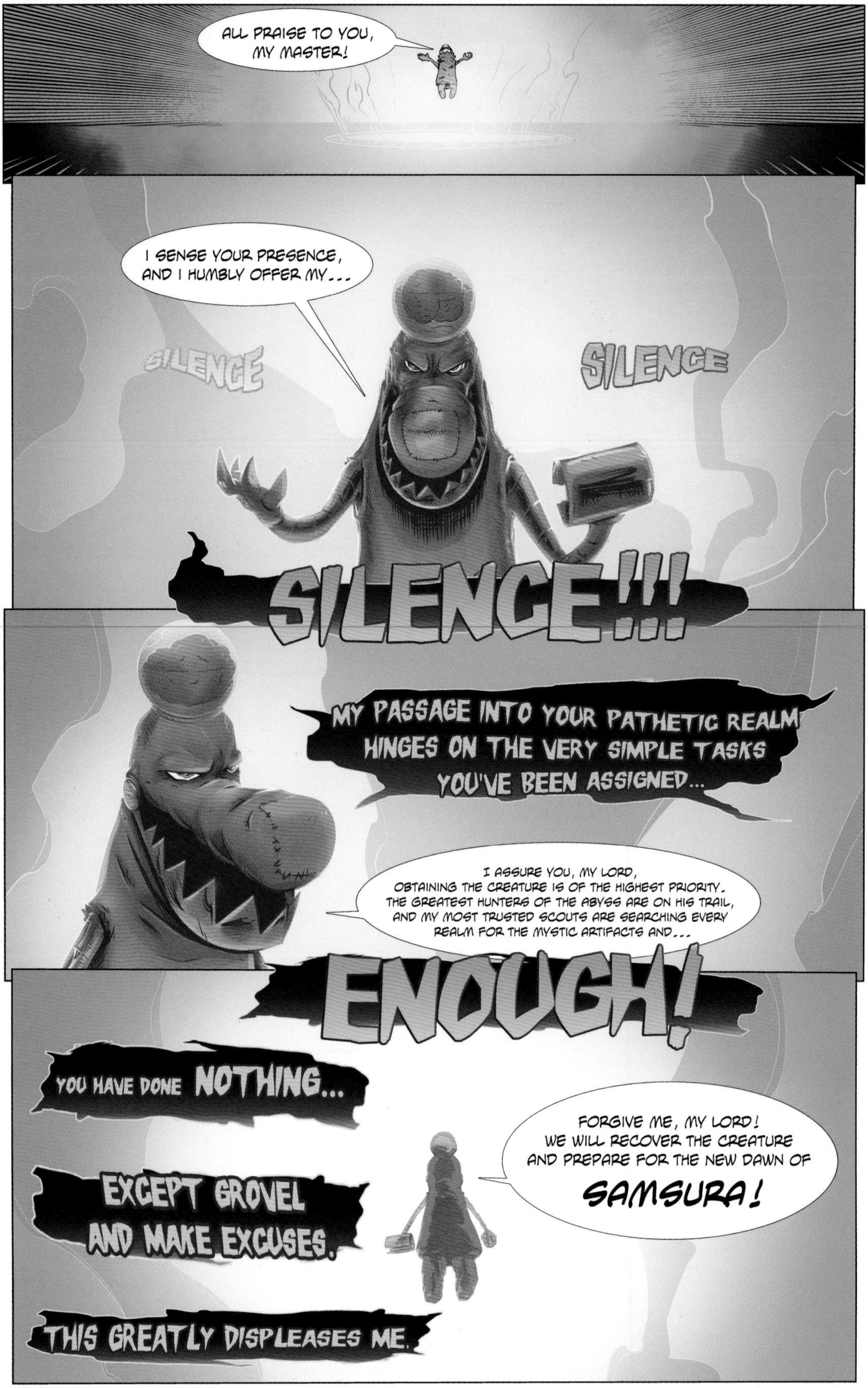
ALL PRAISE TO YOU, MY MASTER!
I SENSE YOUR PRESENCE, AND I HUMBLY OFFER MY...
SILENCE
SILENCE
SILENCE!!!
MY PASSAGE INTO YOUR PATHETIC REALM HINGES ON THE VERY SIMPLE TASKS YOU'VE BEEN ASSIGNED...
I ASSURE YOU, MY LORD, OBTAINING THE CREATURE IS OF THE HIGHEST PRIORITY. THE GREATEST HUNTERS OF THE ABYSS ARE ON HIS TRAIL, AND MY MOST TRUSTED SCOUTS ARE SEARCHING EVERY REALM FOR THE MYSTIC ARTIFACTS AND...
ENOUGH!
YOU HAVE DONE NOTHING...
EXCEPT GROVEL AND MAKE EXCUSES.
THIS GREATLY DISPLEASES ME.
FORGIVE ME, MY LORD! WE WILL RECOVER THE CREATURE AND PREPARE FOR THE NEW DAWN OF SAMSURA!

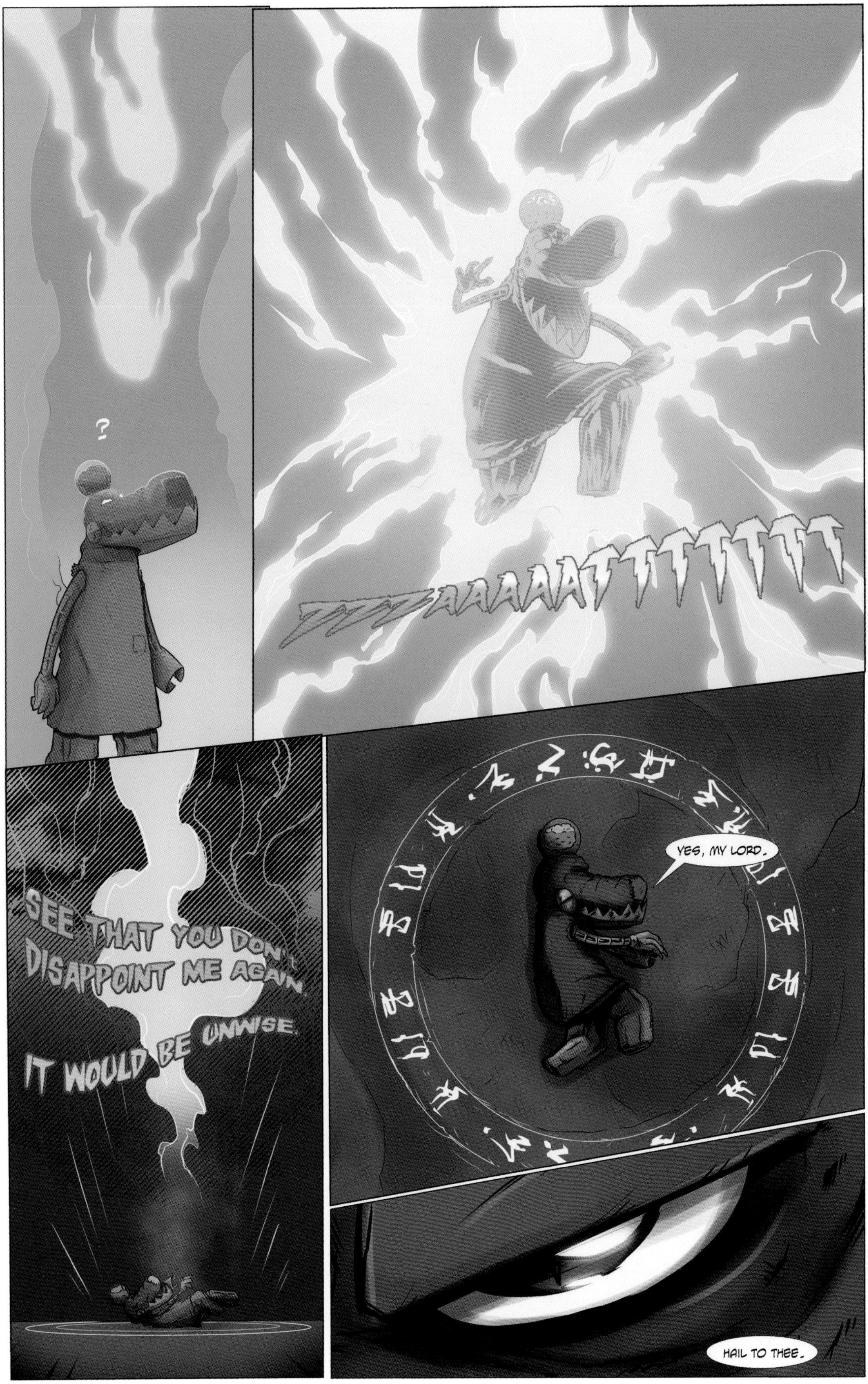
?
ZZZZAAAAATTTTTTTTT
SEE THAT YOU DON'T DISAPPOINT ME AGAIN.
IT WOULD BE UNWISE.
YES, MY LORD.
HAIL TO THEE.

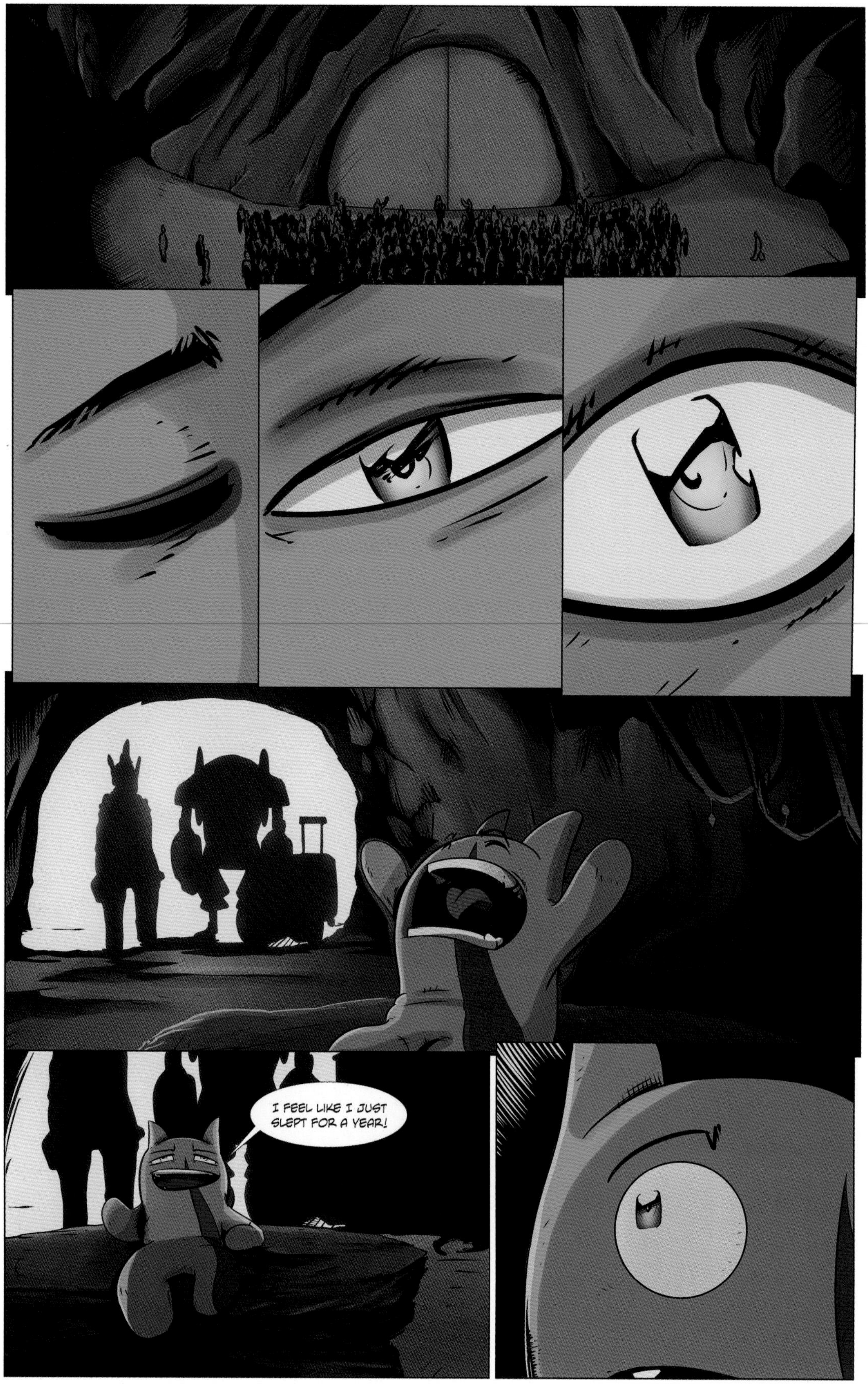
I FEEL LIKE I JUST
SLEPT FOR A YEAR!

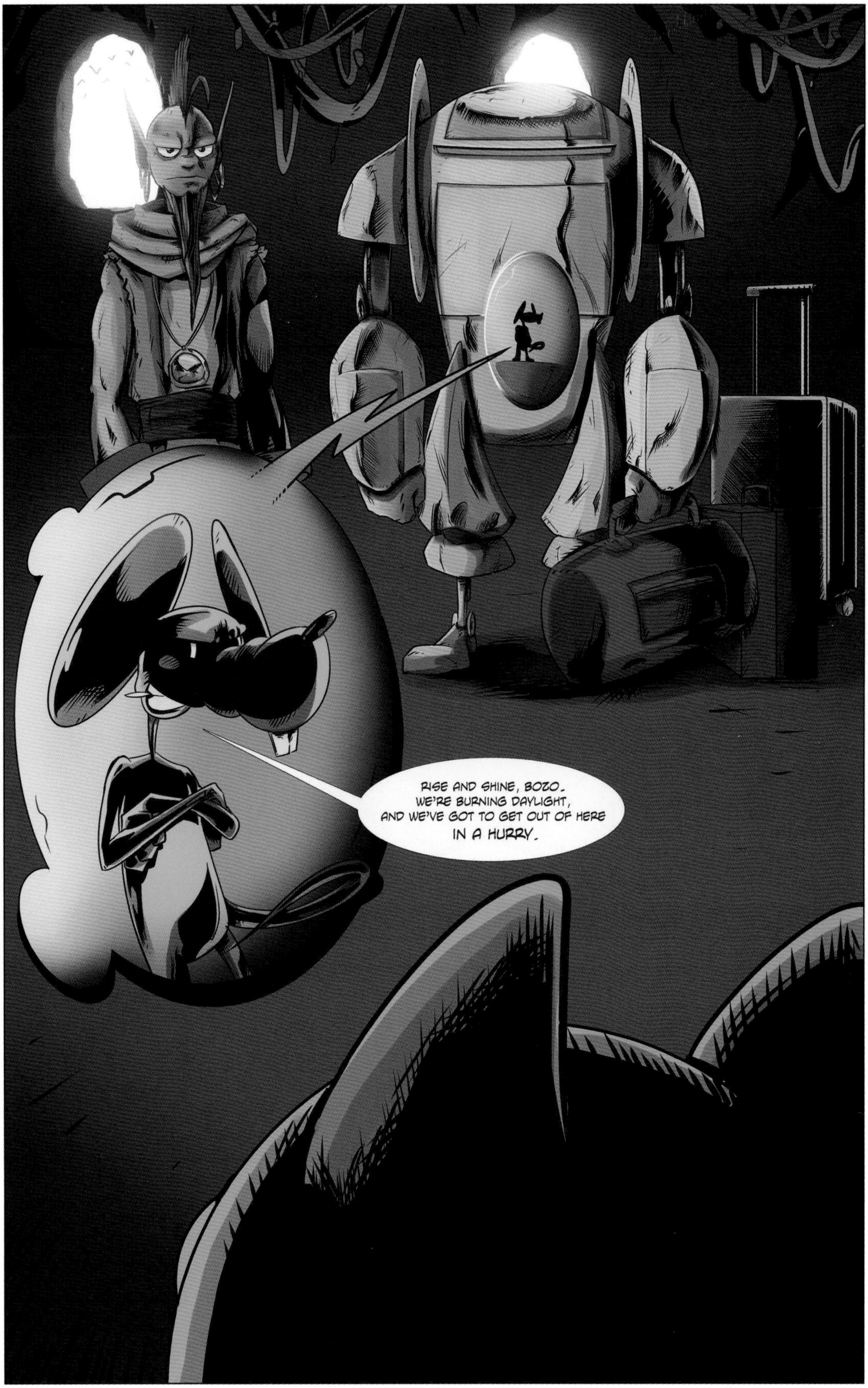
RISE AND SHINE, BOZO. WE'RE BURNING DAYLIGHT, AND WE'VE GOT TO GET OUT OF HERE IN A HURRY.

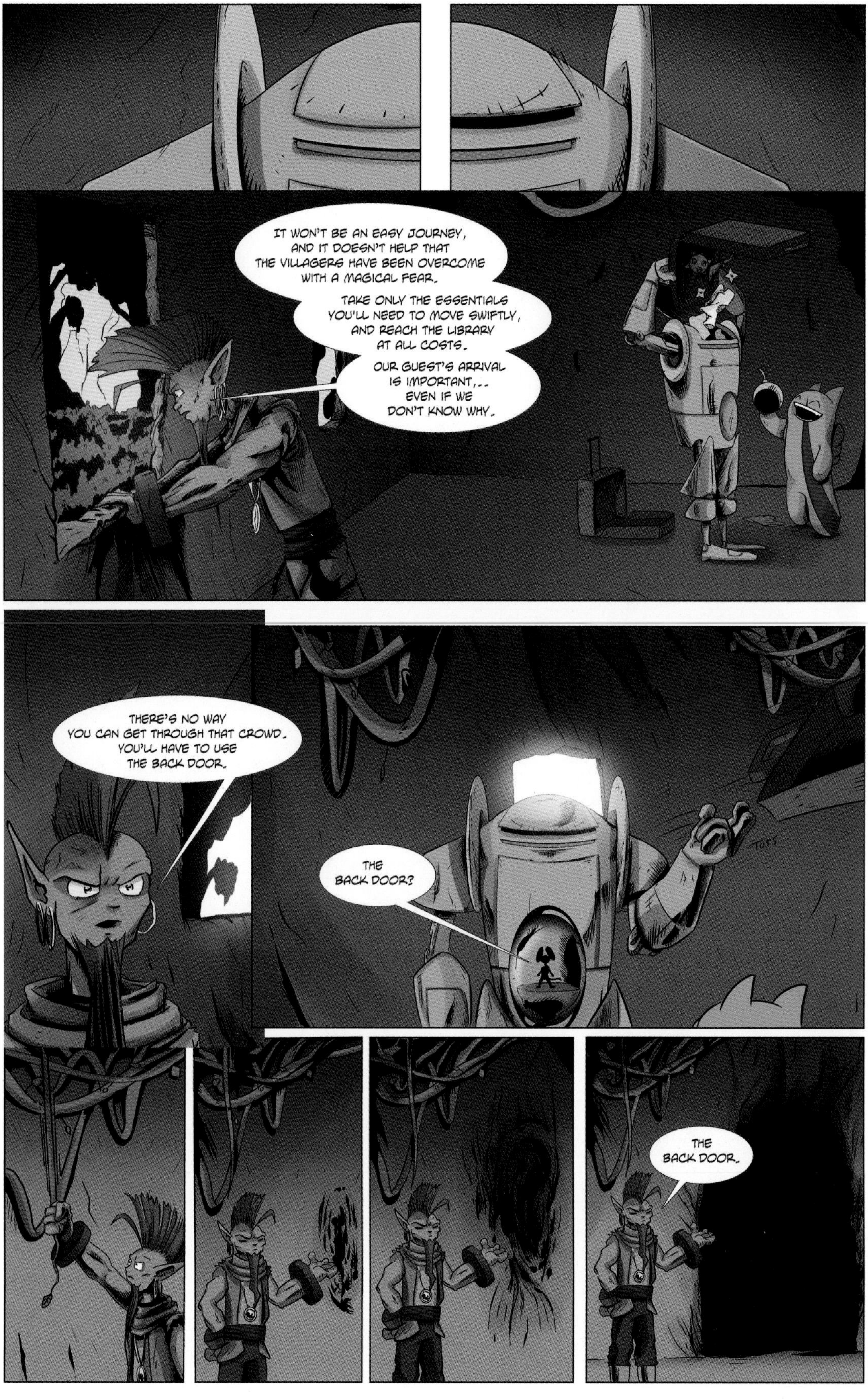
IT WON'T BE AN EASY JOURNEY, AND IT DOESN'T HELP THAT THE VILLAGERS HAVE BEEN OVERCOME WITH A MAGICAL FEAR.
TAKE ONLY THE ESSENTIALS YOU'LL NEED TO MOVE SWIFTLY, AND REACH THE LIBRARY AT ALL COSTS.
OUR GUEST'S ARRIVAL IS IMPORTANT... EVEN IF WE DON'T KNOW WHY.
THERE'S NO WAY YOU CAN GET THROUGH THAT CROWD. YOU'LL HAVE TO USE THE BACK DOOR.
TOSS
THE BACK DOOR?
THE BACK DOOR.

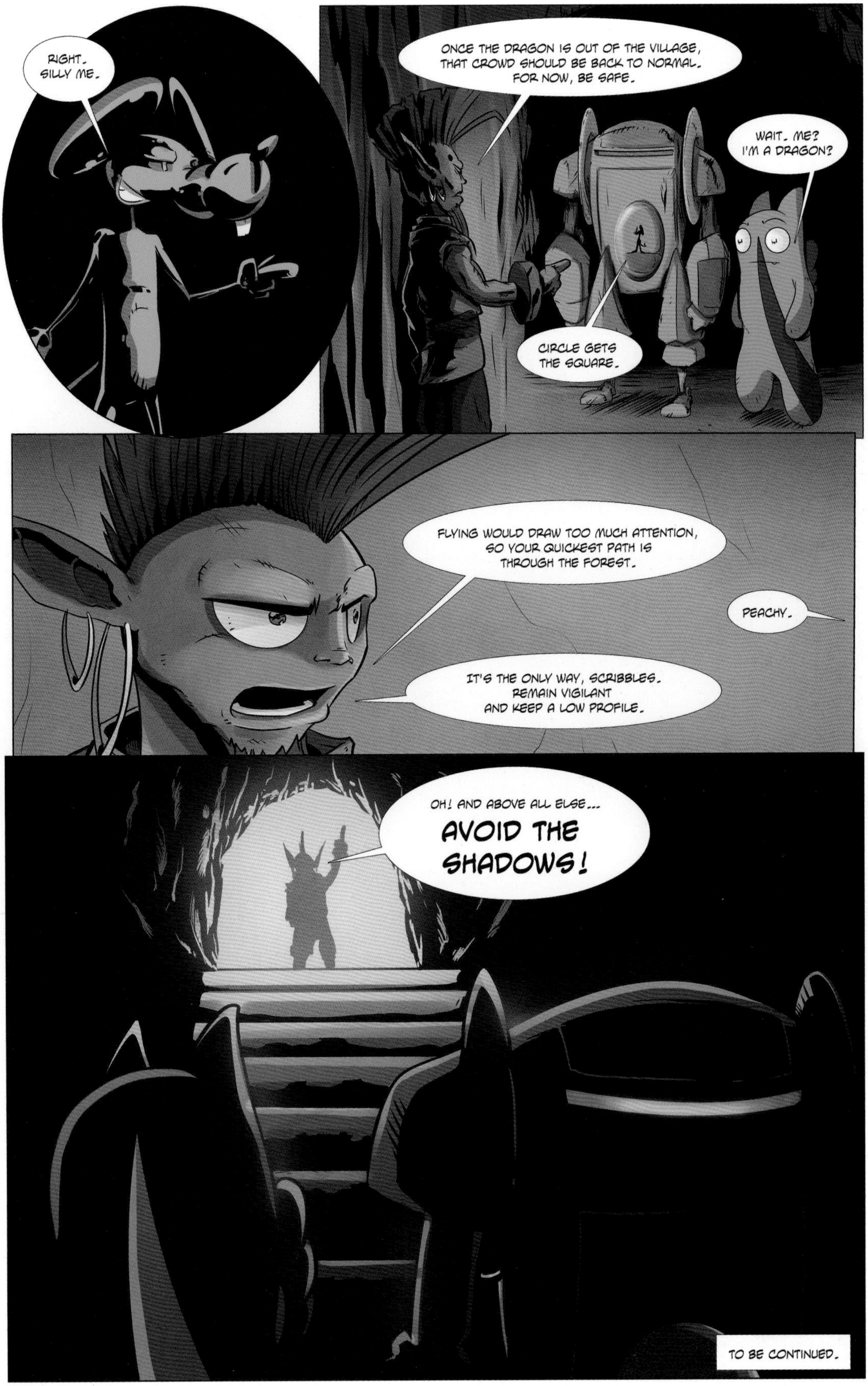
RIGHT. SILLY ME.
ONCE THE DRAGON IS OUT OF THE VILLAGE, THAT CROWD SHOULD BE BACK TO NORMAL. FOR NOW, BE SAFE.
WAIT. ME? I'M A DRAGON?
CIRCLE GETS THE SQUARE.
FLYING WOULD DRAW TOO MUCH ATTENTION, SO YOUR QUICKEST PATH IS THROUGH THE FOREST.
PEACHY.
IT'S THE ONLY WAY, SCRIBBLES. REMAIN VIGILANT AND KEEP A LOW PROFILE.
OH! AND ABOVE ALL ELSE...
AVOID THE SHADOWS!
TO BE CONTINUED.

CHAPTER TWO

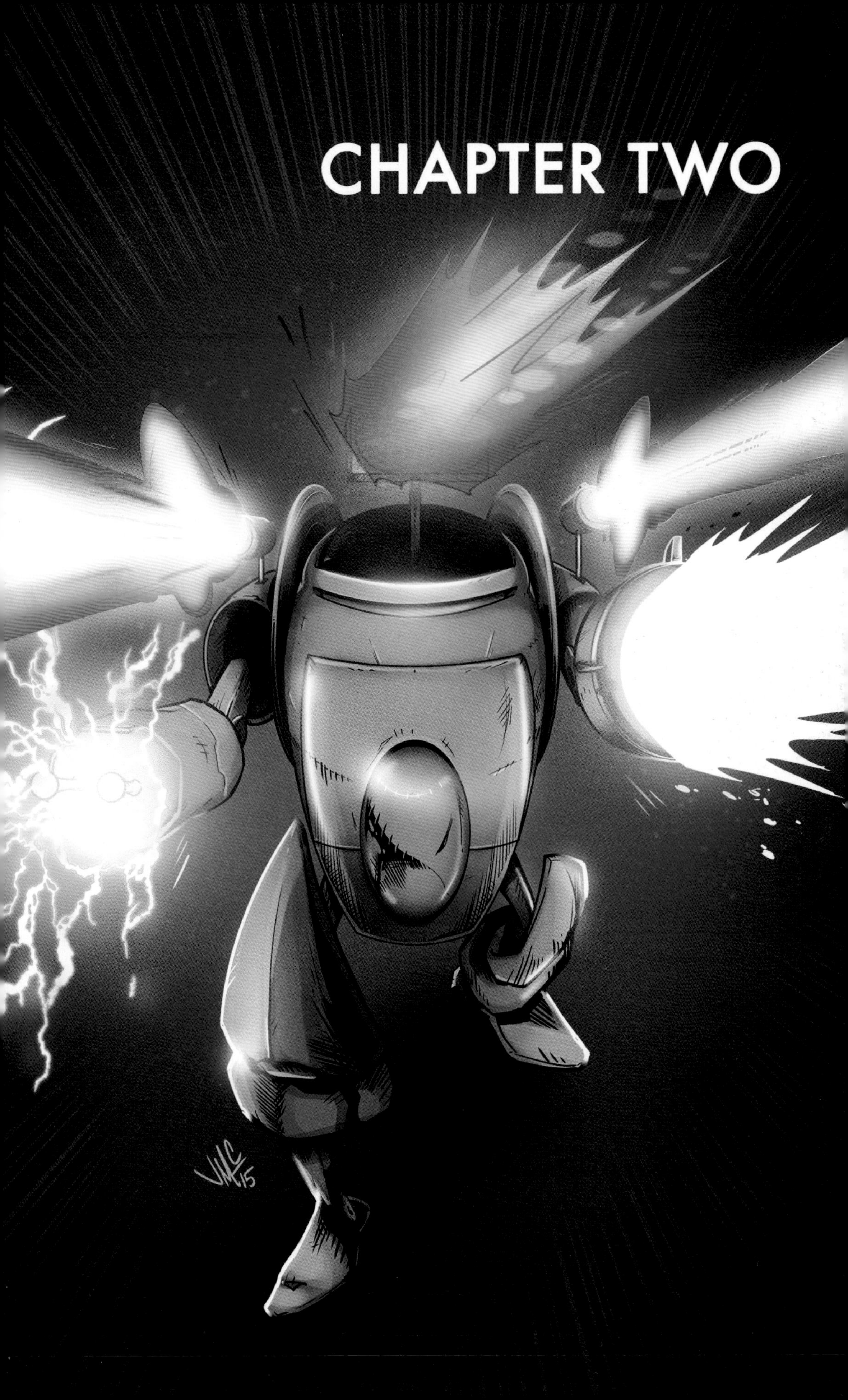

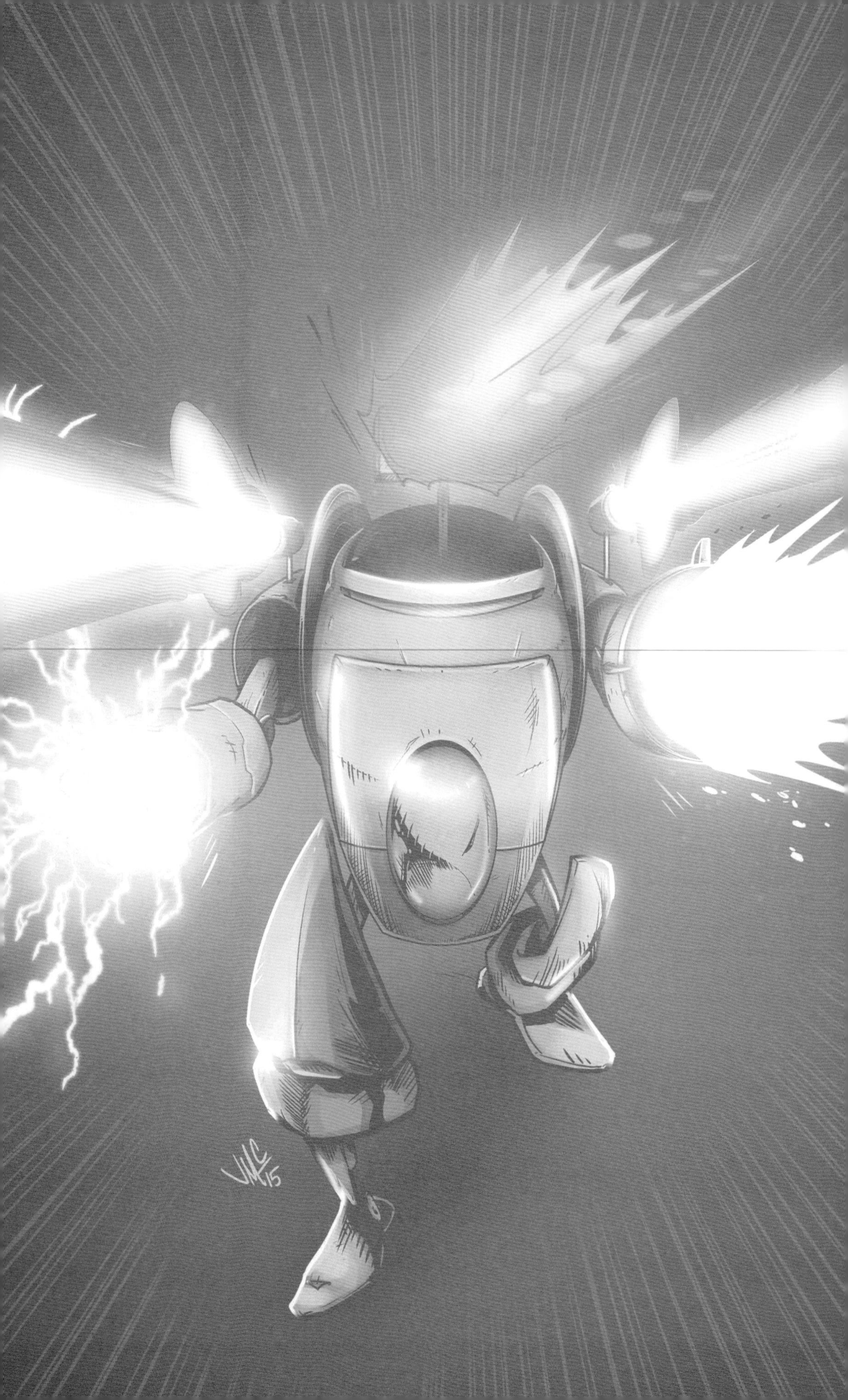

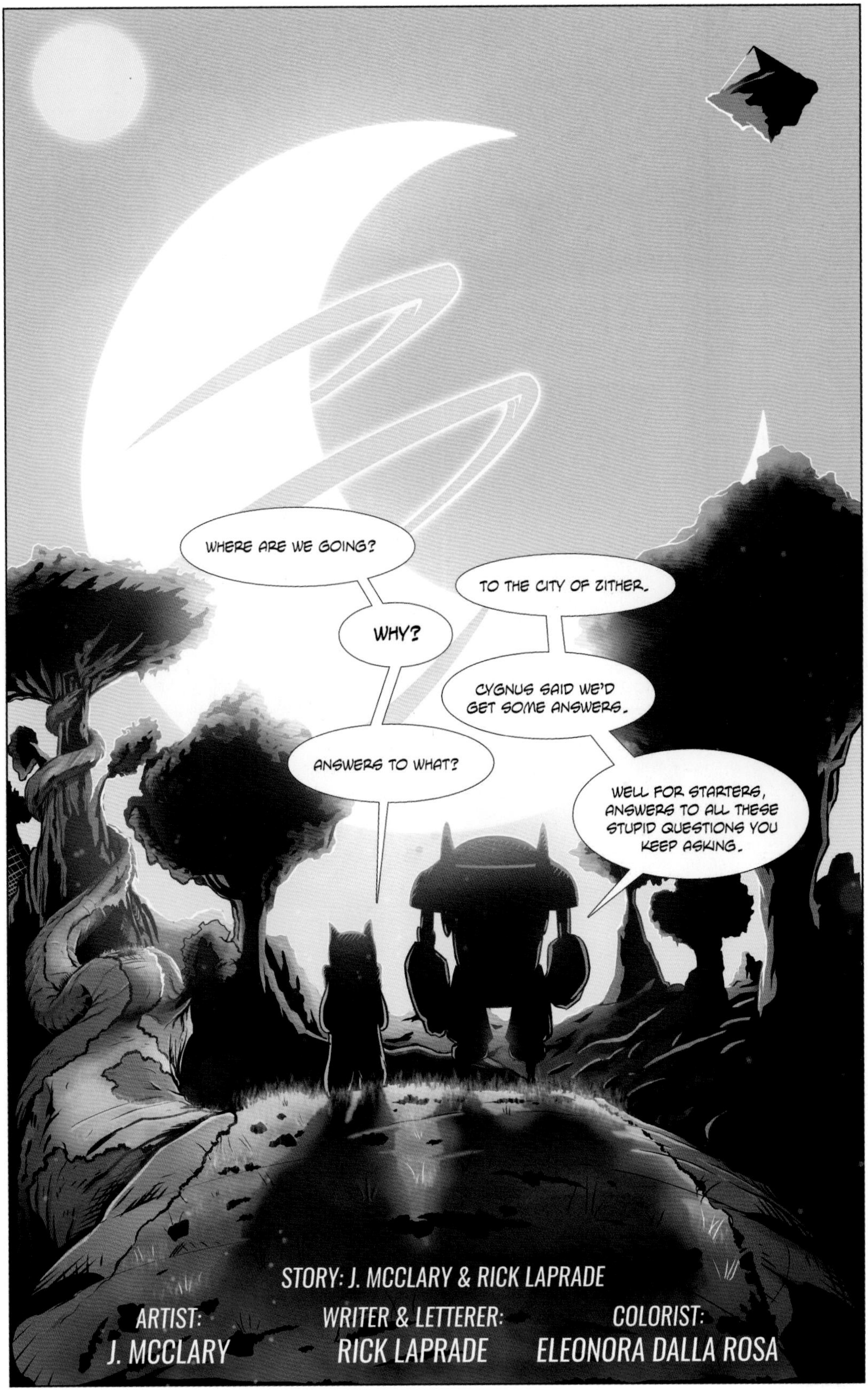
WHERE ARE WE GOING?
WHY?
TO THE CITY OF ZITHER.
CYGNUS SAID WE'D GET SOME ANSWERS.
ANSWERS TO WHAT?
WELL FOR STARTERS, ANSWERS TO ALL THESE STUPID QUESTIONS YOU KEEP ASKING.
STORY: J. MCCLARY & RICK LAPRADE
ARTIST: J. MCCLARY
WRITER & LETTERER: RICK LAPRADE
COLORIST: ELEONORA DALLA ROSA

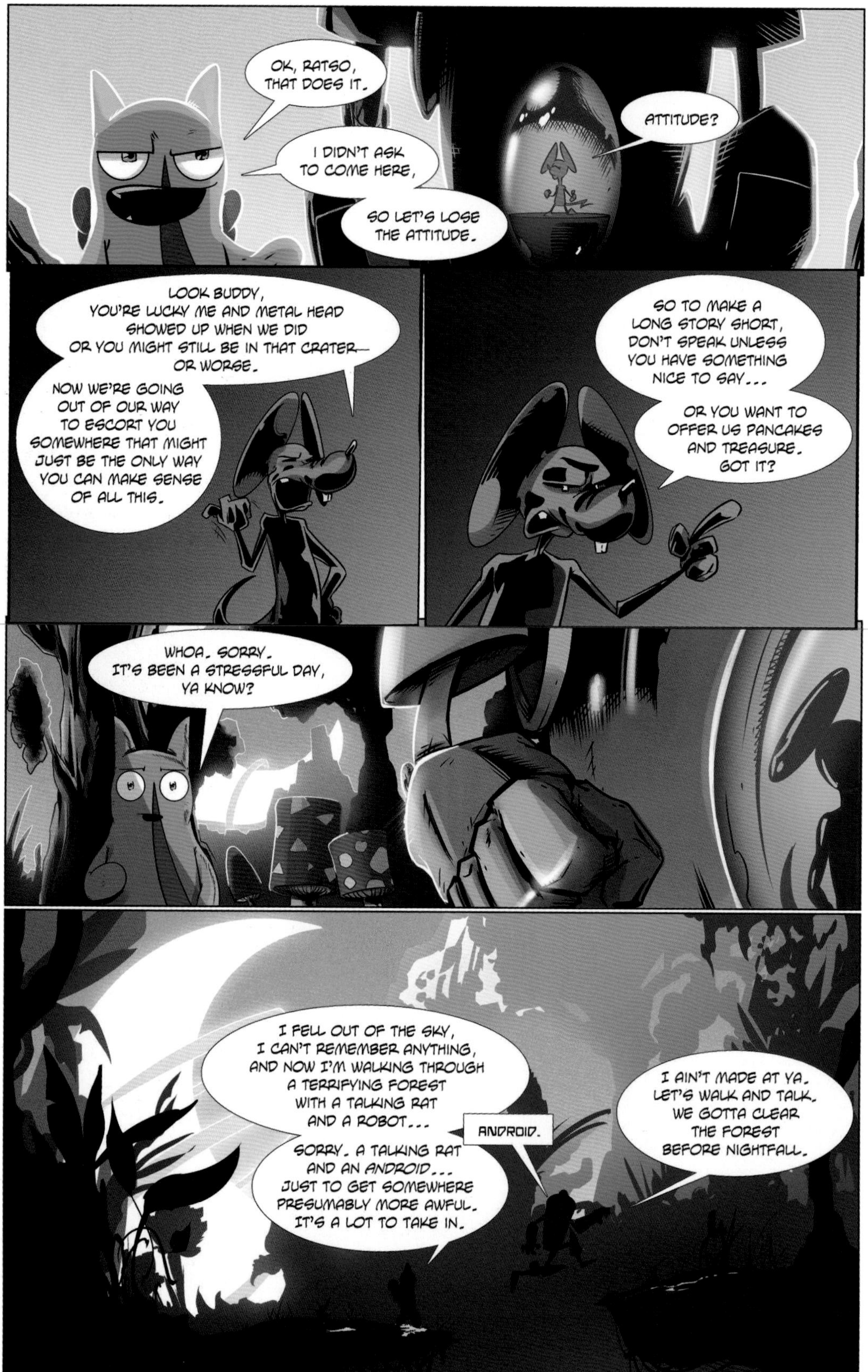

OK, RATSO, THAT DOES IT.
I DIDN'T ASK TO COME HERE,
SO LET'S LOSE THE ATTITUDE.
ATTITUDE?
LOOK BUDDY, YOU'RE LUCKY ME AND METAL HEAD SHOWED UP WHEN WE DID OR YOU MIGHT STILL BE IN THAT CRATER— OR WORSE.
NOW WE'RE GOING OUT OF OUR WAY TO ESCORT YOU SOMEWHERE THAT MIGHT JUST BE THE ONLY WAY YOU CAN MAKE SENSE OF ALL THIS.
SO TO MAKE A LONG STORY SHORT, DON'T SPEAK UNLESS YOU HAVE SOMETHING NICE TO SAY...
OR YOU WANT TO OFFER US PANCAKES AND TREASURE. GOT IT?
WHOA. SORRY. IT'S BEEN A STRESSFUL DAY, YA KNOW?
I FELL OUT OF THE SKY, I CAN'T REMEMBER ANYTHING, AND NOW I'M WALKING THROUGH A TERRIFYING FOREST WITH A TALKING RAT AND A ROBOT...
ANDROID.
SORRY. A TALKING RAT AND AN ANDROID... JUST TO GET SOMEWHERE PRESUMABLY MORE AWFUL. IT'S A LOT TO TAKE IN.
I AIN'T MADE AT YA. LET'S WALK AND TALK. WE GOTTA CLEAR THE FOREST BEFORE NIGHTFALL.

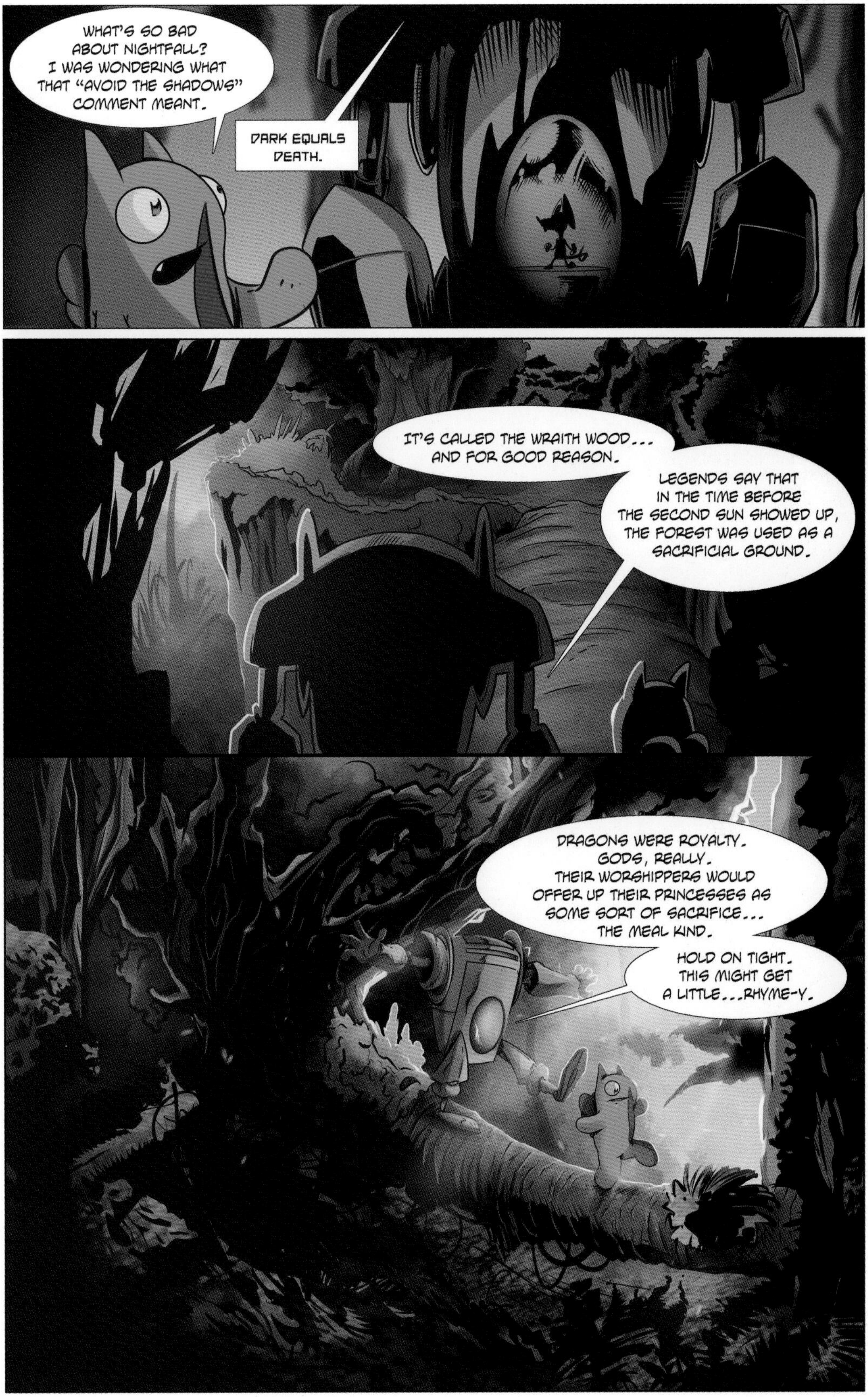

WHAT'S SO BAD ABOUT NIGHTFALL? I WAS WONDERING WHAT THAT "AVOID THE SHADOWS" COMMENT MEANT.
DARK EQUALS DEATH.
IT'S CALLED THE WRAITH WOOD... AND FOR GOOD REASON.
LEGENDS SAY THAT IN THE TIME BEFORE THE SECOND SUN SHOWED UP, THE FOREST WAS USED AS A SACRIFICIAL GROUND.
DRAGONS WERE ROYALTY. GODS, REALLY. THEIR WORSHIPPERS WOULD OFFER UP THEIR PRINCESSES AS SOME SORT OF SACRIFICE... THE MEAL KIND.
HOLD ON TIGHT. THIS MIGHT GET A LITTLE...RHYME-Y.

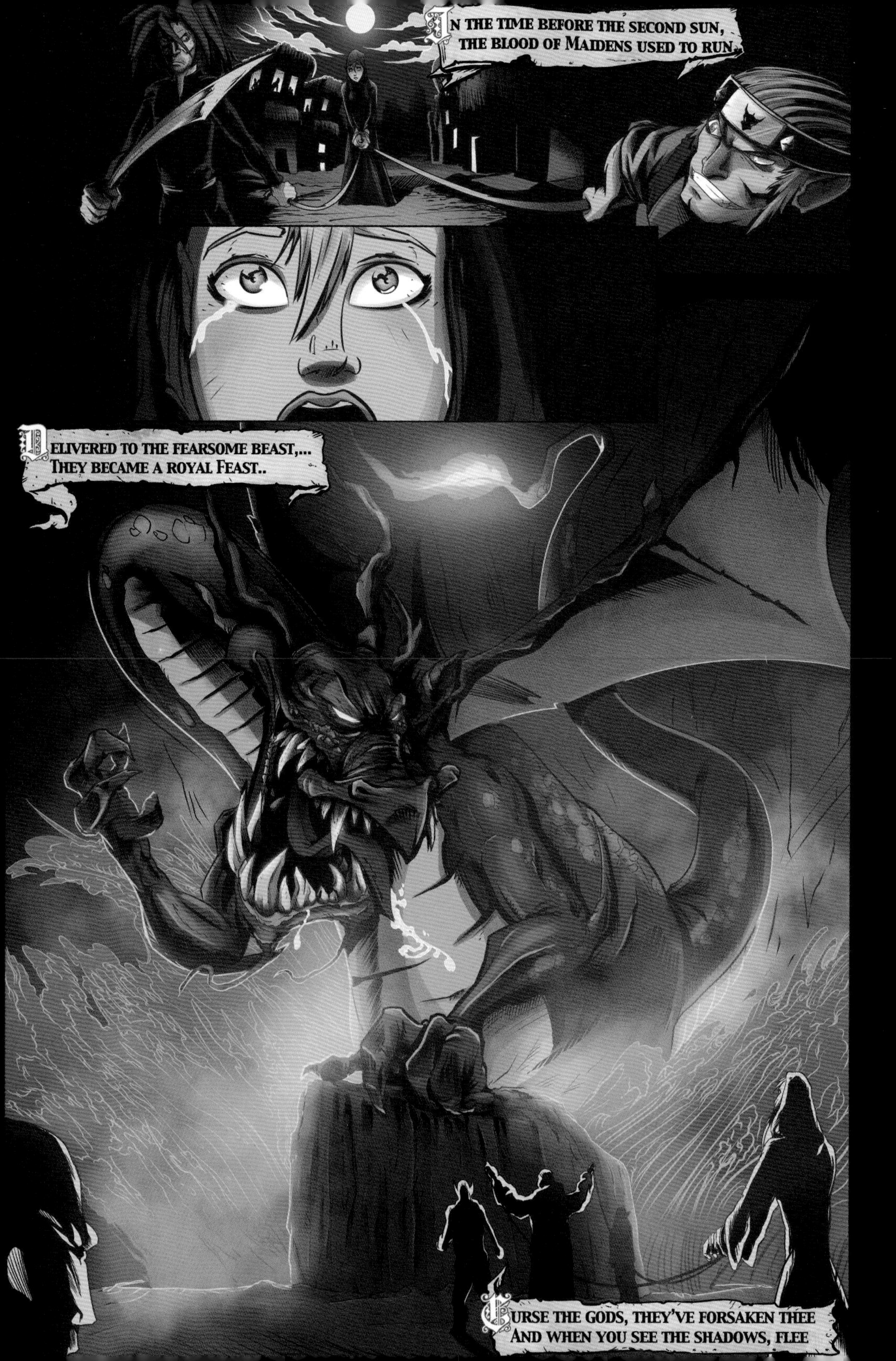
In the time before the second sun,
the blood of Maidens used to run.
Delivered to the fearsome beast,...
They became a royal Feast..
Curse the gods, they've forsaken thee
And when you see the shadows, flee

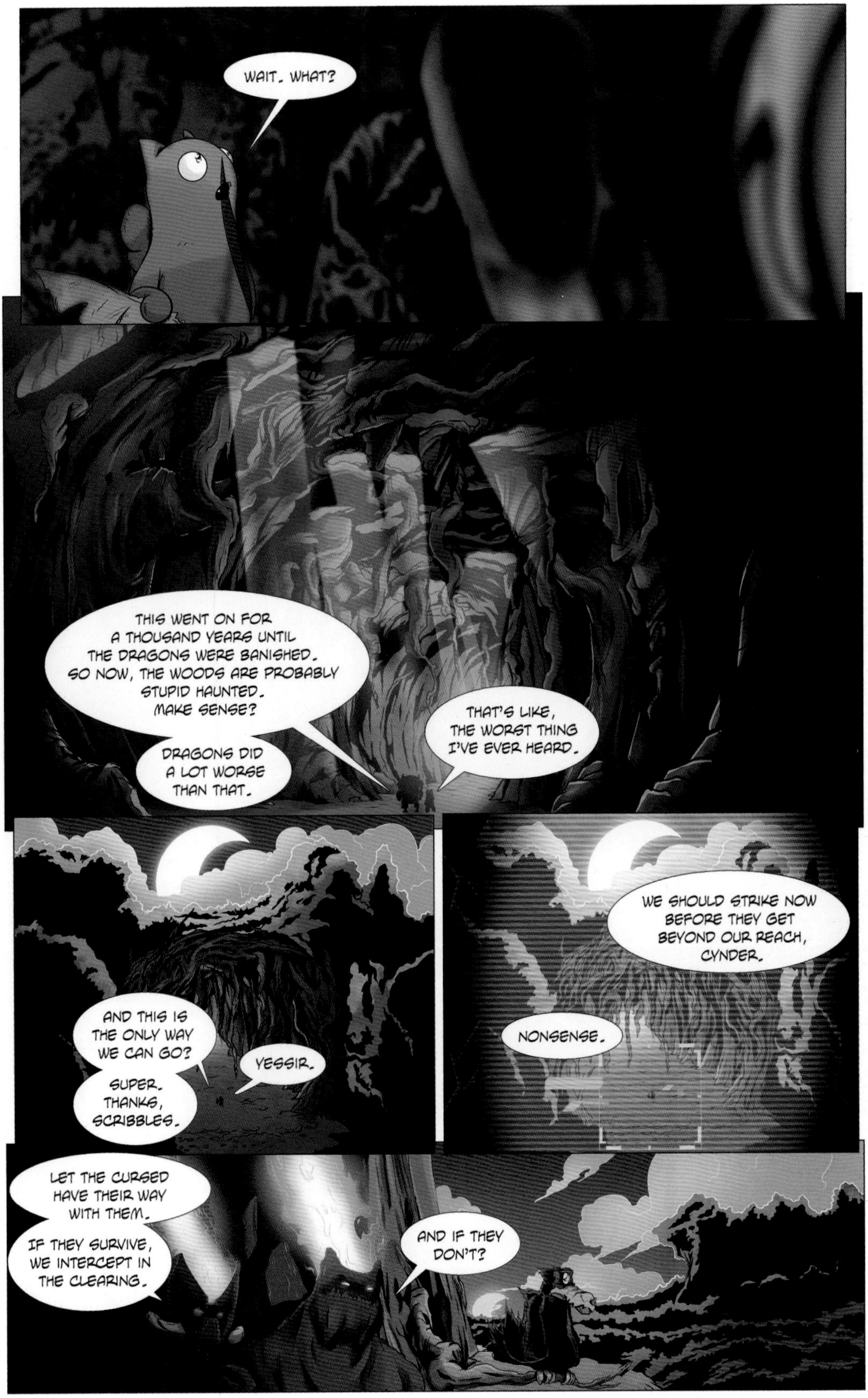
WAIT. WHAT?
THIS WENT ON FOR A THOUSAND YEARS UNTIL THE DRAGONS WERE BANISHED. SO NOW, THE WOODS ARE PROBABLY STUPID HAUNTED. MAKE SENSE?
DRAGONS DID A LOT WORSE THAN THAT.
THAT'S LIKE, THE WORST THING I'VE EVER HEARD.
AND THIS IS THE ONLY WAY WE CAN GO?
YESSIR.
SUPER. THANKS, SCRIBBLES.
WE SHOULD STRIKE NOW BEFORE THEY GET BEYOND OUR REACH, CYNDER.
NONSENSE.
LET THE CURSED HAVE THEIR WAY WITH THEM.
IF THEY SURVIVE, WE INTERCEPT IN THE CLEARING.
AND IF THEY DON'T?

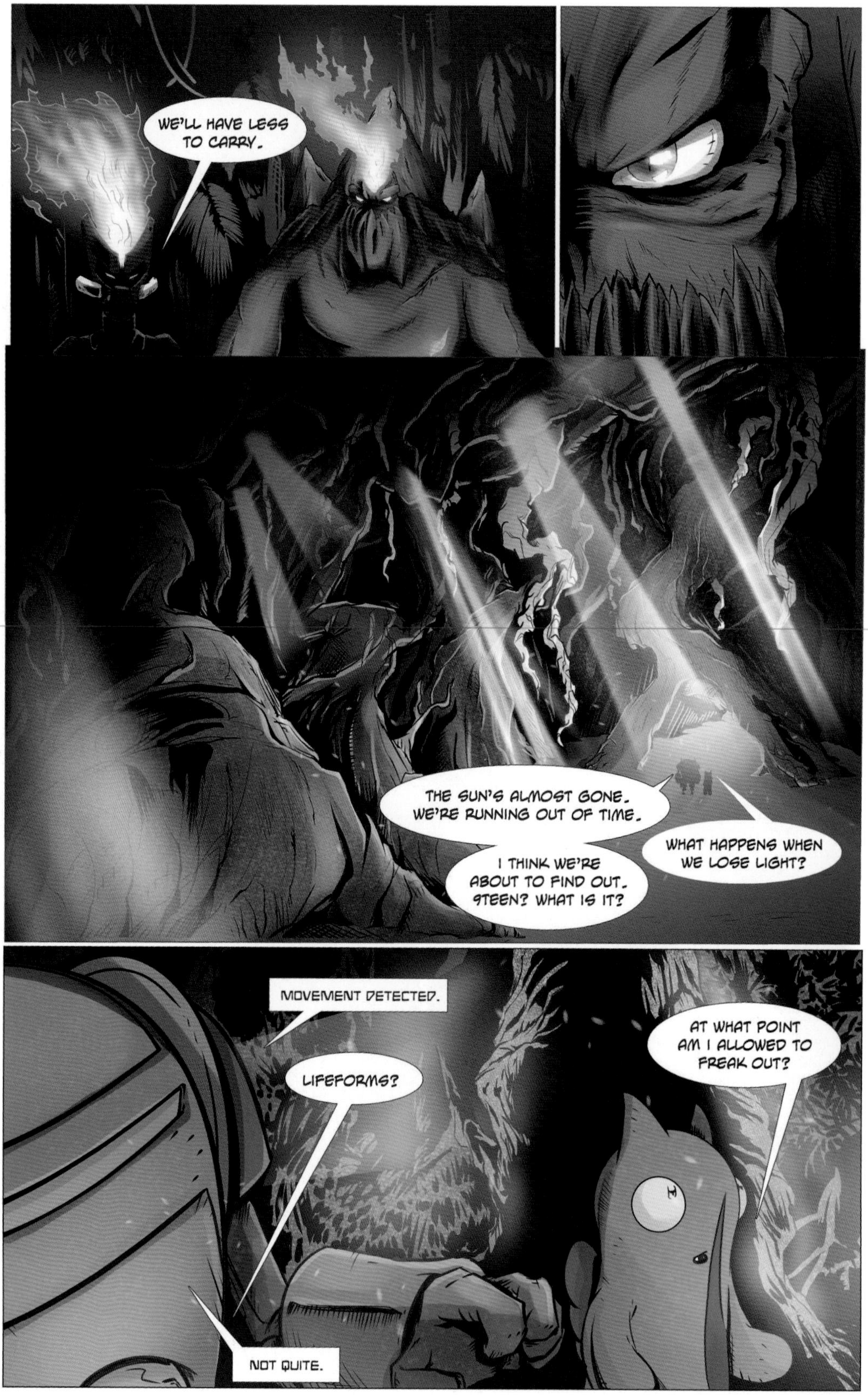
WE'LL HAVE LESS TO CARRY.
THE SUN'S ALMOST GONE. WE'RE RUNNING OUT OF TIME.
WHAT HAPPENS WHEN WE LOSE LIGHT?
I THINK WE'RE ABOUT TO FIND OUT. STEEN? WHAT IS IT?
MOVEMENT DETECTED.
LIFEFORMS?
NOT QUITE.
AT WHAT POINT AM I ALLOWED TO FREAK OUT?

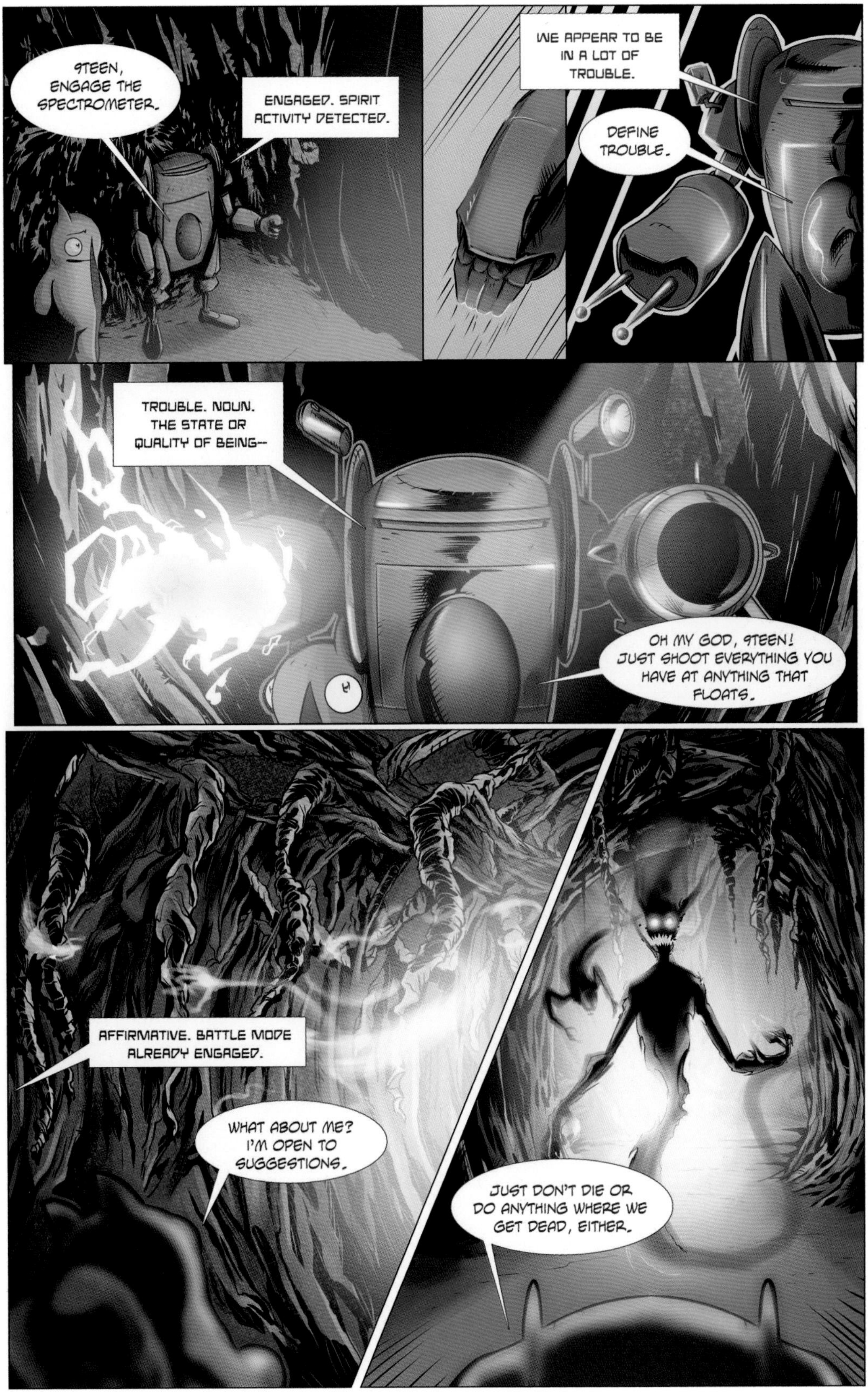
9TEEN, ENGAGE THE SPECTROMETER.
ENGAGED. SPIRIT ACTIVITY DETECTED.
WE APPEAR TO BE IN A LOT OF TROUBLE.
DEFINE TROUBLE.
TROUBLE. NOUN. THE STATE OR QUALITY OF BEING--
OH MY GOD, 9TEEN! JUST SHOOT EVERYTHING YOU HAVE AT ANYTHING THAT FLOATS.
AFFIRMATIVE. BATTLE MODE ALREADY ENGAGED.
WHAT ABOUT ME? I'M OPEN TO SUGGESTIONS.
JUST DON'T DIE OR DO ANYTHING WHERE WE GET DEAD, EITHER.

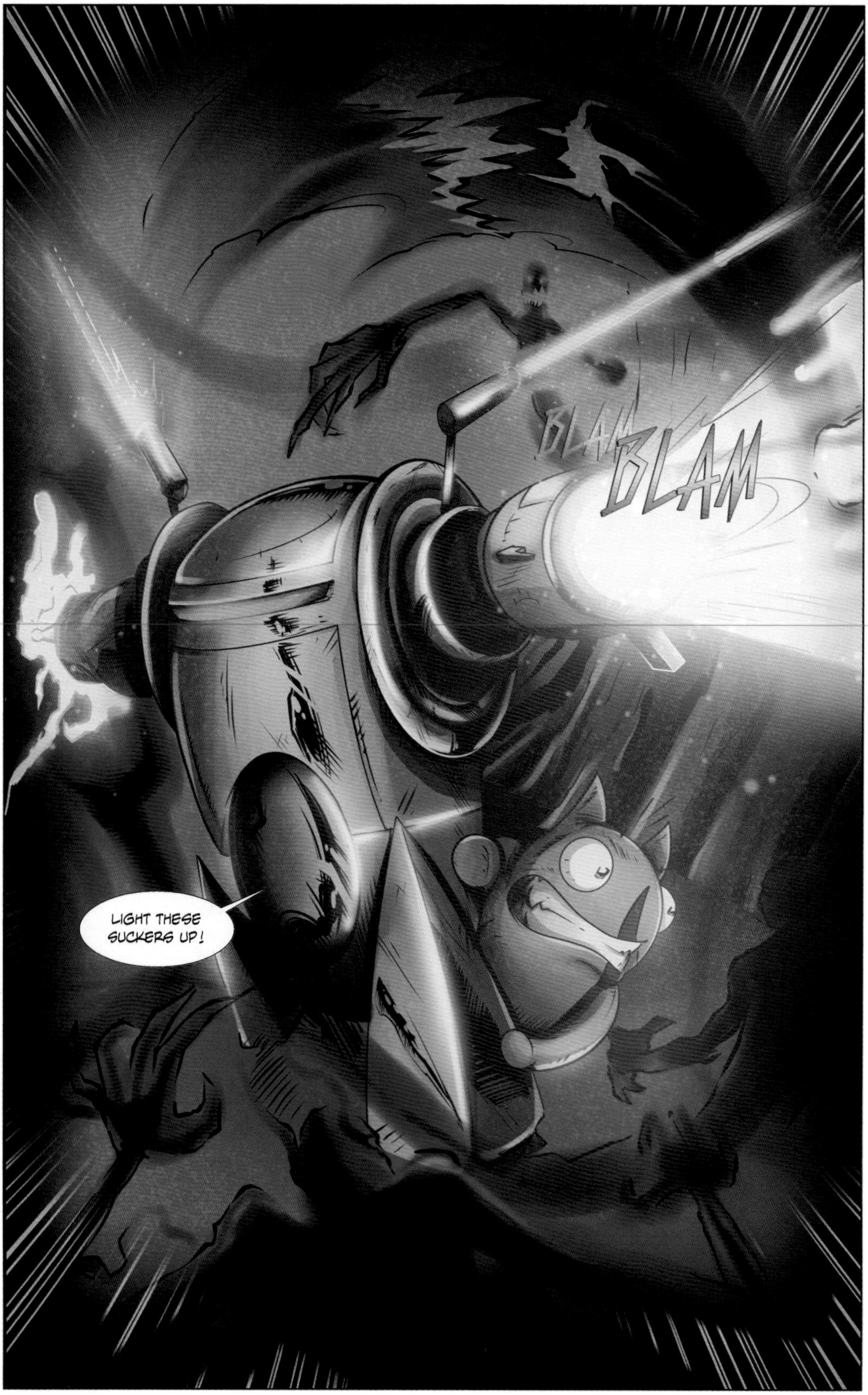
BLAM BLAM
LIGHT THESE SUCKERS UP!

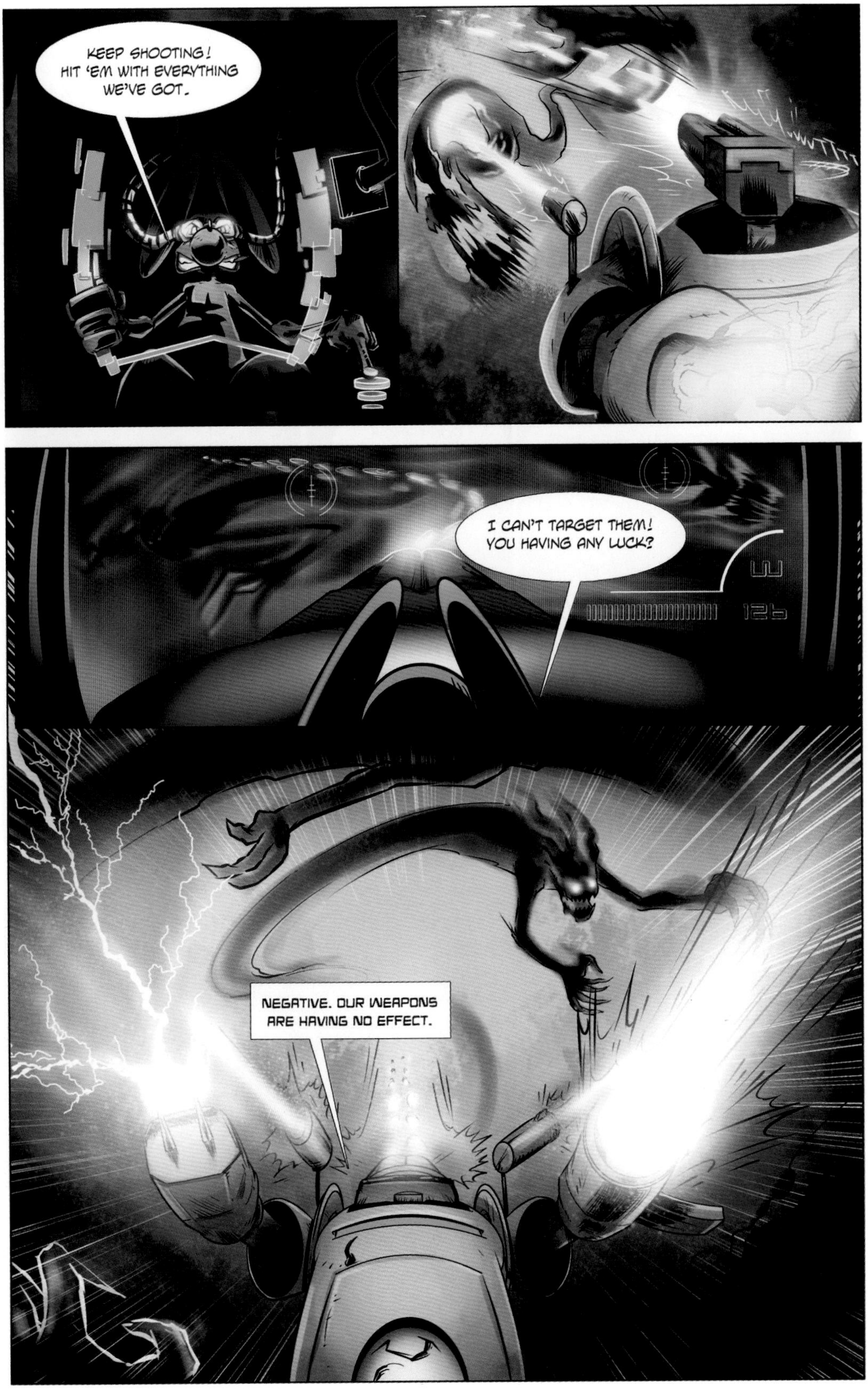
KEEP SHOOTING! HIT 'EM WITH EVERYTHING WE'VE GOT.
I CAN'T TARGET THEM! YOU HAVING ANY LUCK?
NEGATIVE. OUR WEAPONS ARE HAVING NO EFFECT.

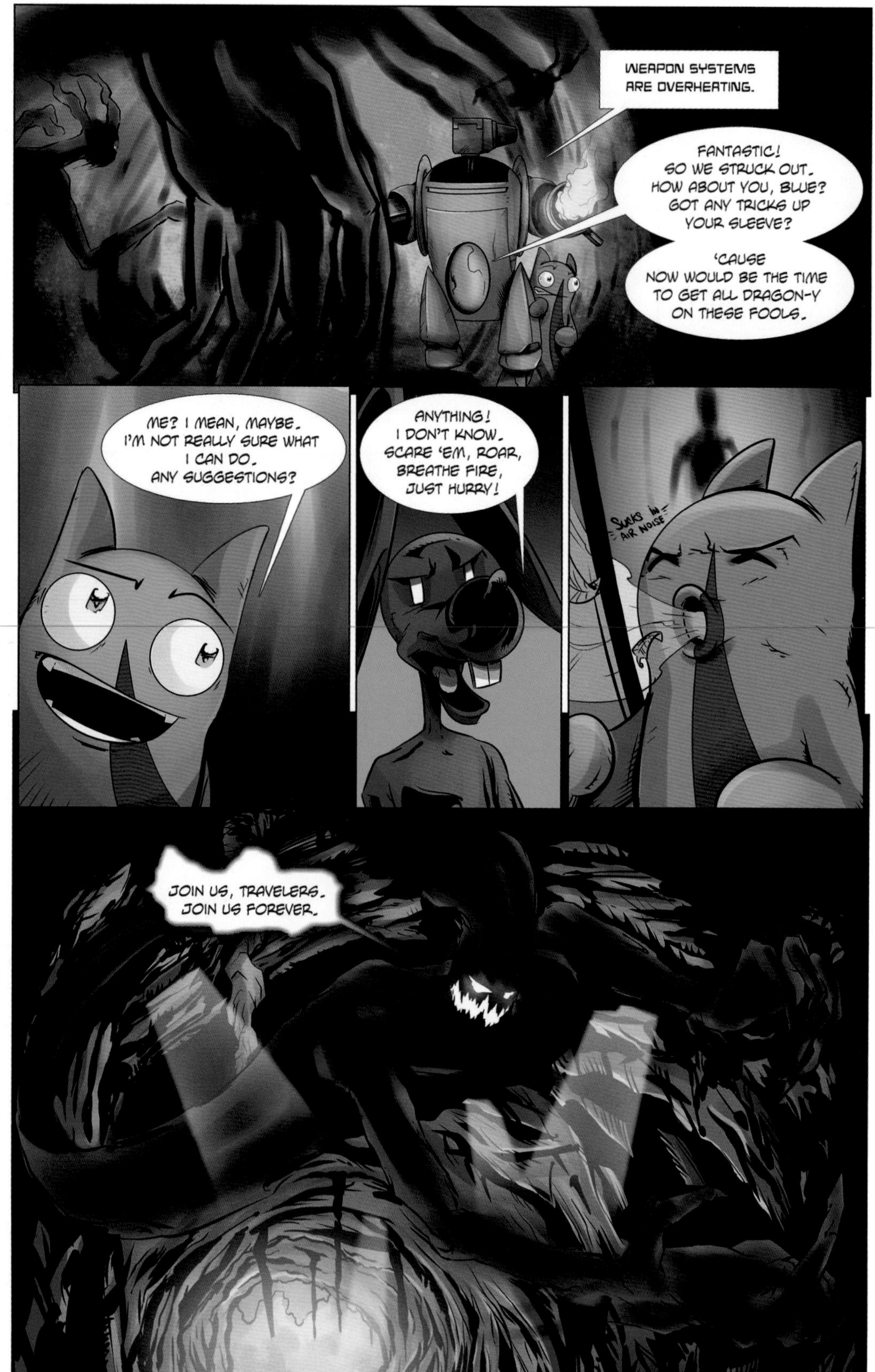
WEAPON SYSTEMS ARE OVERHEATING.
FANTASTIC! SO WE STRUCK OUT. HOW ABOUT YOU, BLUE? GOT ANY TRICKS UP YOUR SLEEVE?
'CAUSE NOW WOULD BE THE TIME TO GET ALL DRAGON-Y ON THESE FOOLS.
ME? I MEAN, MAYBE. I'M NOT REALLY SURE WHAT I CAN DO. ANY SUGGESTIONS?
ANYTHING! I DON'T KNOW. SCARE 'EM, ROAR, BREATHE FIRE, JUST HURRY!
SUCKS IN AIR NOISE
JOIN US, TRAVELERS. JOIN US FOREVER.

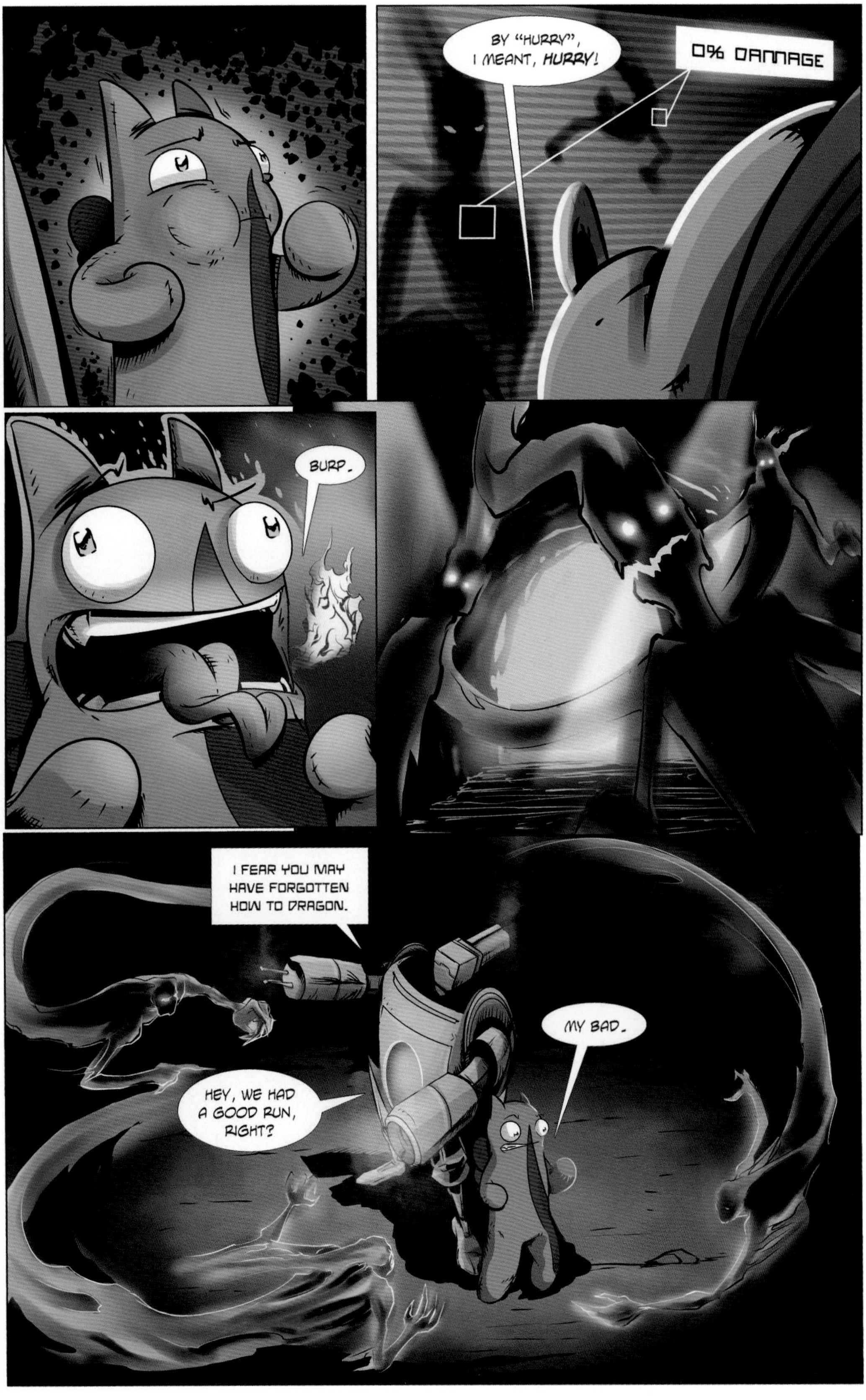
BY "HURRY", I MEANT, HURRY!
0% DAMAGE
BURP.
I FEAR YOU MAY HAVE FORGOTTEN HOW TO DRAGON.
HEY, WE HAD A GOOD RUN, RIGHT?
MY BAD.

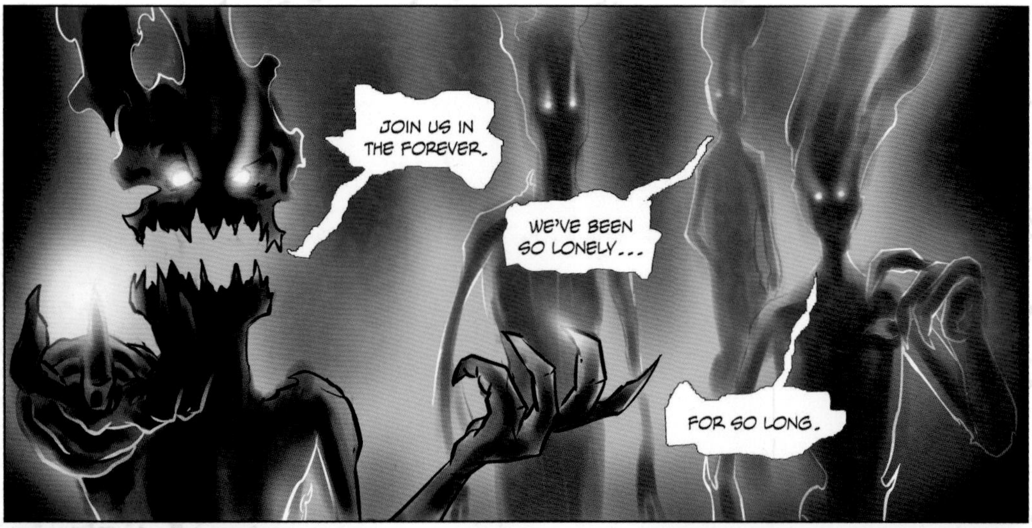
JOIN US IN THE FOREVER.
WE'VE BEEN SO LONELY...
FOR SO LONG.

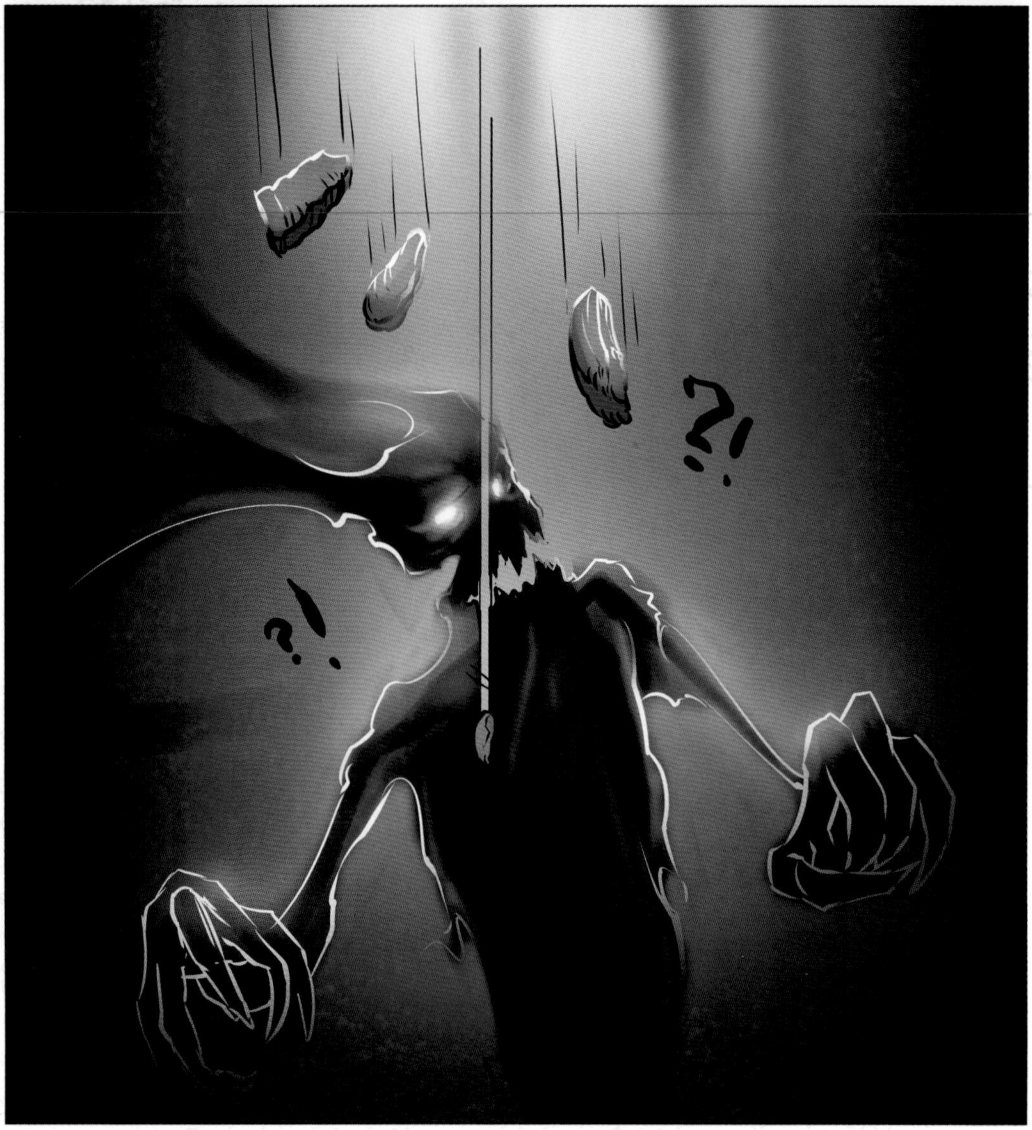
?!
?!

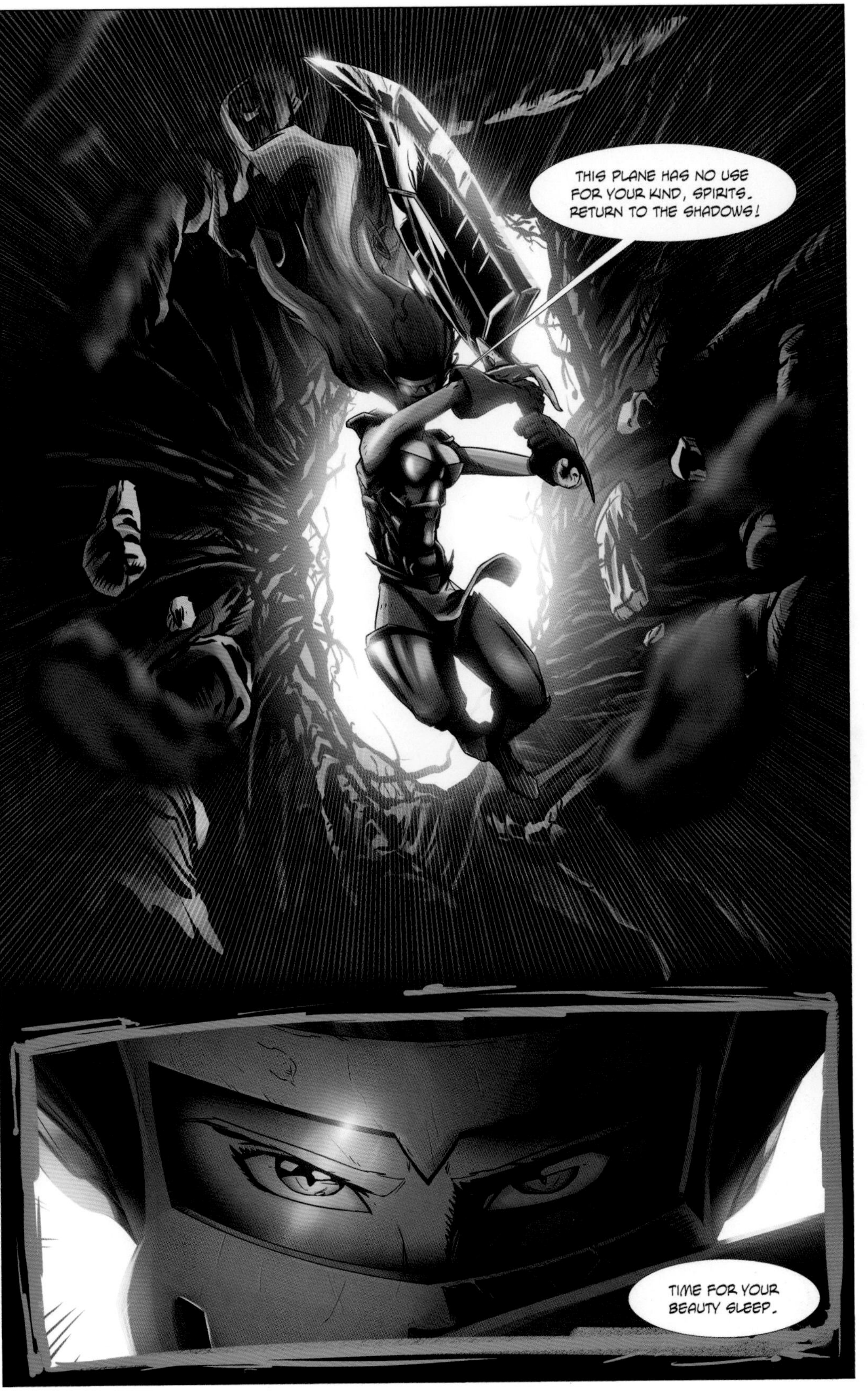
THIS PLANE HAS NO USE FOR YOUR KIND, SPIRITS. RETURN TO THE SHADOWS!
TIME FOR YOUR BEAUTY SLEEP.

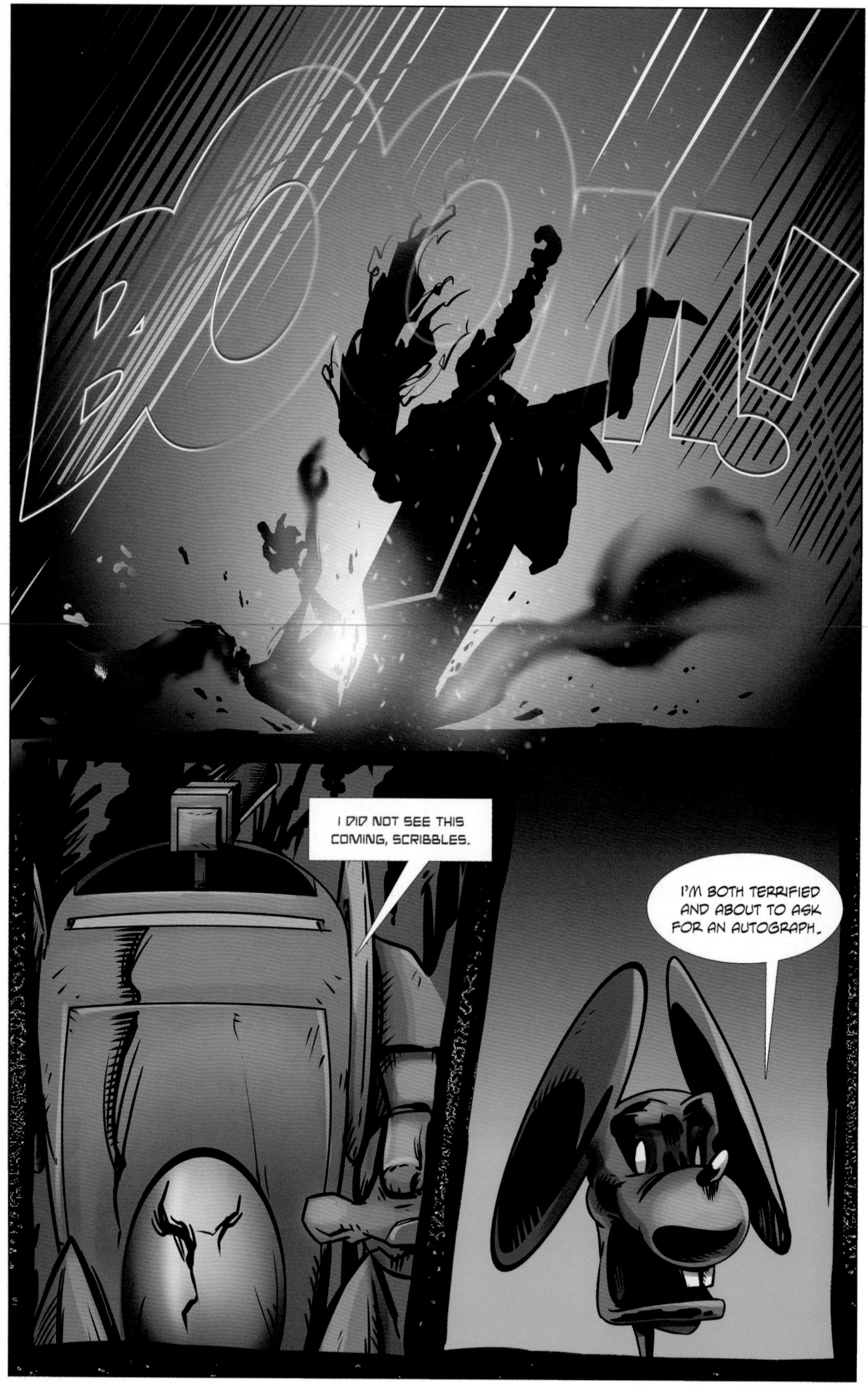
BOOM!
I DID NOT SEE THIS COMING, SCRIBBLES.
I'M BOTH TERRIFIED AND ABOUT TO ASK FOR AN AUTOGRAPH.

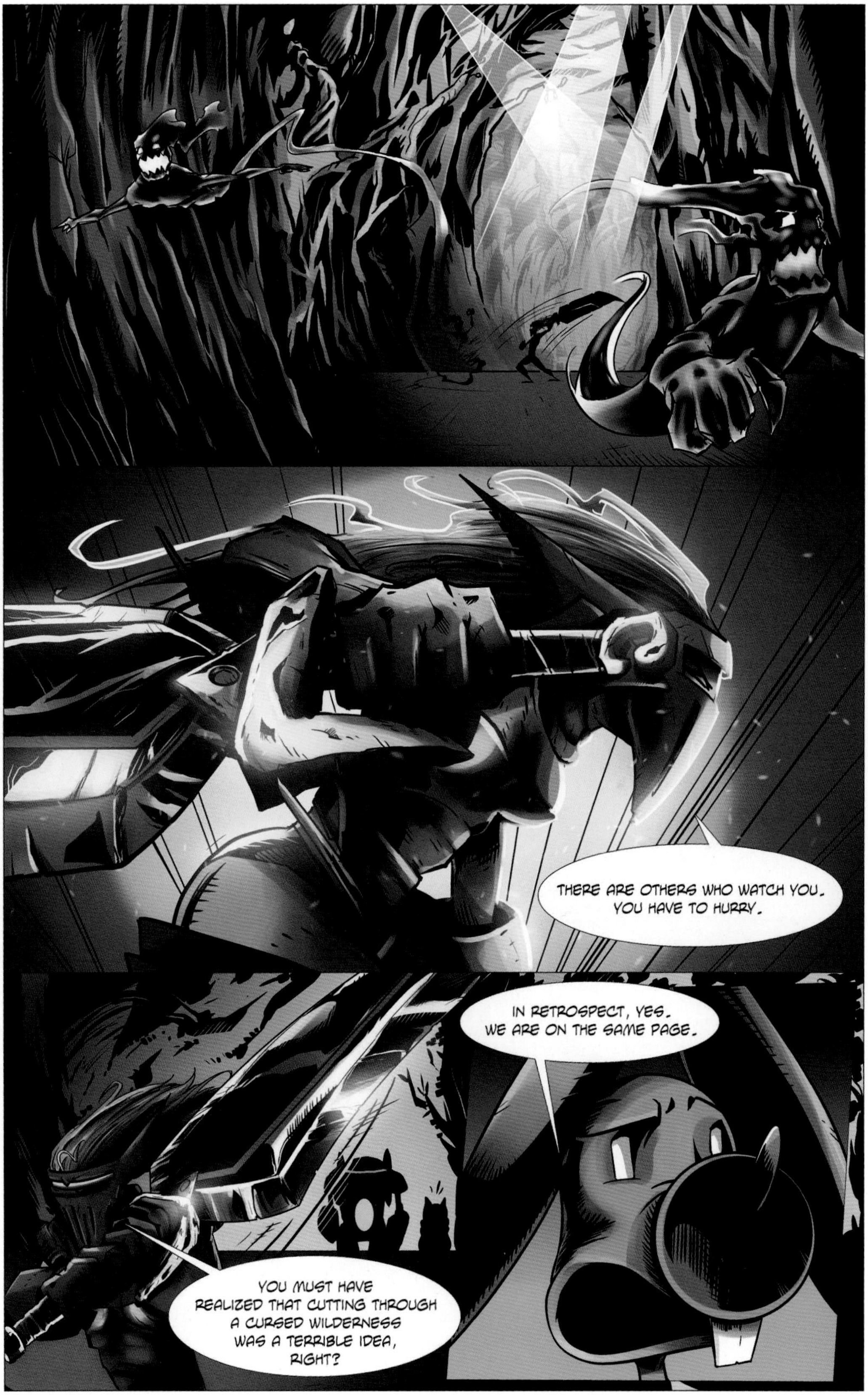
THERE ARE OTHERS WHO WATCH YOU. YOU HAVE TO HURRY.
YOU MUST HAVE REALIZED THAT CUTTING THROUGH A CURSED WILDERNESS WAS A TERRIBLE IDEA, RIGHT?
IN RETROSPECT, YES. WE ARE ON THE SAME PAGE.

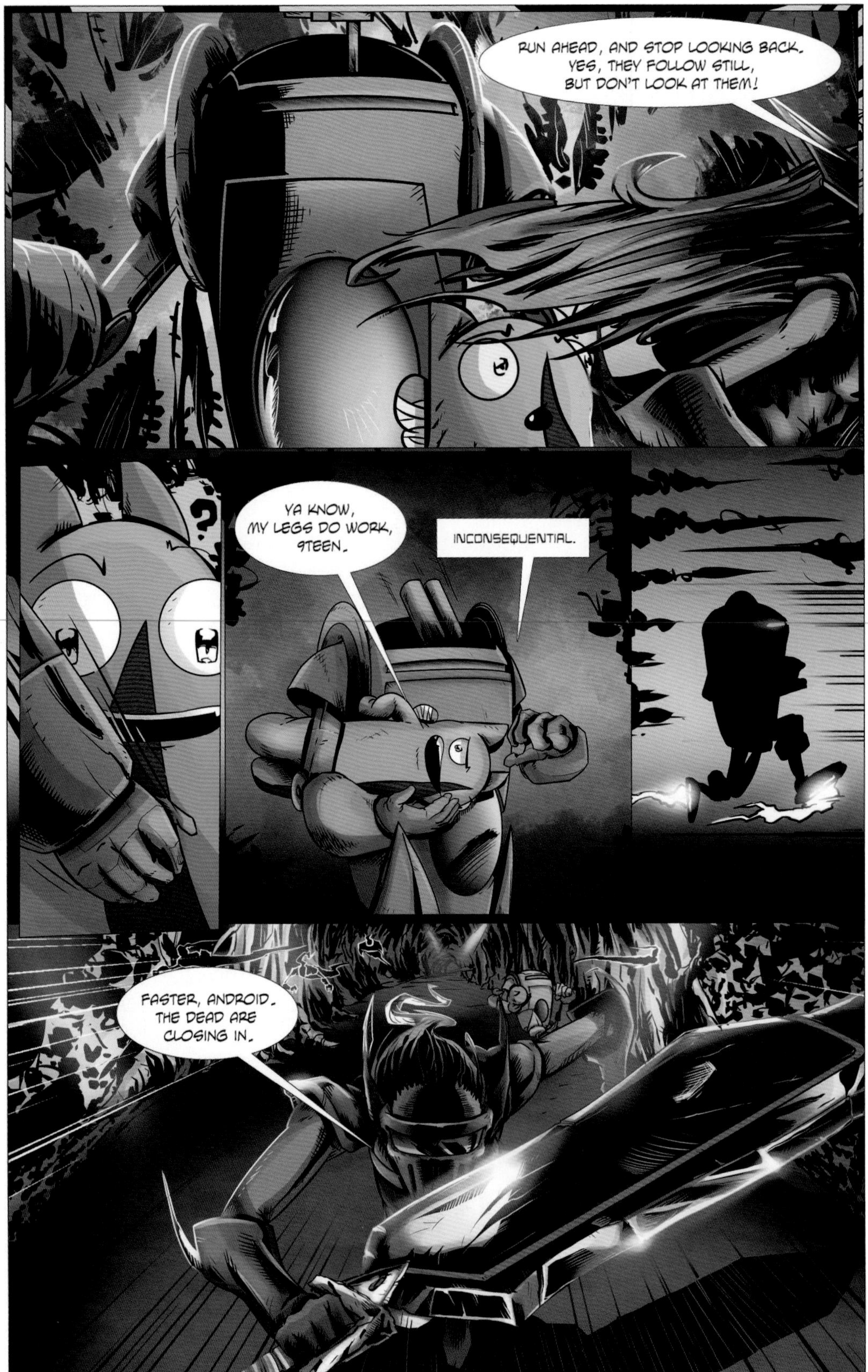
RUN AHEAD, AND STOP LOOKING BACK. YES, THEY FOLLOW STILL, BUT DON'T LOOK AT THEM!
YA KNOW, MY LEGS DO WORK, 9TEEN.
INCONSEQUENTIAL.
FASTER, ANDROID. THE DEAD ARE CLOSING IN.

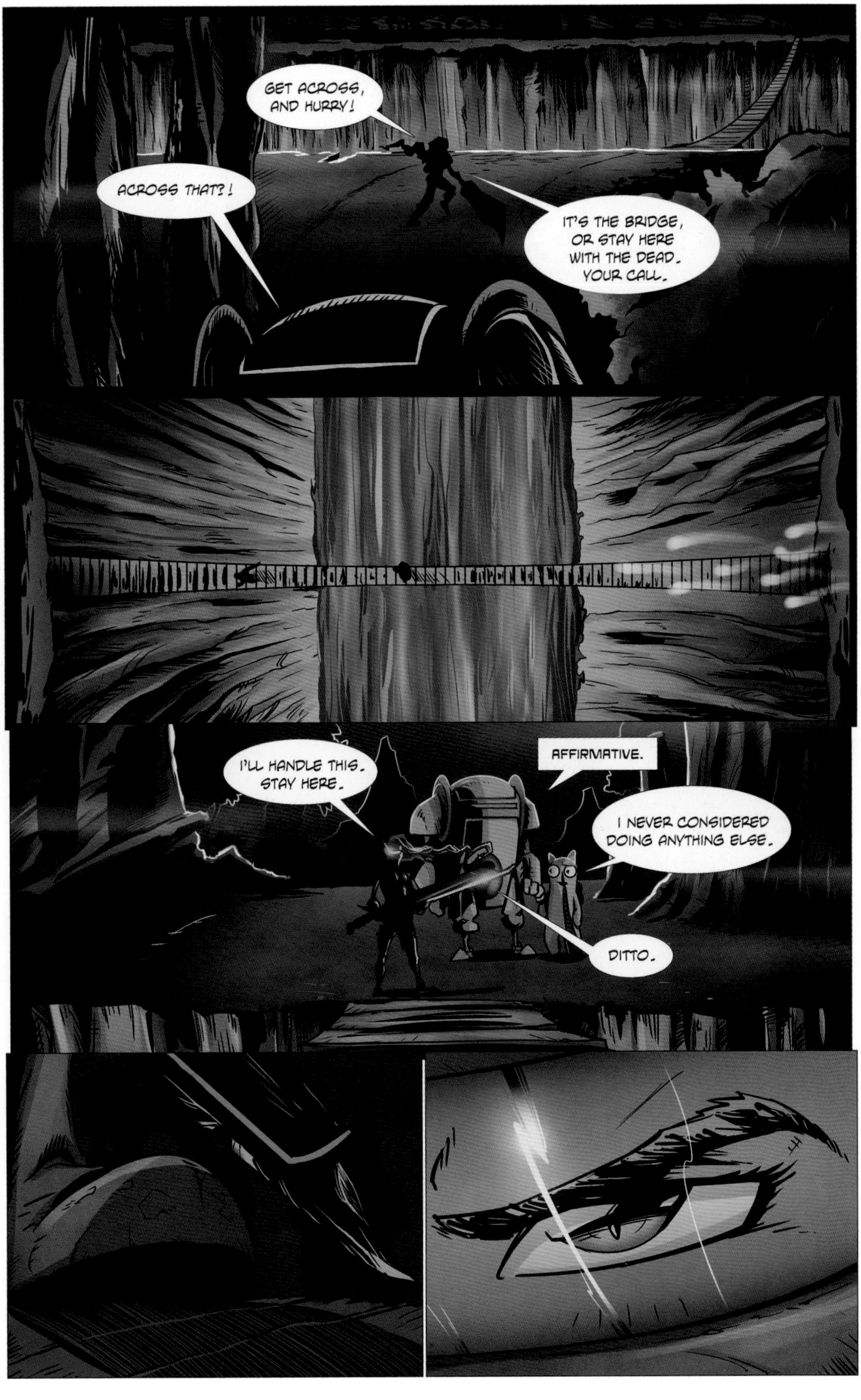
GET ACROSS, AND HURRY!
ACROSS THAT?!
IT'S THE BRIDGE, OR STAY HERE WITH THE DEAD. YOUR CALL.
I'LL HANDLE THIS. STAY HERE.
AFFIRMATIVE.
I NEVER CONSIDERED DOING ANYTHING ELSE.
DITTO.

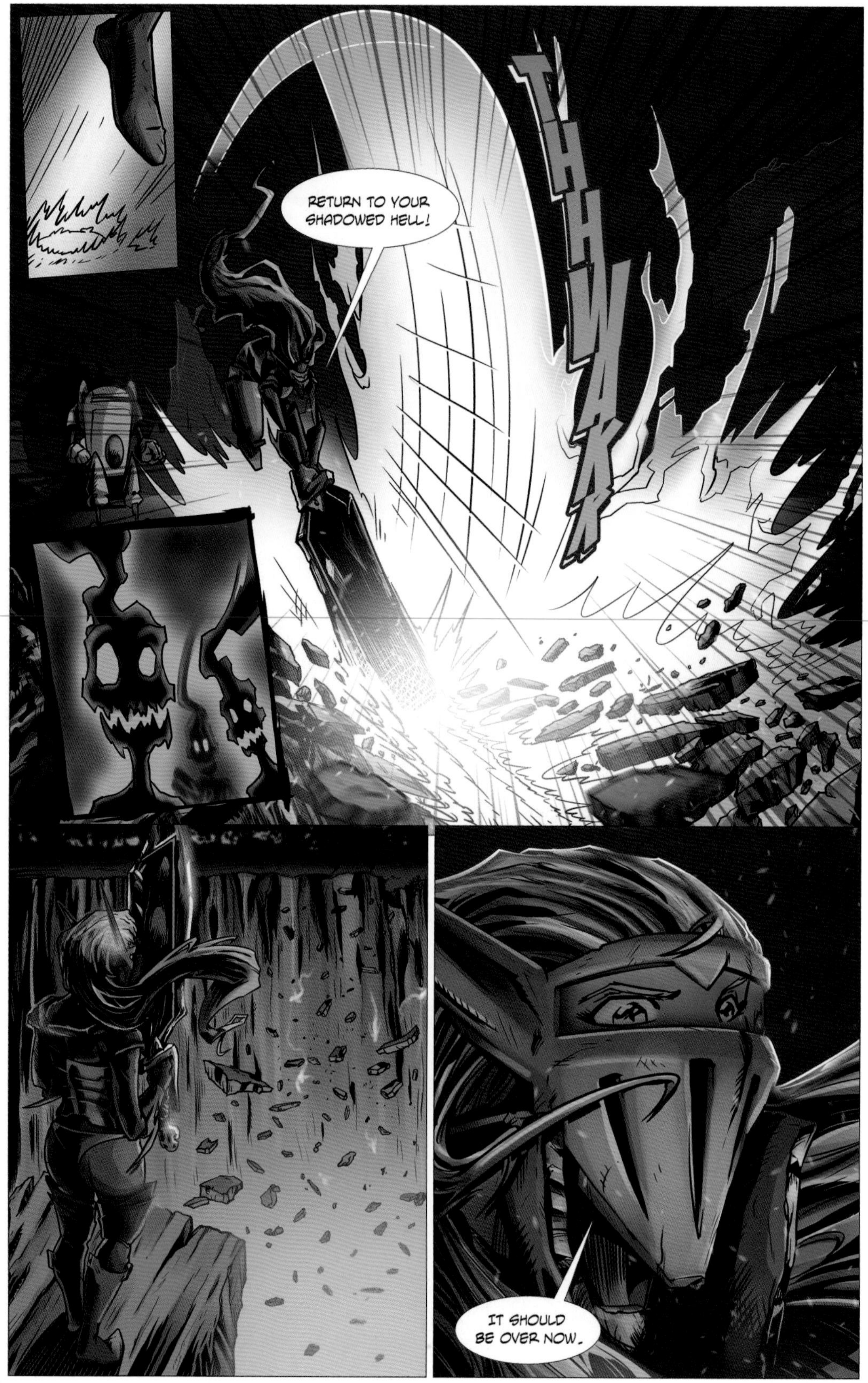
THHWAK
RETURN TO YOUR SHADOWED HELL!
IT SHOULD BE OVER NOW.

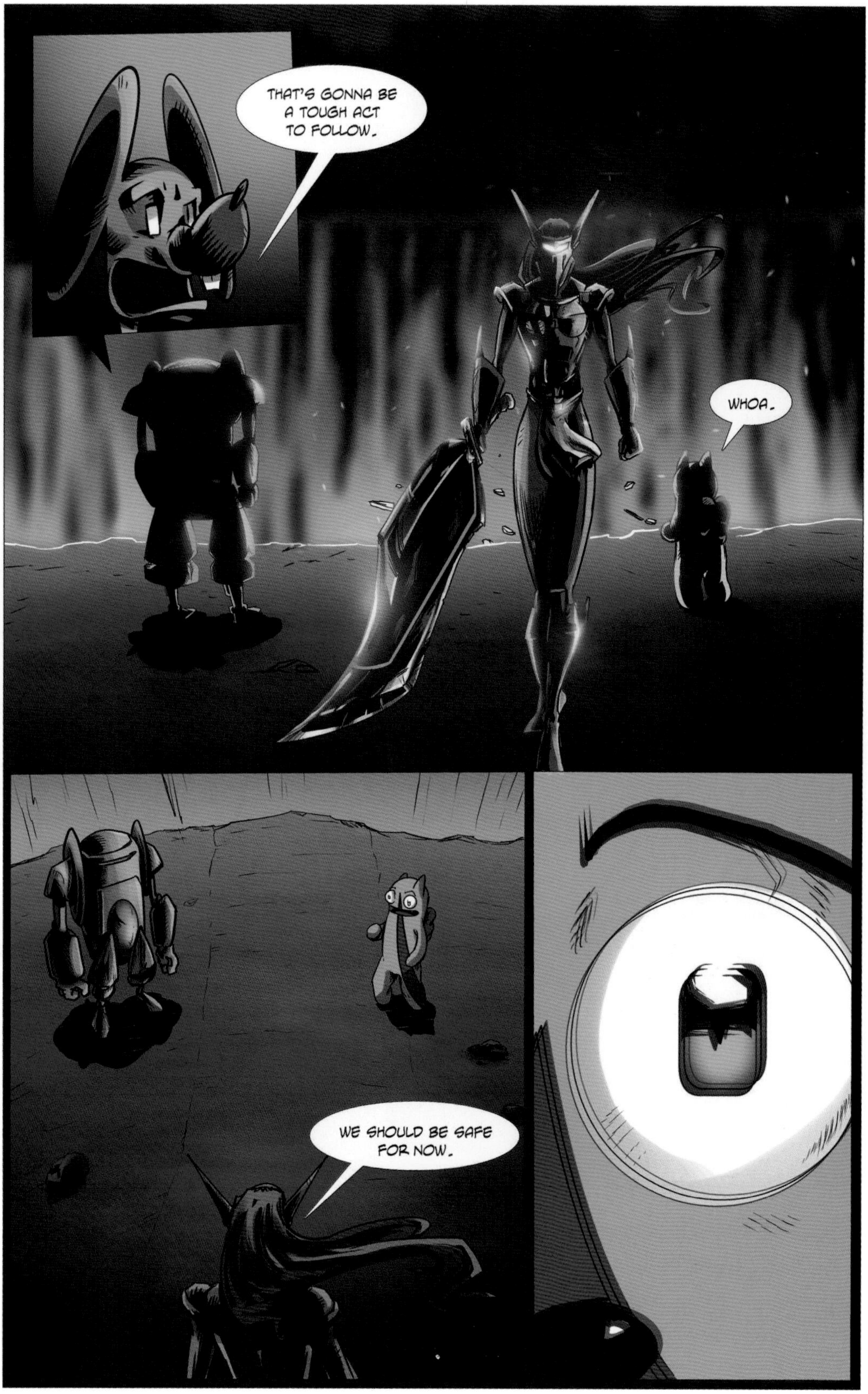
THAT'S GONNA BE A TOUGH ACT TO FOLLOW.
WHOA.
WE SHOULD BE SAFE FOR NOW.

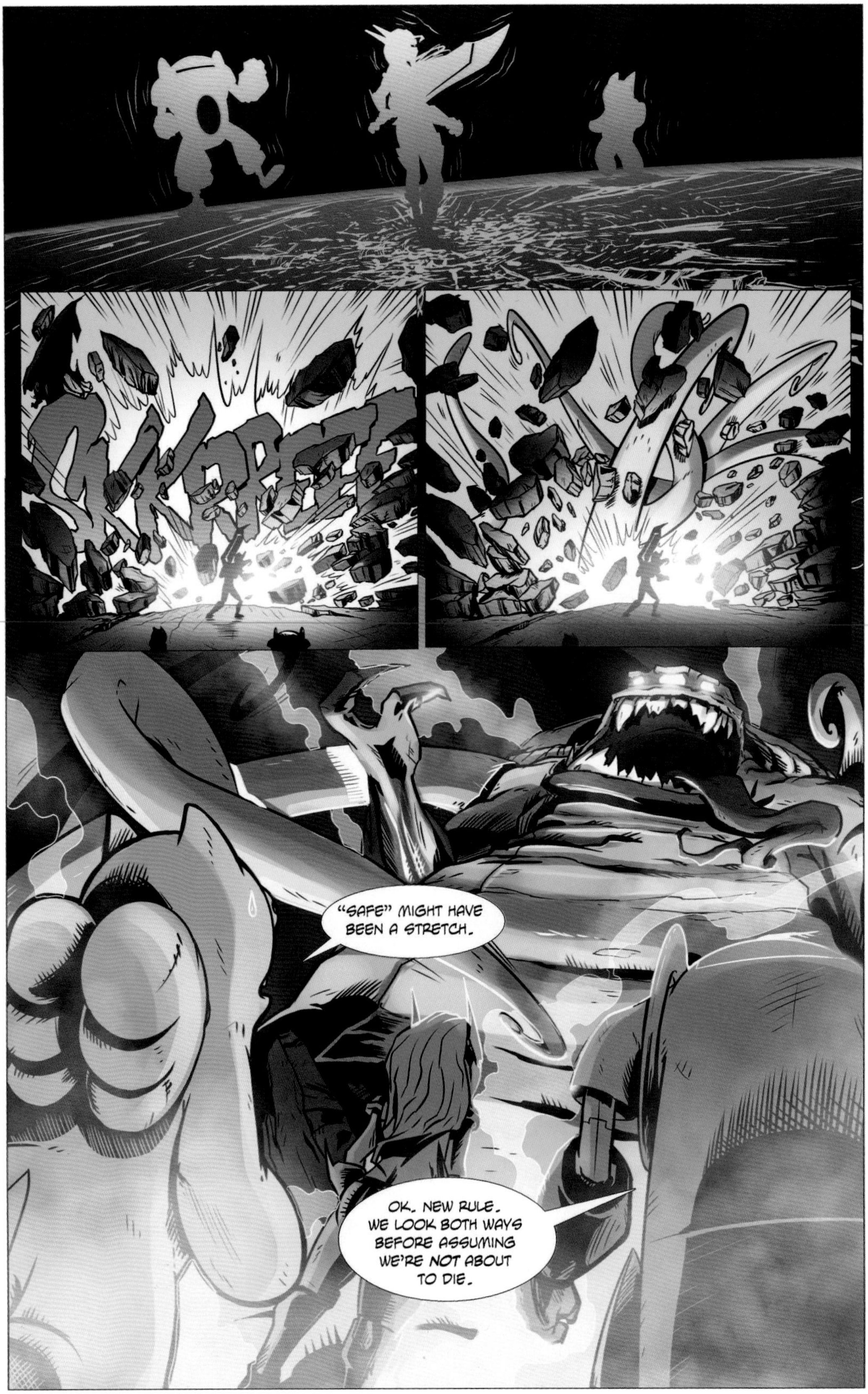
"SAFE" MIGHT HAVE BEEN A STRETCH.
OK. NEW RULE. WE LOOK BOTH WAYS BEFORE ASSUMING WE'RE NOT ABOUT TO DIE.

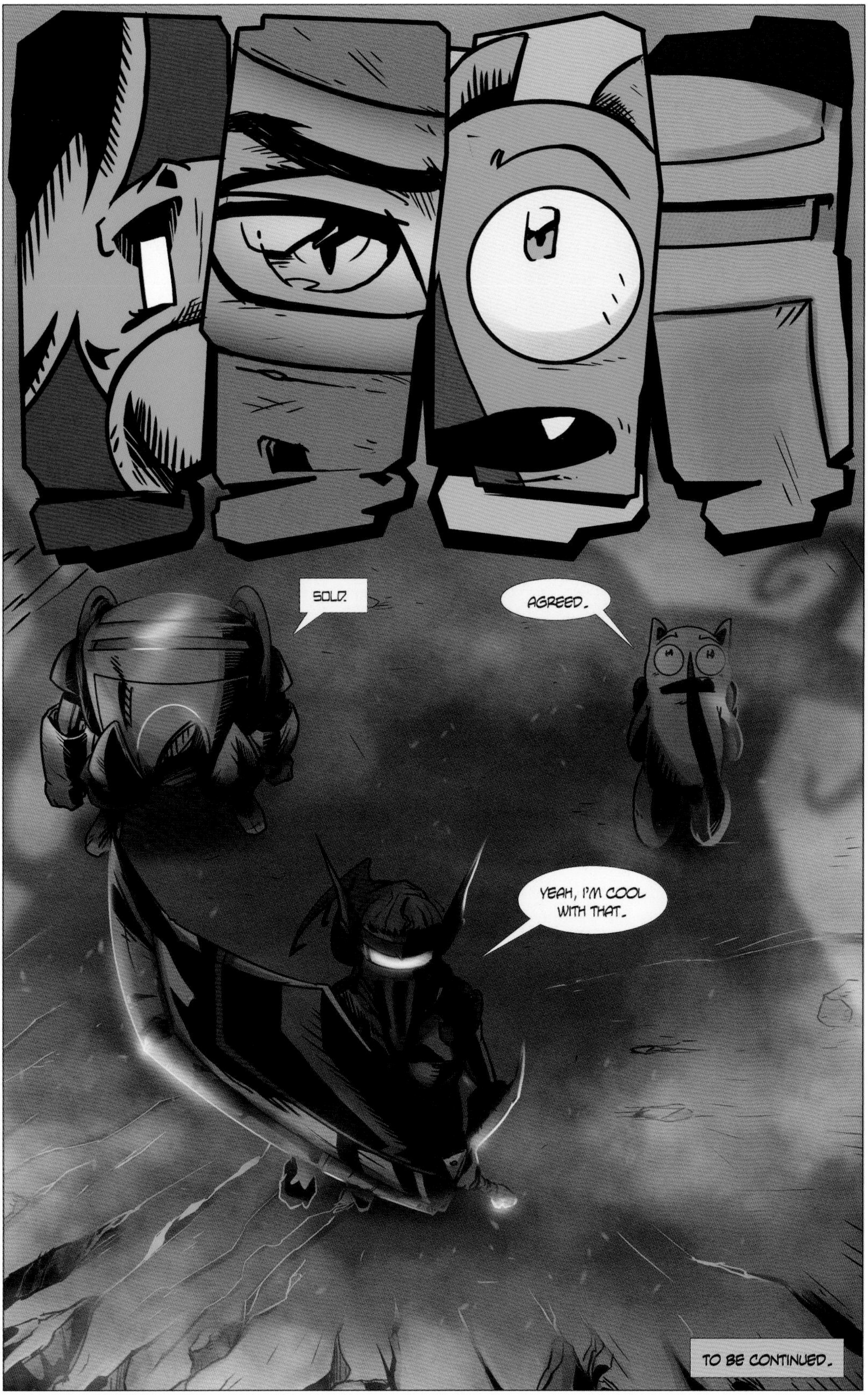
SOLD.
AGREED.
YEAH, I'M COOL WITH THAT.
TO BE CONTINUED.

CHAPTER THREE

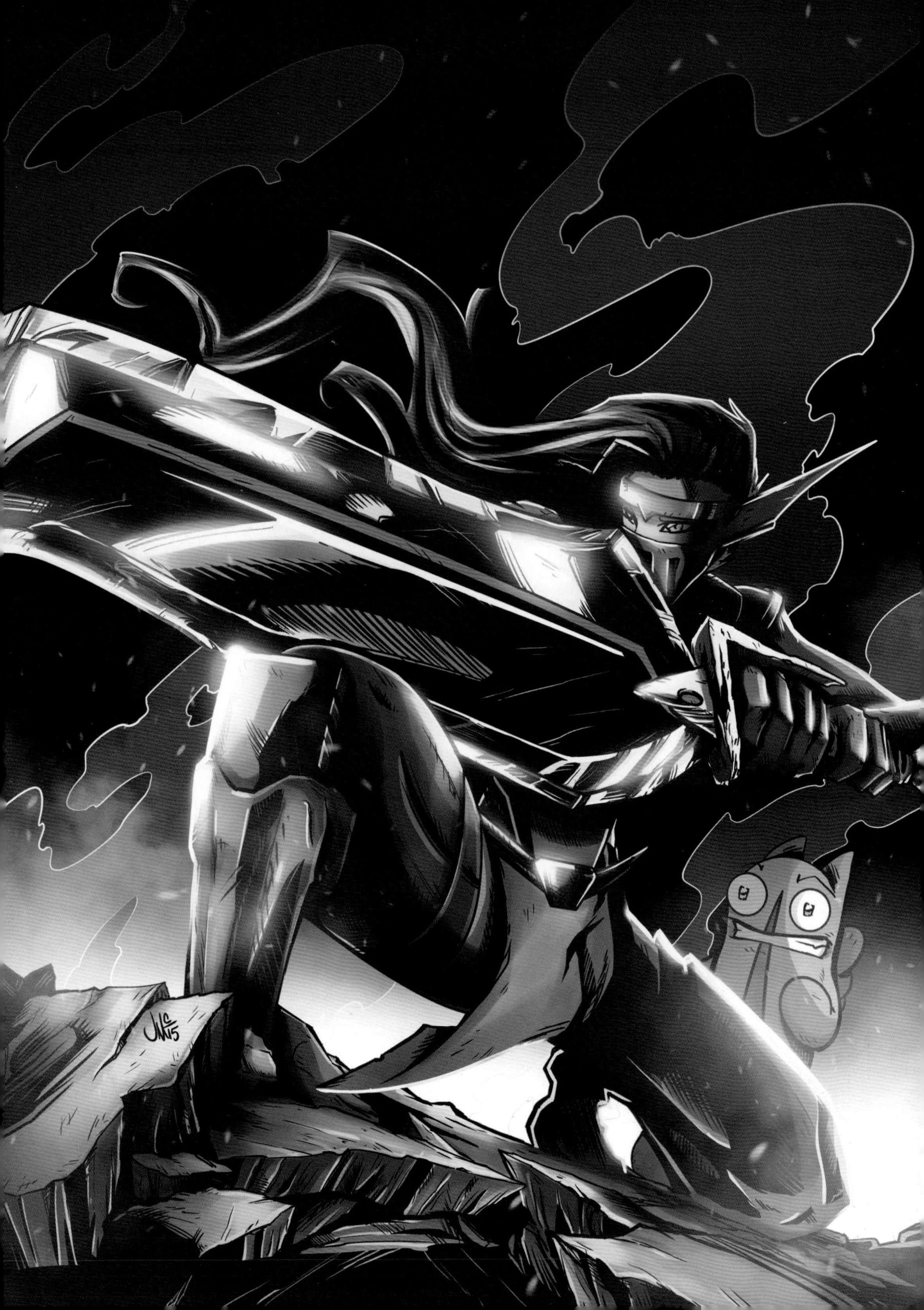

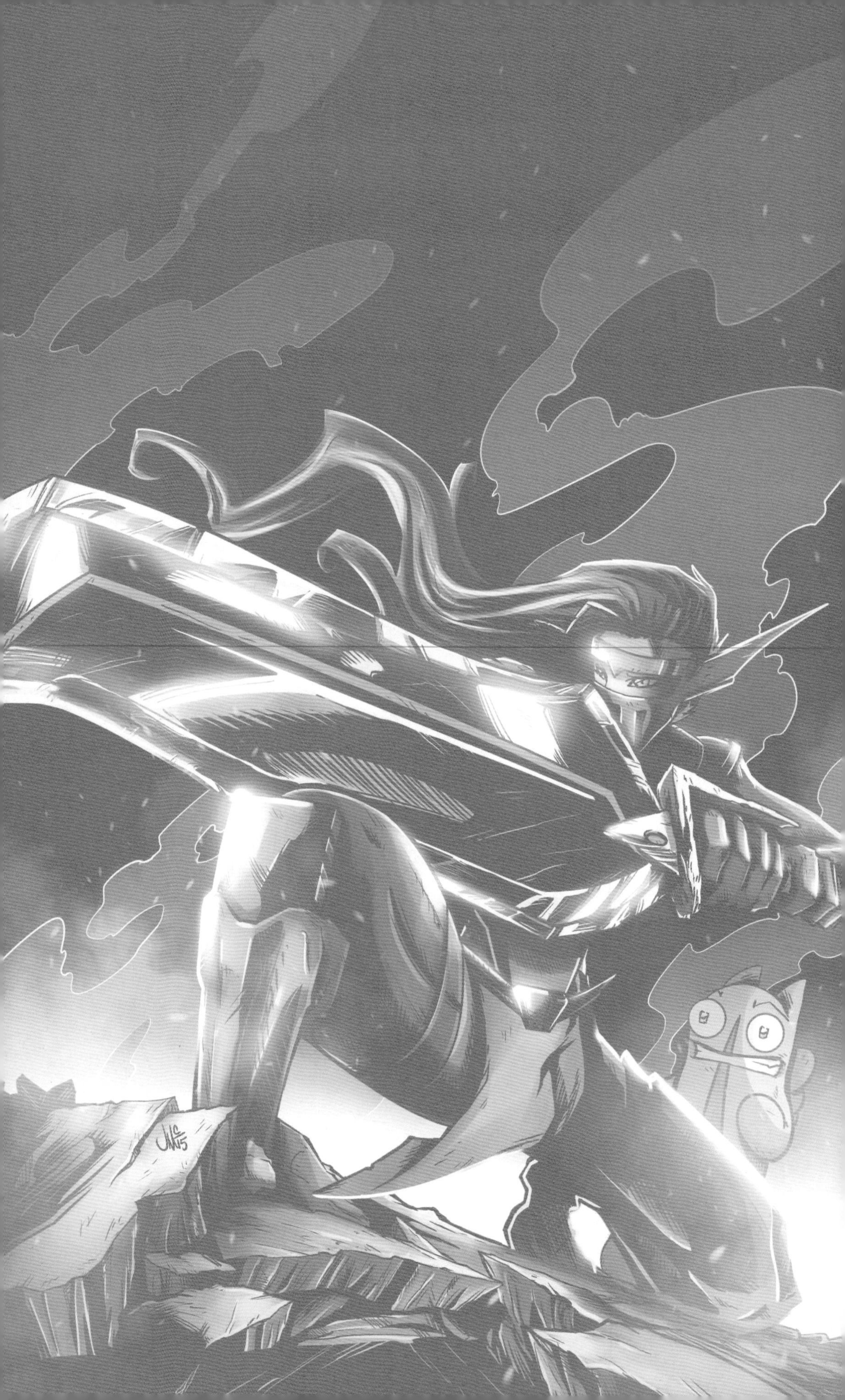

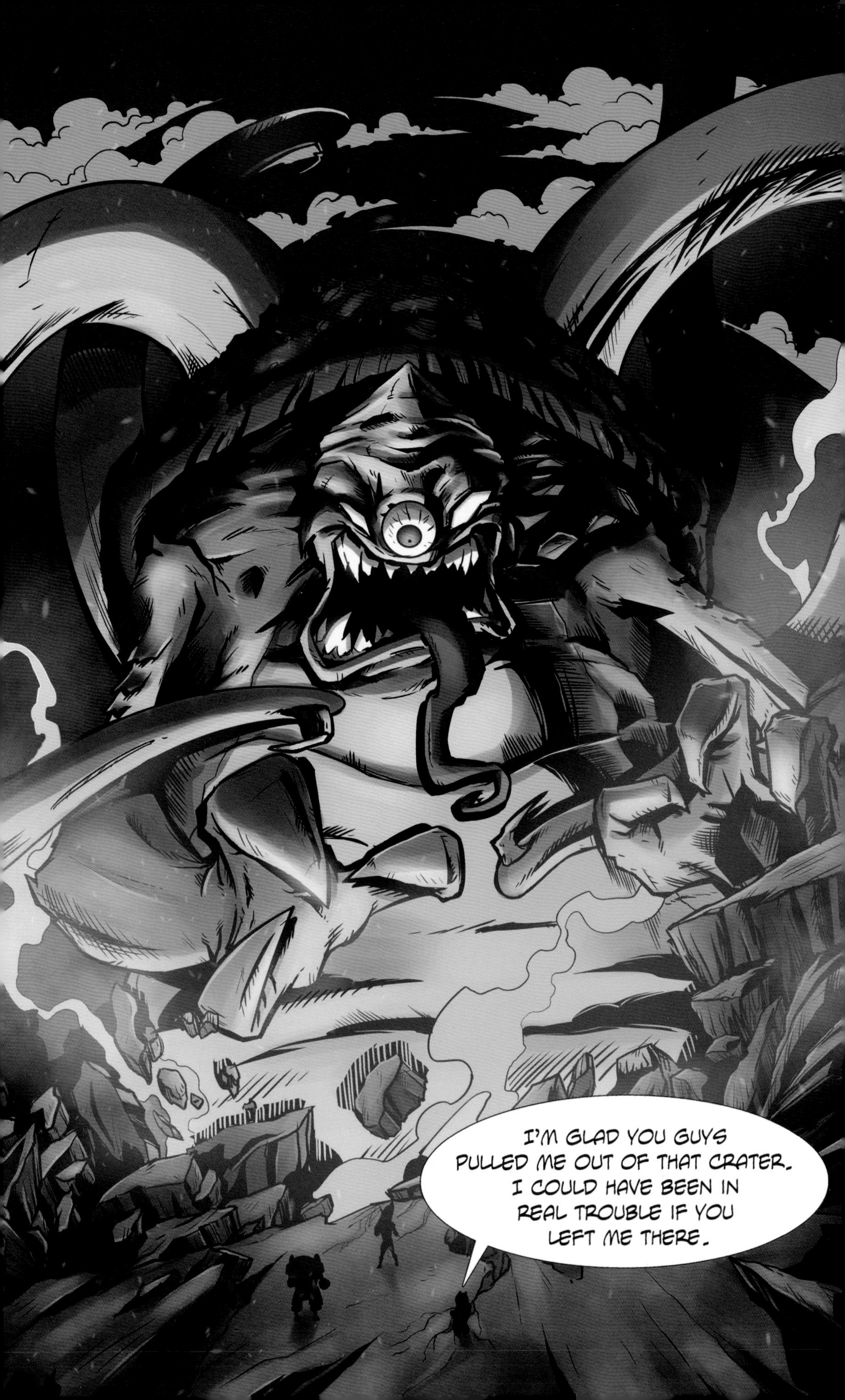
I'M GLAD YOU GUYS PULLED ME OUT OF THAT CRATER. I COULD HAVE BEEN IN REAL TROUBLE IF YOU LEFT ME THERE.

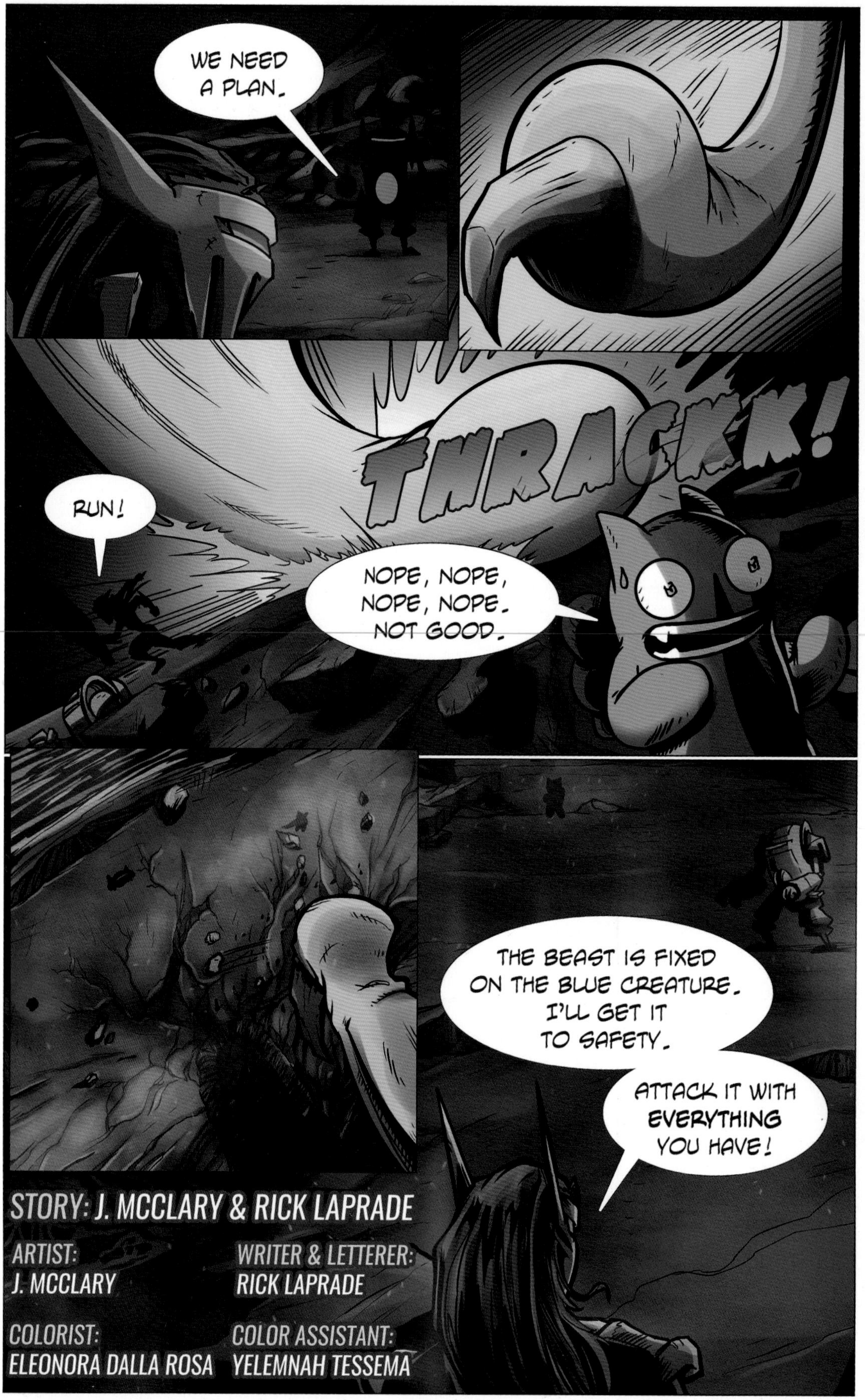
WE NEED A PLAN.
THRACKK!
RUN!
NOPE, NOPE, NOPE, NOPE. NOT GOOD.
THE BEAST IS FIXED ON THE BLUE CREATURE. I'LL GET IT TO SAFETY.
ATTACK IT WITH **EVERYTHING** YOU HAVE!
STORY: J. MCCLARY & RICK LAPRADE
ARTIST: J. MCCLARY
WRITER & LETTERER: RICK LAPRADE
COLORIST: ELEONORA DALLA ROSA
COLOR ASSISTANT: YELEMNAH TESSEMA

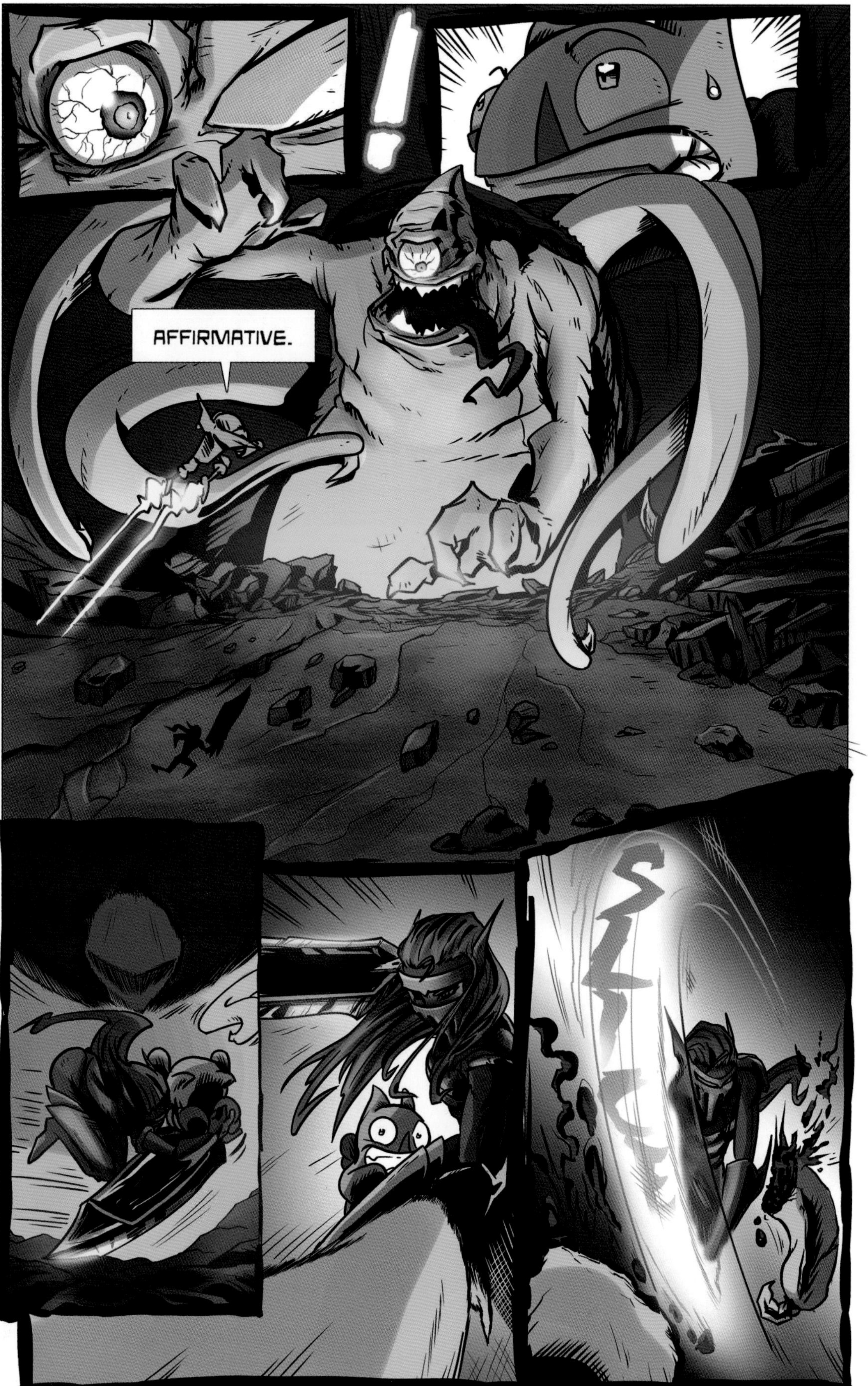
!
AFFIRMATIVE.

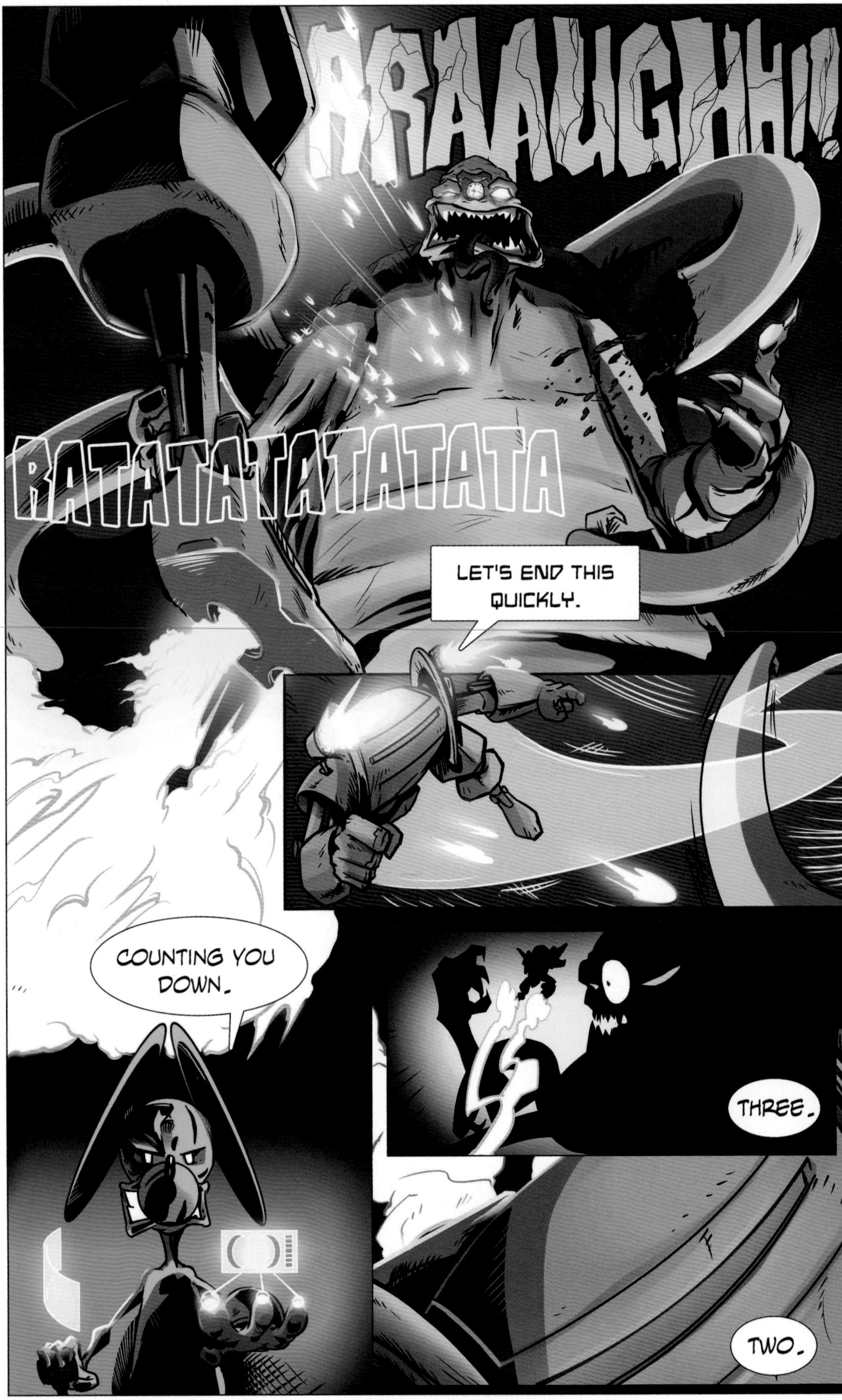
RRAAUGHH!
RATATATATATATA
LET'S END THIS QUICKLY.
COUNTING YOU DOWN.
THREE.
TWO.

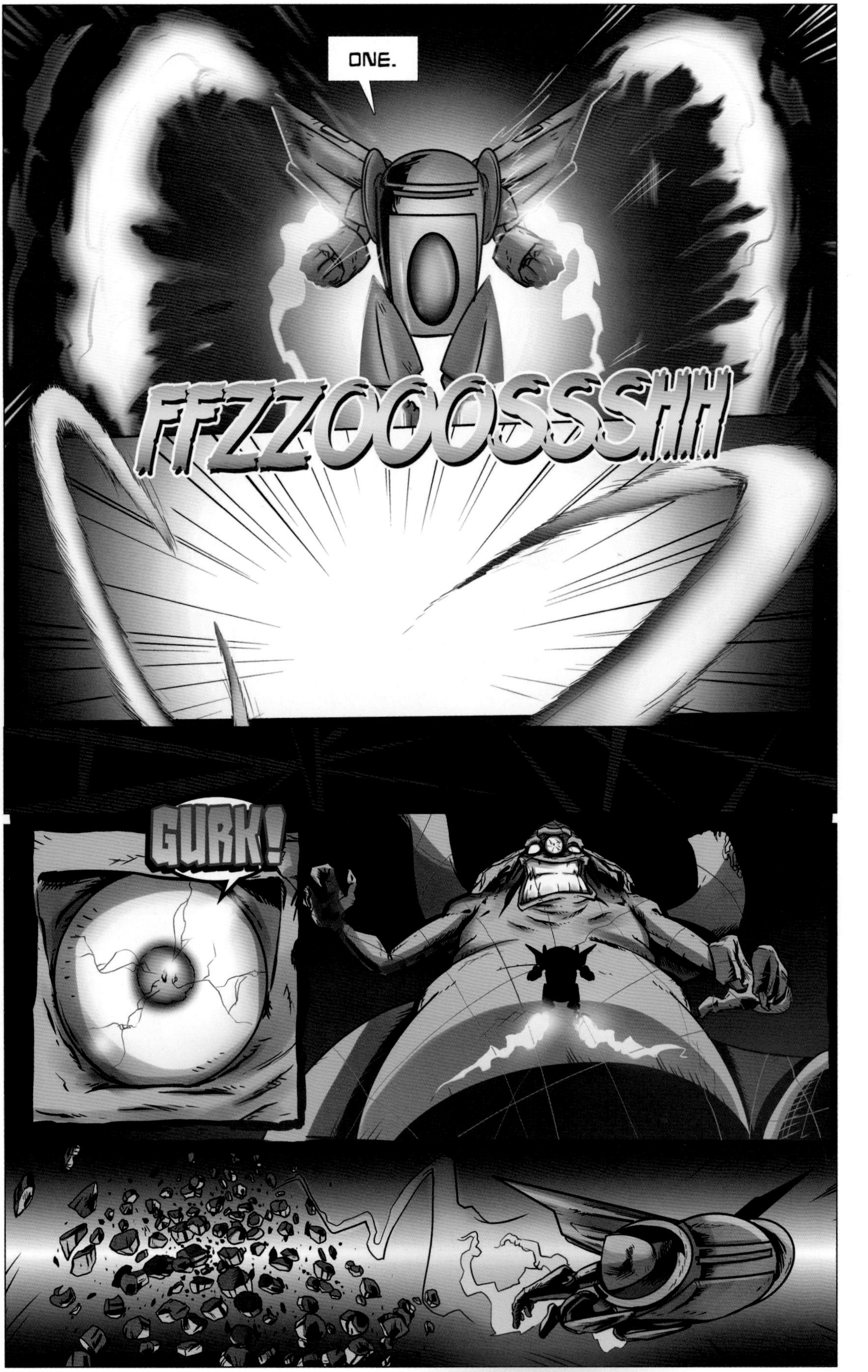

ONE.
FFZZOOOSSSHH
GURK!

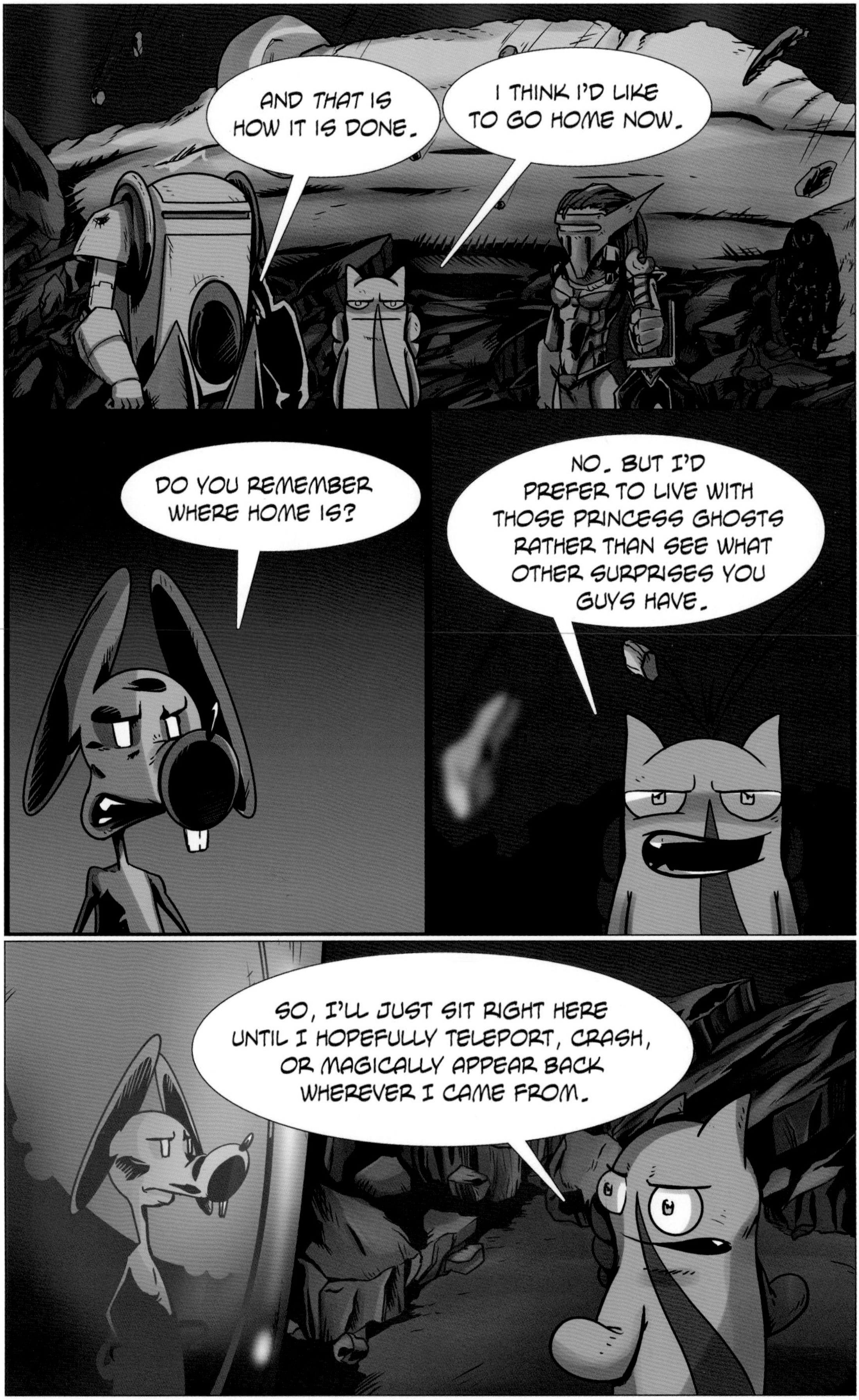
AND THAT IS HOW IT IS DONE.
I THINK I'D LIKE TO GO HOME NOW.
DO YOU REMEMBER WHERE HOME IS?
NO. BUT I'D PREFER TO LIVE WITH THOSE PRINCESS GHOSTS RATHER THAN SEE WHAT OTHER SURPRISES YOU GUYS HAVE.
SO, I'LL JUST SIT RIGHT HERE UNTIL I HOPEFULLY TELEPORT, CRASH, OR MAGICALLY APPEAR BACK WHEREVER I CAME FROM.

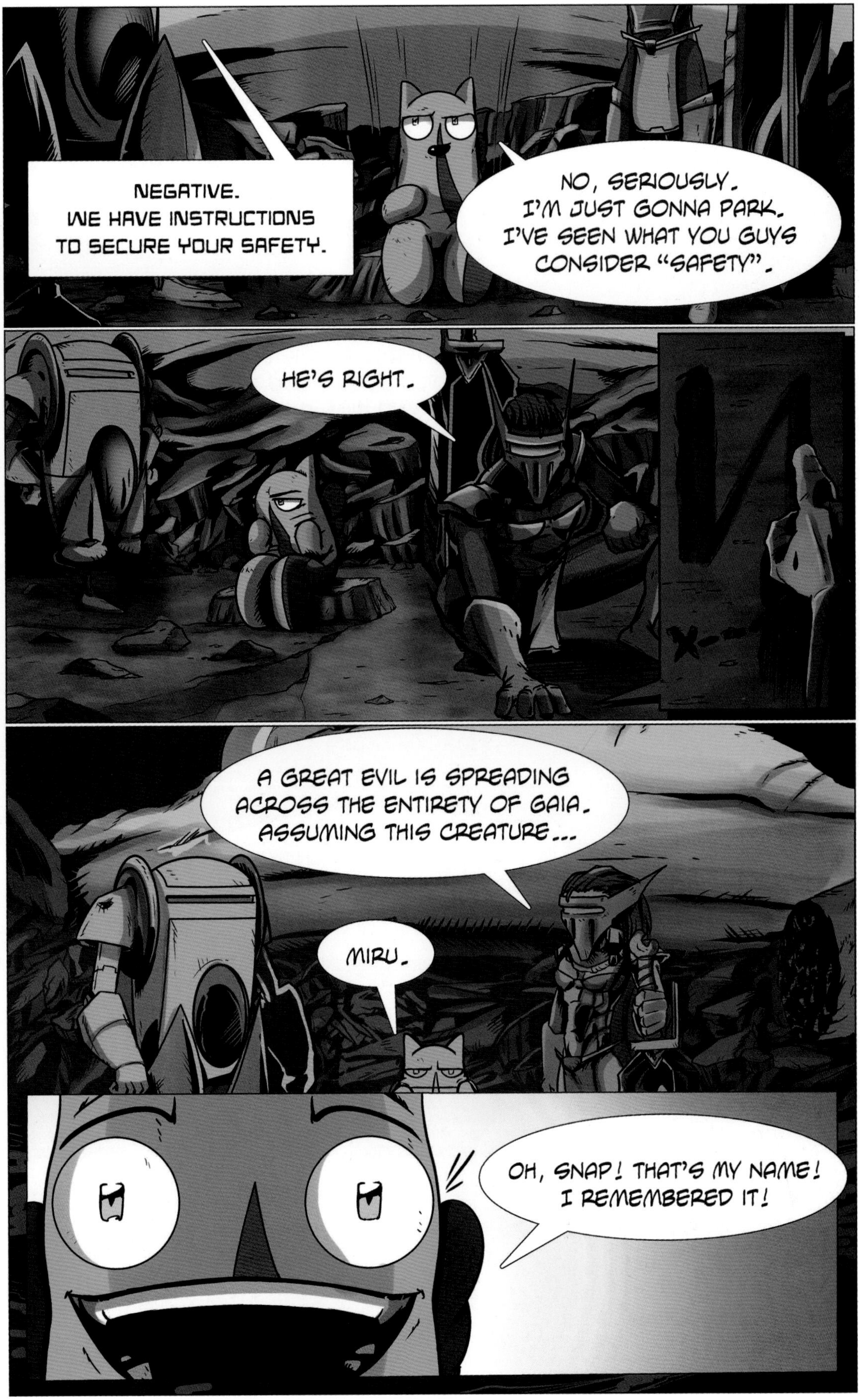
NEGATIVE.
WE HAVE INSTRUCTIONS
TO SECURE YOUR SAFETY.
NO, SERIOUSLY.
I'M JUST GONNA PARK.
I'VE SEEN WHAT YOU GUYS
CONSIDER "SAFETY".
HE'S RIGHT.
A GREAT EVIL IS SPREADING
ACROSS THE ENTIRETY OF GAIA.
ASSUMING THIS CREATURE...
MIRU.
OH, SNAP! THAT'S MY NAME!
I REMEMBERED IT!

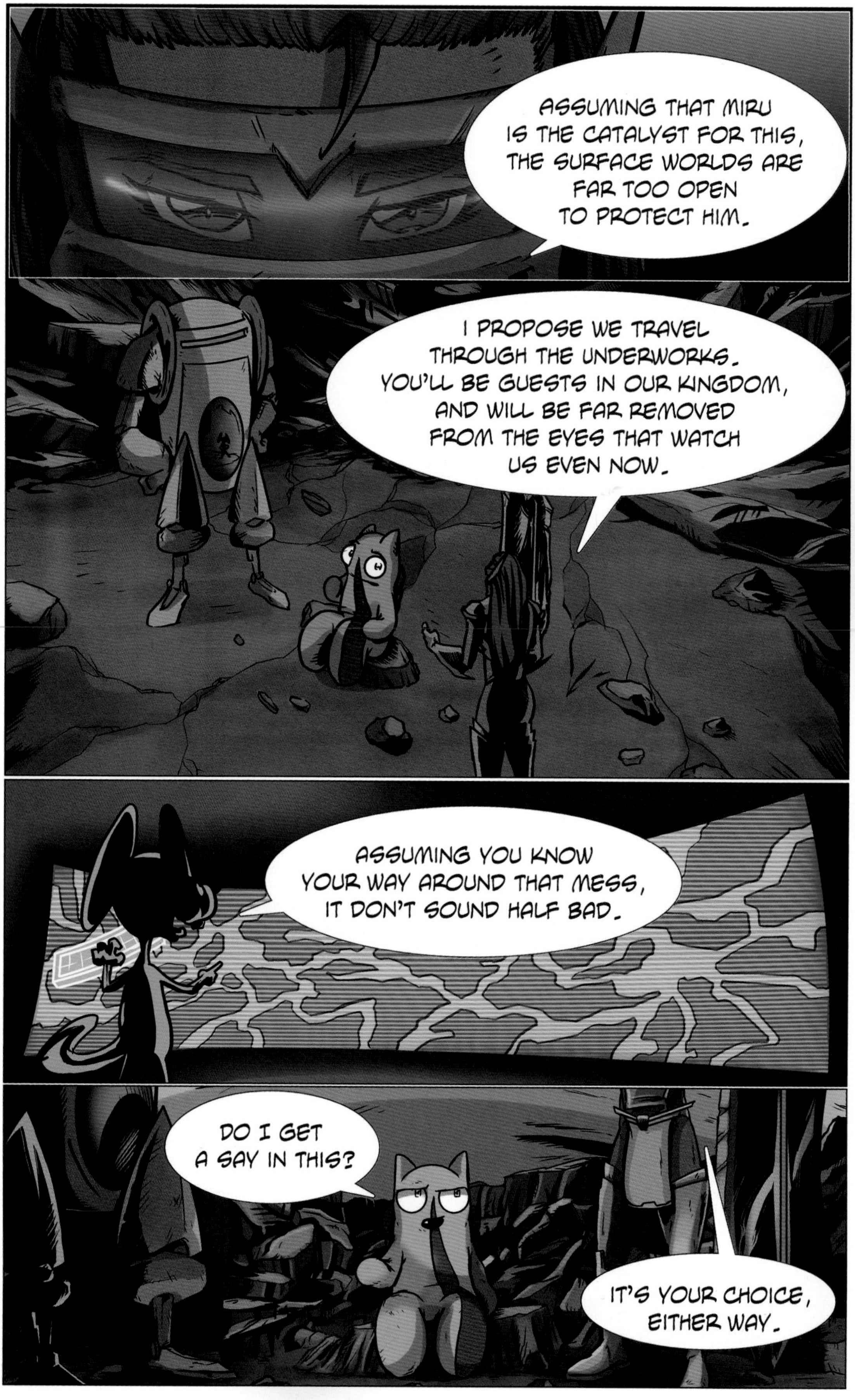
ASSUMING THAT MIRU IS THE CATALYST FOR THIS, THE SURFACE WORLDS ARE FAR TOO OPEN TO PROTECT HIM.
I PROPOSE WE TRAVEL THROUGH THE UNDERWORKS. YOU'LL BE GUESTS IN OUR KINGDOM, AND WILL BE FAR REMOVED FROM THE EYES THAT WATCH US EVEN NOW.
ASSUMING YOU KNOW YOUR WAY AROUND THAT MESS, IT DON'T SOUND HALF BAD.
DO I GET A SAY IN THIS?
IT'S YOUR CHOICE, EITHER WAY.

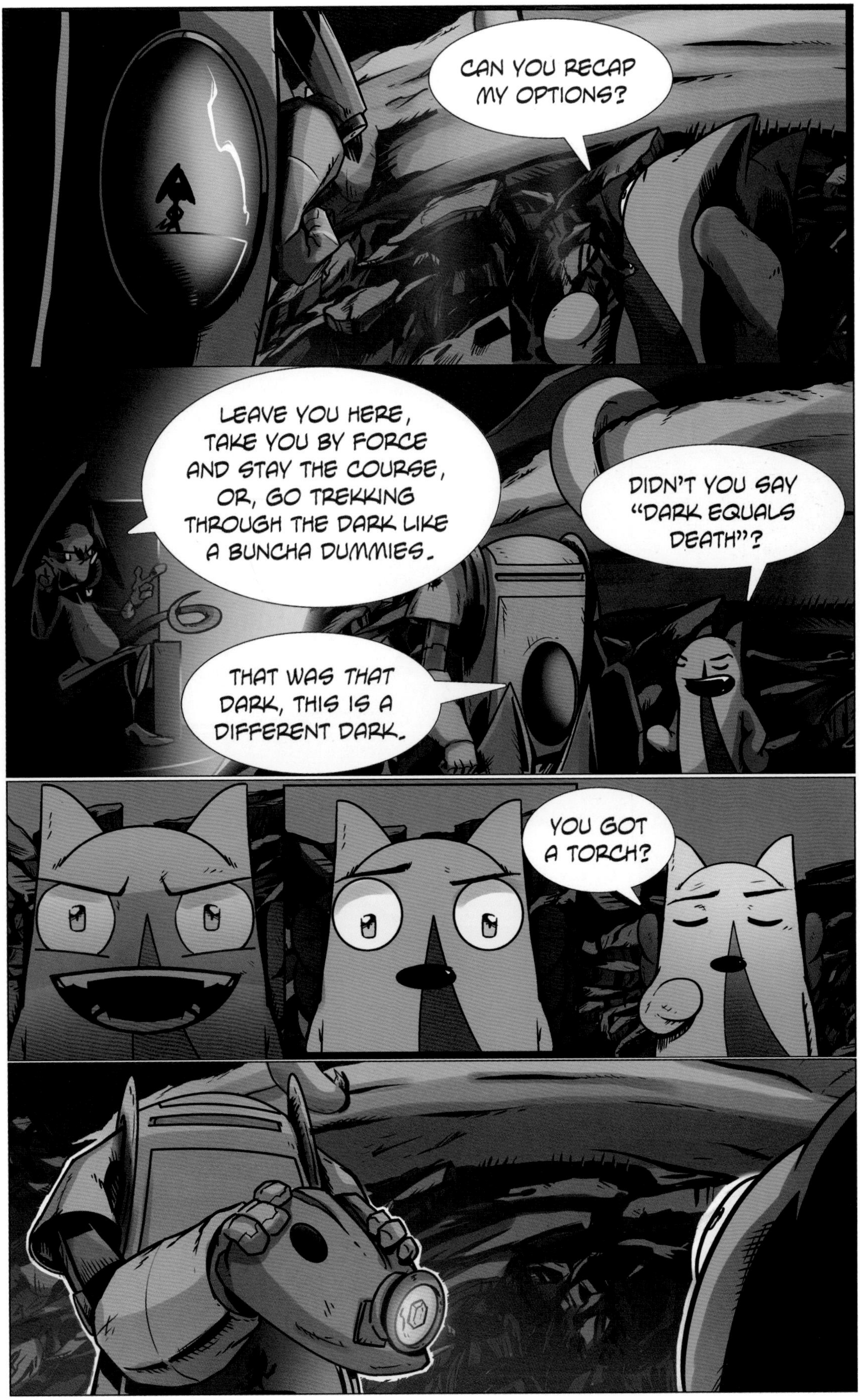
CAN YOU RECAP MY OPTIONS?
LEAVE YOU HERE, TAKE YOU BY FORCE AND STAY THE COURSE, OR, GO TREKKING THROUGH THE DARK LIKE A BUNCHA DUMMIES.
DIDN'T YOU SAY "DARK EQUALS DEATH"?
THAT WAS THAT DARK, THIS IS A DIFFERENT DARK.
YOU GOT A TORCH?

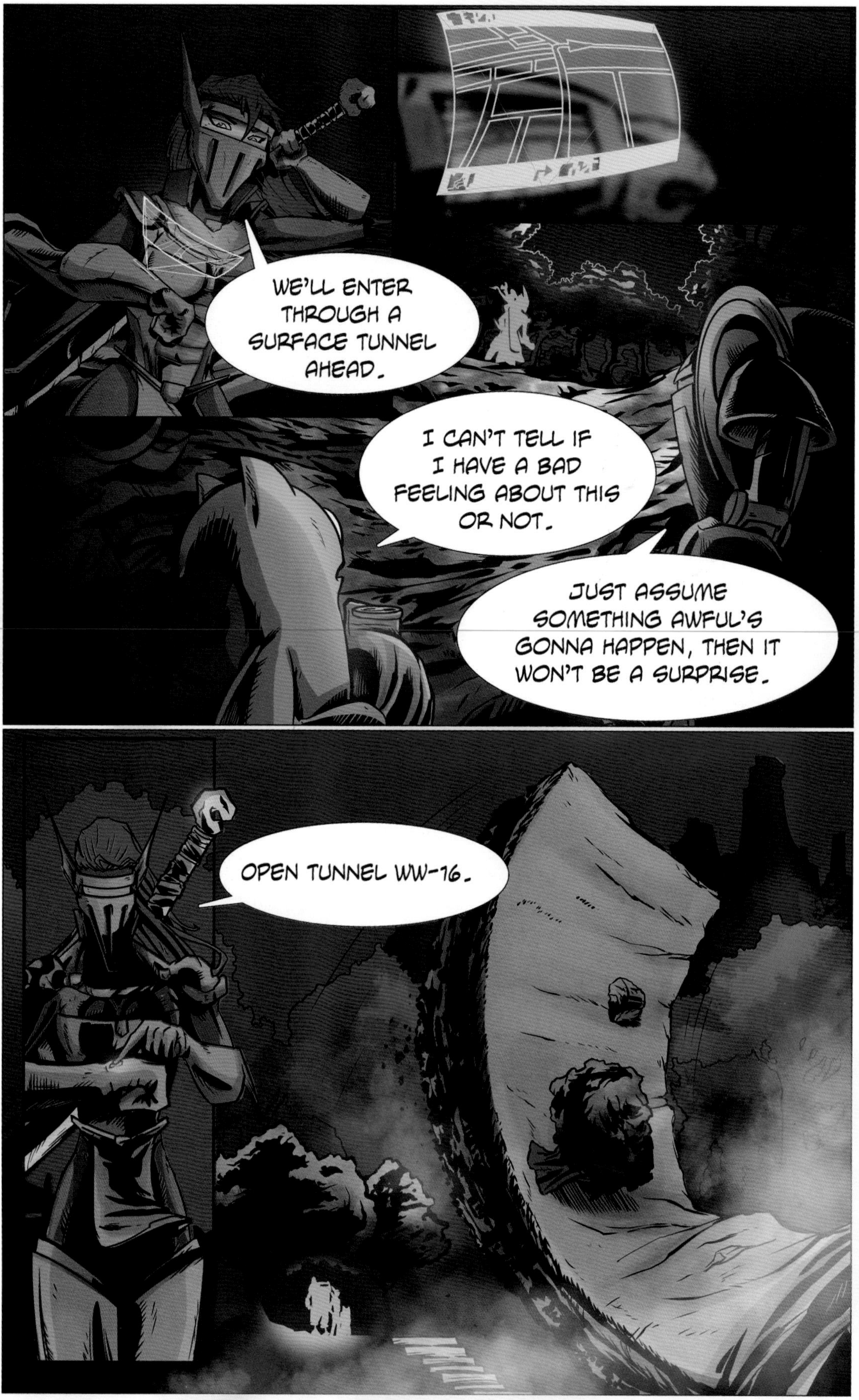
WE'LL ENTER THROUGH A SURFACE TUNNEL AHEAD.
I CAN'T TELL IF I HAVE A BAD FEELING ABOUT THIS OR NOT.
JUST ASSUME SOMETHING AWFUL'S GONNA HAPPEN, THEN IT WON'T BE A SURPRISE.
OPEN TUNNEL WW-16.

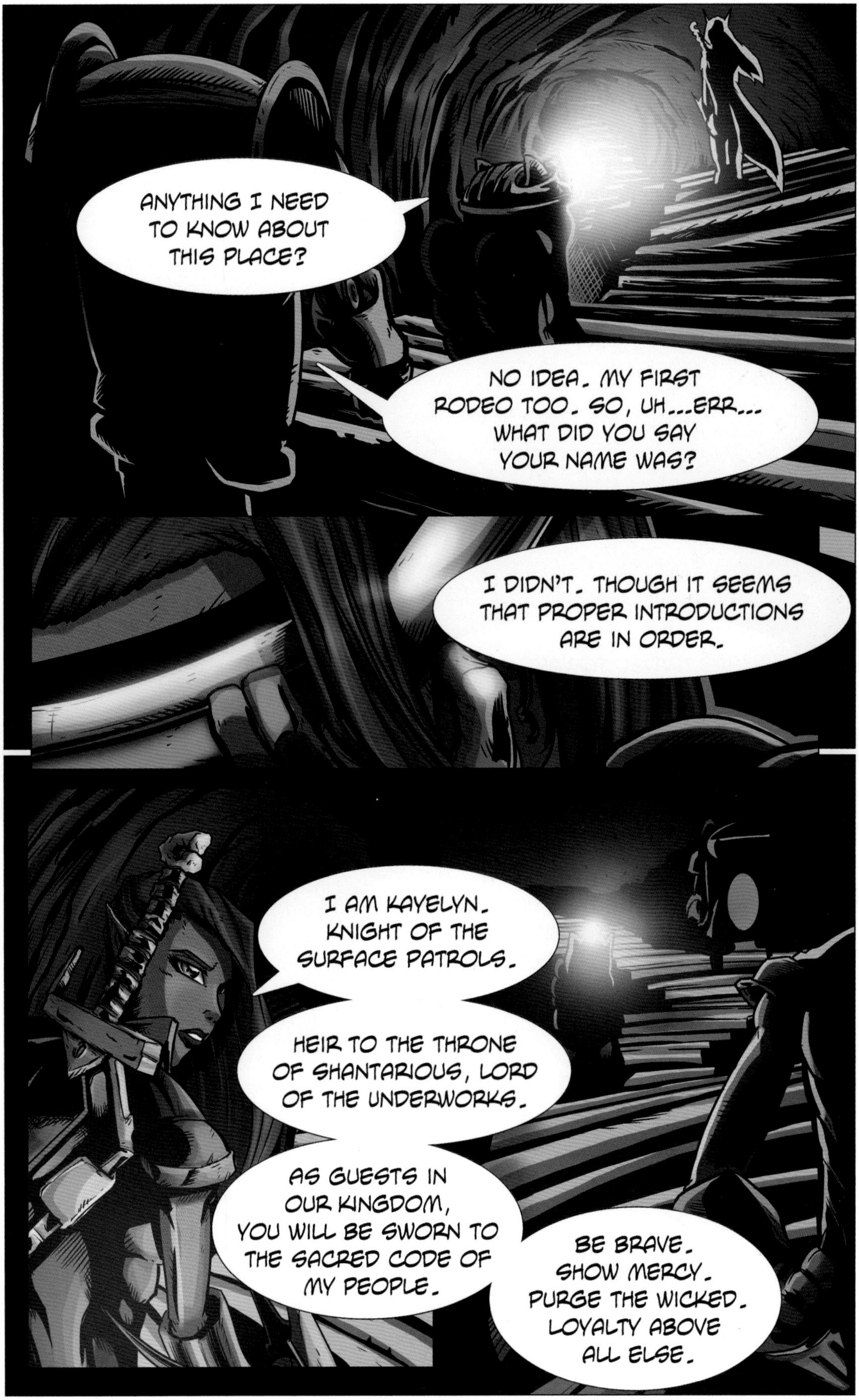
ANYTHING I NEED TO KNOW ABOUT THIS PLACE?
NO IDEA. MY FIRST RODEO TOO. SO, UH...ERR... WHAT DID YOU SAY YOUR NAME WAS?
I DIDN'T. THOUGH IT SEEMS THAT PROPER INTRODUCTIONS ARE IN ORDER.
I AM KAYELYN. KNIGHT OF THE SURFACE PATROLS.
HEIR TO THE THRONE OF SHANTARIOUS, LORD OF THE UNDERWORKS.
AS GUESTS IN OUR KINGDOM, YOU WILL BE SWORN TO THE SACRED CODE OF MY PEOPLE.
BE BRAVE. SHOW MERCY. PURGE THE WICKED. LOYALTY ABOVE ALL ELSE.

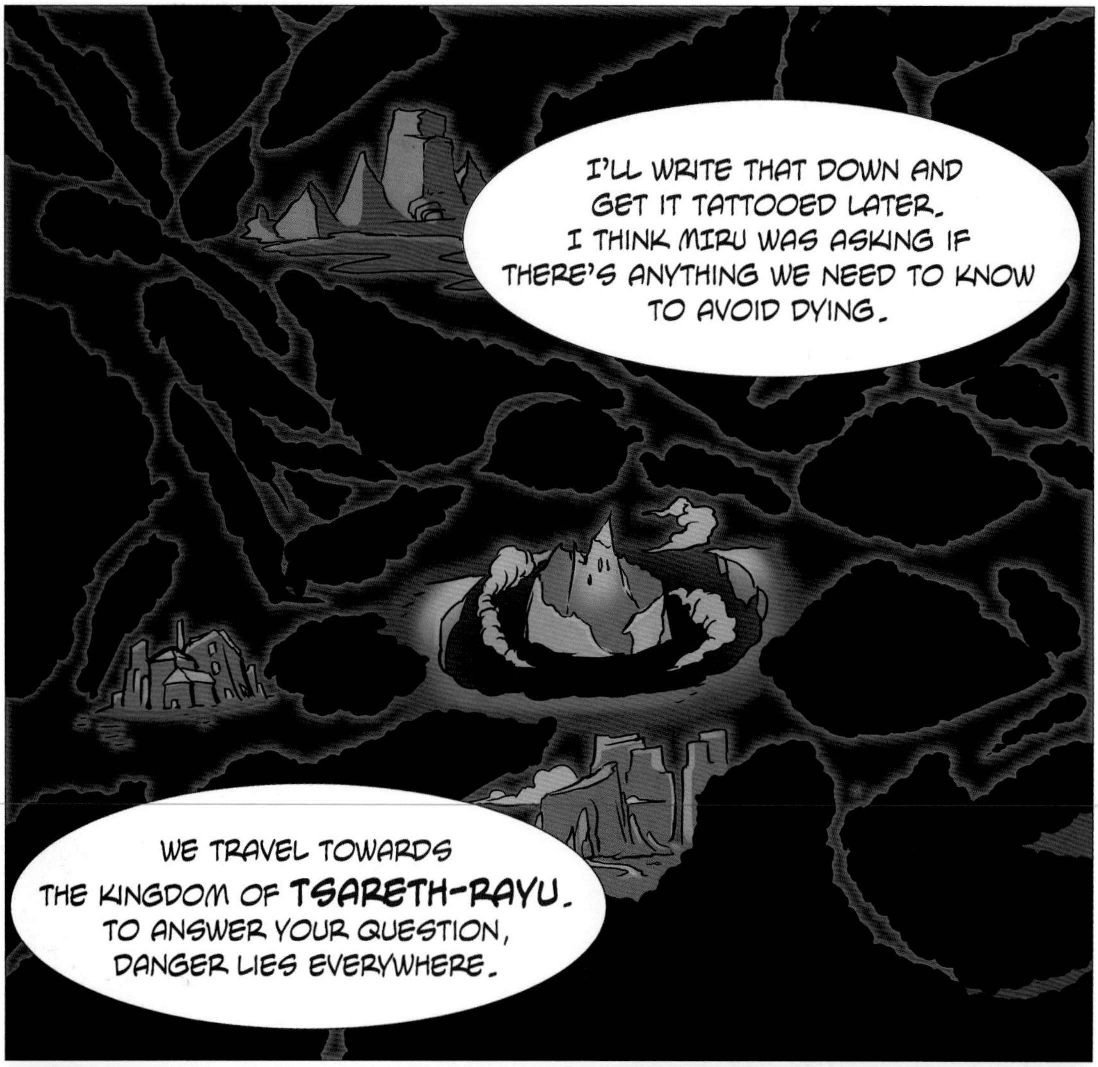
I'LL WRITE THAT DOWN AND GET IT TATTOOED LATER. I THINK MIRU WAS ASKING IF THERE'S ANYTHING WE NEED TO KNOW TO AVOID DYING.
WE TRAVEL TOWARDS THE KINGDOM OF TSARETH-RAYU. TO ANSWER YOUR QUESTION, DANGER LIES EVERYWHERE.

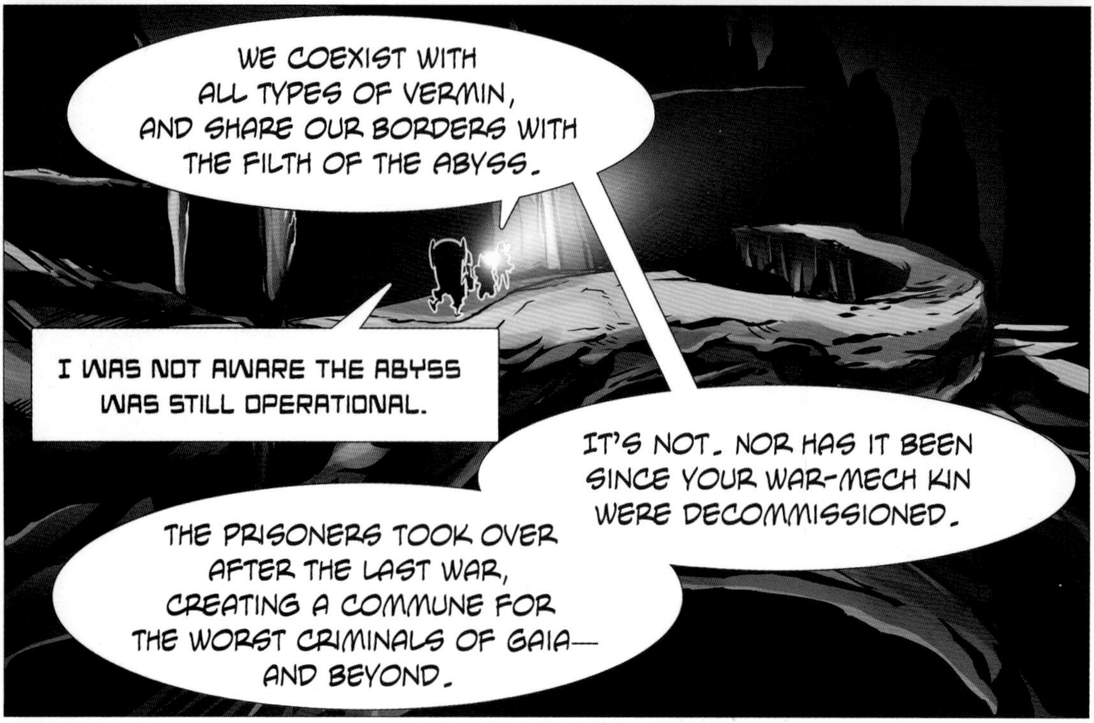
WE COEXIST WITH ALL TYPES OF VERMIN, AND SHARE OUR BORDERS WITH THE FILTH OF THE ABYSS.
I WAS NOT AWARE THE ABYSS WAS STILL OPERATIONAL.
IT'S NOT. NOR HAS IT BEEN SINCE YOUR WAR-MECH KIN WERE DECOMMISSIONED.
THE PRISONERS TOOK OVER AFTER THE LAST WAR, CREATING A COMMUNE FOR THE WORST CRIMINALS OF GAIA— AND BEYOND.

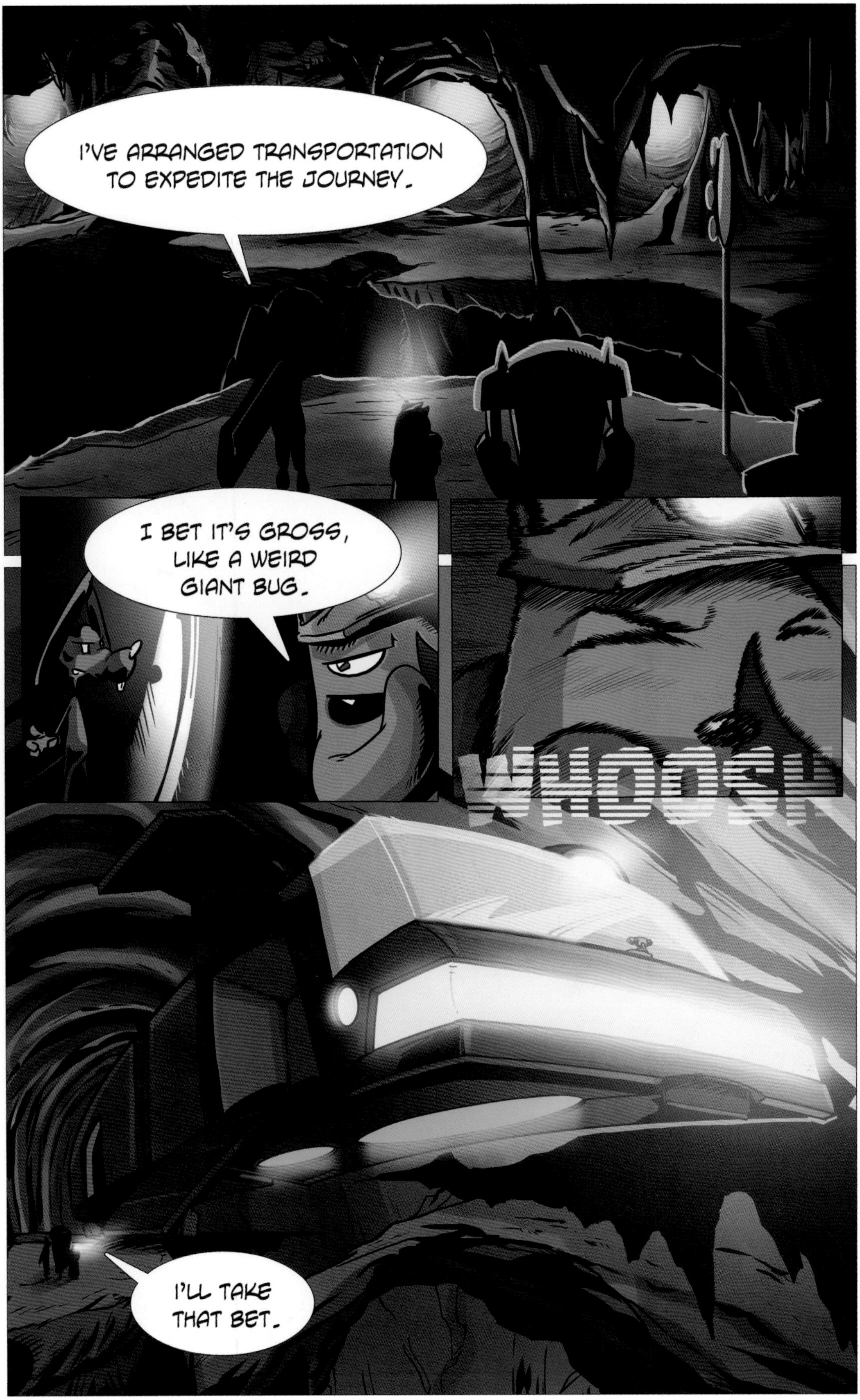
I'VE ARRANGED TRANSPORTATION TO EXPEDITE THE JOURNEY.
I BET IT'S GROSS, LIKE A WEIRD GIANT BUG.
WHOOSH
I'LL TAKE THAT BET.

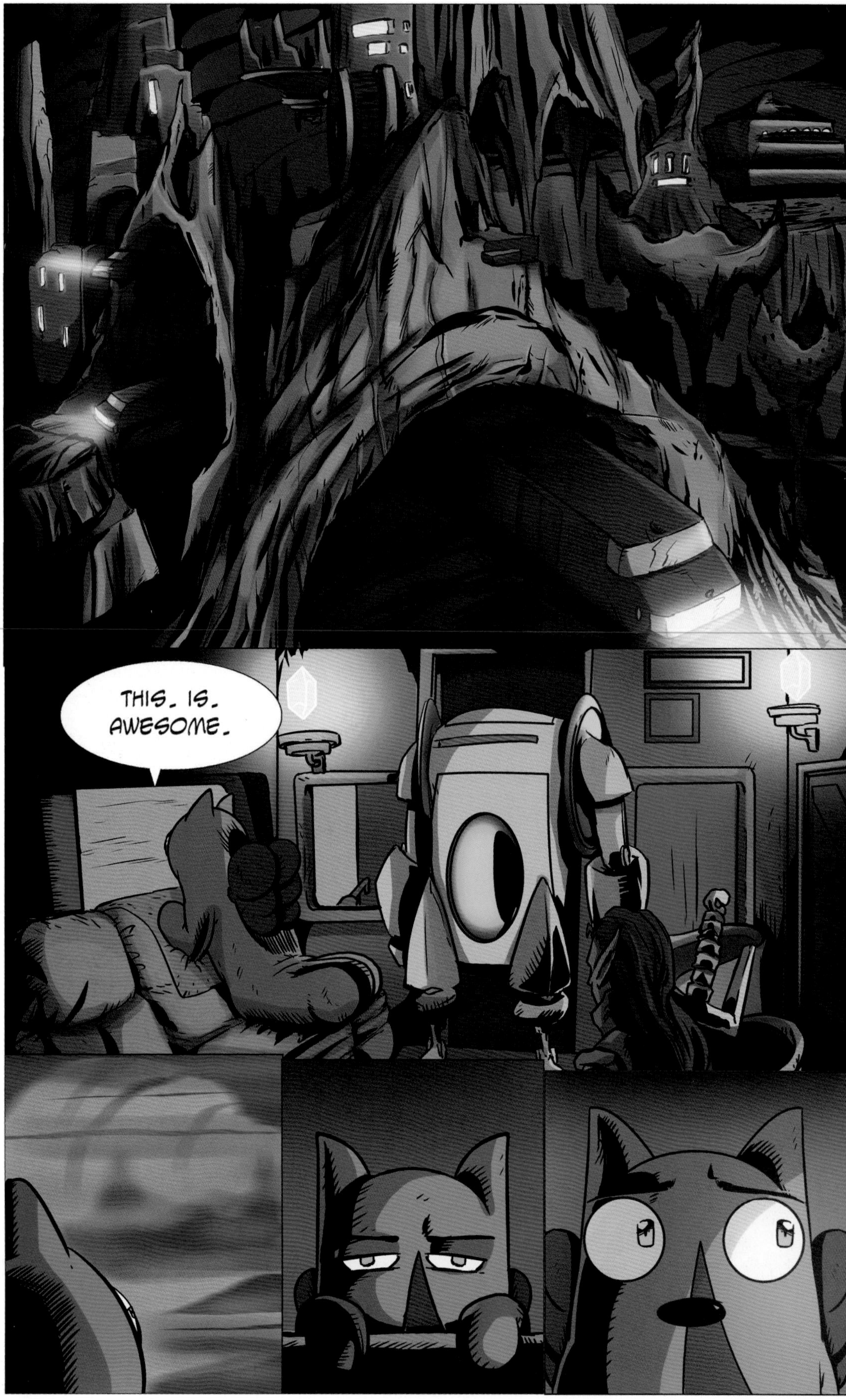
THIS. IS. AWESOME.

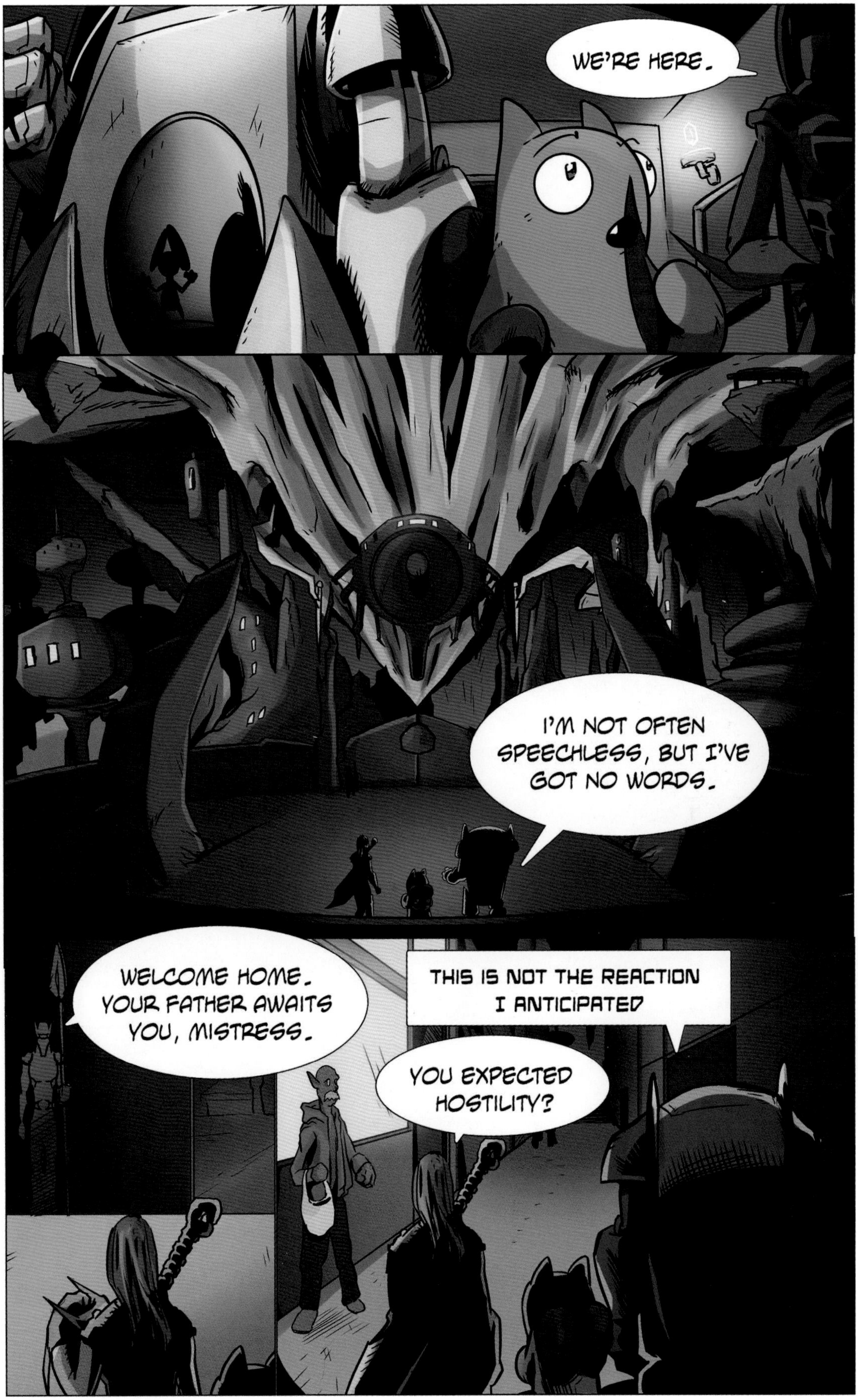
WE'RE HERE.
I'M NOT OFTEN SPEECHLESS, BUT I'VE GOT NO WORDS.
WELCOME HOME. YOUR FATHER AWAITS YOU, MISTRESS.
THIS IS NOT THE REACTION I ANTICIPATED
YOU EXPECTED HOSTILITY?

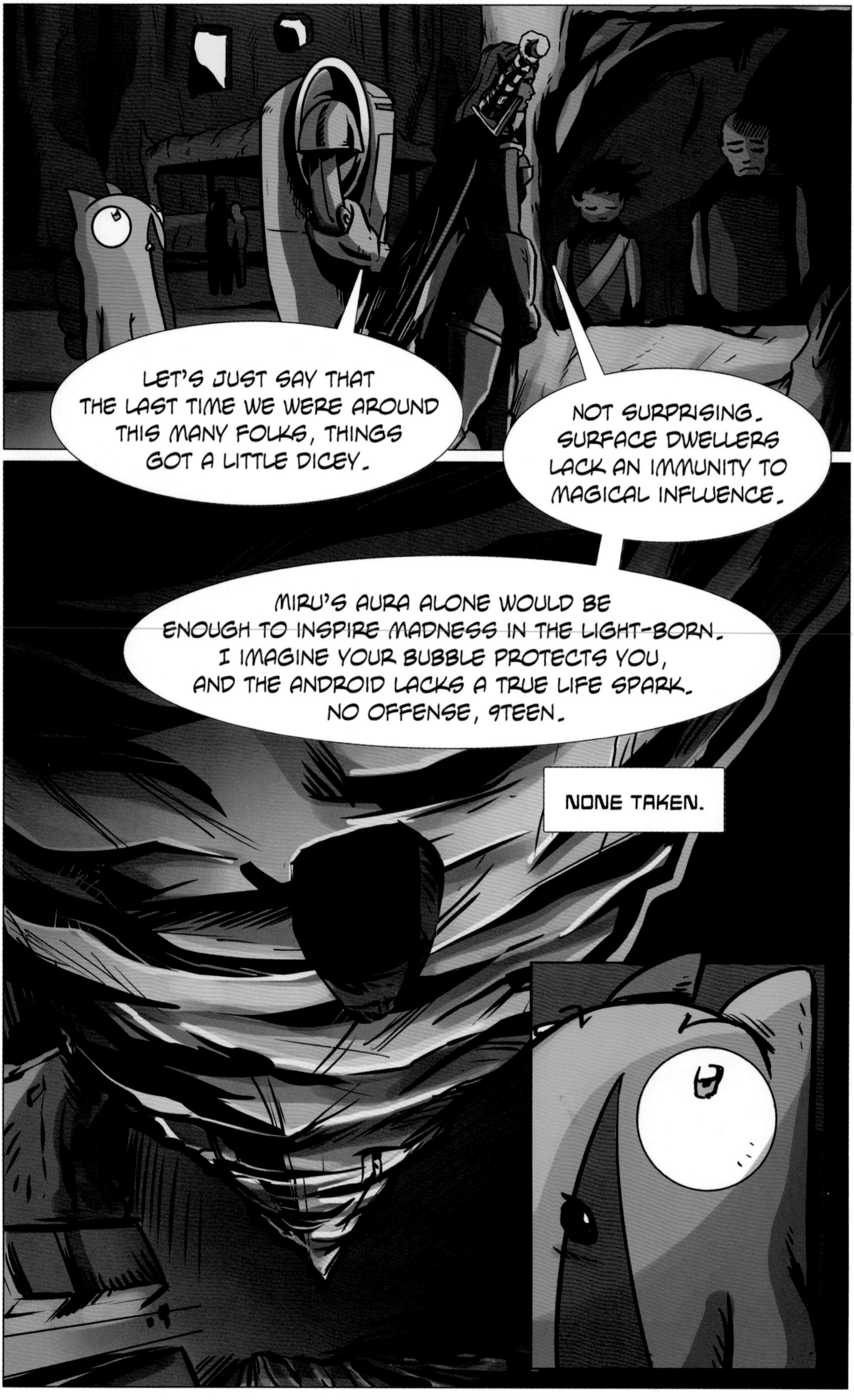
LET'S JUST SAY THAT THE LAST TIME WE WERE AROUND THIS MANY FOLKS, THINGS GOT A LITTLE DICEY.
NOT SURPRISING. SURFACE DWELLERS LACK AN IMMUNITY TO MAGICAL INFLUENCE.
MIRU'S AURA ALONE WOULD BE ENOUGH TO INSPIRE MADNESS IN THE LIGHT-BORN. I IMAGINE YOUR BUBBLE PROTECTS YOU, AND THE ANDROID LACKS A TRUE LIFE SPARK. NO OFFENSE, 9TEEN.
NONE TAKEN.

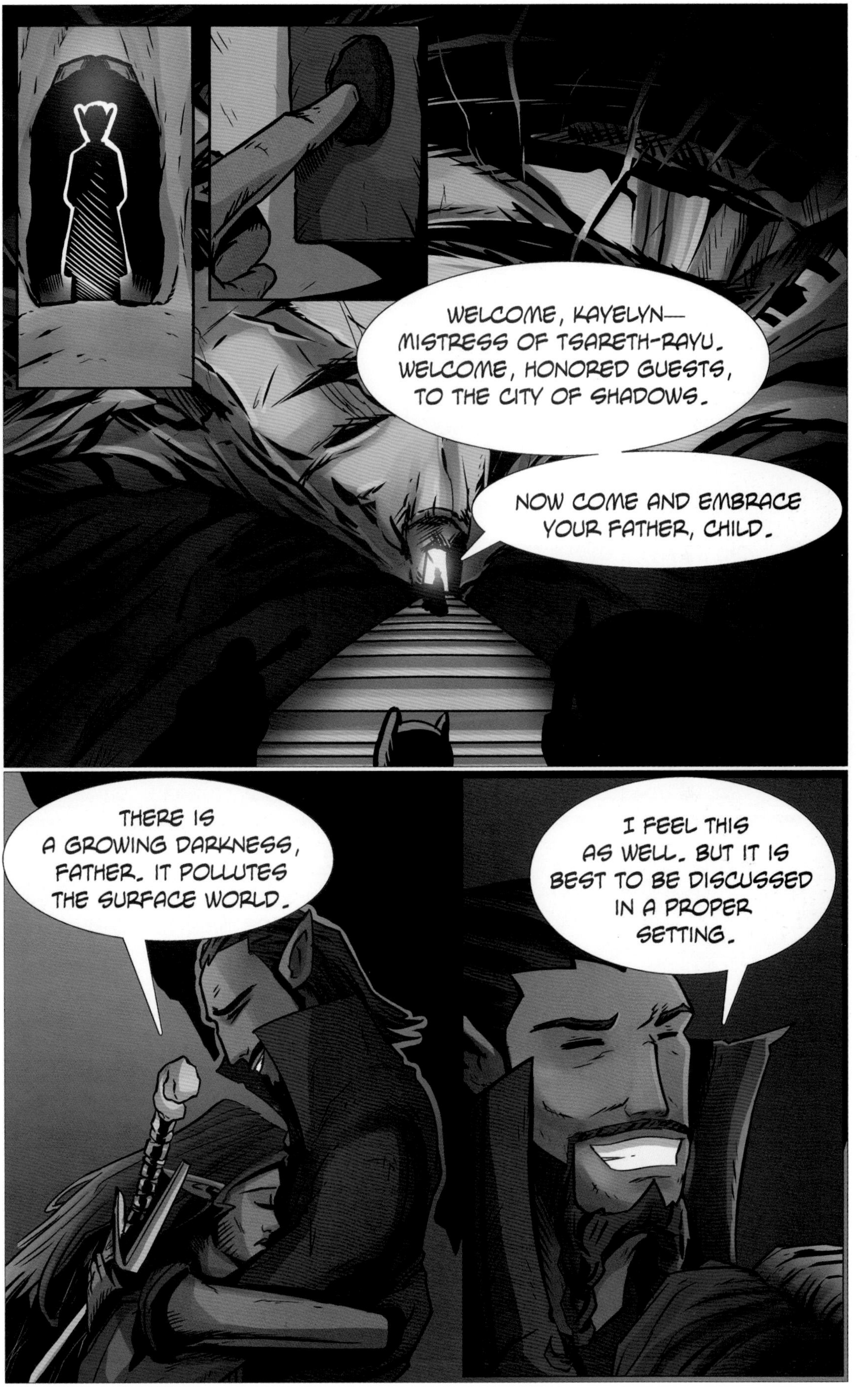
WELCOME, KAYELYN—
MISTRESS OF TSARETH-RAYU. WELCOME, HONORED GUESTS, TO THE CITY OF SHADOWS.
NOW COME AND EMBRACE YOUR FATHER, CHILD.
THERE IS A GROWING DARKNESS, FATHER. IT POLLUTES THE SURFACE WORLD.
I FEEL THIS AS WELL. BUT IT IS BEST TO BE DISCUSSED IN A PROPER SETTING.

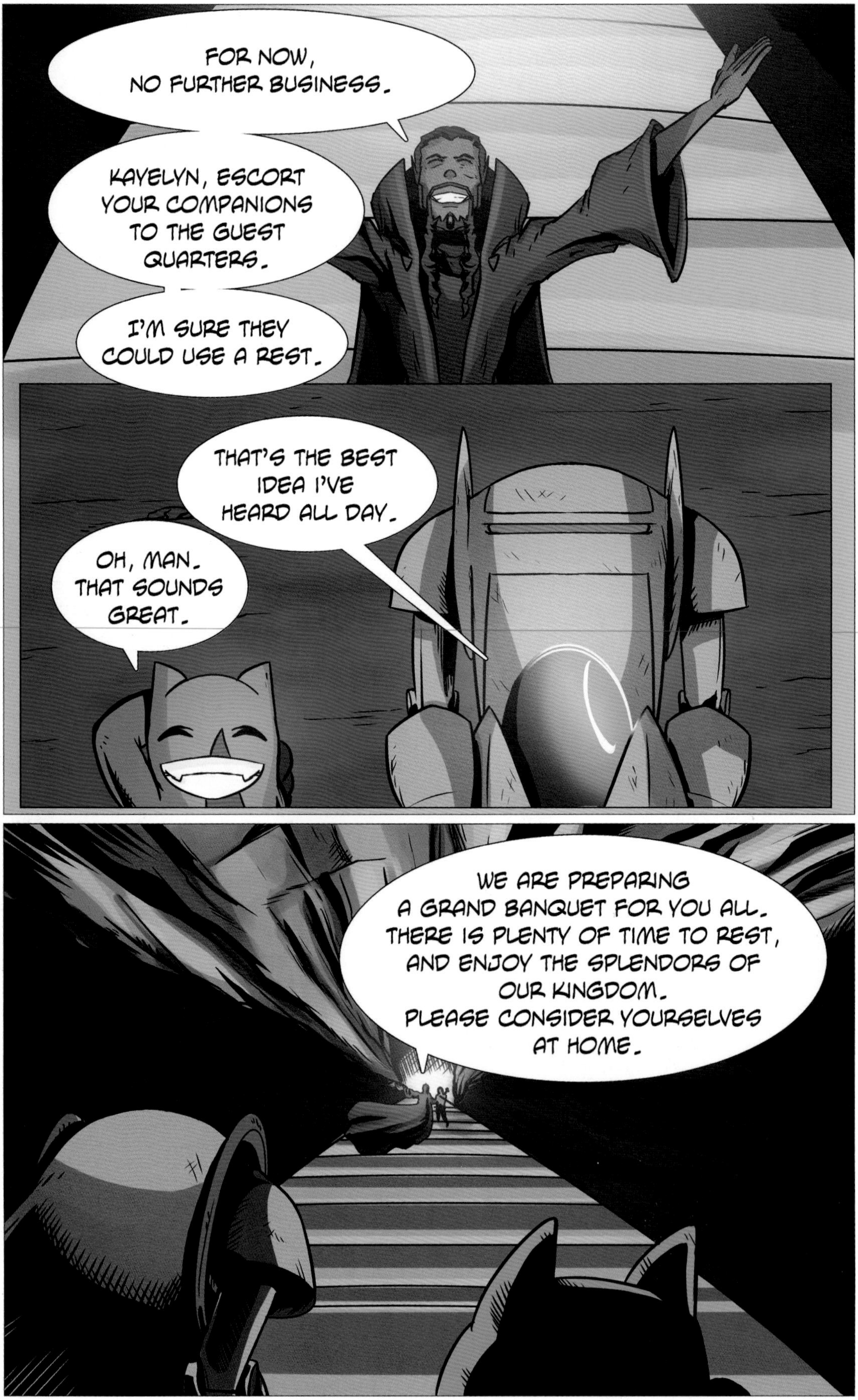
FOR NOW, NO FURTHER BUSINESS.
KAYELYN, ESCORT YOUR COMPANIONS TO THE GUEST QUARTERS.
I'M SURE THEY COULD USE A REST.
THAT'S THE BEST IDEA I'VE HEARD ALL DAY.
OH, MAN. THAT SOUNDS GREAT.
WE ARE PREPARING A GRAND BANQUET FOR YOU ALL. THERE IS PLENTY OF TIME TO REST, AND ENJOY THE SPLENDORS OF OUR KINGDOM. PLEASE CONSIDER YOURSELVES AT HOME.

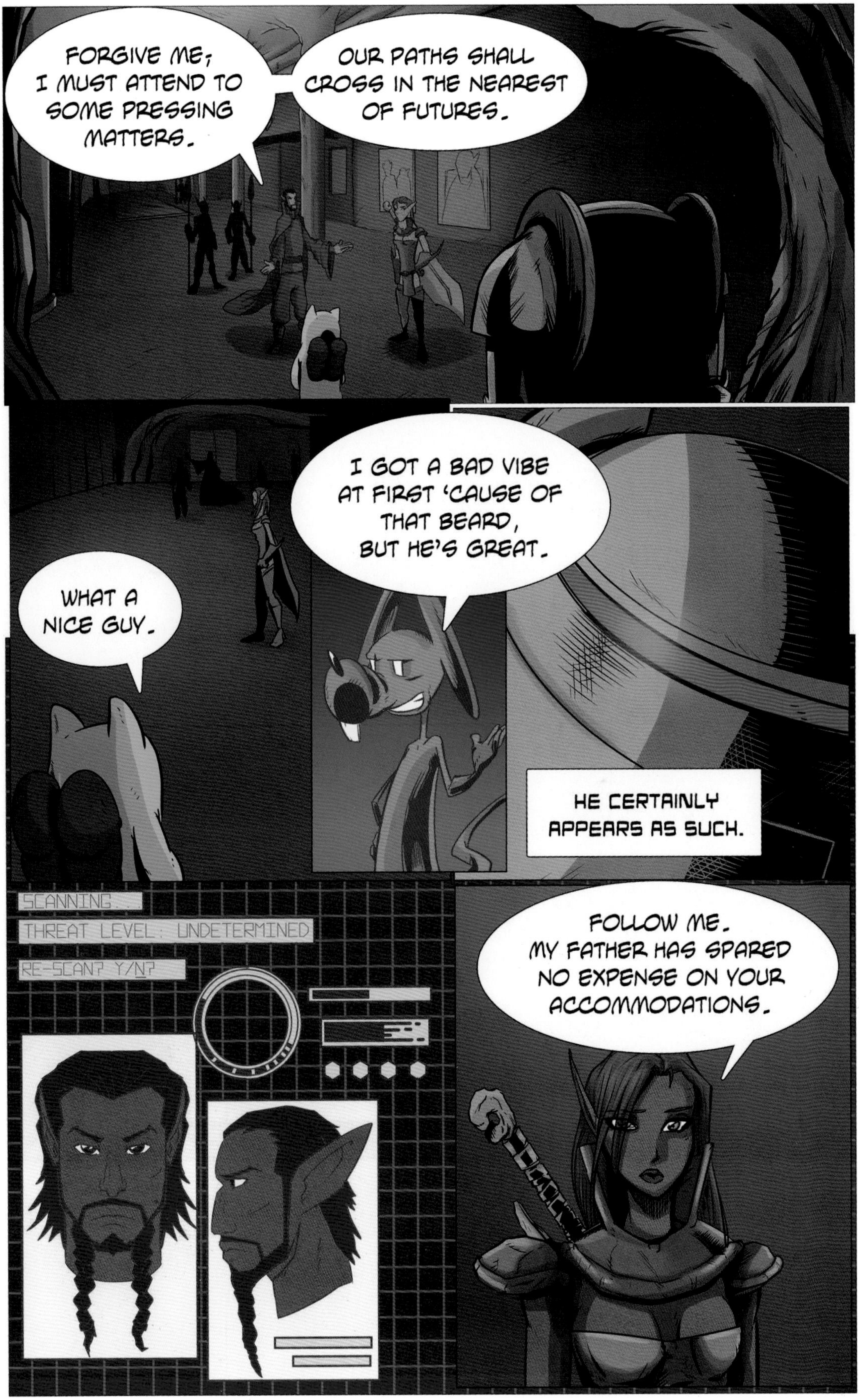
FORGIVE ME; I MUST ATTEND TO SOME PRESSING MATTERS.
OUR PATHS SHALL CROSS IN THE NEAREST OF FUTURES.
WHAT A NICE GUY.
I GOT A BAD VIBE AT FIRST 'CAUSE OF THAT BEARD, BUT HE'S GREAT.
HE CERTAINLY APPEARS AS SUCH.
SCANNING...
THREAT LEVEL: UNDETERMINED
RE-SCAN? Y/N?
FOLLOW ME. MY FATHER HAS SPARED NO EXPENSE ON YOUR ACCOMMODATIONS.

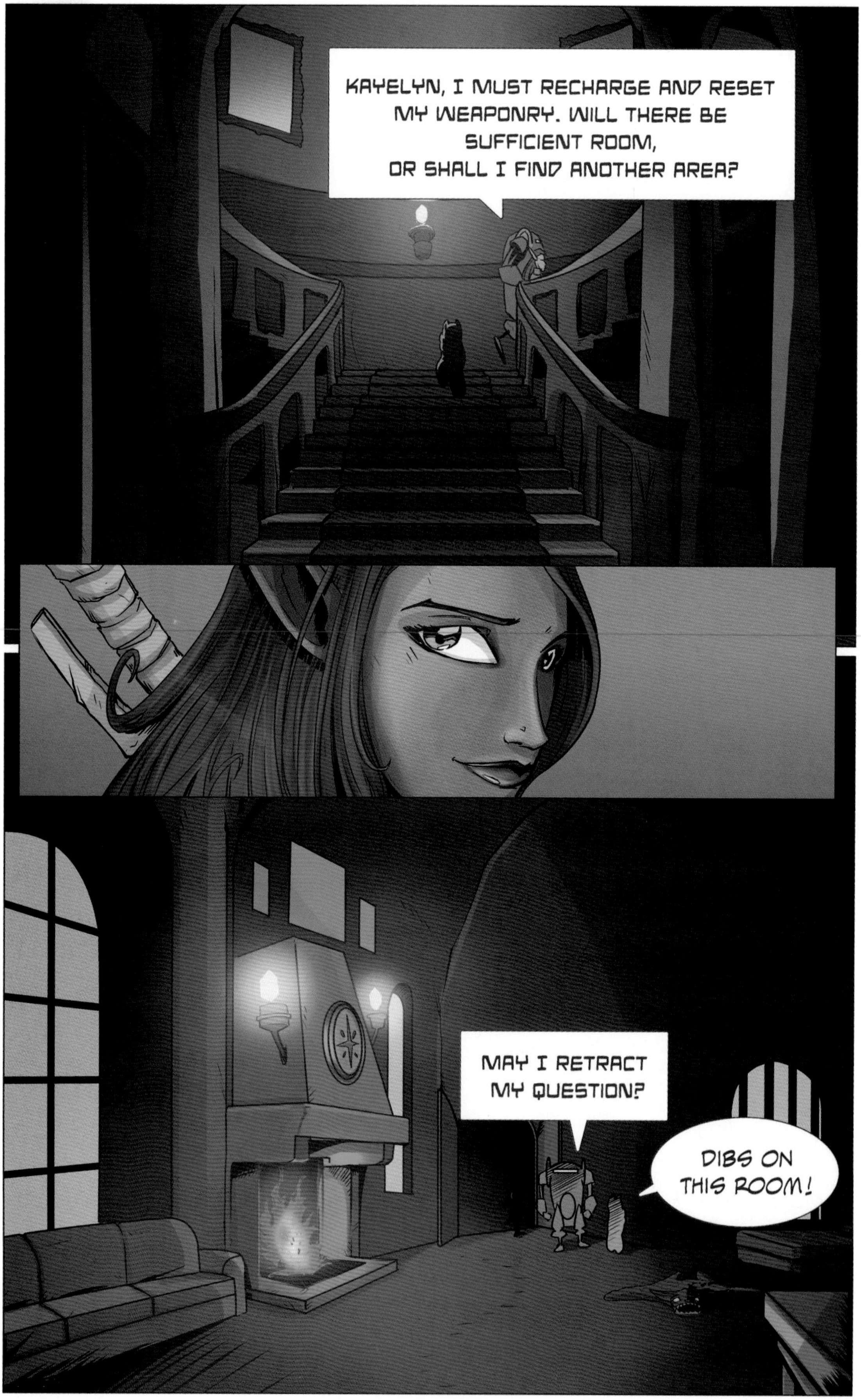
KAYELYN, I MUST RECHARGE AND RESET MY WEAPONRY. WILL THERE BE SUFFICIENT ROOM, OR SHALL I FIND ANOTHER AREA?
MAY I RETRACT MY QUESTION?
DIBS ON THIS ROOM!

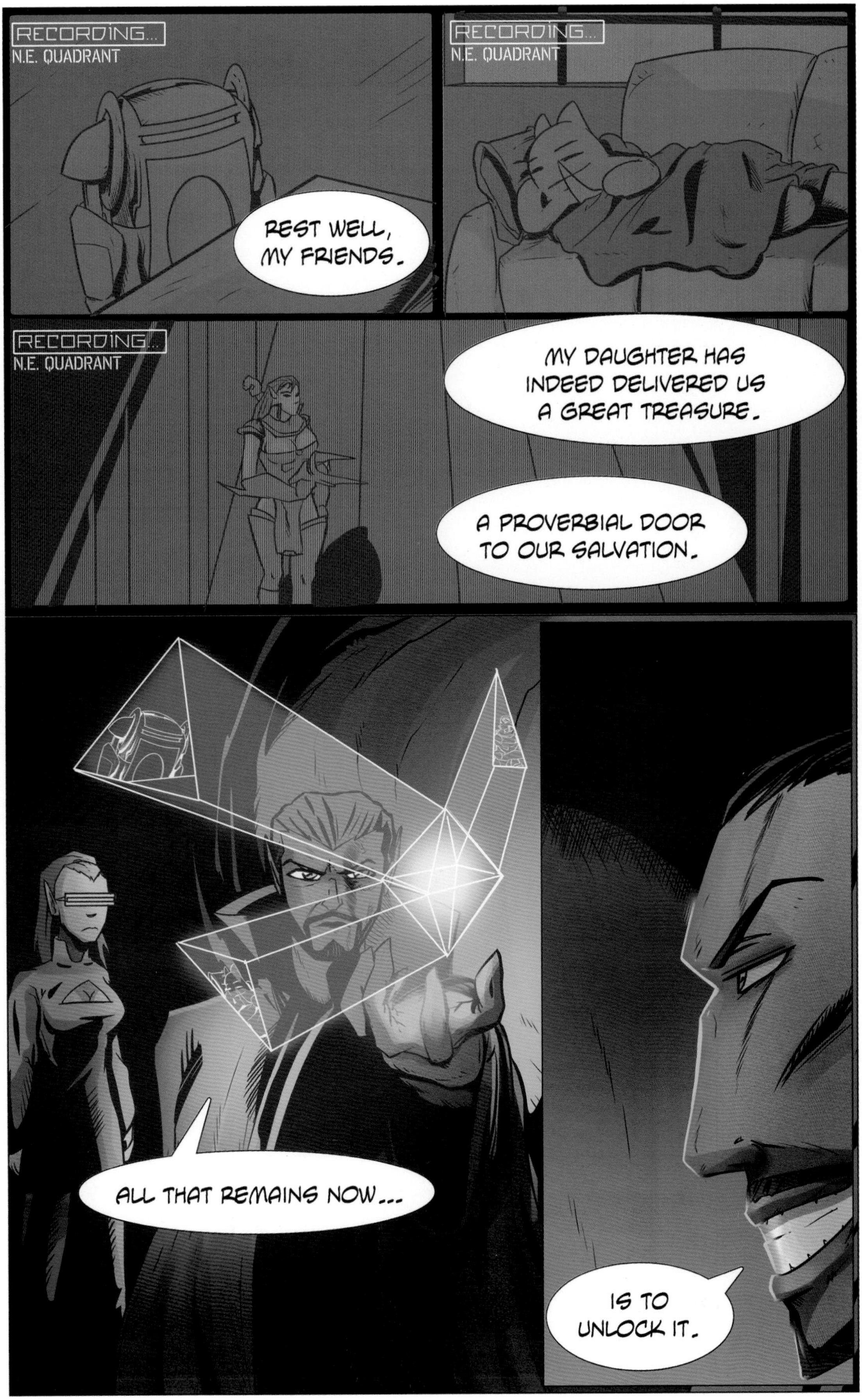
RECORDING...
N.E. QUADRANT
REST WELL, MY FRIENDS.
RECORDING...
N.E. QUADRANT
RECORDING...
N.E. QUADRANT
MY DAUGHTER HAS INDEED DELIVERED US A GREAT TREASURE.
A PROVERBIAL DOOR TO OUR SALVATION.
ALL THAT REMAINS NOW...
IS TO UNLOCK IT.

CHAPTER FOUR

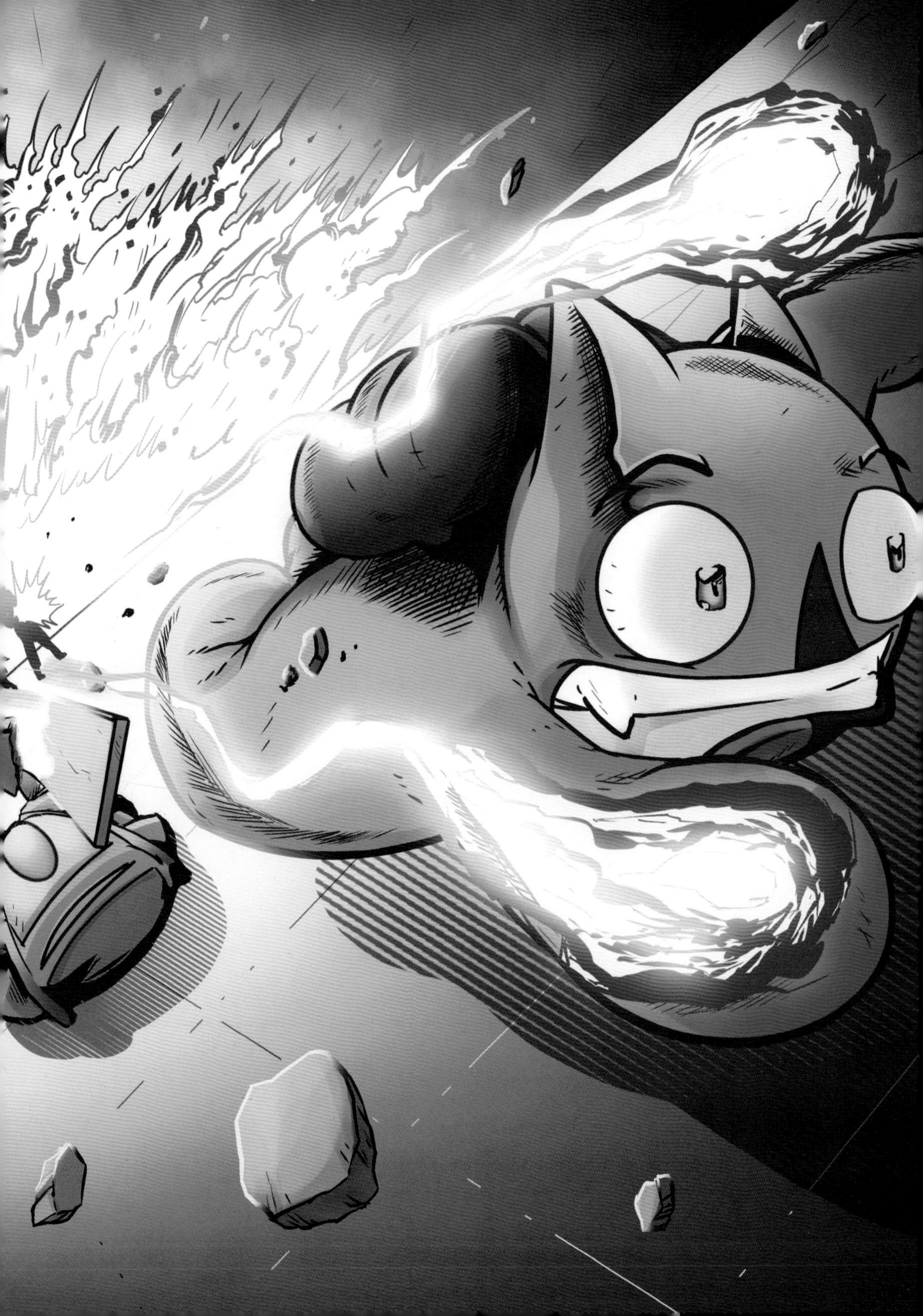

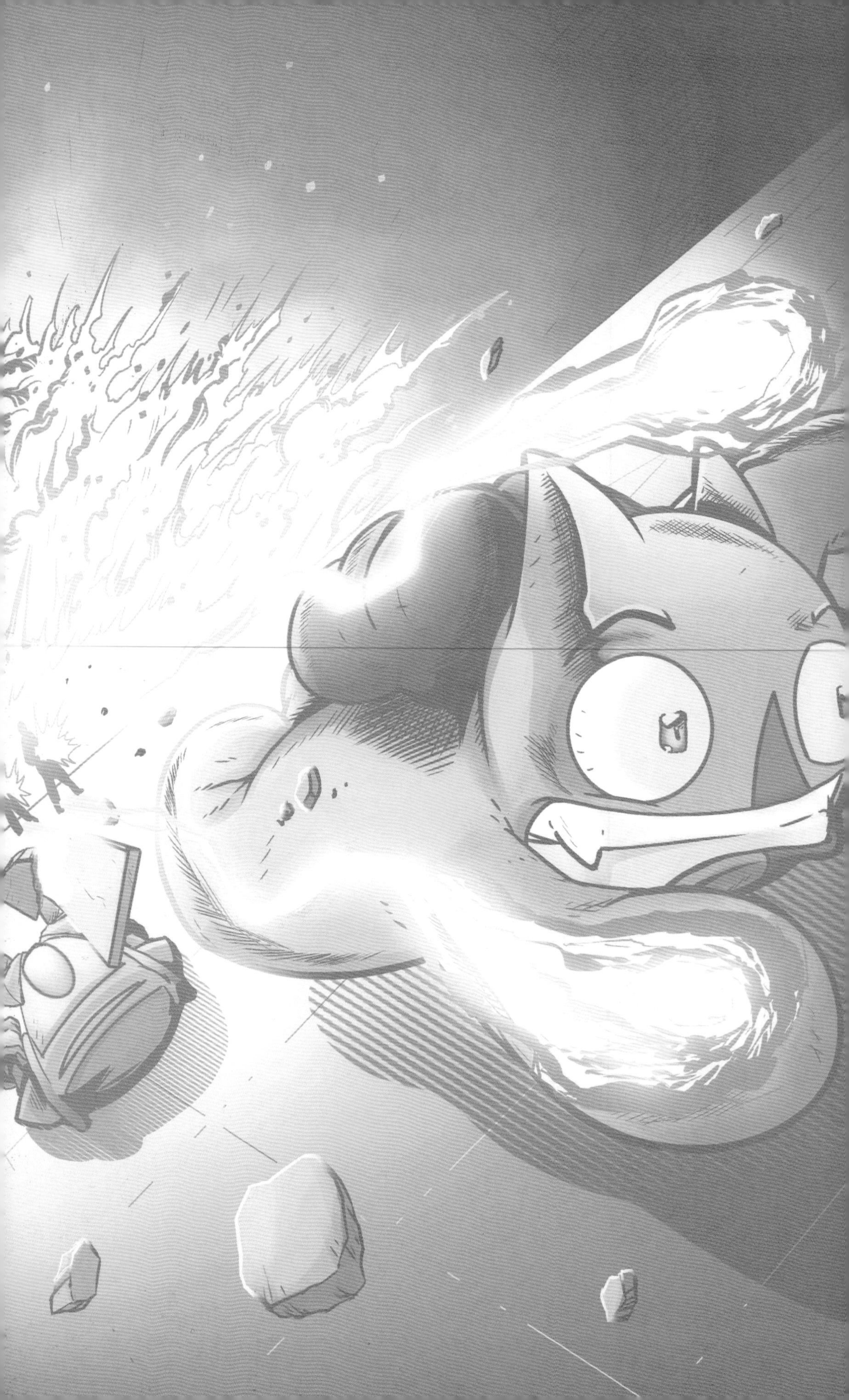

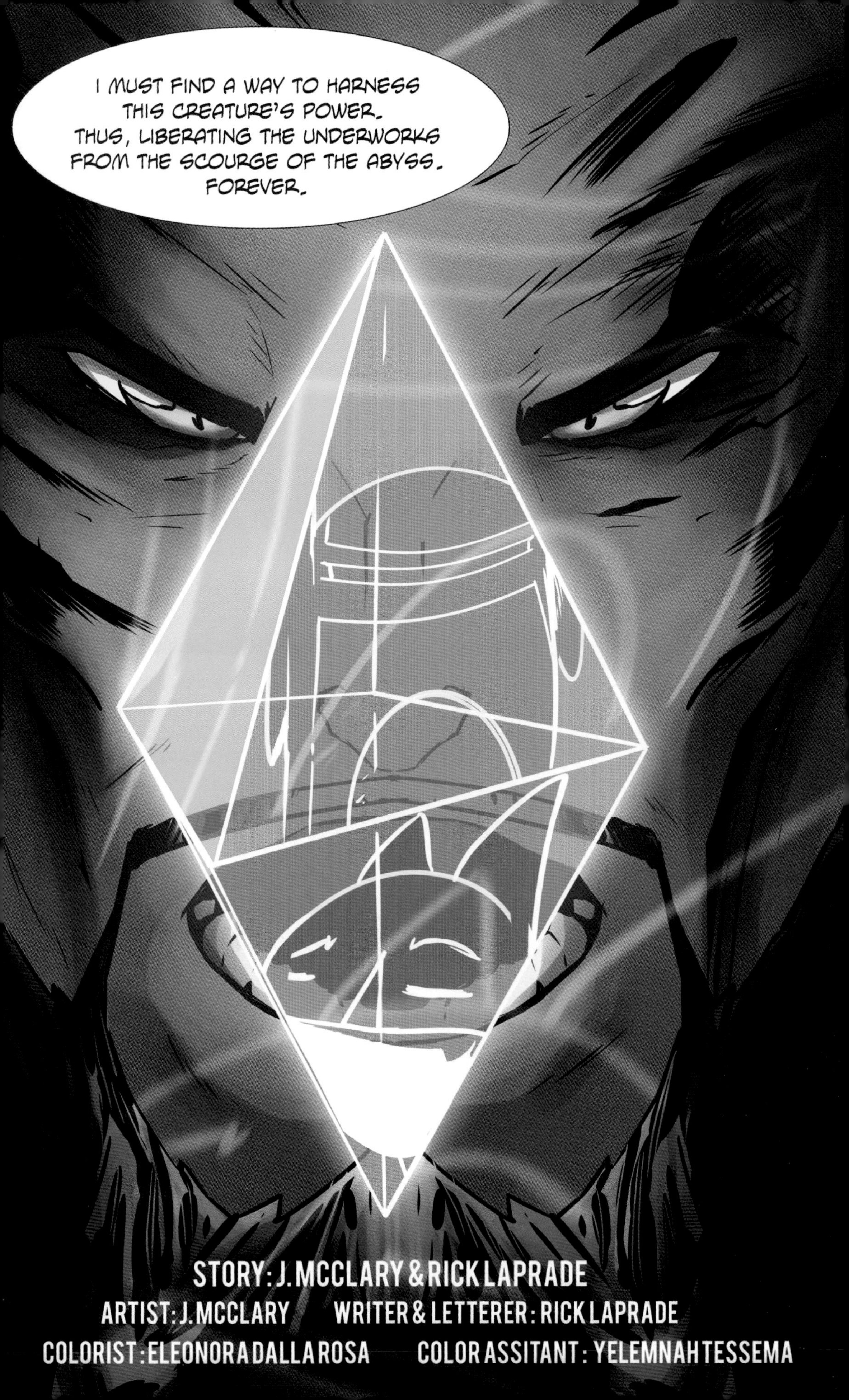
I MUST FIND A WAY TO HARNESS THIS CREATURE'S POWER. THUS, LIBERATING THE UNDERWORKS FROM THE SCOURGE OF THE ABYSS. FOREVER.

STORY: J. MCCLARY & RICK LAPRADE
ARTIST: J. MCCLARY   WRITER & LETTERER: RICK LAPRADE
COLORIST: ELEONORA DALLA ROSA   COLOR ASSITANT: YELEMNAH TESSEMA

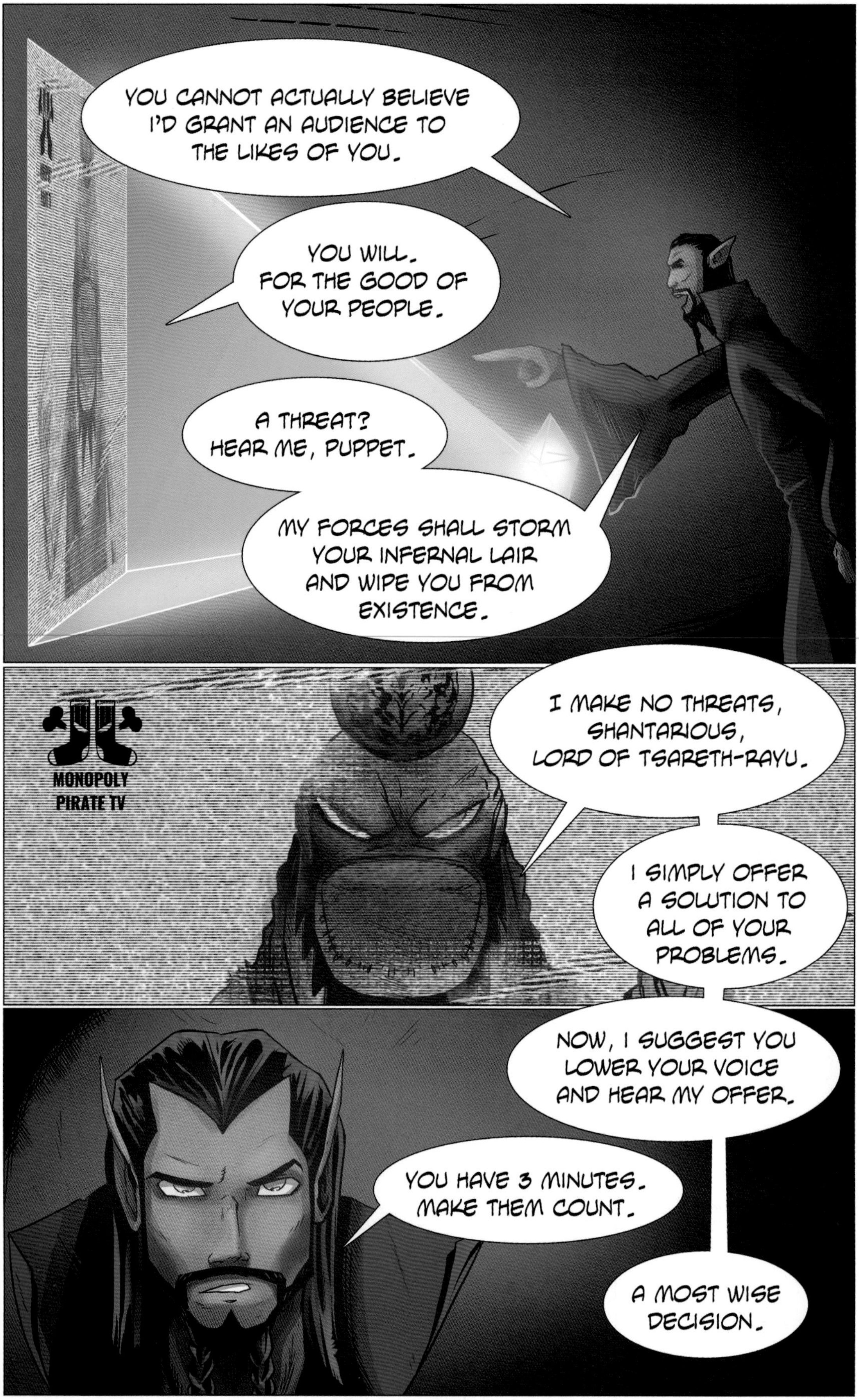
YOU CANNOT ACTUALLY BELIEVE I'D GRANT AN AUDIENCE TO THE LIKES OF YOU.
YOU WILL. FOR THE GOOD OF YOUR PEOPLE.
A THREAT? HEAR ME, PUPPET.
MY FORCES SHALL STORM YOUR INFERNAL LAIR AND WIPE YOU FROM EXISTENCE.
MONOPOLY PIRATE TV
I MAKE NO THREATS, SHANTARIOUS, LORD OF TSARETH-RAYU.
I SIMPLY OFFER A SOLUTION TO ALL OF YOUR PROBLEMS.
NOW, I SUGGEST YOU LOWER YOUR VOICE AND HEAR MY OFFER.
YOU HAVE 3 MINUTES. MAKE THEM COUNT.
A MOST WISE DECISION.

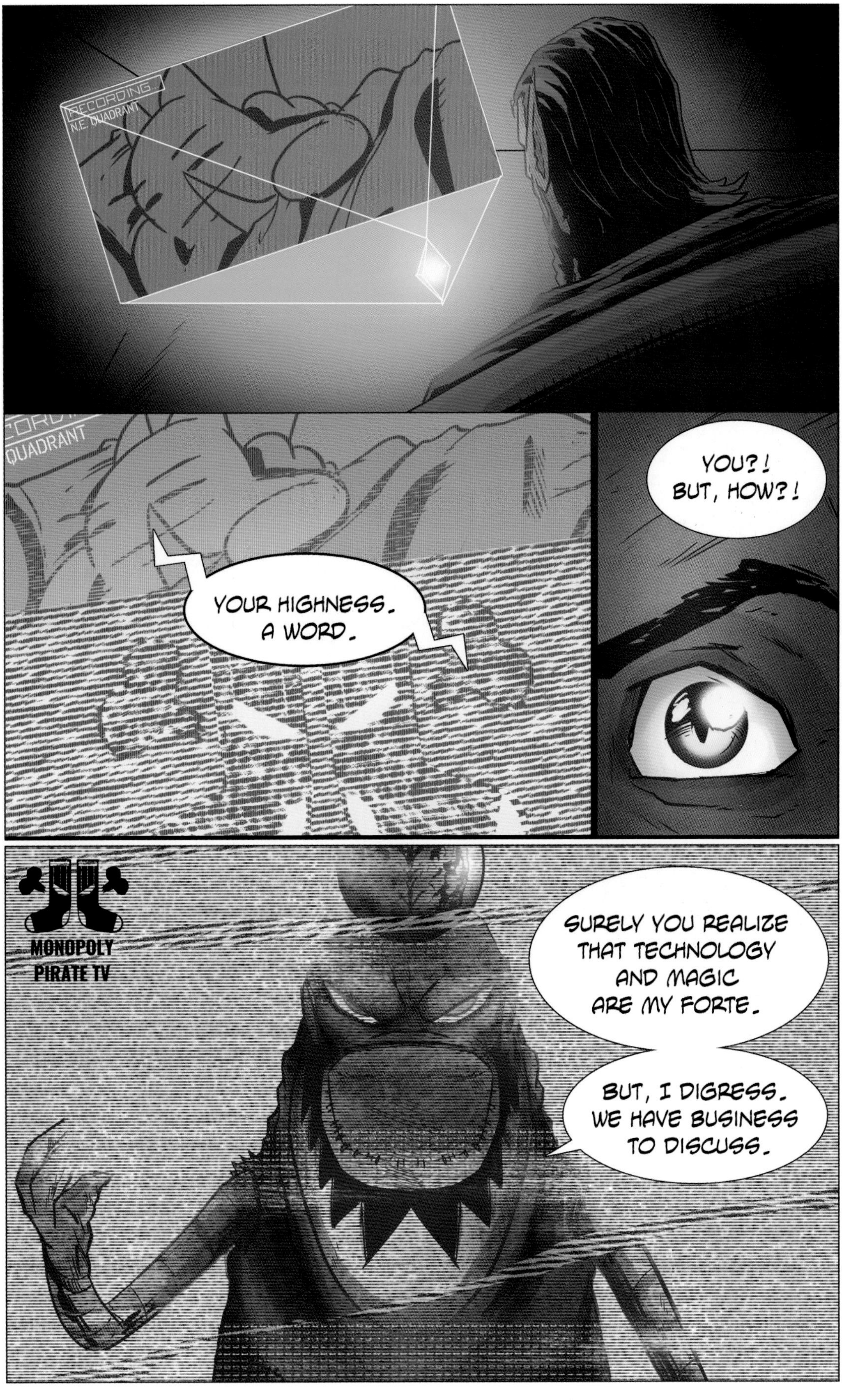
RECORDING..
N.E. QUADRANT
YOUR HIGHNESS. A WORD.
YOU?! BUT, HOW?!
SURELY YOU REALIZE THAT TECHNOLOGY AND MAGIC ARE MY FORTE.
BUT, I DIGRESS. WE HAVE BUSINESS TO DISCUSS.
MONOPOLY PIRATE TV

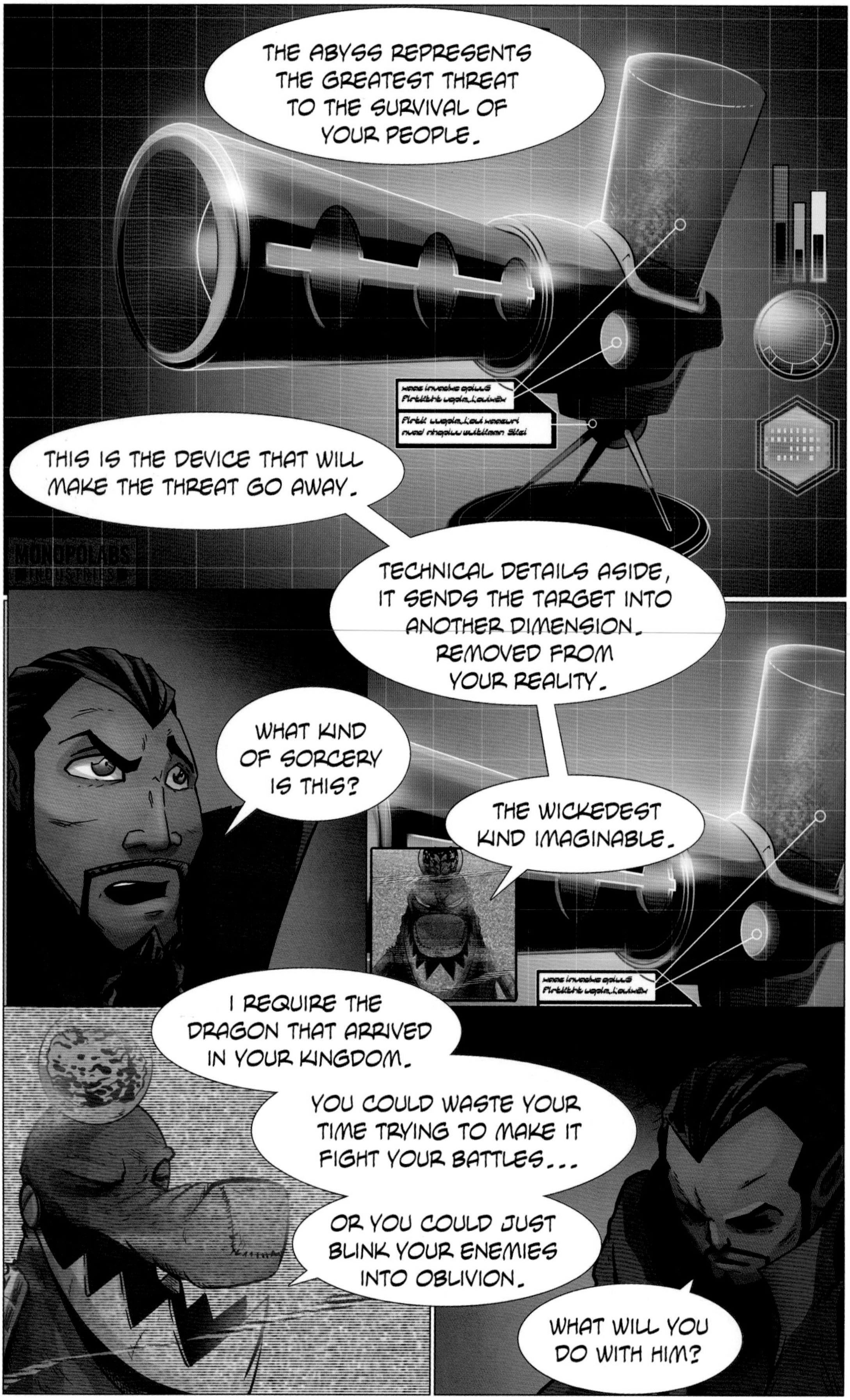
THE ABYSS REPRESENTS THE GREATEST THREAT TO THE SURVIVAL OF YOUR PEOPLE.
THIS IS THE DEVICE THAT WILL MAKE THE THREAT GO AWAY.
MONOPOLABS INDUSTRIES
TECHNICAL DETAILS ASIDE, IT SENDS THE TARGET INTO ANOTHER DIMENSION. REMOVED FROM YOUR REALITY.
WHAT KIND OF SORCERY IS THIS?
THE WICKEDEST KIND IMAGINABLE.
I REQUIRE THE DRAGON THAT ARRIVED IN YOUR KINGDOM.
YOU COULD WASTE YOUR TIME TRYING TO MAKE IT FIGHT YOUR BATTLES...
OR YOU COULD JUST BLINK YOUR ENEMIES INTO OBLIVION.
WHAT WILL YOU DO WITH HIM?

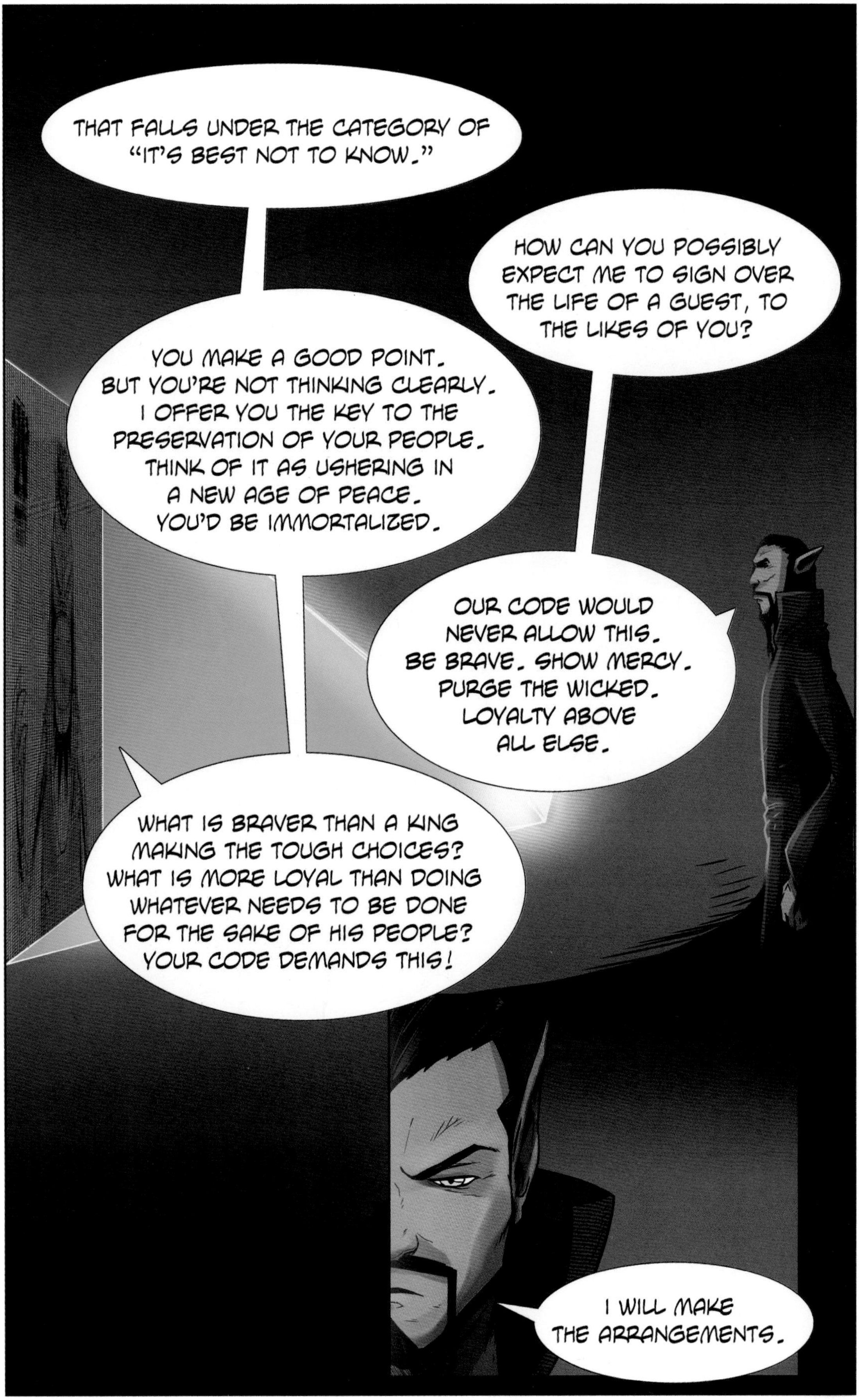
THAT FALLS UNDER THE CATEGORY OF "IT'S BEST NOT TO KNOW."
HOW CAN YOU POSSIBLY EXPECT ME TO SIGN OVER THE LIFE OF A GUEST, TO THE LIKES OF YOU?
YOU MAKE A GOOD POINT. BUT YOU'RE NOT THINKING CLEARLY. I OFFER YOU THE KEY TO THE PRESERVATION OF YOUR PEOPLE. THINK OF IT AS USHERING IN A NEW AGE OF PEACE. YOU'D BE IMMORTALIZED.
OUR CODE WOULD NEVER ALLOW THIS. BE BRAVE. SHOW MERCY. PURGE THE WICKED. LOYALTY ABOVE ALL ELSE.
WHAT IS BRAVER THAN A KING MAKING THE TOUGH CHOICES? WHAT IS MORE LOYAL THAN DOING WHATEVER NEEDS TO BE DONE FOR THE SAKE OF HIS PEOPLE? YOUR CODE DEMANDS THIS!
I WILL MAKE THE ARRANGEMENTS.

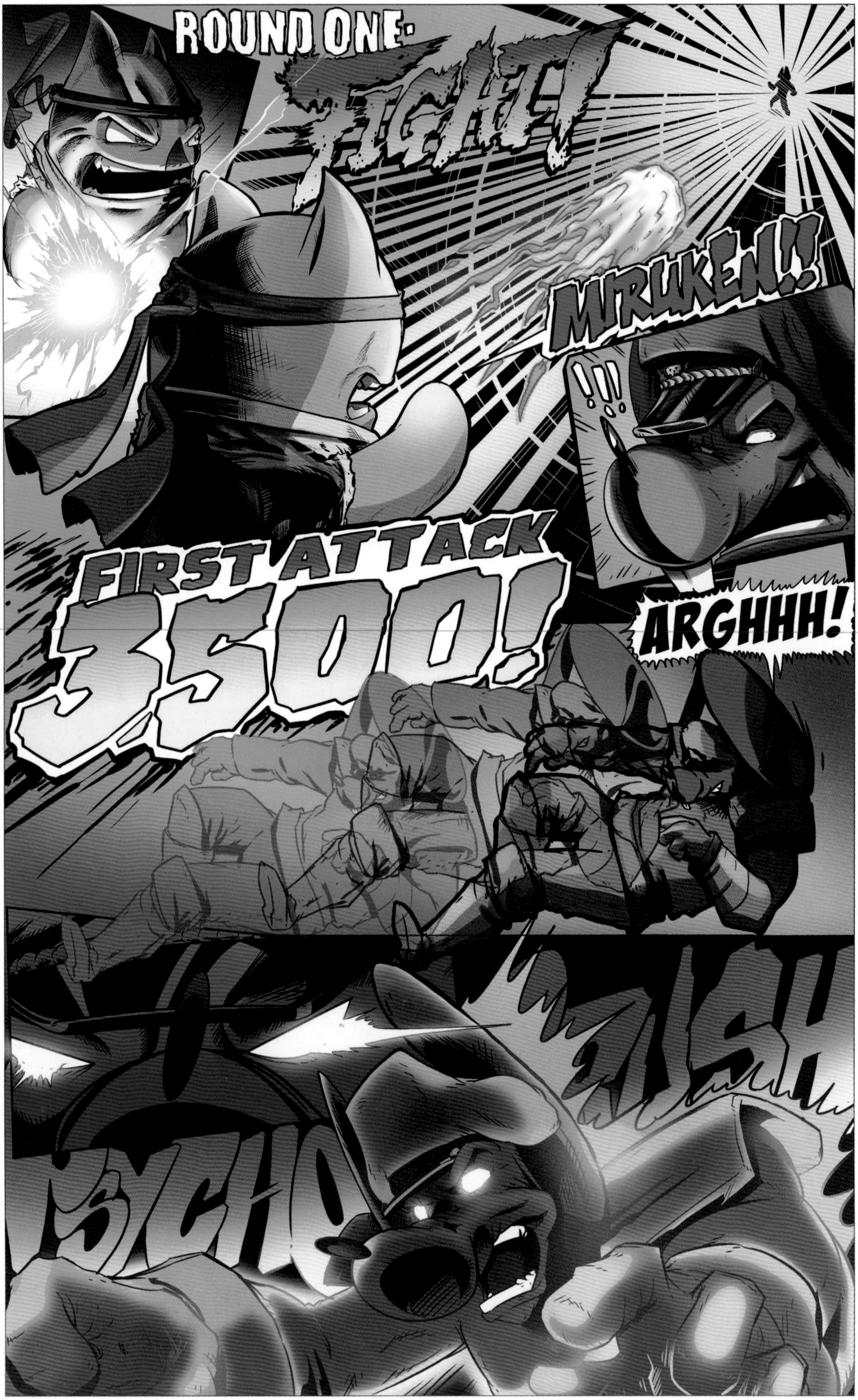
ROUND ONE:
FIGHT!
MIRUKEN!!
!!!
FIRST ATTACK
3500!
ARGHHH!

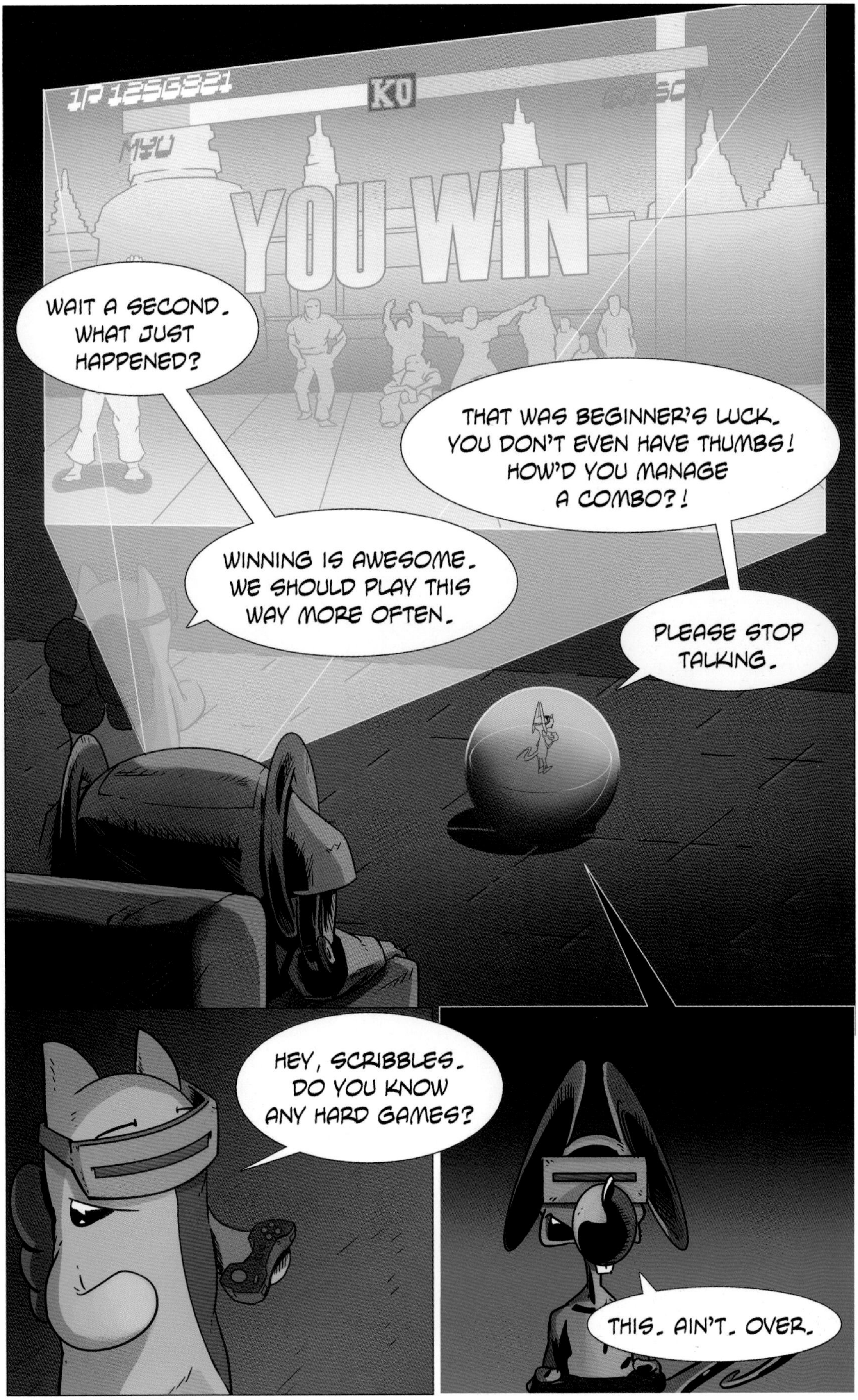
1P 1256821
KO
YOU WIN
WAIT A SECOND. WHAT JUST HAPPENED?
THAT WAS BEGINNER'S LUCK. YOU DON'T EVEN HAVE THUMBS! HOW'D YOU MANAGE A COMBO?!
WINNING IS AWESOME. WE SHOULD PLAY THIS WAY MORE OFTEN.
PLEASE STOP TALKING.
HEY, SCRIBBLES. DO YOU KNOW ANY HARD GAMES?
THIS. AIN'T. OVER.

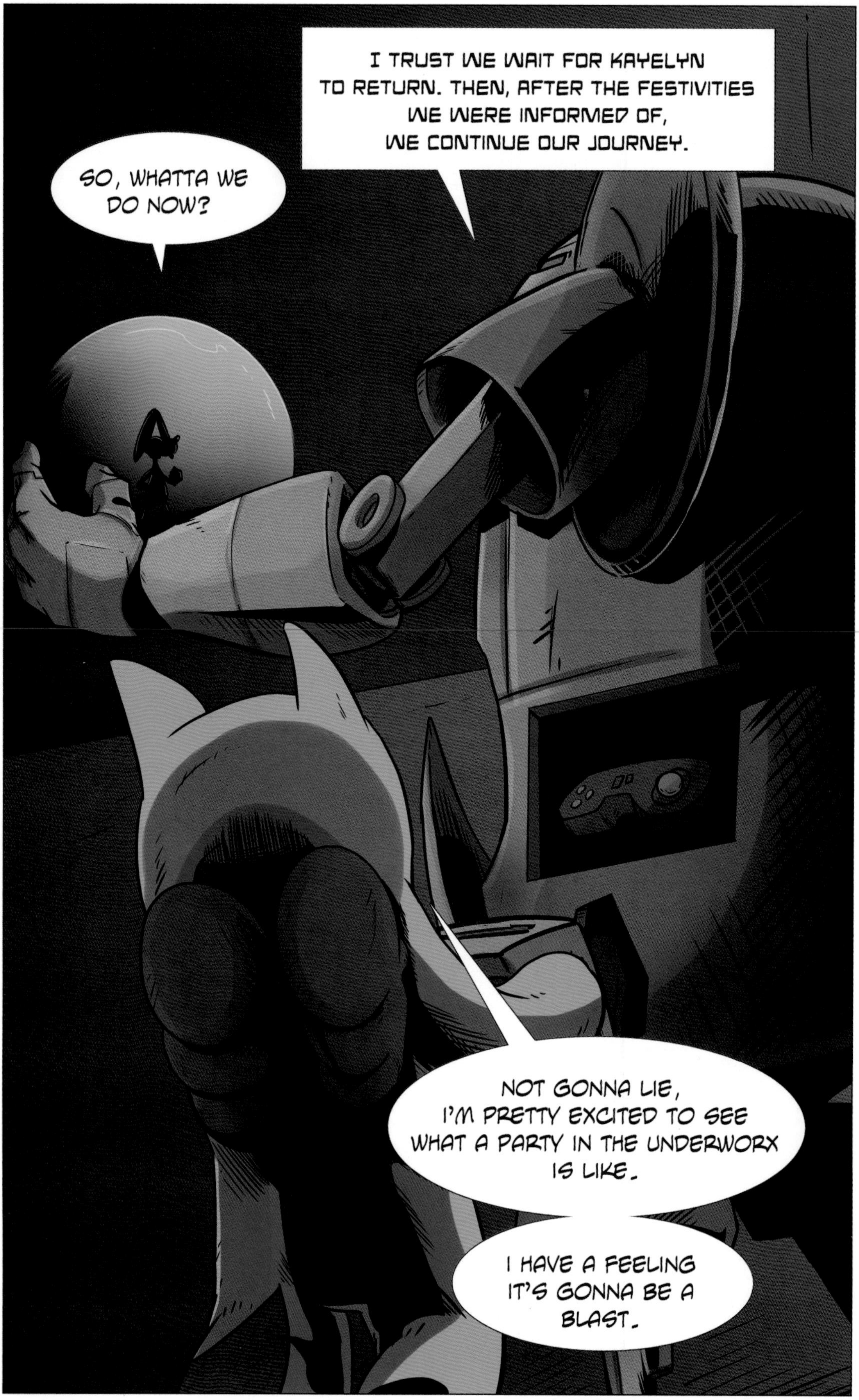
SO, WHATTA WE DO NOW?
I TRUST WE WAIT FOR KAYELYN TO RETURN. THEN, AFTER THE FESTIVITIES WE WERE INFORMED OF, WE CONTINUE OUR JOURNEY.
NOT GONNA LIE, I'M PRETTY EXCITED TO SEE WHAT A PARTY IN THE UNDERWORX IS LIKE.
I HAVE A FEELING IT'S GONNA BE A BLAST.

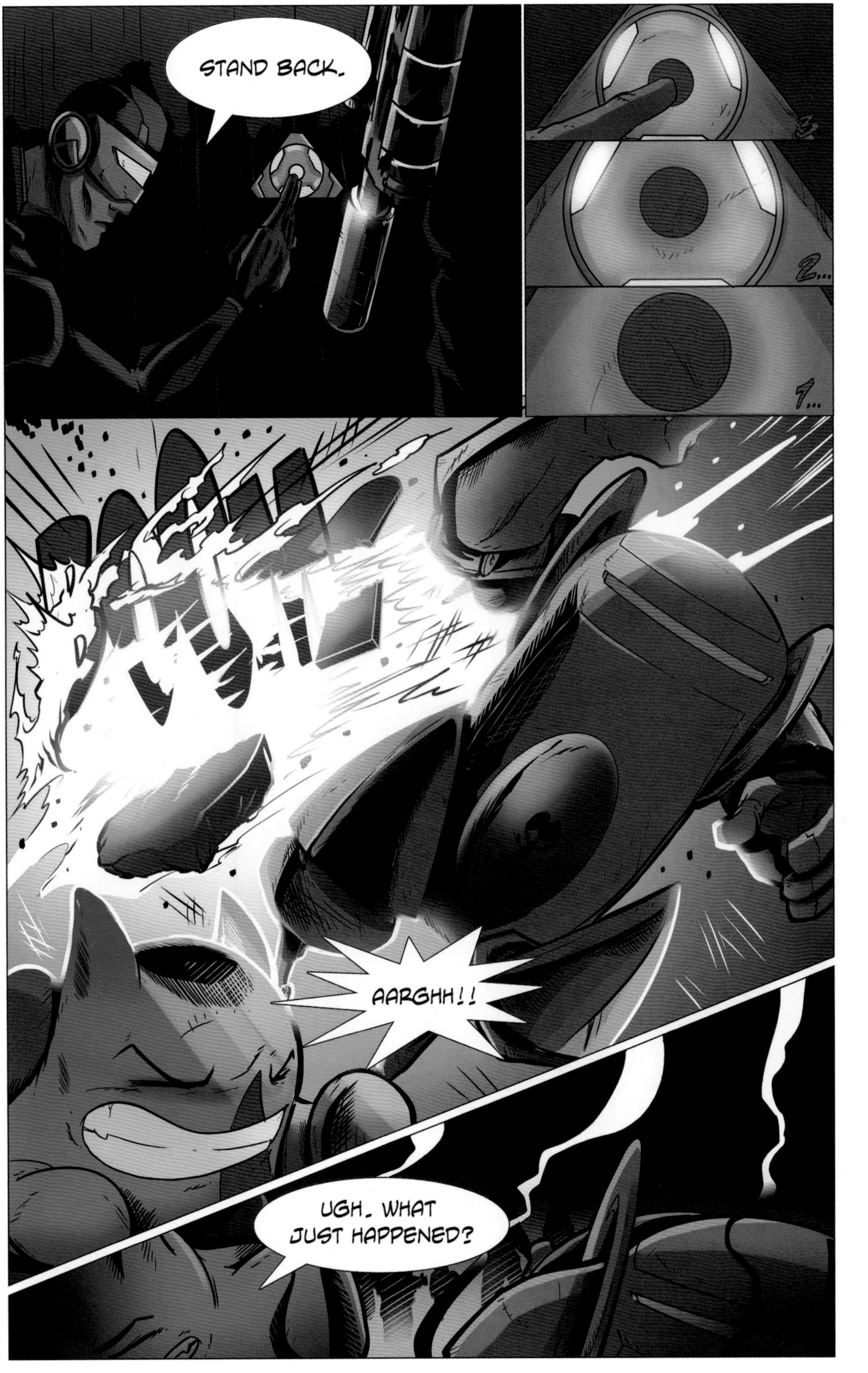
STAND BACK.
3...
2...
1...
AARGHH!!
UGH. WHAT JUST HAPPENED?

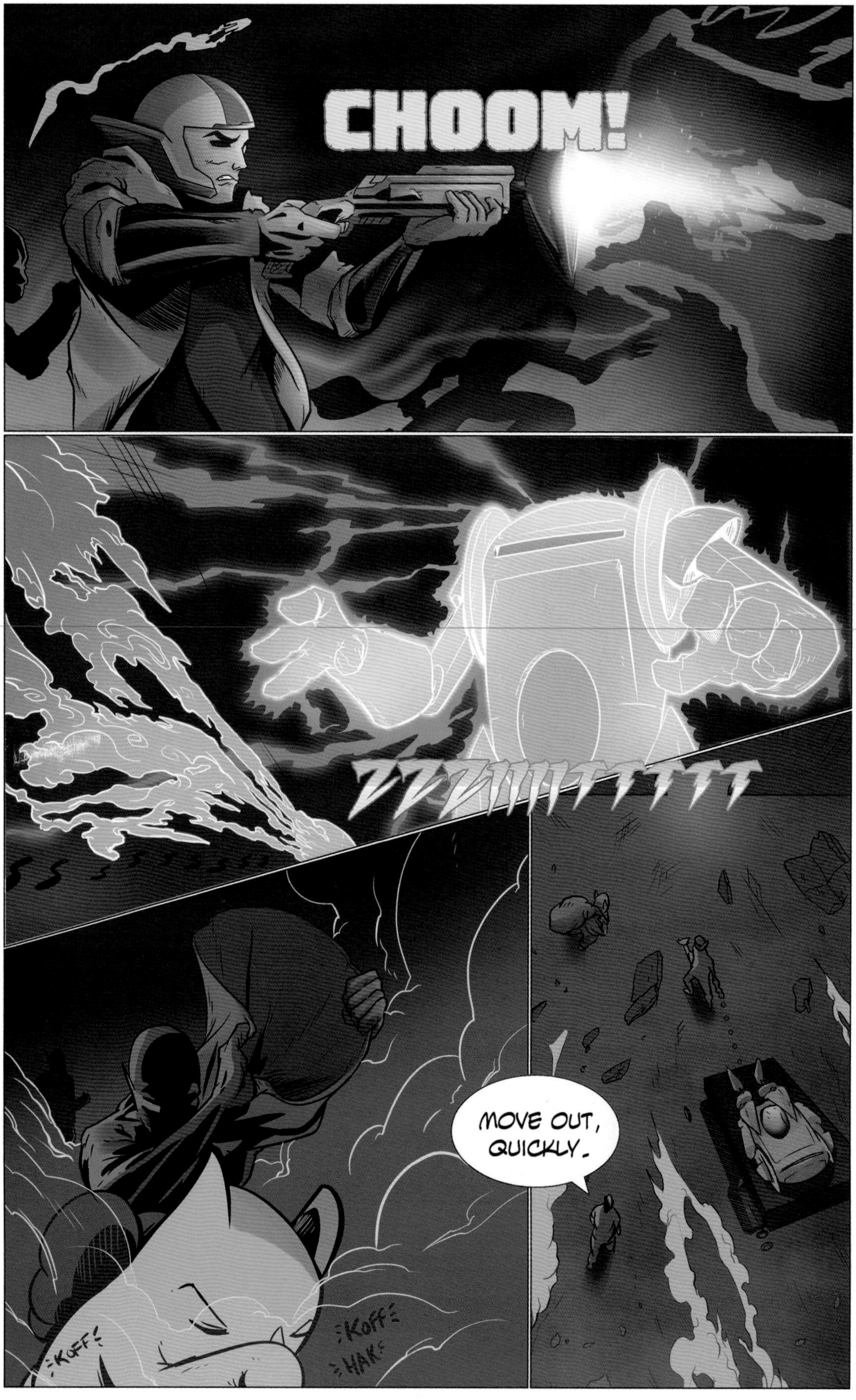
CHOOM!
ZZZIIIIITTTTT
SSSSSSSSSSS
MOVE OUT, QUICKLY.
KOFF
KOFF
HAK

WHAT IN THE #%&!?

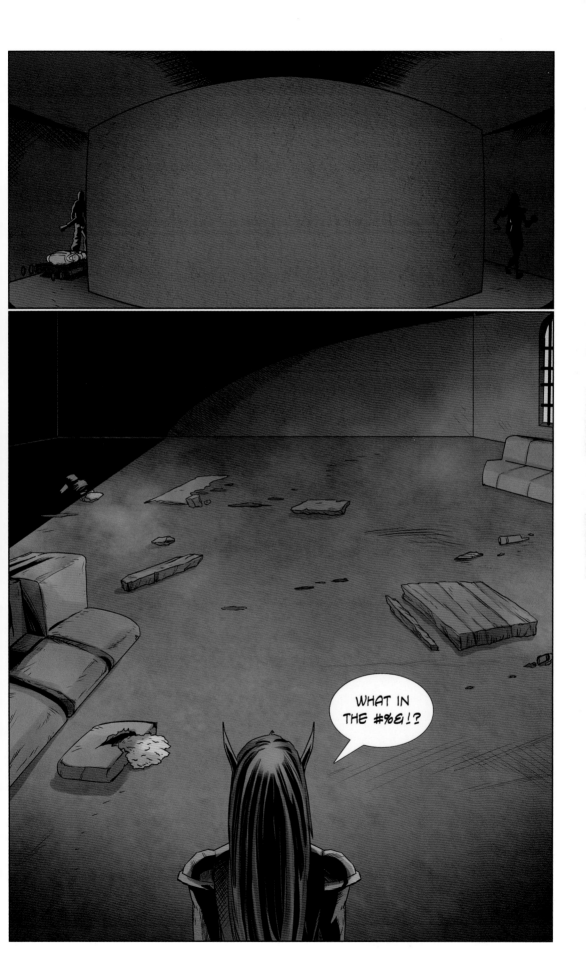

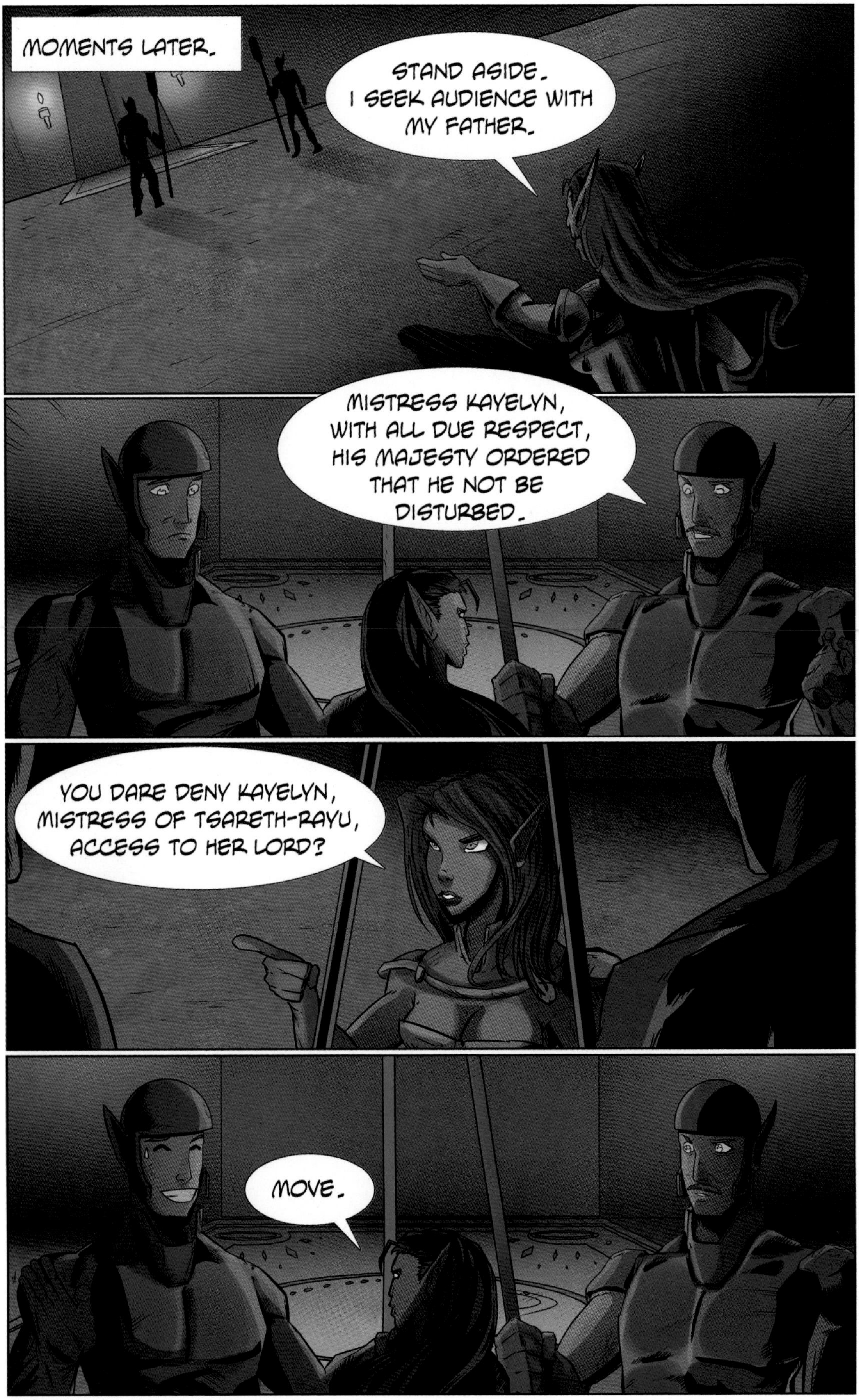
MOMENTS LATER.
STAND ASIDE. I SEEK AUDIENCE WITH MY FATHER.
MISTRESS KAYELYN, WITH ALL DUE RESPECT, HIS MAJESTY ORDERED THAT HE NOT BE DISTURBED.
YOU DARE DENY KAYELYN, MISTRESS OF TSARETH-RAYU, ACCESS TO HER LORD?
MOVE.

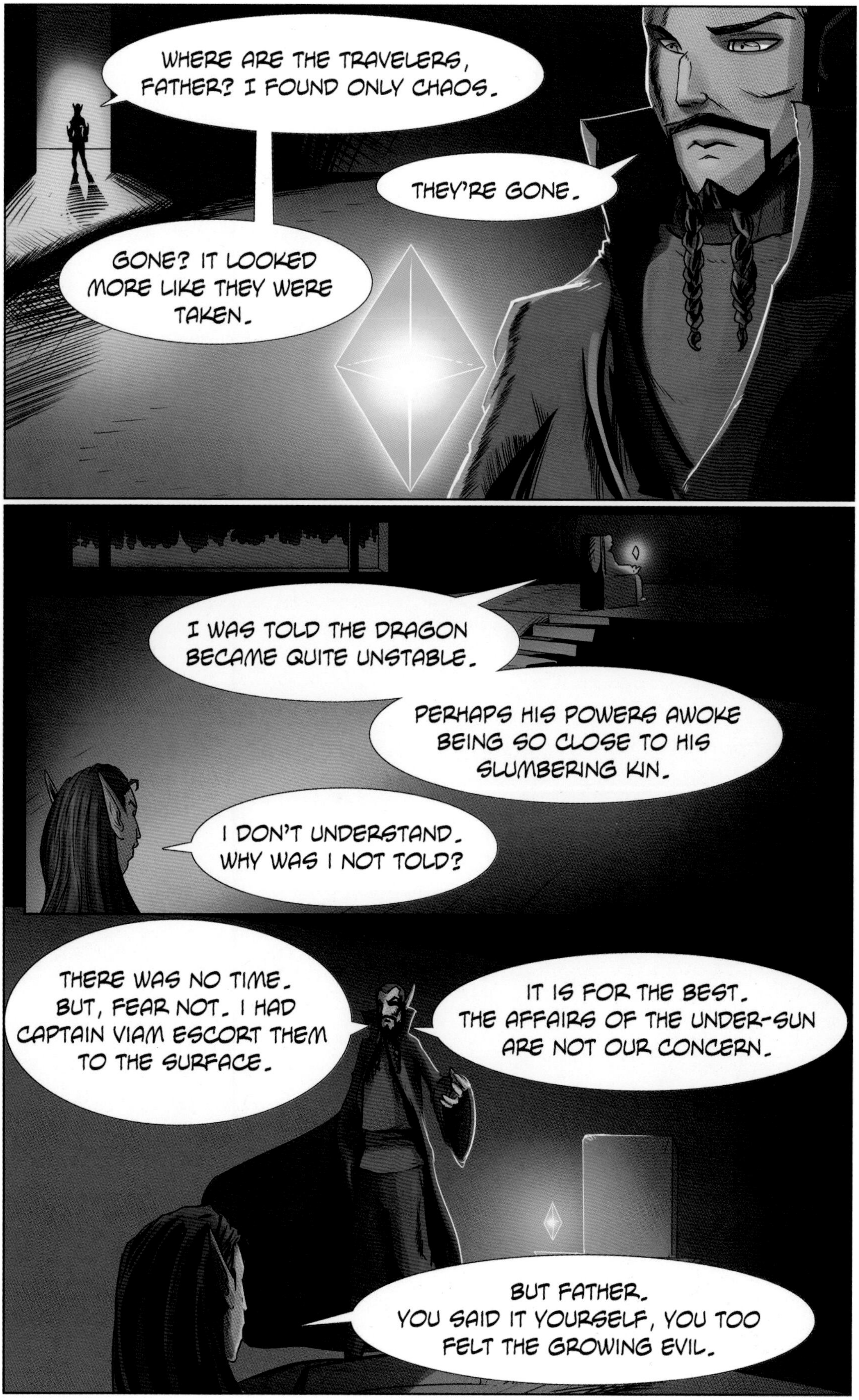
WHERE ARE THE TRAVELERS, FATHER? I FOUND ONLY CHAOS.
THEY'RE GONE.
GONE? IT LOOKED MORE LIKE THEY WERE TAKEN.
I WAS TOLD THE DRAGON BECAME QUITE UNSTABLE.
PERHAPS HIS POWERS AWOKE BEING SO CLOSE TO HIS SLUMBERING KIN.
I DON'T UNDERSTAND. WHY WAS I NOT TOLD?
THERE WAS NO TIME. BUT, FEAR NOT. I HAD CAPTAIN VIAM ESCORT THEM TO THE SURFACE.
IT IS FOR THE BEST. THE AFFAIRS OF THE UNDER-SUN ARE NOT OUR CONCERN.
BUT FATHER. YOU SAID IT YOURSELF, YOU TOO FELT THE GROWING EVIL.

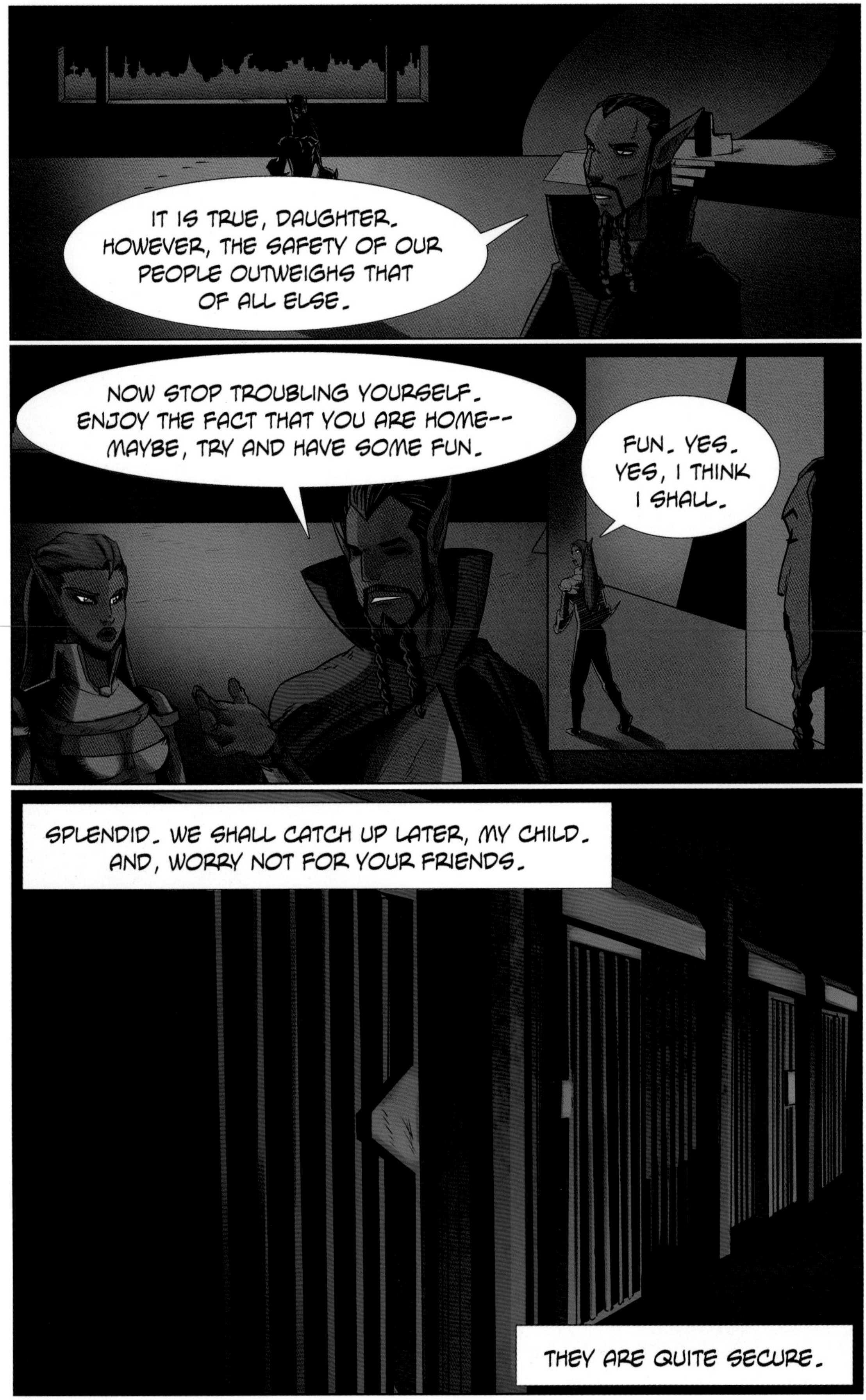
IT IS TRUE, DAUGHTER. HOWEVER, THE SAFETY OF OUR PEOPLE OUTWEIGHS THAT OF ALL ELSE.
NOW STOP TROUBLING YOURSELF. ENJOY THE FACT THAT YOU ARE HOME-- MAYBE, TRY AND HAVE SOME FUN.
FUN. YES. YES, I THINK I SHALL.
SPLENDID. WE SHALL CATCH UP LATER, MY CHILD. AND, WORRY NOT FOR YOUR FRIENDS.
THEY ARE QUITE SECURE.

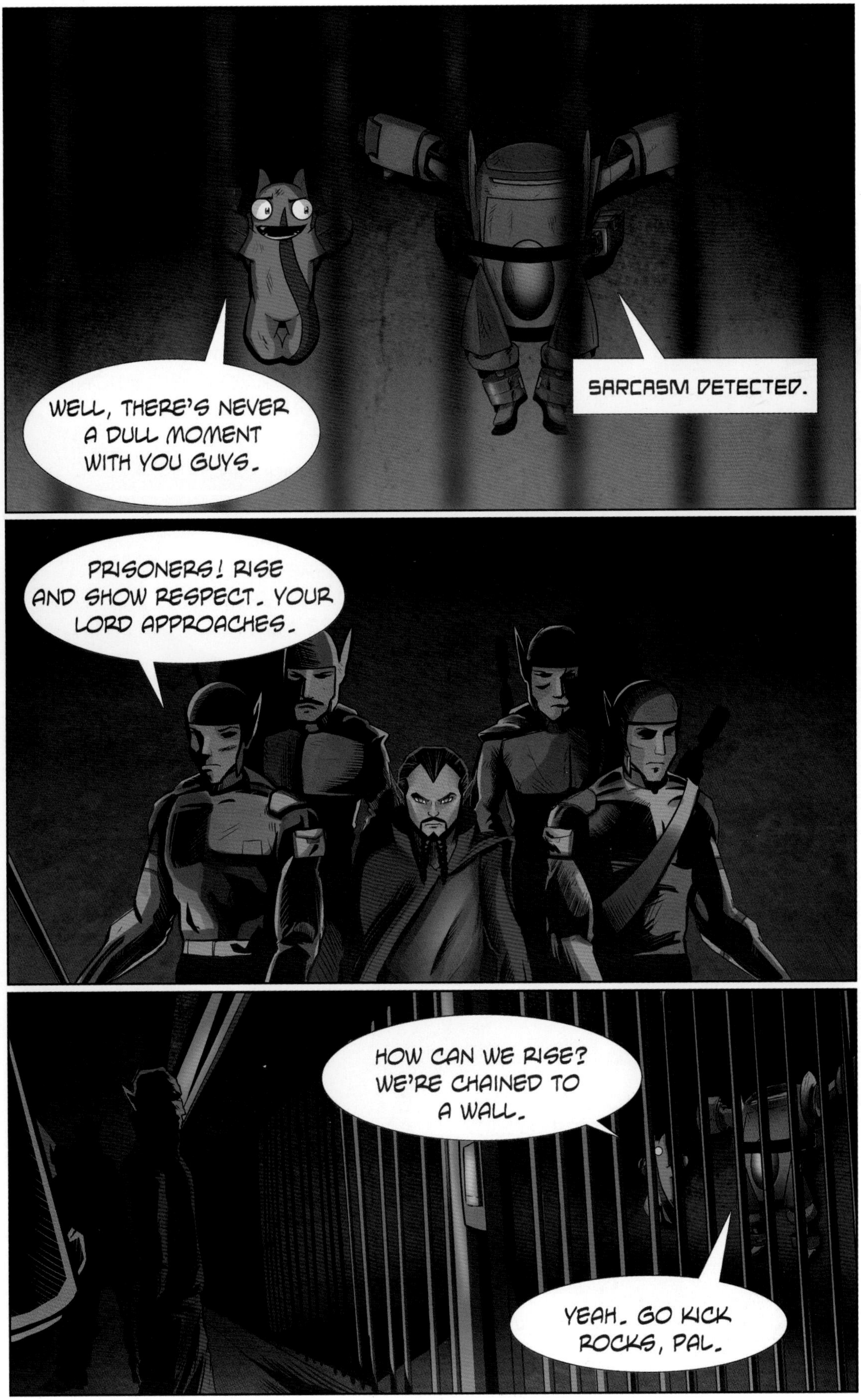
WELL, THERE'S NEVER A DULL MOMENT WITH YOU GUYS.
SARCASM DETECTED.
PRISONERS! RISE AND SHOW RESPECT. YOUR LORD APPROACHES.
HOW CAN WE RISE? WE'RE CHAINED TO A WALL.
YEAH. GO KICK ROCKS, PAL.

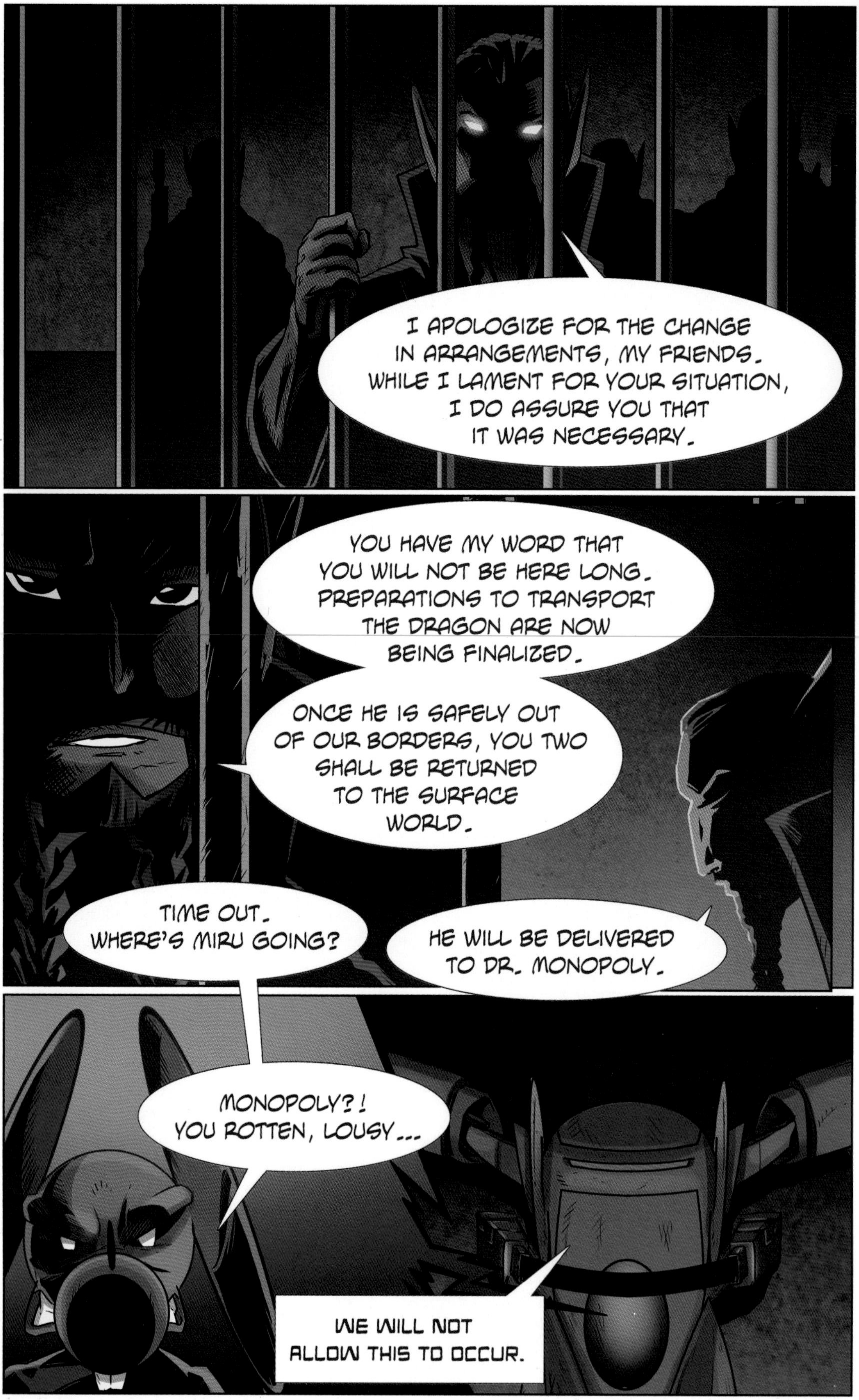
I APOLOGIZE FOR THE CHANGE IN ARRANGEMENTS, MY FRIENDS. WHILE I LAMENT FOR YOUR SITUATION, I DO ASSURE YOU THAT IT WAS NECESSARY.
YOU HAVE MY WORD THAT YOU WILL NOT BE HERE LONG. PREPARATIONS TO TRANSPORT THE DRAGON ARE NOW BEING FINALIZED.
ONCE HE IS SAFELY OUT OF OUR BORDERS, YOU TWO SHALL BE RETURNED TO THE SURFACE WORLD.
TIME OUT. WHERE'S MIRU GOING?
HE WILL BE DELIVERED TO DR. MONOPOLY.
MONOPOLY?! YOU ROTTEN, LOUSY...
WE WILL NOT ALLOW THIS TO OCCUR.

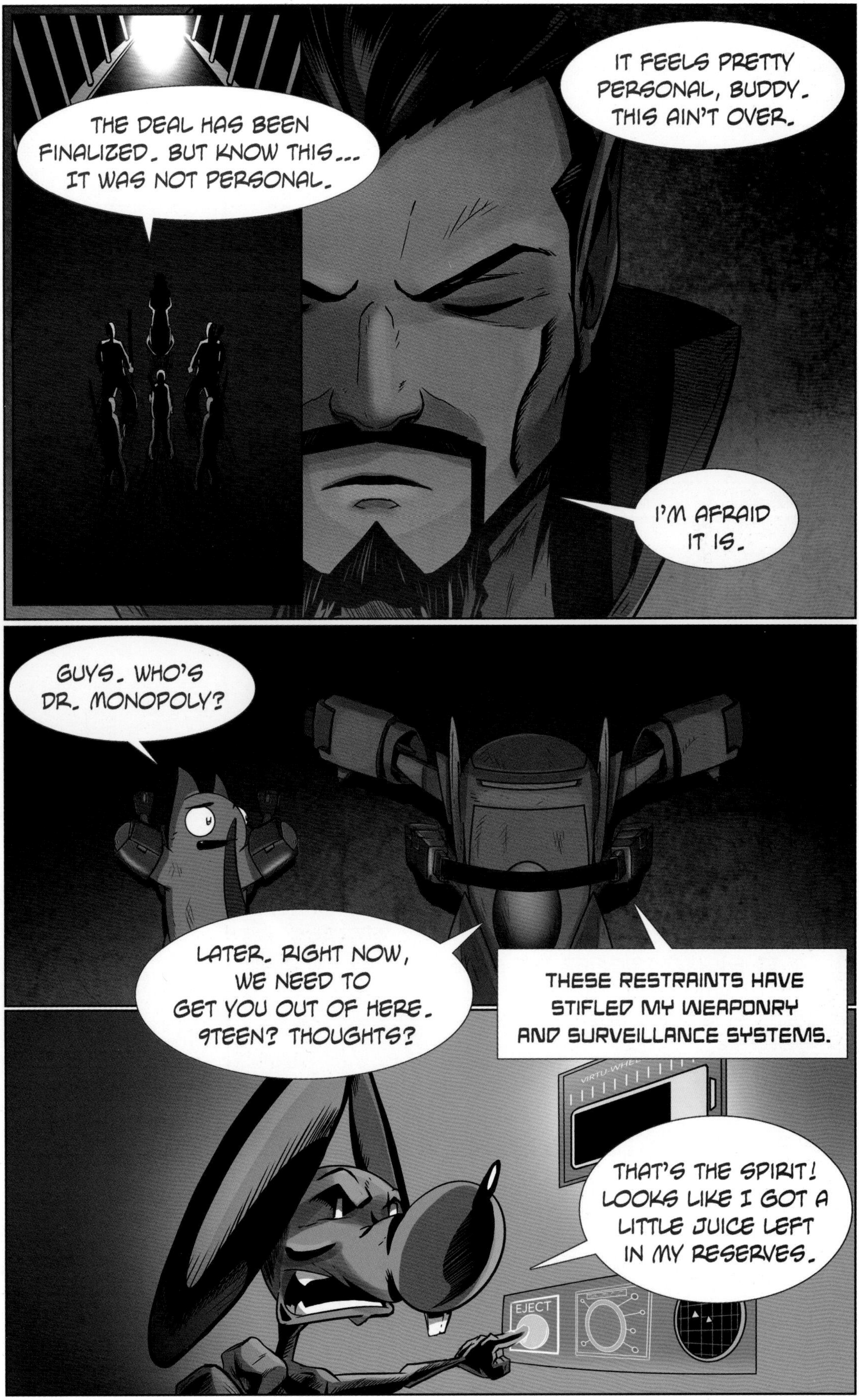
THE DEAL HAS BEEN FINALIZED. BUT KNOW THIS... IT WAS NOT PERSONAL.
IT FEELS PRETTY PERSONAL, BUDDY. THIS AIN'T OVER.
I'M AFRAID IT IS.
GUYS. WHO'S DR. MONOPOLY?
LATER. RIGHT NOW, WE NEED TO GET YOU OUT OF HERE. 9TEEN? THOUGHTS?
THESE RESTRAINTS HAVE STIFLED MY WEAPONRY AND SURVEILLANCE SYSTEMS.
THAT'S THE SPIRIT! LOOKS LIKE I GOT A LITTLE JUICE LEFT IN MY RESERVES.
EJECT

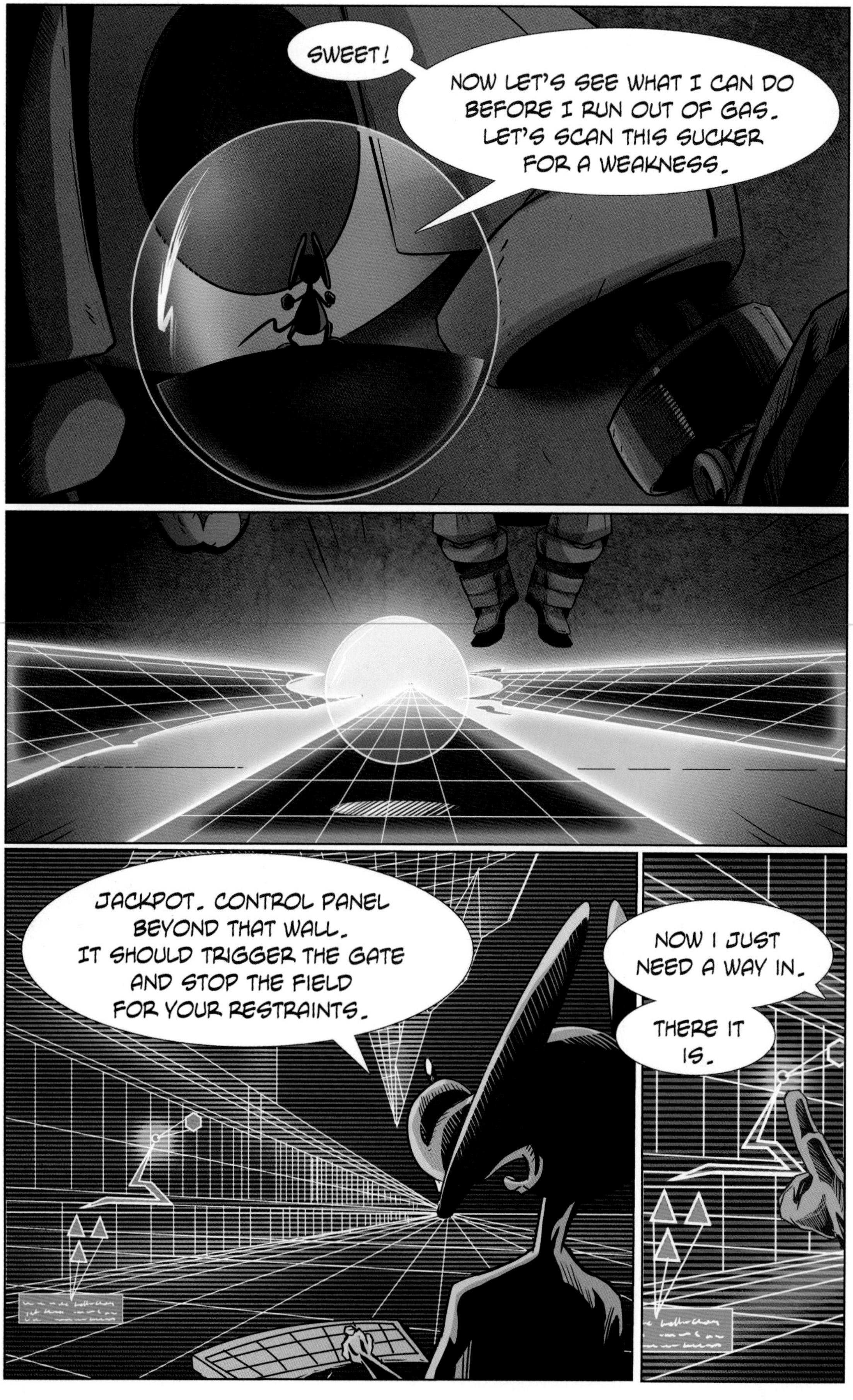
SWEET!
NOW LET'S SEE WHAT I CAN DO BEFORE I RUN OUT OF GAS. LET'S SCAN THIS SUCKER FOR A WEAKNESS.
JACKPOT. CONTROL PANEL BEYOND THAT WALL. IT SHOULD TRIGGER THE GATE AND STOP THE FIELD FOR YOUR RESTRAINTS.
NOW I JUST NEED A WAY IN.
THERE IT IS.

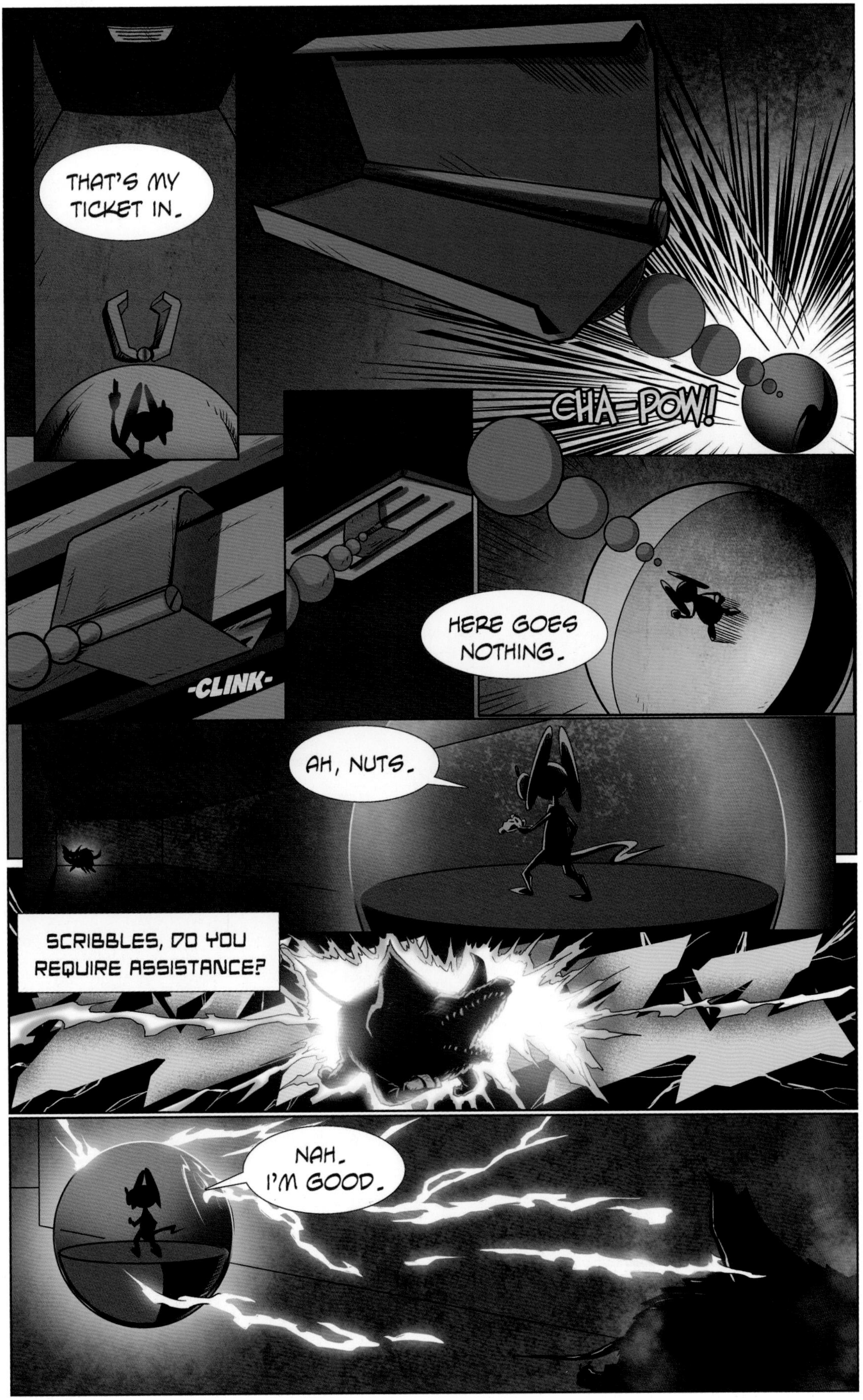
THAT'S MY TICKET IN.
CHA-POW!
-CLINK-
HERE GOES NOTHING.
AH, NUTS.
SCRIBBLES, DO YOU REQUIRE ASSISTANCE?
NAH. I'M GOOD.

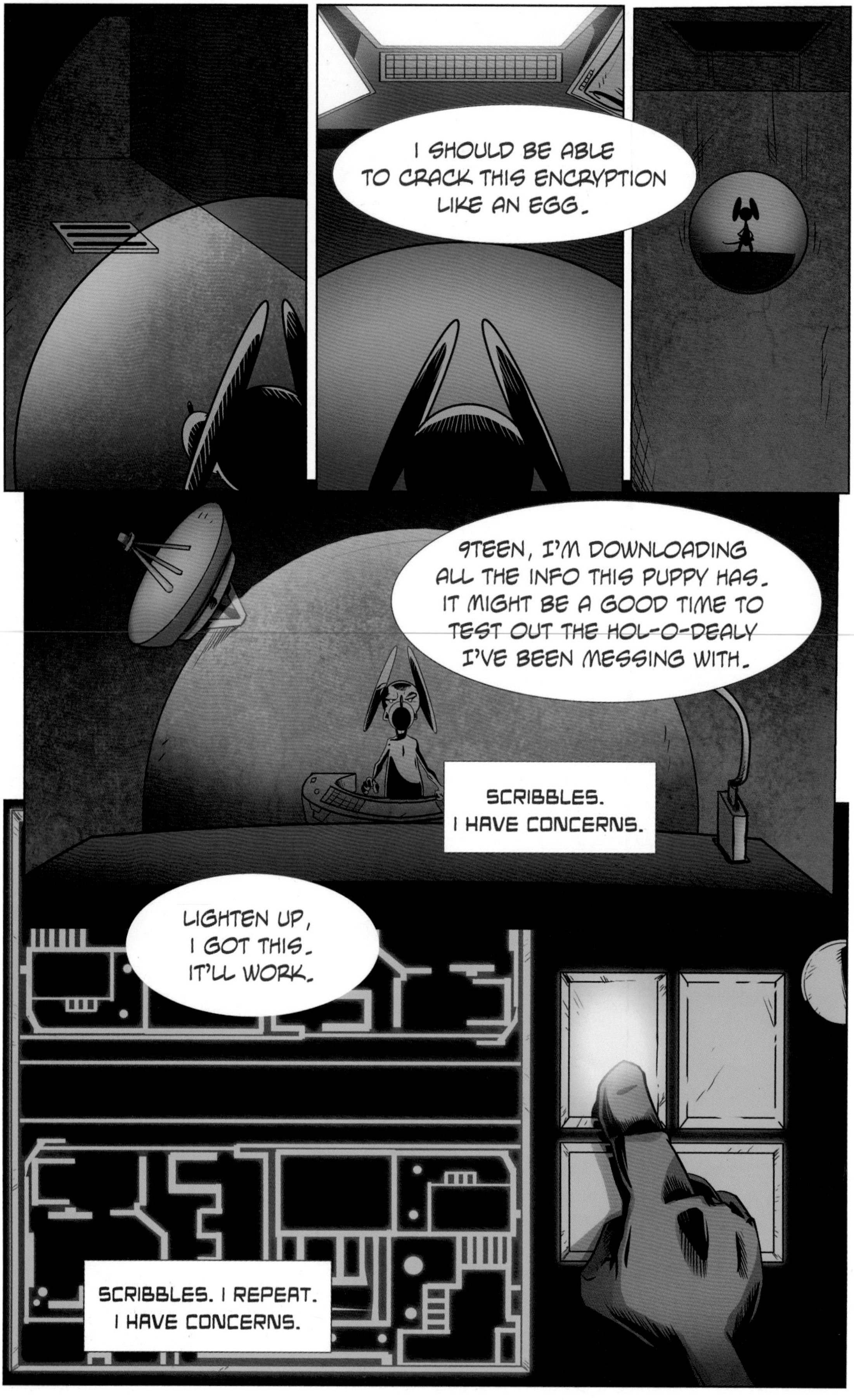
I SHOULD BE ABLE TO CRACK THIS ENCRYPTION LIKE AN EGG.
9TEEN, I'M DOWNLOADING ALL THE INFO THIS PUPPY HAS. IT MIGHT BE A GOOD TIME TO TEST OUT THE HOL-O-DEALY I'VE BEEN MESSING WITH.
SCRIBBLES. I HAVE CONCERNS.
LIGHTEN UP, I GOT THIS. IT'LL WORK.
SCRIBBLES. I REPEAT. I HAVE CONCERNS.

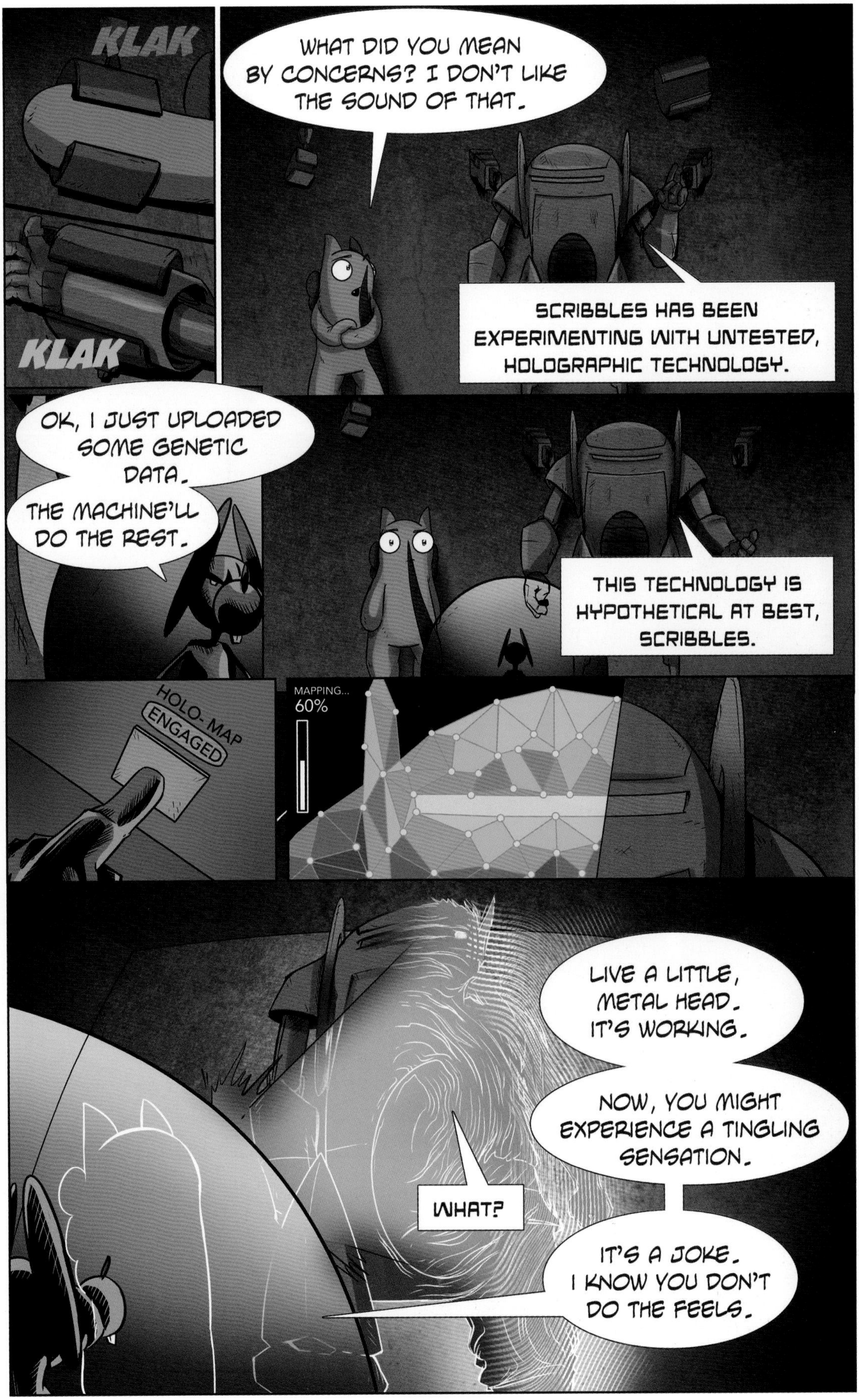
KLAK
KLAK
WHAT DID YOU MEAN BY CONCERNS? I DON'T LIKE THE SOUND OF THAT.
SCRIBBLES HAS BEEN EXPERIMENTING WITH UNTESTED, HOLOGRAPHIC TECHNOLOGY.
OK, I JUST UPLOADED SOME GENETIC DATA.
THE MACHINE'LL DO THE REST.
THIS TECHNOLOGY IS HYPOTHETICAL AT BEST, SCRIBBLES.
HOLO-MAP ENGAGED
MAPPING...
60%
LIVE A LITTLE, METAL HEAD. IT'S WORKING.
NOW, YOU MIGHT EXPERIENCE A TINGLING SENSATION.
WHAT?
IT'S A JOKE. I KNOW YOU DON'T DO THE FEELS.

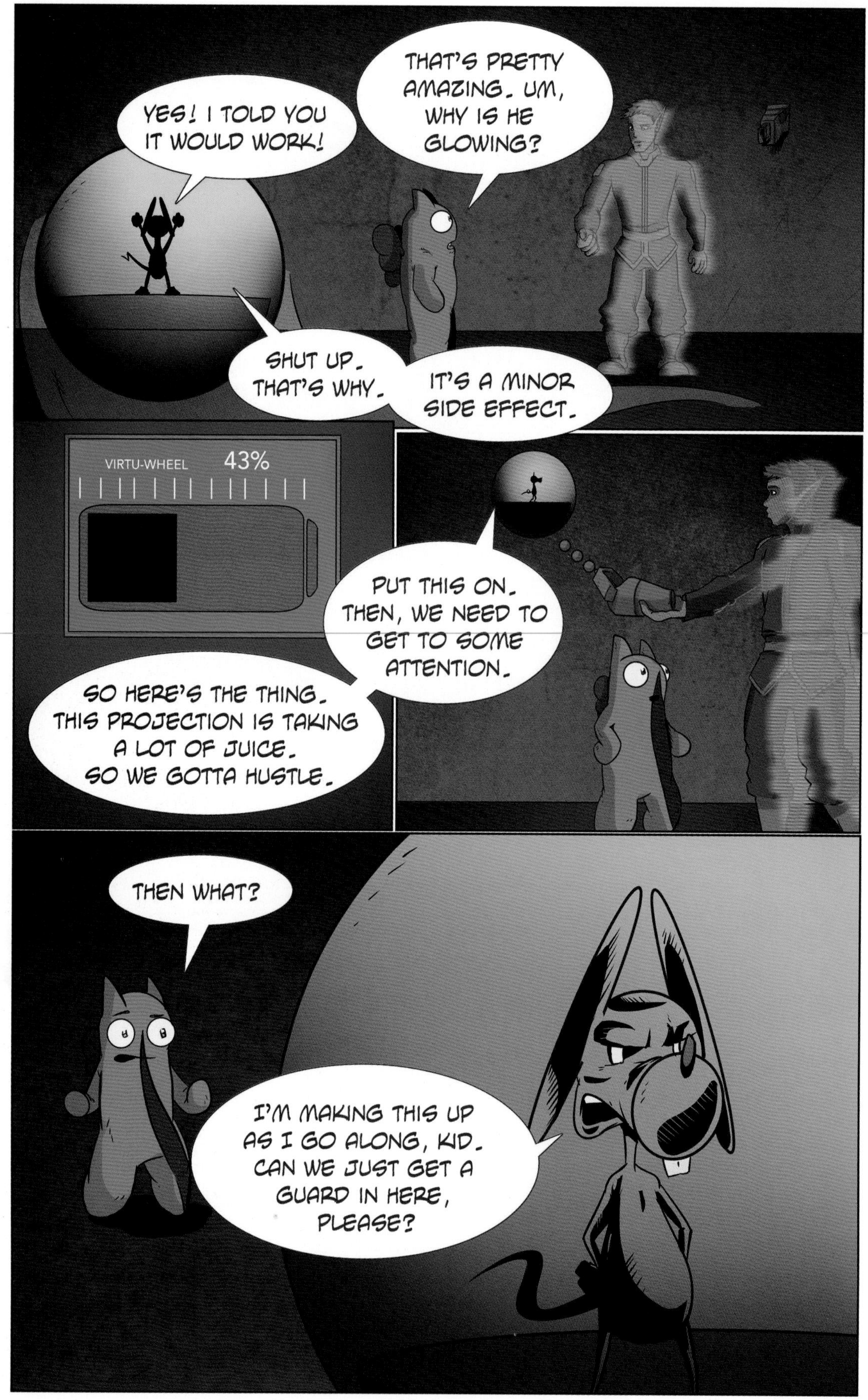
YES! I TOLD YOU IT WOULD WORK!
THAT'S PRETTY AMAZING. UM, WHY IS HE GLOWING?
SHUT UP. THAT'S WHY.
IT'S A MINOR SIDE EFFECT.
VIRTU-WHEEL 43%
PUT THIS ON. THEN, WE NEED TO GET TO SOME ATTENTION.
SO HERE'S THE THING. THIS PROJECTION IS TAKING A LOT OF JUICE. SO WE GOTTA HUSTLE.
THEN WHAT?
I'M MAKING THIS UP AS I GO ALONG, KID. CAN WE JUST GET A GUARD IN HERE, PLEASE?

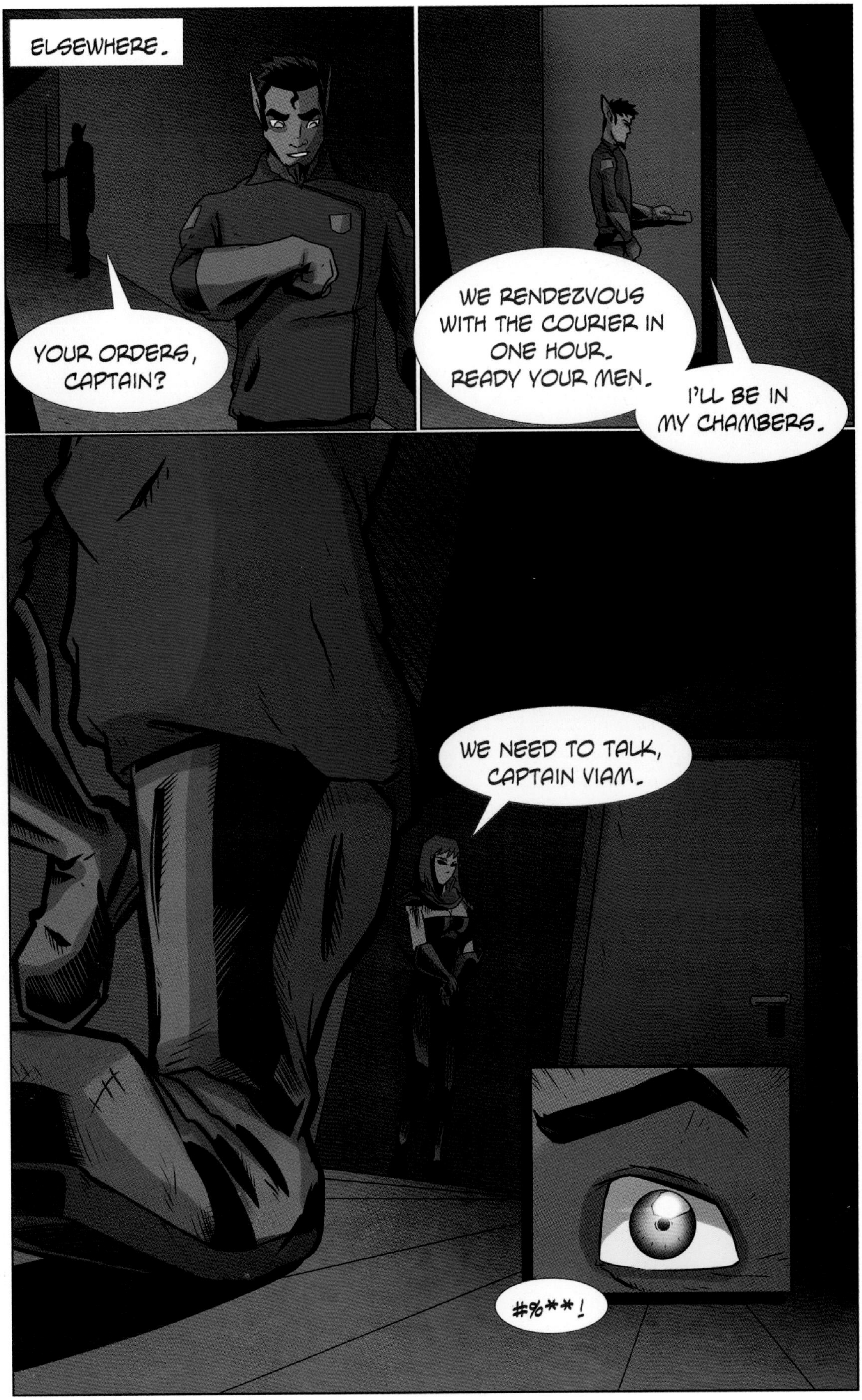
ELSEWHERE.
YOUR ORDERS, CAPTAIN?
WE RENDEZVOUS WITH THE COURIER IN ONE HOUR. READY YOUR MEN.
I'LL BE IN MY CHAMBERS.
WE NEED TO TALK, CAPTAIN VIAM.
#%**!

CHAPTER FIVE

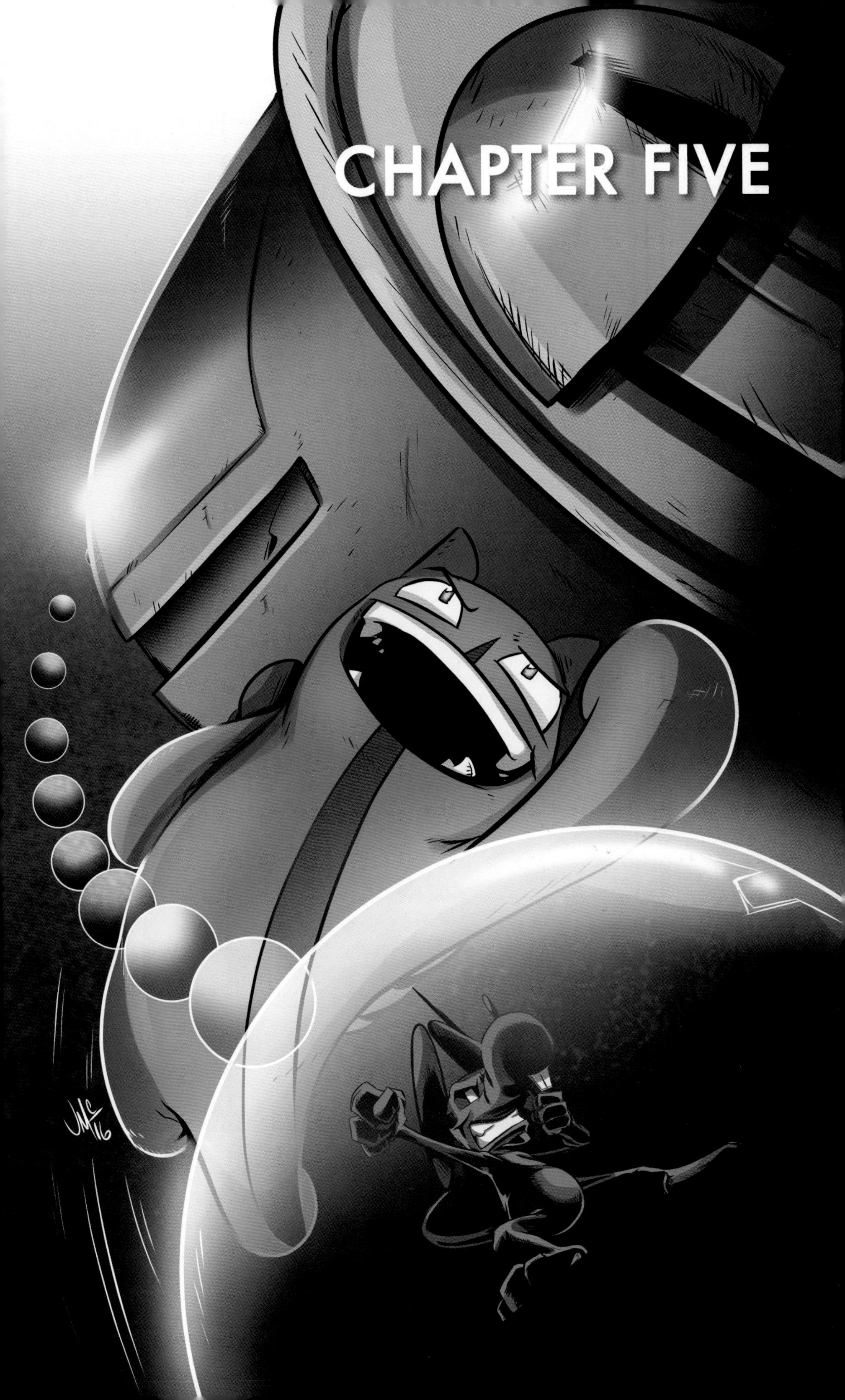

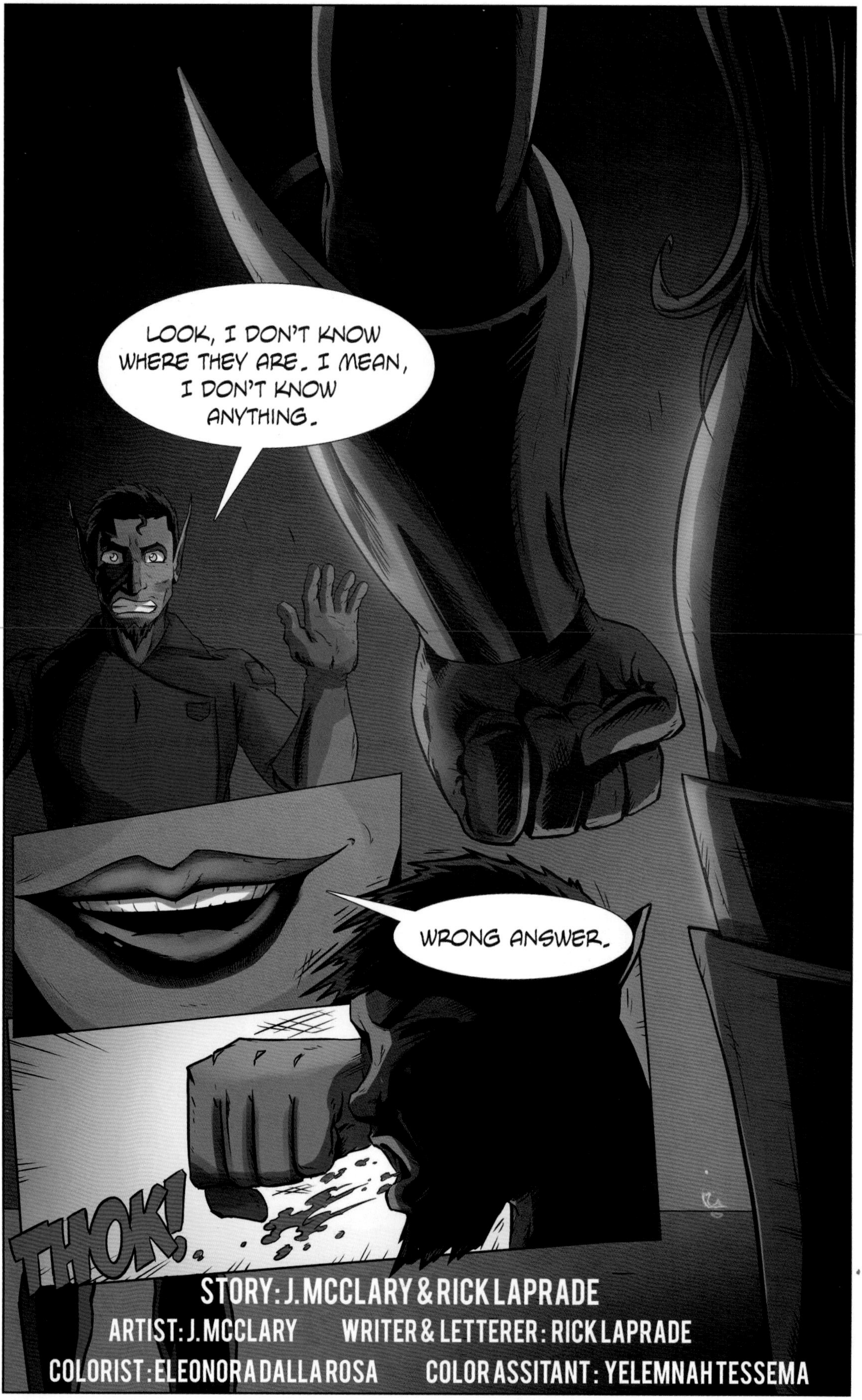
LOOK, I DON'T KNOW WHERE THEY ARE. I MEAN, I DON'T KNOW ANYTHING.
WRONG ANSWER.
THOK!

STORY: J. MCCLARY & RICK LAPRADE

ARTIST: J. MCCLARY WRITER & LETTERER: RICK LAPRADE

COLORIST: ELEONORA DALLA ROSA COLOR ASSITANT: YELEMNAH TESSEMA

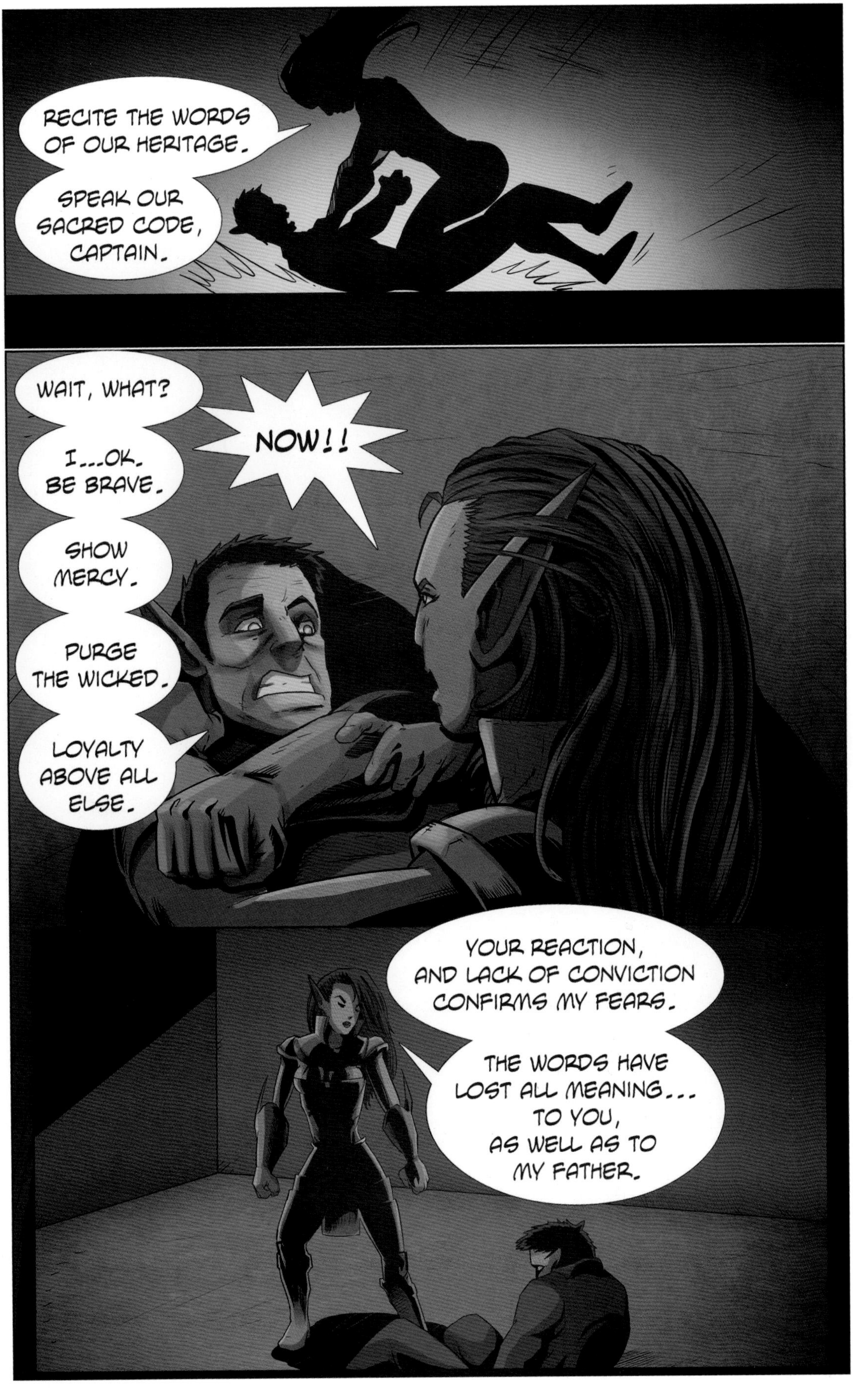
RECITE THE WORDS OF OUR HERITAGE.
SPEAK OUR SACRED CODE, CAPTAIN.
WAIT, WHAT?
NOW!!
I...OK. BE BRAVE.
SHOW MERCY.
PURGE THE WICKED.
LOYALTY ABOVE ALL ELSE.
YOUR REACTION, AND LACK OF CONVICTION CONFIRMS MY FEARS.
THE WORDS HAVE LOST ALL MEANING... TO YOU, AS WELL AS TO MY FATHER.

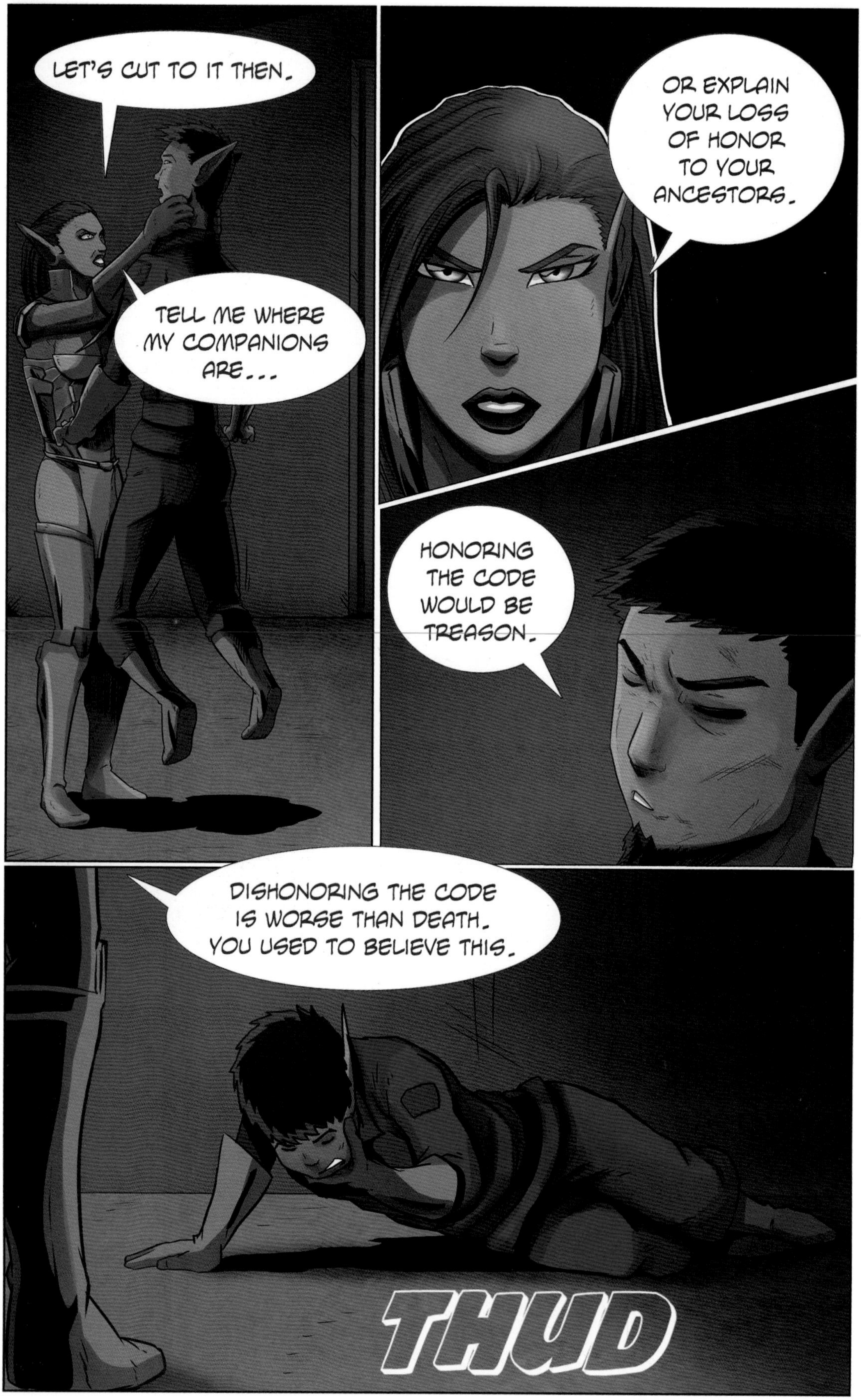
LET'S CUT TO IT THEN.
TELL ME WHERE MY COMPANIONS ARE...
OR EXPLAIN YOUR LOSS OF HONOR TO YOUR ANCESTORS.
HONORING THE CODE WOULD BE TREASON.
DISHONORING THE CODE IS WORSE THAN DEATH. YOU USED TO BELIEVE THIS.
THUD

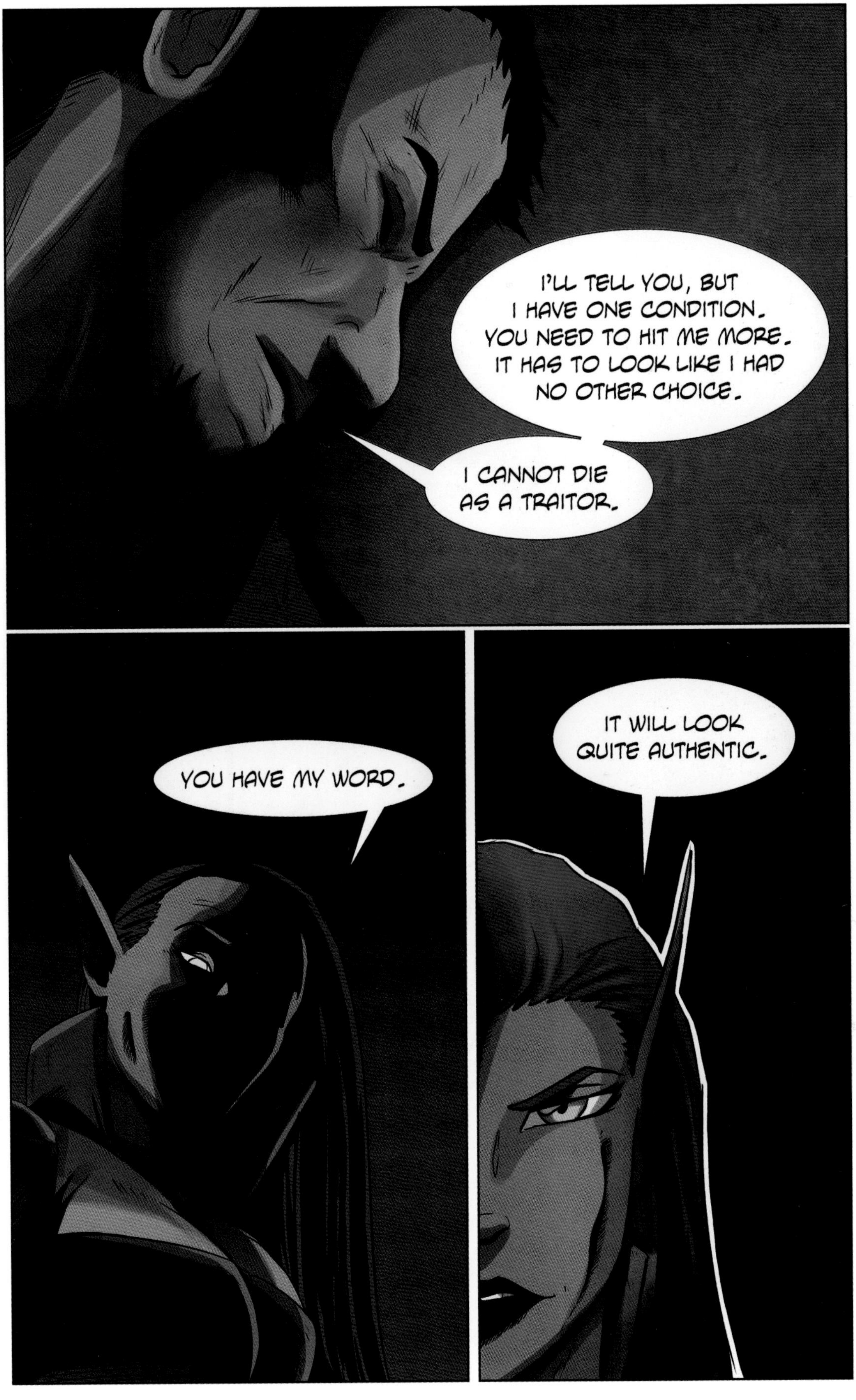
I'LL TELL YOU, BUT I HAVE ONE CONDITION. YOU NEED TO HIT ME MORE. IT HAS TO LOOK LIKE I HAD NO OTHER CHOICE.
I CANNOT DIE AS A TRAITOR.
YOU HAVE MY WORD.
IT WILL LOOK QUITE AUTHENTIC.

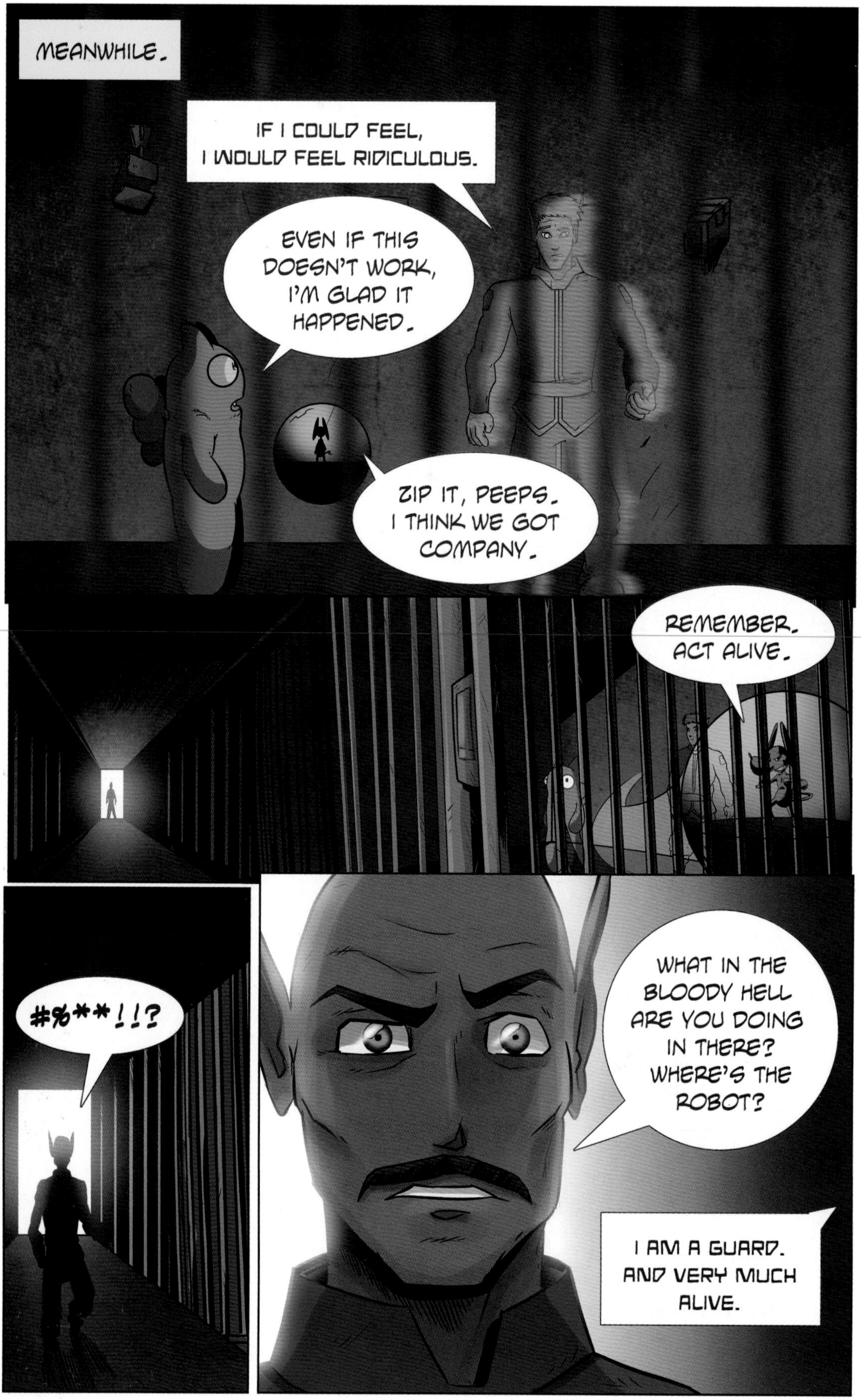
MEANWHILE.
IF I COULD FEEL, I WOULD FEEL RIDICULOUS.
EVEN IF THIS DOESN'T WORK, I'M GLAD IT HAPPENED.
ZIP IT, PEEPS. I THINK WE GOT COMPANY.
REMEMBER. ACT ALIVE.
#%**!!?
WHAT IN THE BLOODY HELL ARE YOU DOING IN THERE? WHERE'S THE ROBOT?
I AM A GUARD. AND VERY MUCH ALIVE.

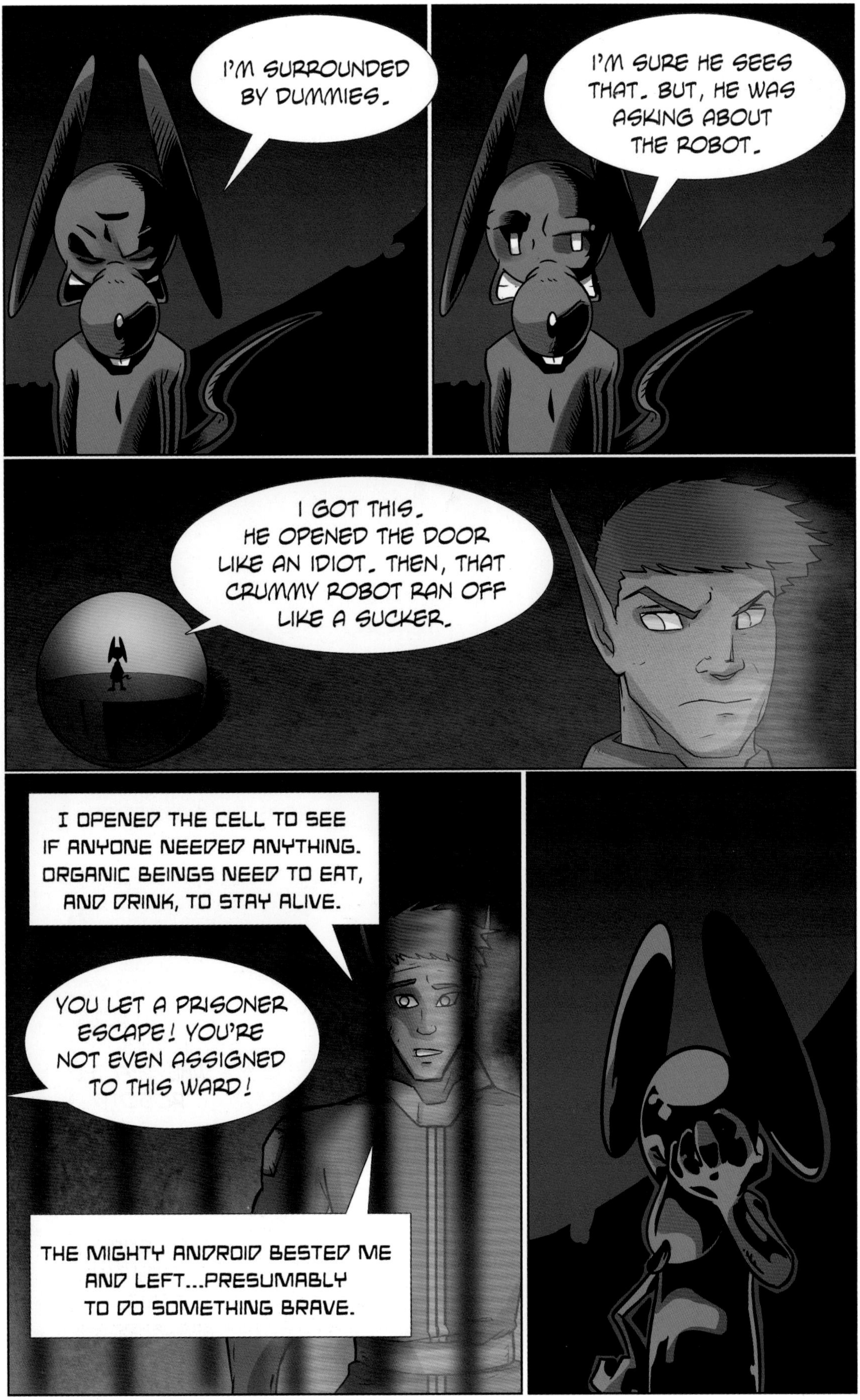
I'M SURROUNDED BY DUMMIES.
I'M SURE HE SEES THAT. BUT, HE WAS ASKING ABOUT THE ROBOT.
I GOT THIS. HE OPENED THE DOOR LIKE AN IDIOT. THEN, THAT CRUMMY ROBOT RAN OFF LIKE A SUCKER.
I OPENED THE CELL TO SEE IF ANYONE NEEDED ANYTHING. ORGANIC BEINGS NEED TO EAT, AND DRINK, TO STAY ALIVE.
YOU LET A PRISONER ESCAPE! YOU'RE NOT EVEN ASSIGNED TO THIS WARD!
THE MIGHTY ANDROID BESTED ME AND LEFT...PRESUMABLY TO DO SOMETHING BRAVE.

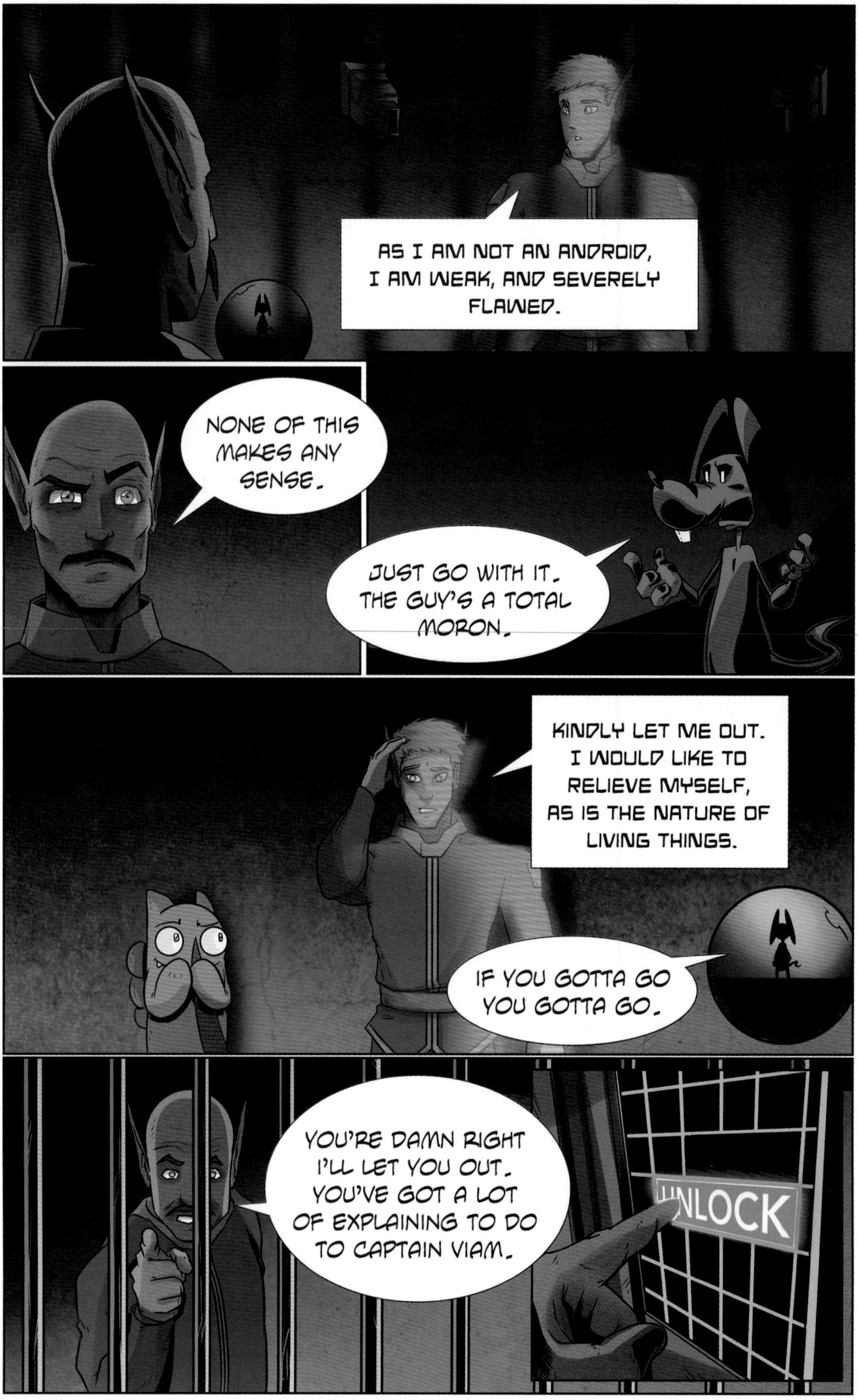
AS I AM NOT AN ANDROID, I AM WEAK, AND SEVERELY FLAWED.
NONE OF THIS MAKES ANY SENSE.
JUST GO WITH IT. THE GUY'S A TOTAL MORON.
KINDLY LET ME OUT. I WOULD LIKE TO RELIEVE MYSELF, AS IS THE NATURE OF LIVING THINGS.
IF YOU GOTTA GO YOU GOTTA GO.
YOU'RE DAMN RIGHT I'LL LET YOU OUT. YOU'VE GOT A LOT OF EXPLAINING TO DO TO CAPTAIN VIAM.
UNLOCK

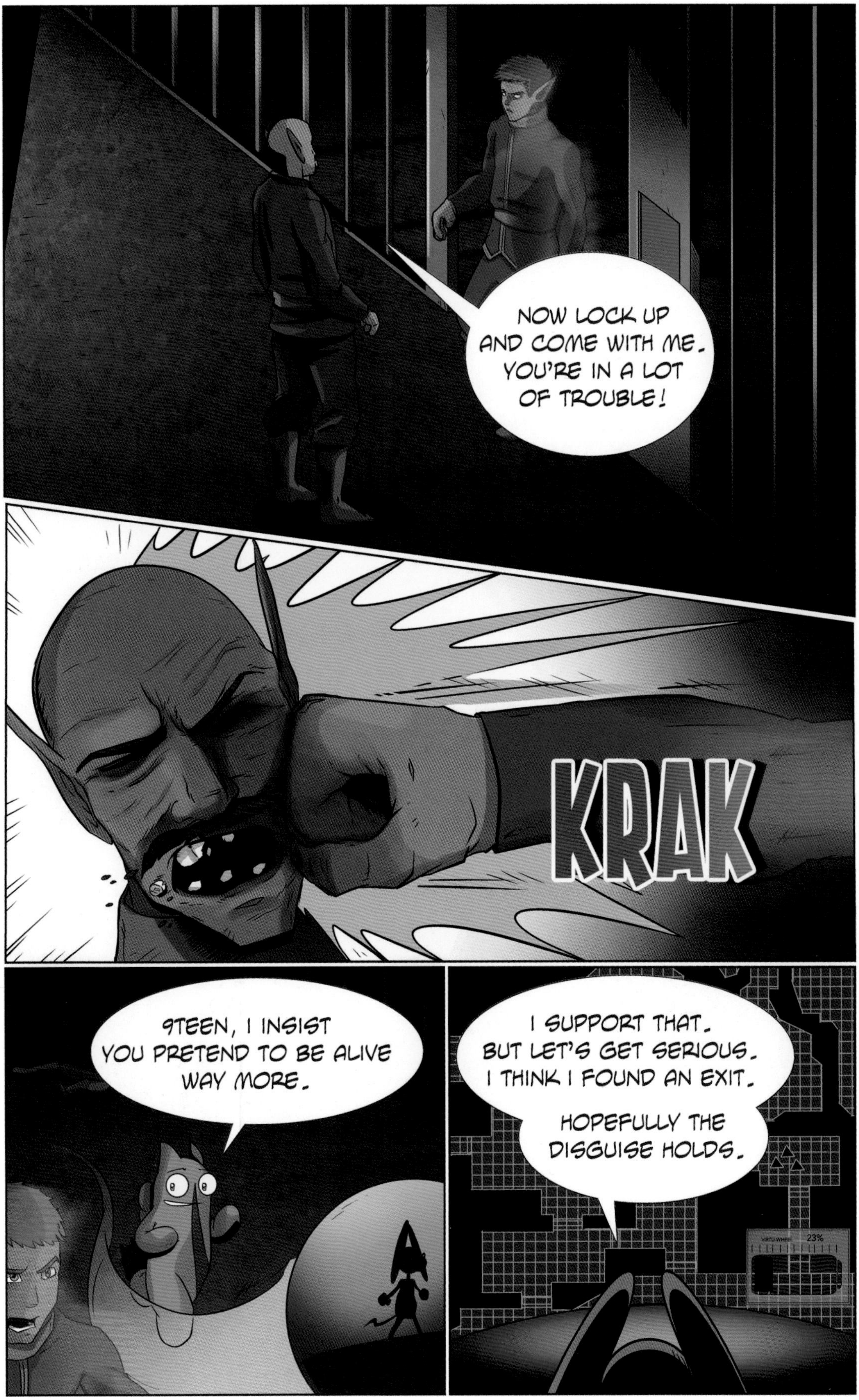
NOW LOCK UP AND COME WITH ME. YOU'RE IN A LOT OF TROUBLE!
KRAK
9TEEN, I INSIST YOU PRETEND TO BE ALIVE WAY MORE.
I SUPPORT THAT. BUT LET'S GET SERIOUS. I THINK I FOUND AN EXIT.
HOPEFULLY THE DISGUISE HOLDS.
VIRTU-WHEEL 23%

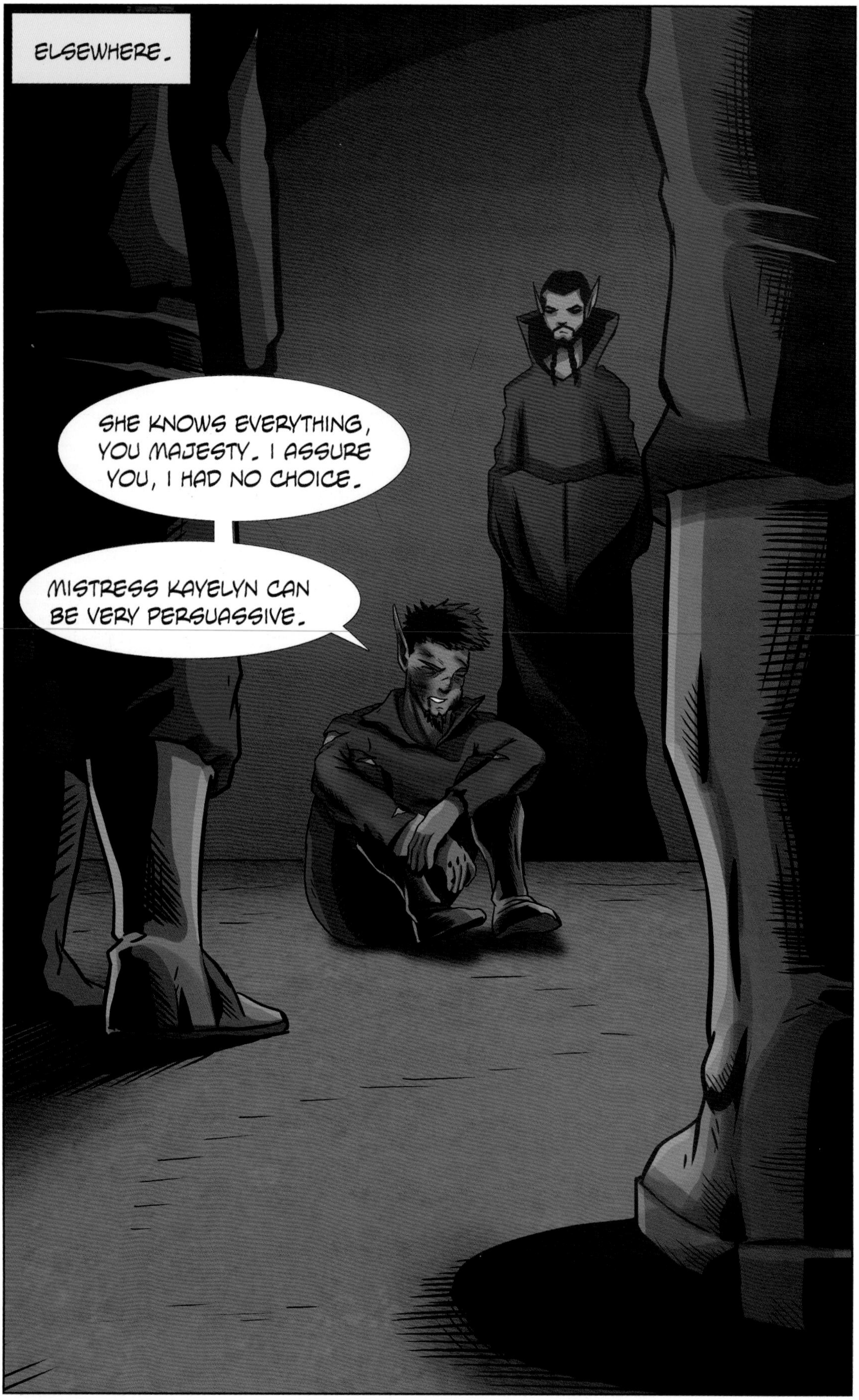
ELSEWHERE.
SHE KNOWS EVERYTHING, YOU MAJESTY. I ASSURE YOU, I HAD NO CHOICE.
MISTRESS KAYELYN CAN BE VERY PERSUASSIVE.

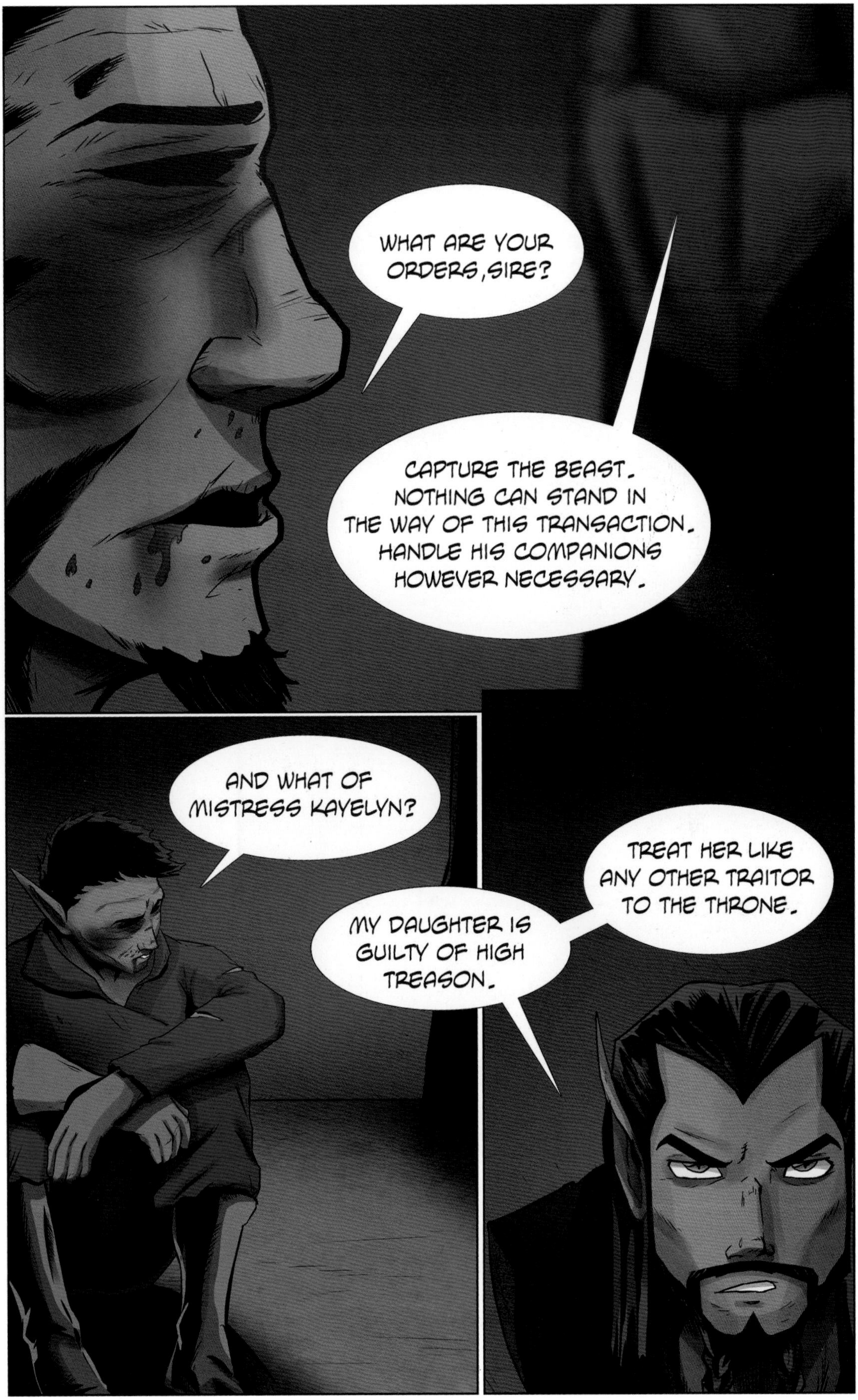
WHAT ARE YOUR ORDERS, SIRE?
CAPTURE THE BEAST. NOTHING CAN STAND IN THE WAY OF THIS TRANSACTION. HANDLE HIS COMPANIONS HOWEVER NECESSARY.
AND WHAT OF MISTRESS KAYELYN?
MY DAUGHTER IS GUILTY OF HIGH TREASON.
TREAT HER LIKE ANY OTHER TRAITOR TO THE THRONE.

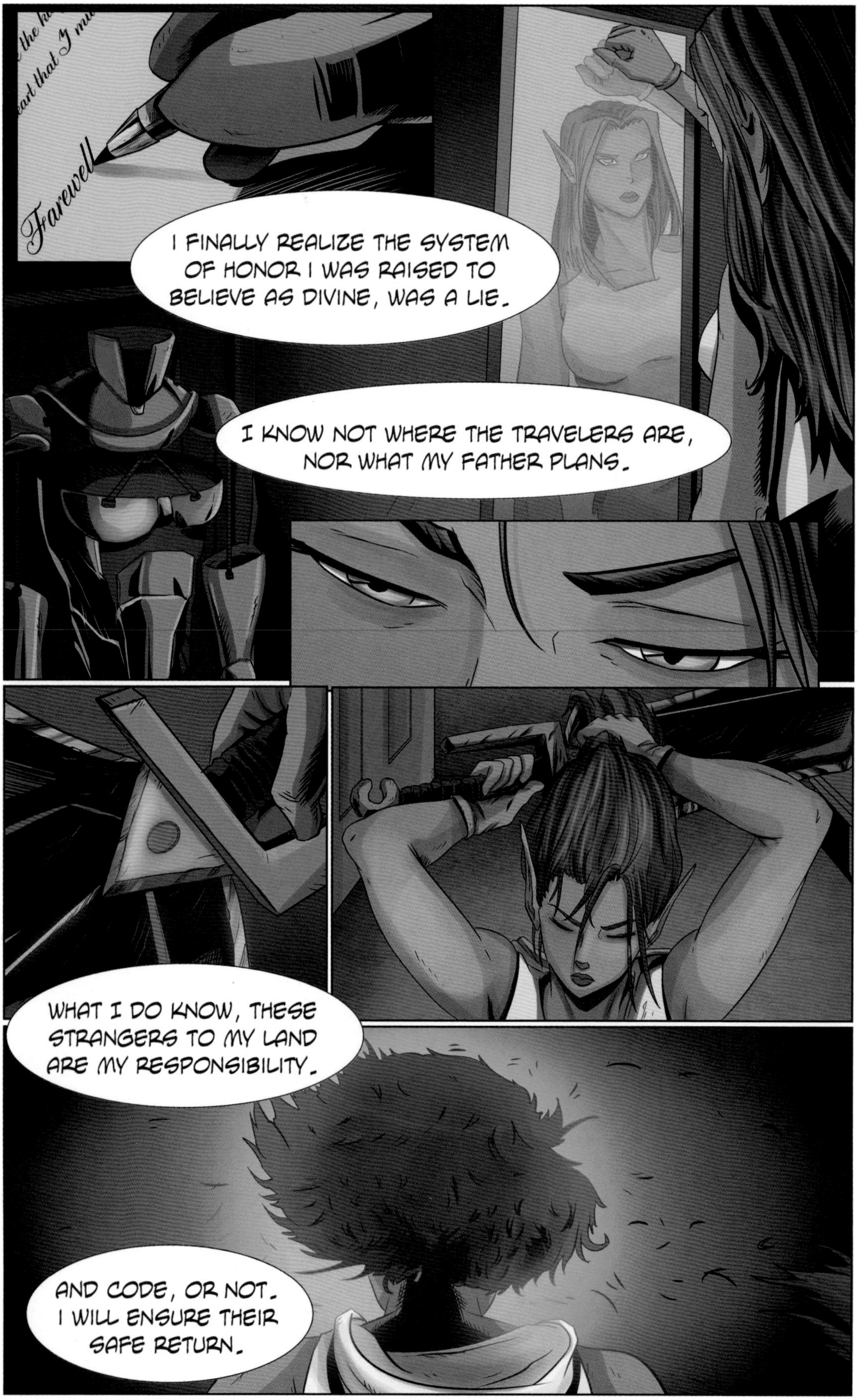
Farewell
I FINALLY REALIZE THE SYSTEM OF HONOR I WAS RAISED TO BELIEVE AS DIVINE, WAS A LIE.
I KNOW NOT WHERE THE TRAVELERS ARE, NOR WHAT MY FATHER PLANS.
WHAT I DO KNOW, THESE STRANGERS TO MY LAND ARE MY RESPONSIBILITY.
AND CODE, OR NOT. I WILL ENSURE THEIR SAFE RETURN.

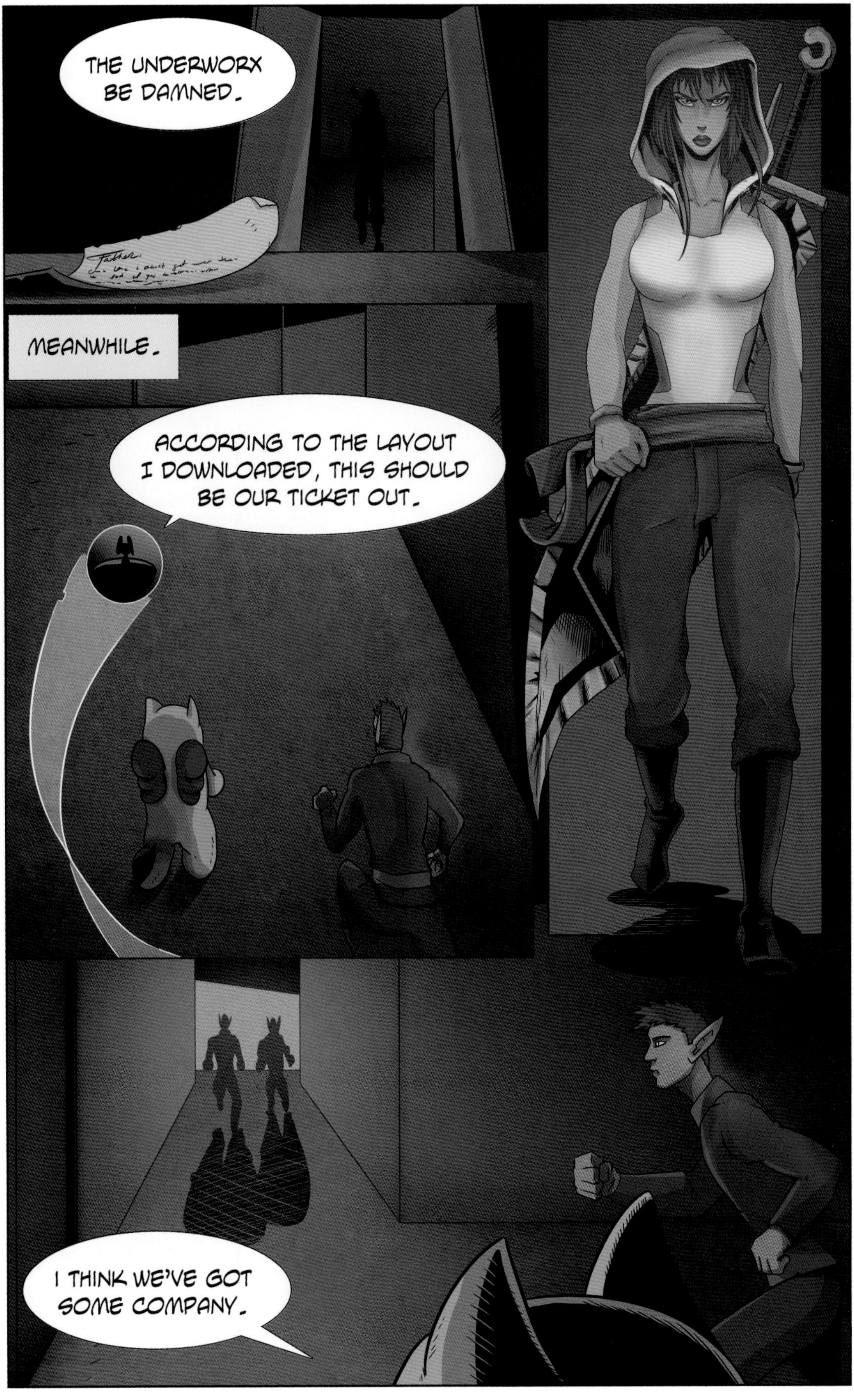
THE UNDERWORX BE DAMNED.
MEANWHILE.
ACCORDING TO THE LAYOUT I DOWNLOADED, THIS SHOULD BE OUR TICKET OUT.
I THINK WE'VE GOT SOME COMPANY.

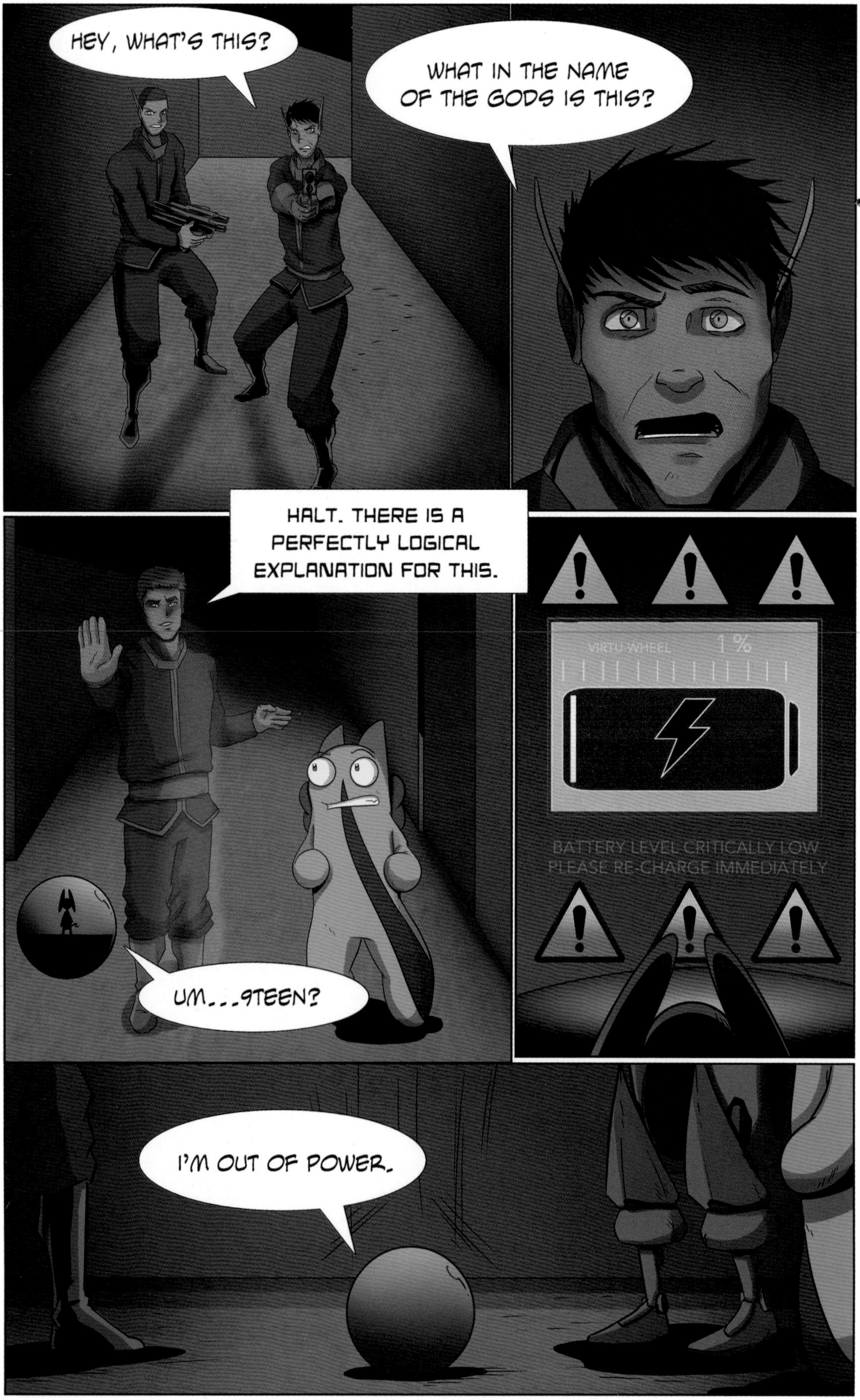
HEY, WHAT'S THIS?
WHAT IN THE NAME OF THE GODS IS THIS?
HALT. THERE IS A PERFECTLY LOGICAL EXPLANATION FOR THIS.
UM...9TEEN?
VIRTU-WHEEL 1%
BATTERY LEVEL CRITICALLY LOW
PLEASE RE-CHARGE IMMEDIATELY
I'M OUT OF POWER.

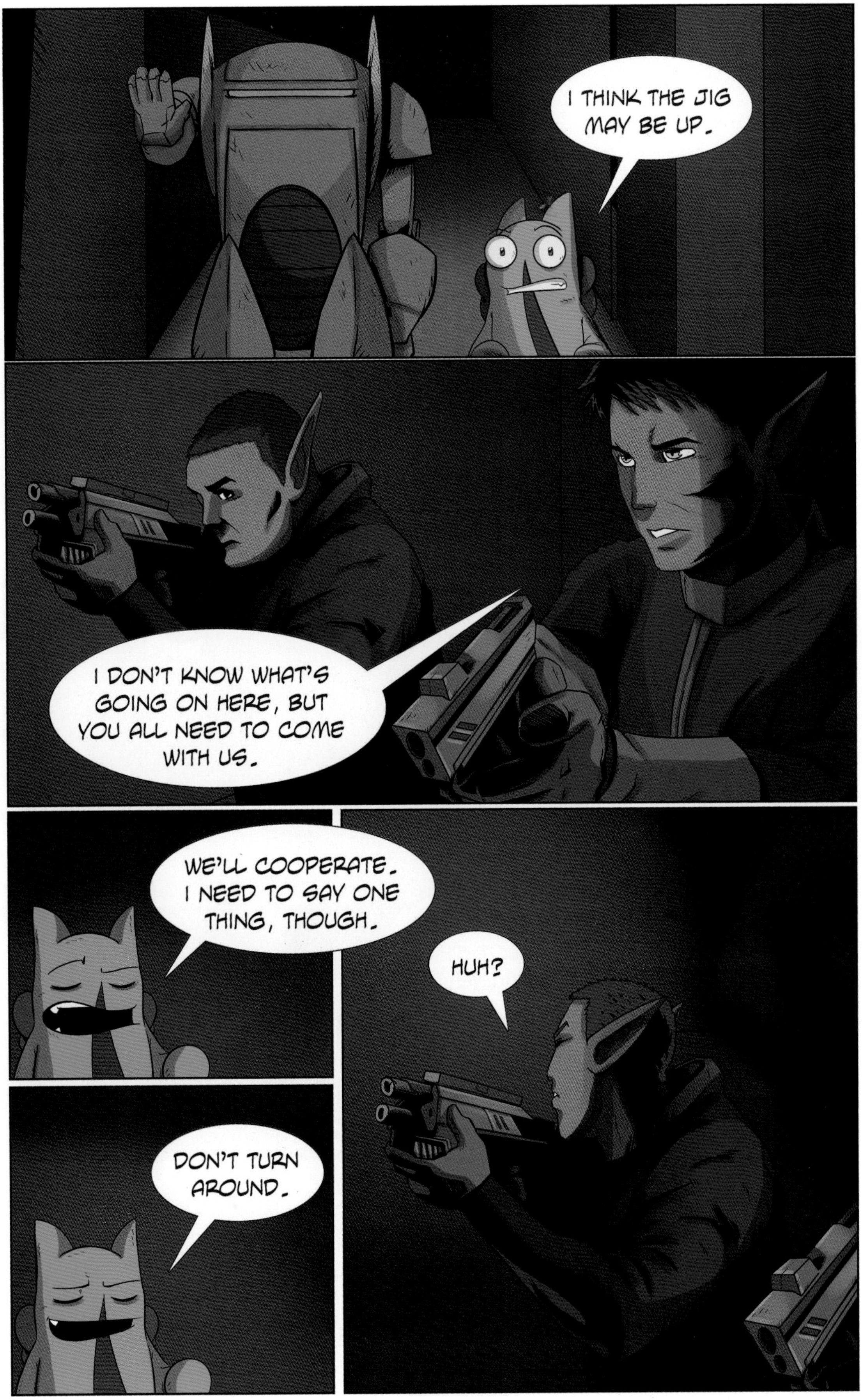
I THINK THE JIG MAY BE UP.
I DON'T KNOW WHAT'S GOING ON HERE, BUT YOU ALL NEED TO COME WITH US.
WE'LL COOPERATE. I NEED TO SAY ONE THING, THOUGH.
HUH?
DON'T TURN AROUND.

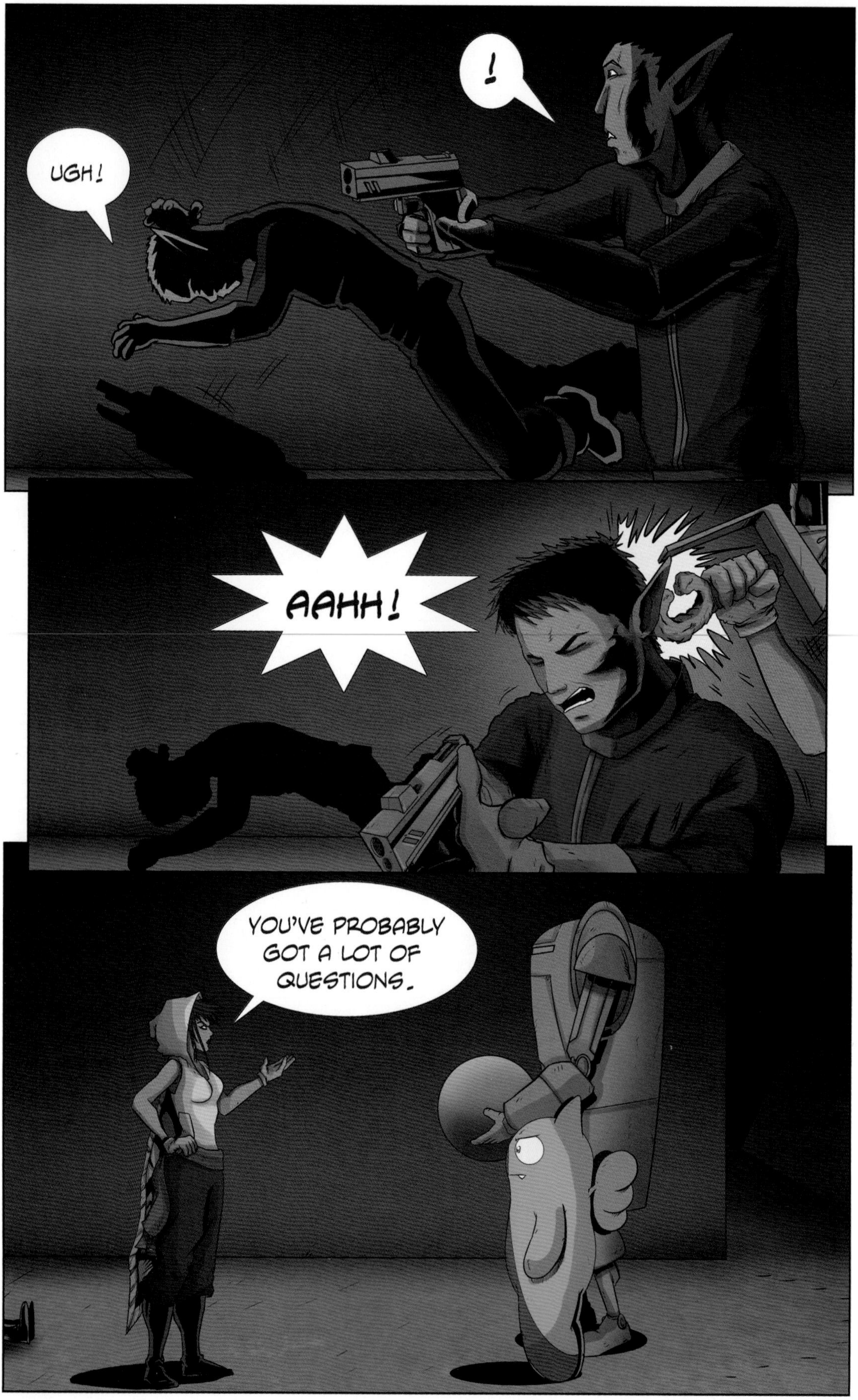
UGH!
!
AAHH!
YOU'VE PROBABLY GOT A LOT OF QUESTIONS.

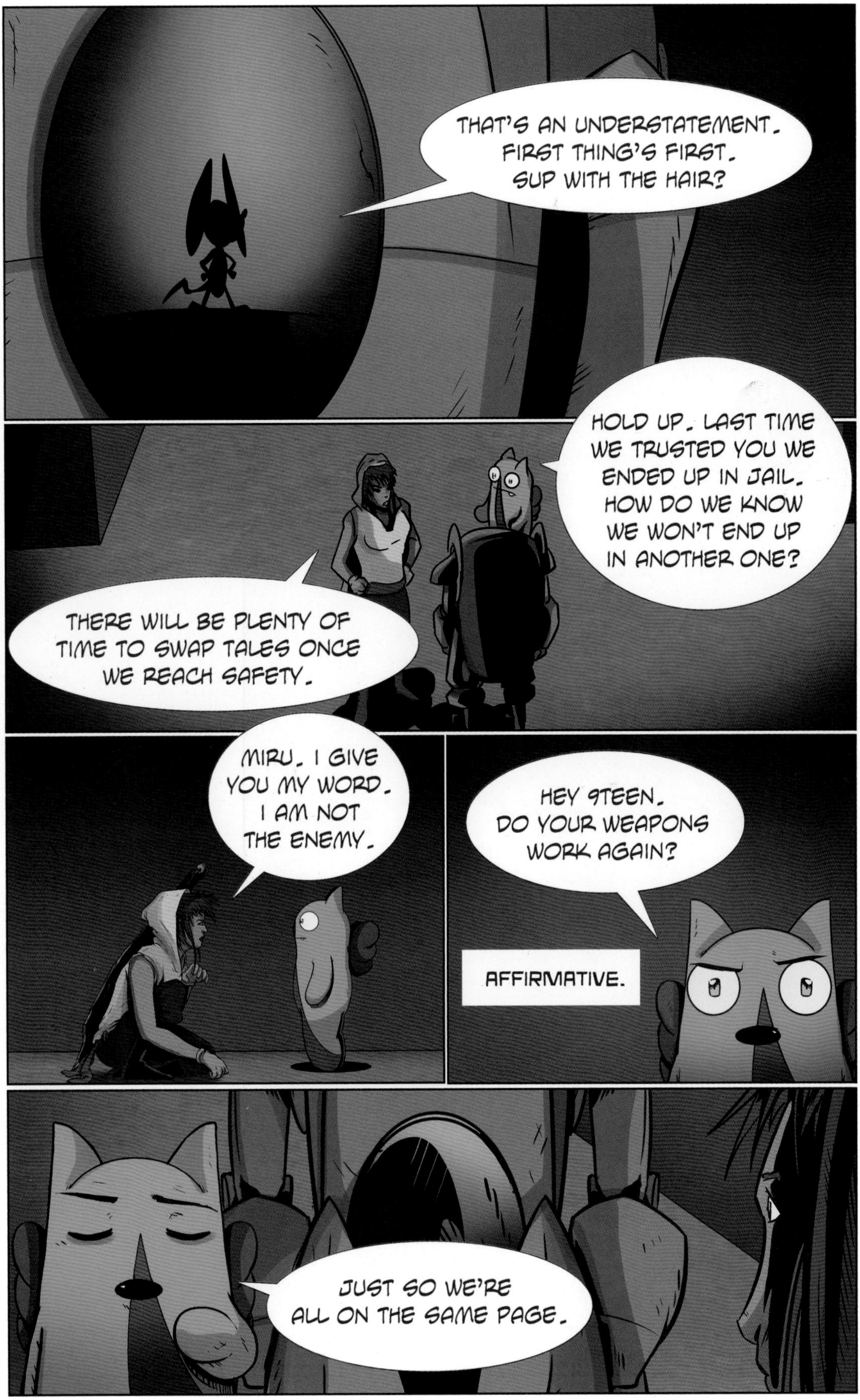
THAT'S AN UNDERSTATEMENT. FIRST THING'S FIRST. SUP WITH THE HAIR?
HOLD UP. LAST TIME WE TRUSTED YOU WE ENDED UP IN JAIL. HOW DO WE KNOW WE WON'T END UP IN ANOTHER ONE?
THERE WILL BE PLENTY OF TIME TO SWAP TALES ONCE WE REACH SAFETY.
MIRU. I GIVE YOU MY WORD. I AM NOT THE ENEMY.
HEY 9TEEN. DO YOUR WEAPONS WORK AGAIN?
AFFIRMATIVE.
JUST SO WE'RE ALL ON THE SAME PAGE.

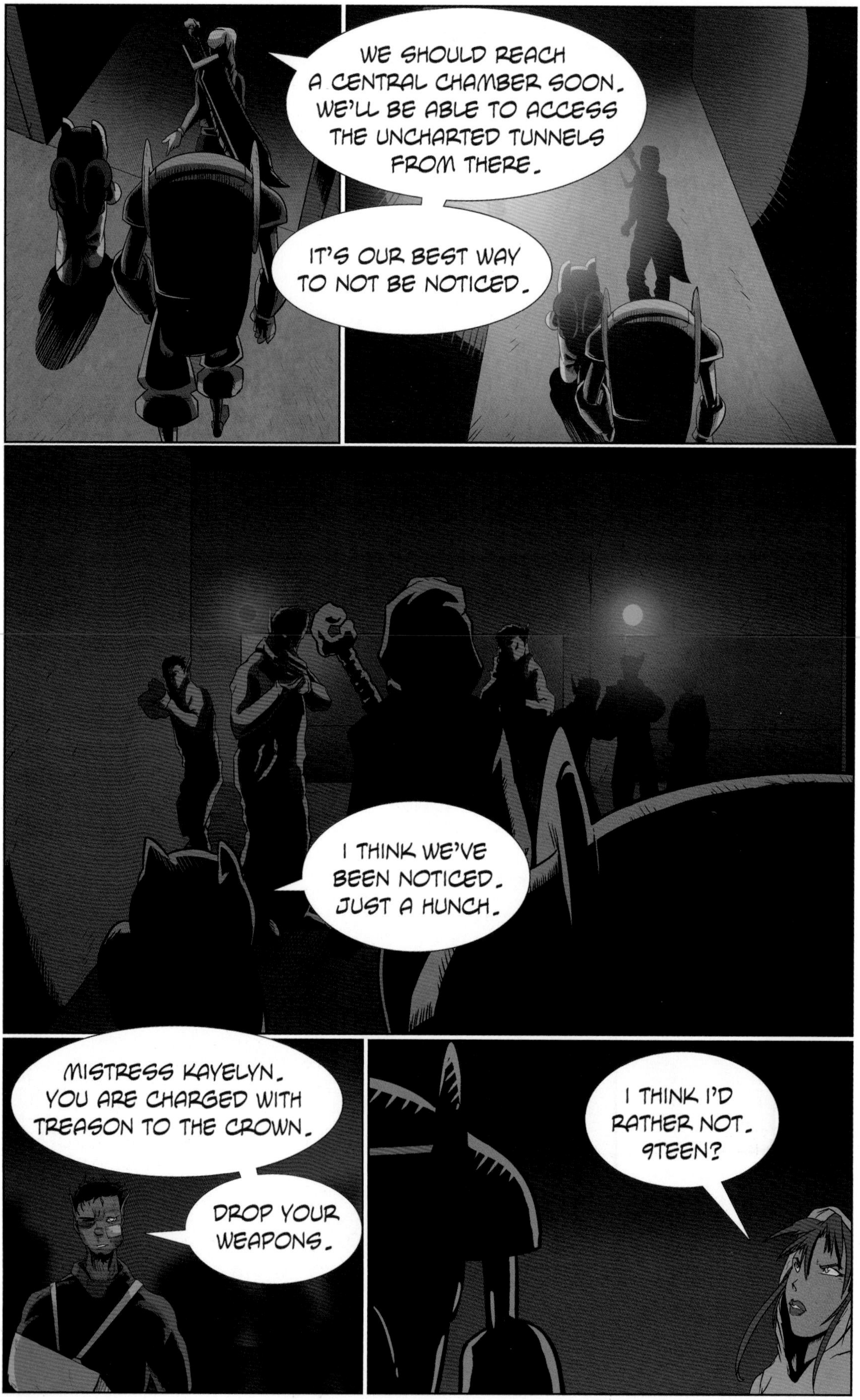
WE SHOULD REACH A CENTRAL CHAMBER SOON. WE'LL BE ABLE TO ACCESS THE UNCHARTED TUNNELS FROM THERE.
IT'S OUR BEST WAY TO NOT BE NOTICED.
I THINK WE'VE BEEN NOTICED. JUST A HUNCH.
MISTRESS KAYELYN. YOU ARE CHARGED WITH TREASON TO THE CROWN.
DROP YOUR WEAPONS.
I THINK I'D RATHER NOT. 9TEEN?

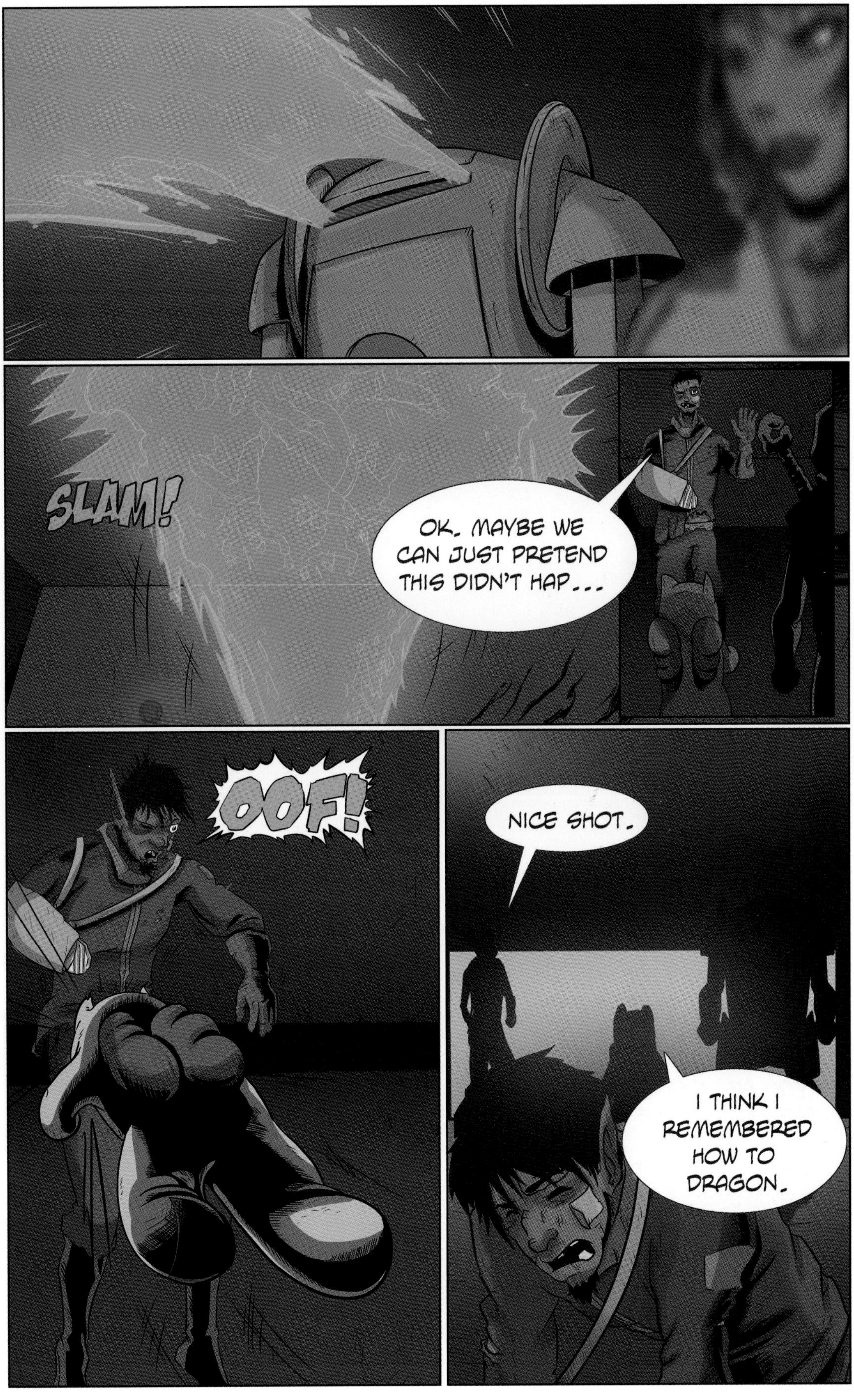
SLAM!
OK. MAYBE WE CAN JUST PRETEND THIS DIDN'T HAP...
OOF!
NICE SHOT.
I THINK I REMEMBERED HOW TO DRAGON.

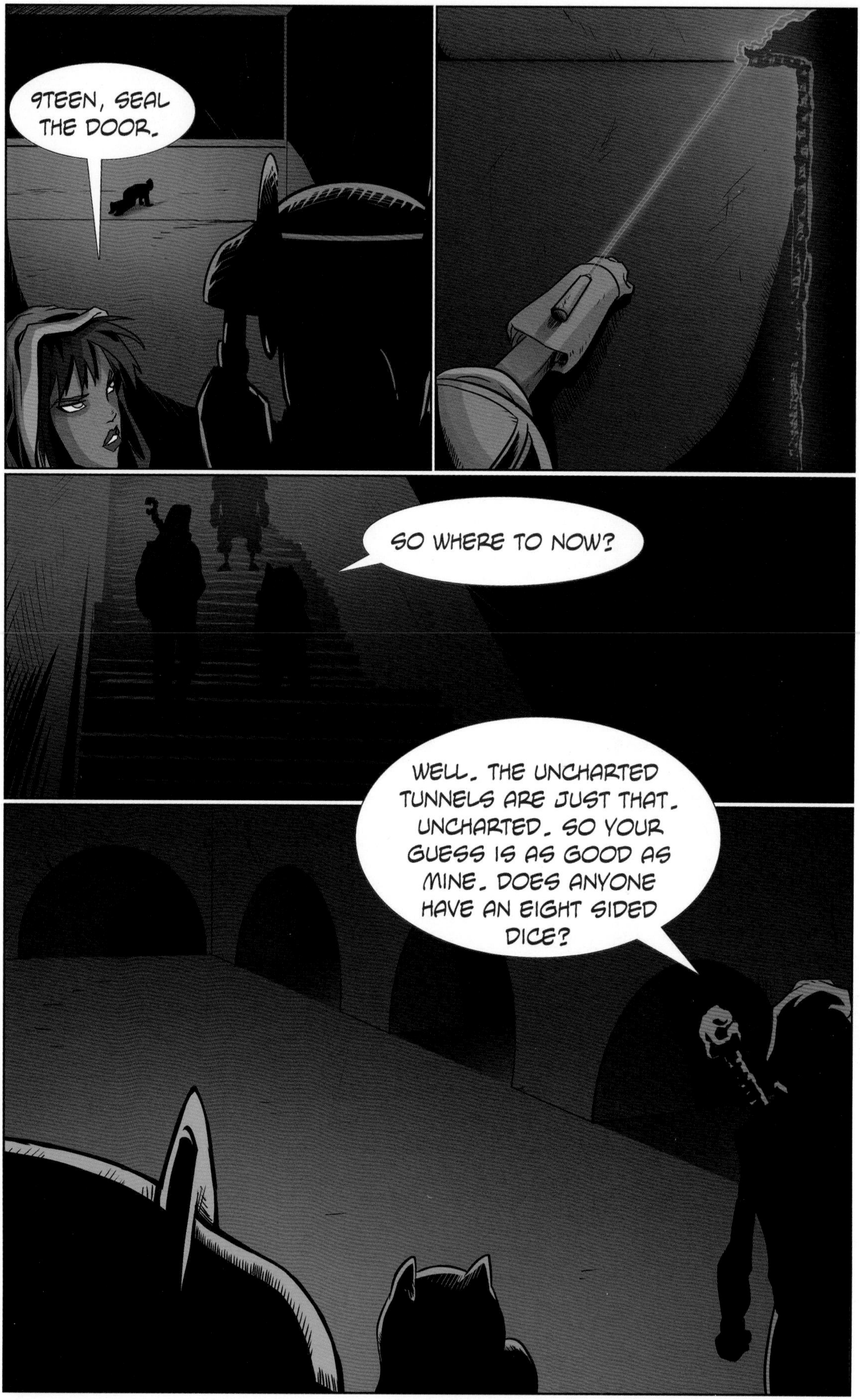

9TEEN, SEAL THE DOOR.

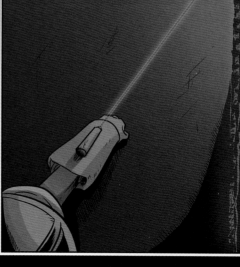

SO WHERE TO NOW?

WELL. THE UNCHARTED TUNNELS ARE JUST THAT. UNCHARTED. SO YOUR GUESS IS AS GOOD AS MINE. DOES ANYONE HAVE AN EIGHT SIDED DICE?

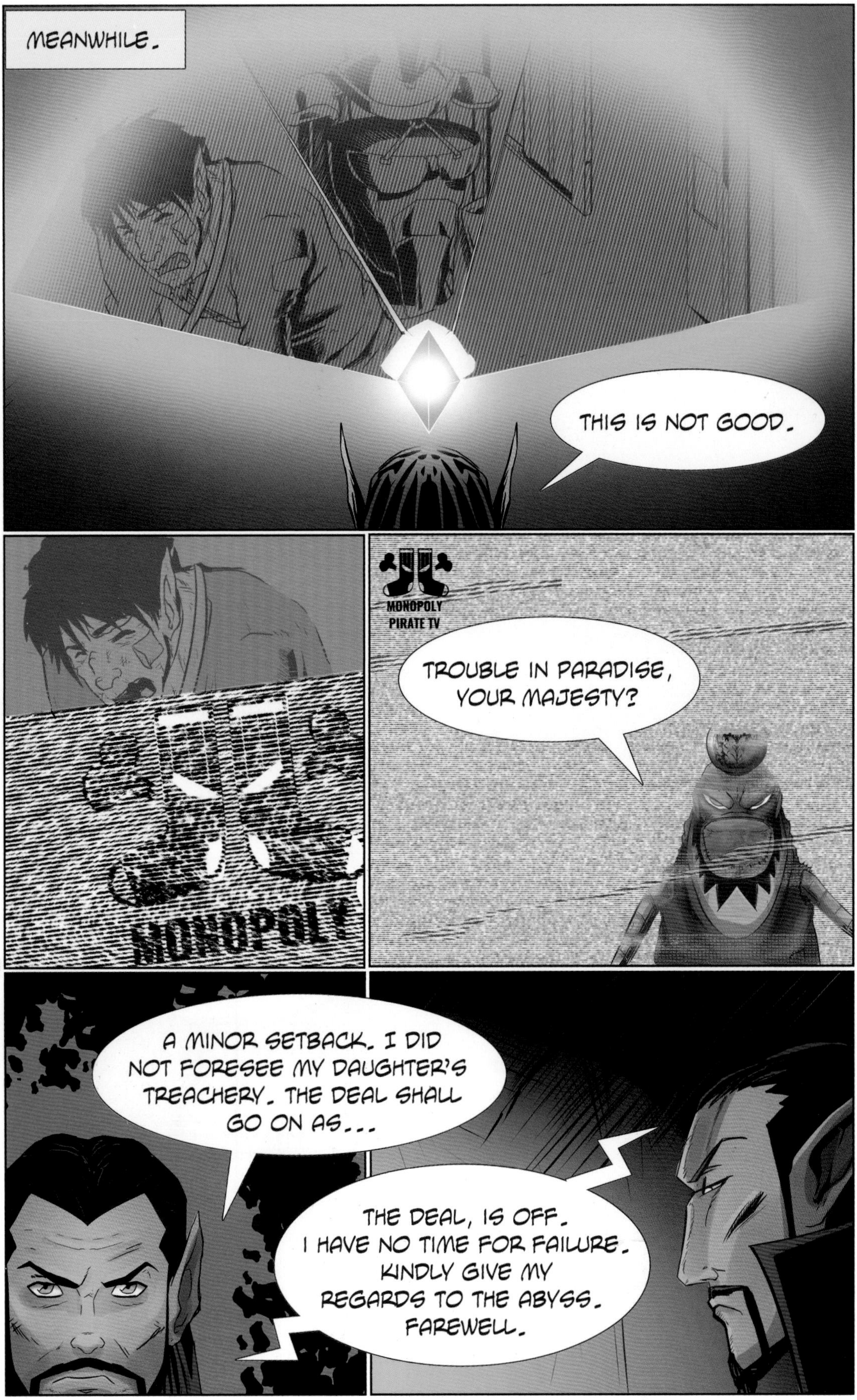
MEANWHILE.
THIS IS NOT GOOD.
MONOPOLY PIRATE TV
MONOPOLY
TROUBLE IN PARADISE, YOUR MAJESTY?
A MINOR SETBACK. I DID NOT FORESEE MY DAUGHTER'S TREACHERY. THE DEAL SHALL GO ON AS...
THE DEAL, IS OFF. I HAVE NO TIME FOR FAILURE. KINDLY GIVE MY REGARDS TO THE ABYSS. FAREWELL.

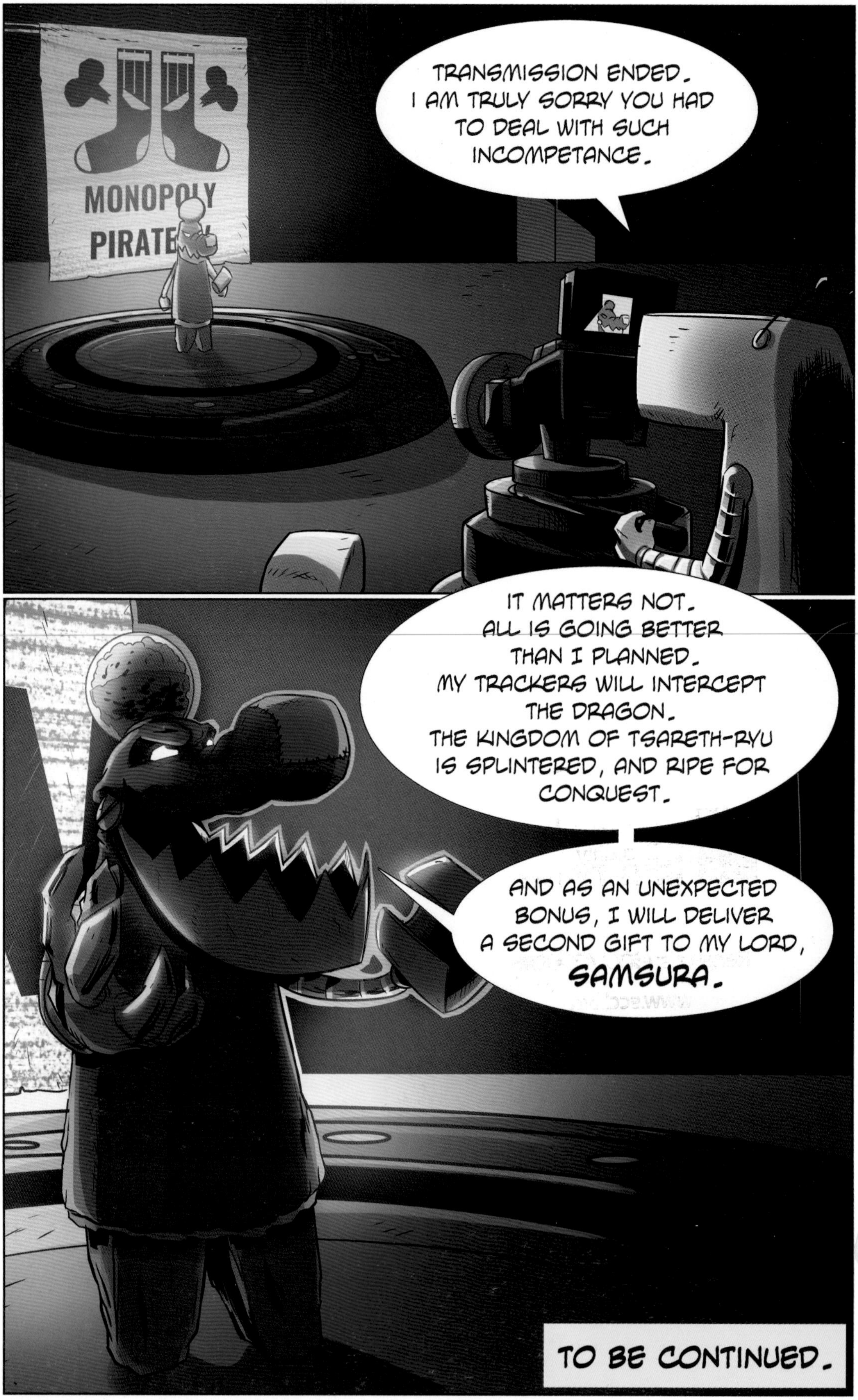
TRANSMISSION ENDED. I AM TRULY SORRY YOU HAD TO DEAL WITH SUCH INCOMPETANCE.
IT MATTERS NOT. ALL IS GOING BETTER THAN I PLANNED. MY TRACKERS WILL INTERCEPT THE DRAGON. THE KINGDOM OF TSARETH-RYU IS SPLINTERED, AND RIPE FOR CONQUEST.
AND AS AN UNEXPECTED BONUS, I WILL DELIVER A SECOND GIFT TO MY LORD, **SAMSURA.**
TO BE CONTINUED.